THE LAST DOG IN FRANCE

A TALE OF THE FRENCH RESISTANCE AND THEIR ESCAPE LINE IN WWII

John Van Wyck Gould

Bloomington, IN   Milton Keynes, UK

authorHOUSE™

AuthorHouse™
1663 Liberty Drive, Suite 200
Bloomington, IN 47403
www.authorhouse.com
Phone: 1-800-839-8640

AuthorHouse™ UK Ltd.
500 Avebury Boulevard
Central Milton Keynes, MK9 2BE
www.authorhouse.co.uk
Phone: 08001974150

First published by AuthorHouse 8/1/2006

ISBN: 1-4259-3884-1 (sc)

Library of Congress Control Number: 2006904447

Printed in the United States of America
Bloomington, Indiana

This book is printed on acid-free paper.

FOREWARD
AND
ACKNOWLEDGEMENTS

At the core, this is a tale of suspense and love more than a war story, but is set against the historical backdrop of World War II and the French Resistance.

Before we begin, a few comments are called for regarding those dreadful years. Many of us have forgotten what an extraordinary era this was, an era in which the world tried to compress too much history into too little time. It is impossible to describe with credible sensitivity the depth of misery and the war. Dry and unfeeling as they may be, statistics tell us that approximately sixty million people died in the war, half of whom were innocent civilians, and millions more starved in the world-wide "Great Depression."

One might refer to the war and depression years as the Roosevelt-Hitler era, since they both came to power in 1933 and died in 1945 within one month of each other. The changes that shook our world during this short period were extraordinary—invasions and occupations of no less than twenty-three countries; the rise and fall of Nazi Germany and the Japanese Empire; Mussolini's adventures in Africa; the Spanish civil war; the Holocaust; the atom bomb; the Marshall Plan; the Nuremberg trials; the "Iron Curtain;" the creation of an Israeli state; the breakup of the British Empire—just to mention a few. At times it may seem that W.W.II and the decade leading up to it have been overworked subjects, but the events were so momentous and fascinating, I believe they will never be overworked or even fully explored.

In fashioning this tale, I have woven the fiction around a number of true events: The Caves of St.-Pierre were a hiding place for the French Resistance, although briefly. To survive, many of the French Resistance lived off the land, eating whatever they could get their hands on, including insects, small animals like squirrels—and dogs. Hermann Goering and other Nazi leaders plundered more than one hundred billion Reichmarks'[1] worth of gold, silver, diamonds, francs, kopecks, rubles, gilders, kroner, priceless art work, and goods of every description, including food and staples needed for survival, from Germany's occupied countries. Goering siphoned off some fifty million for himself, most of it in the form of art masterpieces—Titians, Rubens, Van Dycks, Goyas—a fact well documented. Not so well documented was where it all went. The Reich Marshal went to his grave by his own hand without satisfactorily explaining the tangled story. At the Nuremberg trials he was so arrogant and unresponsive that the American Chief Justice Jackson, at one point in the proceedings, threw down his earphones in disgust and adjourned the trial for the day.

Much of the stolen art and wealth passed through multiple hands and even blackmailers before it ended up in Goering's Karinhall estate. To this day, scholars and investigators have been unable to completely untangle the complicated transactions. Several of the masterpieces have shown up in Russia some fifty years later. Goering was known to be a shrewd art bargainer who bought and sold numerous pieces at substantial profits. In fact, much of the time, he became so absorbed in his art collecting that he neglected his duties as chief of the Luftwaffe. He claimed to have paid for his acquisitions legally, but the truth is he stole a great deal of the treasure from the Jews when it became "ownerless," as he called it, when the Jews fled or were shipped off to Auschwitz and Dachau.

Because of the immense power of Nazi leaders, the "Quislings" of many of the occupied countries raided their own national treasures and gifted invaluable art works to the Nazis in order to curry favor.

American troops discovered loot worth more than a million dollars buried by Heinrich Himmler under a barn near Berchtesgaden. Among other Nazi buried treasures found by American forces were 100 tons of gold and silver, five billion German Reichmarks, two million U.S. dollars, four million Norwegian kroner, one hundred million French francs, and countless pieces of priceless art hidden in a mine shaft in Merkers, Belgium. To this day, rumors persist that Nazi treasure is still buried in the Obersalzburg Bavarian Alps. As recently as 1997, The Netherlands announced it has opened an investigation into the whereabouts of some 75 tons of gold, still unaccounted for, from the 145 tons stolen by the Nazis in World War II.

In this tale, I have portrayed a fictional character with a made-up name, Marshal Heidendorff, intended to represent any one of a number of Nazi leaders who were responsible for the rape of the occupied countries and the brutal killings of millions of innocent civilians. One other fictional character in this tale is SS Hauptsturmfuehrer (equivalent of Captain) Otto Streikler, but I have chosen to simply refer to him as Captain (or Kapitan if addressed by a fellow German).

While part of this novel is based on pure speculation about the hiding of Nazi treasure, a number of real historical events have been woven in, although slightly fictionalized to fit the plot: for example, the French Resistance and their "Escape Line," which successfully smuggled approximately 2,500 RAF and U.S. downed airmen out of France; the simple BBC radio code; the traitorous French Milice; and the Flemish house painter, who stole a set of plans of Germany's "Atlantic Wall" defenses.

In writing this novel, I have not attempted textbook precision. There are many well-known historical persons referred to in this book. There are also many fictional characters. The dialog is fabricated and any resemblance to real conversations is purely coincidental; also any resemblance to real persons (except for references to well-known historical figures) is purely coincidental.

I have never visited the Caves of St.-Pierre, but I have visited other caves in France, from which my cave descriptions are derived. To better fit the story, I have moved the St.-Pierre caves a few miles from their real location near Amiens to my mythical village of St.-Pierre-du-Bois. Sir Charles Atwater and Sir Hugh Effington-Peugh are fictional heads of British Intelligence and the British Embassy in Spain respectively, although it is interesting to note that the landed aristocracy filled many of the high-level positions in the British war effort.

The village of St.-Pierre-du-Bois, the central location of this tale, is fictional, but it could have been any one of hundreds of similar villages that were engulfed in the fighting in Normandy.

A word of explanation may be helpful about the term "Reichmark". The currency of Nazi Germany in the 1930s and throughout WWII, the Reichmark became practically worthless upon Germany's defeat.

However, in 1945, the Allies, in collaboration with the new West German government, artificially supported the currency and issued Westmarks, paying one Westmark for every ten Reichmarks. The Westmark was later called the Deutschemark as it is known today.

During the war, the Nazis paid many of the French and the peoples of other occupied countries in Reichmarks for some of the services and goods they were forced to provide—those that had not been stolen outright without compensation. Although hardly adequate, some recompense was due these oppressed people after the war, and was provided to a small extent by the issuance of Westmarks.

To a considerable degree, I have relied on my own memory of events in the 1940s, which occurred during my lifetime and during my service in the US Navy in WWII. These memories are admittedly a bit foggy; but I have also relied on a number of more dependable sources. Like most Americans who lived through "The War," my information sources (thought to be unimpeachable at the time) were LIFE and TIME magazines. The other references to which I am indebted are: The Rise and Fall of The Third Reich by William L. Shirer; The Resistance by Russell Miller, And The Walls Came Tumbling Down by Jack Fishman (in which the Caves of St.-Pierre are mentioned), the editors of Time-Life books; and The New York Times.

I would like to acknowledge the help from numerous friends who read and assisted me with this work: especially Michelle Van Slyke who grew up in France at the time of the German occupation and whose father participated in the Resistance; Sheila Rabe, a distinguished writer; and my good friend, William M. Jenkins, who inspired a portion of this story about the planning for D-Day. Awarded the Navy Cross and the Croix-de-Guerre for his extraordinary accomplishments at D-Day, his real-life story is a good deal more dramatic than my fiction.

In spite of using some factual historical situations, this book is a work of fiction.

John Gould

PROLOGE

1987

Christmas Eve

LYON, FRANCE

Otto Streikler peered through the bars of the tiny cell window and watched sleet forming on the sill. The once powerful officer of the Third Reich now stood tense in prison stripes, face gaunt, his faded blue eyes squinting as he waited. A trickle of melted snow dripped off the edge of the sill, seeped through a hair-crack, and ran down the inside wall. The smell of damp concrete, mixed with the ever-present prison odors of stale urine and sweat, permeated the cell.

A young, potbellied guard, making his three p.m. rounds, rattled his nightstick against the bars of the heavy steel door of Otto's cell. He shook his head and made a circular motion with his forefinger around his left ear.

"So they think I'm crazy. Well, let them think what they like," Otto muttered. Indifferent, he returned to his vigil at the window. He knew the guard would move on, wouldn't speak, and would be satisfied with a cursory inspection.

A maximum-security facility, the prison housed France's worst war criminals, and the jailers showed their contempt for Otto and the other Nazi prisoners by disdainful silence. They spoke only to issue orders.

A crunch of gravel sounded from the driveway, announcing the arrival of a black Renault, which circled and parked in front of the prison entrance. Otto strained closer to the window. A large man, wearing a black robe and porkpie hat, stepped from the car. Otto grunted and nodded with satisfaction as he watched the priest drop the ignition keys into the right pocket of his robe, leaving the Renault unlocked.

During the forty-one years Otto had been in prison, the priest had never faltered in his routine. Always, on three religious holidays, Easter, All Saint's Day, and Christmas Eve, the priest had driven up a few minutes before or after three p.m. and walked from cell to cell, offering prayers to the inmates. In the past, when the priest approached his cell, Otto had sneered and turned his back. The priest would offer, "*Dieu vous benisse, mon fils*"—God bless you my son. It was always the same.

Then earlier this year, on All Saint's Day, an idea had begun to take shape. Otto noticed, as the priest grew older, that the cleric bore a remarkable physical resemblance to him. Both he and the priest were large-framed, in their sixties, with palsied hands and graying hair. There were differences, but Otto knew he could find a way around them. In the last two months he had grown a small, gray beard and trimmed it exactly like the priest's. As for eyeglasses, when the time came, he would simply exchange his own wire spectacles for the cleric's dark horn-rims. To affect the priest's voice would be more difficult. Even after hearing nothing but French for forty-one years, Otto had trouble mimicking a French accent. He had practiced the one phrase he'd heard a hundred times from the priest, *Dieu vous benisse, mon fil*, until he had it perfected.

One other preparation had required intense physical effort. Night after night, for two months, he had struggled to loosen the leg of the steel table in his cell. Two nights ago he had succeeded. Now he was ready.

When Otto had first arrived at the Lyon facility, he had looked forward to the company of other prisoners. Some were collaborators, Frenchmen turned by their conquerors into traitors called *Milice*. Others, like Otto, were German Nazis, several of whom had died in prison. The most recent inmate, Klaus Barbi, "The Butcher of Lyon," had been extradited from Bolivia in 1983 and sentenced by a Lyon court to life imprisonment. Barbi, responsible for the deaths of 4,000 persons and the deportation of 7,500 others, had personally tortured and murdered French prisoners and ordered the death of Resistance leader, Jean Moulin.

Otto had never caught sight of Barbi, but had followed the newspaper accounts of the trial and the sentencing. Barbi had been unrepentant and refused to express remorse. Otto would like to have talked to him—to learn whether he too had been driven to acts of violence by the Fuehrer—or whether he was the evil, self-motivated killer portrayed by the French courts.

However, except for a meager thirty minutes a day alone outside in the prison yard, Otto and the other prisoners had been locked in cramped, isolated cells with no opportunity to communicate. In the beginning, Otto had attempted to tap out a code, but the gray concrete walls were a foot thick, and no sound could be transmitted. The only contacts allowed with the outside world were newspapers and the writing of letters, which were censored. From the newspapers he had learned that his nemesis, the damnable American, was now living in St.-Pierre-du-Bois, France.

Without family or friends, Otto neither sent nor received mail. He had passed the time dreaming of his childhood love, Ilsa, and the beautiful French woman. In forty-one years there had been plenty of time to go over the past in spite of his failing memory. His favorite memory that he played over and over like a broken record was of Ilsa, the pretty little ten-year old with the golden curls and the blue-green eyes. She had smiled at him when they played kickball in the shabby dirt yard with a dozen other children, and Otto had protected her from some of the bigger children who played rough. One day, tragedy struck. A particularly mean older boy slammed into her, throwing her against a rock wall, nearly killing her. Ilsa fell into a coma, from which she never recovered. The older boy lied, and blamed Otto for attempted homicide. He was taken before a Magistrate, who found him guilty and sent him to a reform school. Even his mother had not believed him nor stood up for him. From that day on, Otto nursed a hatred for the entire human race, except for Ilsa, whose memory he treasured like a golden idol. Ironically, the reform school had led to bigger things for Otto. Chosen along with a dozen delinquents, he was plucked from the school and sent to a special program to train for Hitler's newly formed SS.

And then there was the beautiful French girl who looked so much like Ilsa—the same golden hair and blue-green eyes. He struggled to remember now—*yes—her name—her name—ah yes—Renee—that was it*. But she was a spy, wasn't she? She had ruined everything.

When his thoughts turned to the American officer, his features would contort, and his lips would form the silent words, "Some day, some way I will even the score." His memory had gone fuzzy on many things, but one detail stuck in his mind—the gun, a Walther— wrapped in oilcloth, buried under the barn in St.-Pierre.

He would lie on the hard, springless bunk and stare at the single light bulb on the ceiling, watching a cockroach, his only companion, going around and around and around. His eyes would widen, the pupils dilated, and the roach would go out of focus. Lips moving without words and hands shaking, he would relive the glory days of the Third Reich and the time Adolph Hitler had shaken his hand. And those damned Nuremberg judges. *They wouldn't believe I was forced to do those things. I was only following orders. A good soldier. I would have been shot if I hadn't.*

Then, in his more lucid moments, Otto's thoughts would revert to the American who had caused him so much grief—and now to planning his escape.

At 3:04 p.m. on this Christmas Eve, the priest approached Otto's cell, shook his head, and turned to walk on. When Otto called out, "bless me, Father," the surprised guard, who accompanied the cleric, turned and stared at Otto. He hadn't heard ten words from the sullen Nazi in the last year. He looked toward the priest, who nodded his approval, shrugged and unlocked the sliding iron door. The priest, with a slight backward wave of his hand, dismissed the guard and stepped inside the cell. The door clanged shut as the guard locked it behind him.

Otto, who, over many holidays, had watched the priest disappear into the opposite cell to pray, knew the routine. The guard would resume his rounds, not to return for four or five minutes. Even for war criminals, prayers were accorded a short time of privacy.

Starting to sweat, Otto tightened his grip on the steel table leg held behind his back. He calculated, given a one-minute safety margin, he had three or four minutes at the most.

When the priest made the sign of the cross and looked down at the open bible in his hand, Otto raised the steel leg and smashed the porkpie-covered head with his shaky arm. The cleric made no sound as he collapsed into Otto's grasp. *Good, no blood.* Otto grimaced. He knew from experience head wounds bleed profusely if you hit too hard.

Feverishly, Otto threw the priest on the prison cot and pulled the glasses, hat, shoes, and robe from the limp body. These he tossed onto the steel table. Moving rapidly, hands shaking, he removed his own clothes—striped prison shirt, pants, wire-rimmed spectacles—and clumsily transformed priest to prisoner. He propped the cleric on the cot with his back against the corner wall, facing the window.

A clang rang out, and the bars of the neighboring cell rattled and echoed in the hall. The guard was running his nightstick against the grate and returning sooner than usual. In a frenzy of motion, Otto pulled on the black robe, slid into the shoes, jammed the porkpie hat on his head, and was donning the horn-rimmed glasses when the guard peered into the cell.

"Dieu vous benisse, mon fils." Otto bent to retrieve the fallen bible as he intoned the blessing to the figure on the cot. The guard paused, then faced away as Otto finished adjusting the hat and robe. *"Dieu vous benisse, mon fils,"* Otto repeated in his practiced voice. His nerves were now calm and steady. *"Dieu vous benisse, mon fils,"* once more. He tapped on the cell door, the signal the priest had used to tell the guard he was ready to move on. Because Otto's was the last cell to receive prayer, it was his signal to leave the prison.

The guard smiled and slid open the bars to the cell. When they reached the second exit, Otto blessed the guard one more time and was politely ushered to the outer gate. The guard spoke briefly to the Sergeant at the gate, and the steel doors slid open with a grinding moan.

Otto scoffed inwardly. The whole process was ridiculously easy. *In an efficient German prison I'd never get away with such a thing.*

The pot-bellied guard took his arm. "Watch your step, Father. The ground is slippery." He glanced down at the cleric's shoes and stopped abruptly. "Your shoes are untied, Father." Otto felt a shiver of panic, but, after a moment's hesitation, the guard smiled, squatted, and began to tie the shoes.

"*Merci, mon fils,*" Otto said. *The imbecile.* He touched the guard lightly on the head and repeated the blessing. The ties of the shoes had been flapping against the concrete floor the entire walk to the prison door, which the guard had not noticed until now. The guard straightened. "There, that's better." He escorted Otto to the black Renault, opened the door, and helped him in.

Seated behind the wheel, Otto fumbled with the priest's massive key ring until he finally found a key that fit the ignition. The guard leaned over, put his hand on the door latch and squinted through the side window. He frowned at Otto, then shrugged and waited patiently. From somewhere came the sound of a dog barking.

Otto was sweating. Had he forgotten how to drive? He finally found a key that fit. The car jerked, coughed, and died. His shaky hand jingled the keys as he tried again, this time remembering to use the clutch. At last the car came to a purr.

The guard leaned toward the window. "Thank you for coming, Father," he said. "*Joyeux Noel.*"

"*Oui, et vous, un Joyeux Noel,*" Otto muttered with his best attempt at a French accent.

The Renault jerked forward, skidded on the icy gravel, then righted and sped northward into the past.

—

CHAPTER ONE

1940

Nazis Invade Holland, Belgium,
Luxembourg By Land And Air;
Dikes Opened; Allies Rush Aid
<u>New York Times</u>, May 10, 1940

ST.-PIERRE-DU-BOIS, FRANCE

The distant rattle of gunfire and the rumble of approaching tanks ruined the beautiful spring day in the sleepy Normandy town of St.-Pierre-du-Bois. Now, on the Brousard farm, sensations of cold fear replaced the usual springtime delights in the fragrance of blossoming apple trees.

Renee Brousard heard the news. The Germans had crushed Holland and Belgium in less than three weeks and had now broken through the French main line of defense. To her, it seemed every villager, frozen in fear and disbelief, had their ears glued to a radio. Normally, in May, Renee would have been tending her beehives, but now she and her brother, Henri, hunched over their radio, listening to BBC. Renee had discovered the BBC broadcasts to be more accurate and complete than their French counterparts, and, after her year of studying in England, she understood the language like a native.

Adding to the sick, empty feeling forming in the pit of her stomach, her father, whose life had been shattered, fighting in World War I, now turned inward and spoke to no one. To the eighteen-year-old Renee, it seemed the anchor in her life had slipped away into some deep abyss.

Now she knew the time had come to open the mysterious letter from Sir Charles, a letter she had hidden under the lid of a beehive. She had been warned. If the letter fell into the wrong hands, it would cause a serious international incident and ruin Sir Charles. She had been instructed to hide it with extreme care and open it only if Germany invaded France—otherwise burn it.

Making a lame excuse to her brother, she slipped out of the house to the apple orchard, gingerly lifted the lid of a hive, extracted a large brown envelope, and began to read.

June 30, 1939

Dearest Renee,

> *You will be reading this letter only if France has been invaded, a circumstance I have predicted for several years. I have been making the case in Parliament that England must prepare for the inevitable. But few will listen, and, in fact, I have been branded something of a warmonger, as if I, and not Hitler, was fomenting this war.*

> *With the information I have at this time, I can predict with some certainty that France will fall to the Nazi invaders, and that it will happen much more quickly than anyone has predicted. The French government is so proud and stubborn. Not only are they unwilling to listen, especially to an Englishman, but they would be enraged if this letter leaked out, probably causing an international incident. Hence, I am sure you will now understand the reason why I did not want it opened until and unless France is actually invaded, and why it must be destroyed after you have memorized the information you will find below.*

> *I have chosen you to be a courier for this extremely important secret information for several reasons:*

> *- No one would suspect an innocent, eighteen-year-old schoolgirl of being a courier of these high-level intelligence matters.*

- You are intelligent enough to memorize this material, and it must be memorized flawlessly.

- You have a command of both the French and English languages, which will be essential to our success.

- You live in the part of France closest to England, our logical future contact zone whether by radio or by land, sea, or air.

- Most importantly, I trust you and trust your judgment implicitly.

You may not yet realize the seriousness of the situation and the critical importance of your help, but I am sure you will as soon as Hitler unleashes his vicious attacks against France and England – and, I believe, half the civilized world.

If there is to be any chance of beating Hitler at his gruesome game, France must continue to resist from within. Guerrilla warfare has been proven to be extremely effective in tying up large numbers of enemy troops. At the very least, French resistance must provide vital intelligence on troop movements, fortifications, and weapons production if England is to have a chance of survival and of eventually freeing France. Safe houses will be needed for British agents and escapees. There will be a critical need to disrupt German communications systems and traffic arteries such as bridges, railroad lines, transmission lines, etc. The list of needs is long and will become much longer.

Of course, I am concerned about your safety, Renee, so I do not want you involved beyond passing this information along to three contacts that I know to be willing participants in a potential resistance movement. These contacts are all located reasonably close to your home in St.-Pierre, so you should be able to reach them with minimum risk. There must be no written record of these names and addresses, so I repeat this letter must be destroyed, and these names must be memorized. They are:

> *Mme. Anice Roulen   Msr. Geo. Etienne   Msr. H. Pouilon*
>
> *27 Rue de Marse   19 Rue de Palois   Hotel de Ville*
>
> *Caen   Saint-Lo   Cherbourg*

> *British intelligence will monitor the following short-wave frequencies for messages transmitted from these sources: 1698 and 1783 kcs. The frequencies will be changed from time to time, and the new ones will be indicated by the code laid out below, which will cover all information, requests, and instructions from our end.*

> *As long as the Germans do not discover what we are doing, we will simply use BBC broadcasts, which will appear to be ordinary news. In fact, it will be exactly that, except we will insert certain key words, which will signal a message to follow. Any such message will be repeated on the 6 p.m. and 9 p.m. news. It will be a simple code, and we will stick with it only as long as it remains undetected. We believe the Germans will not look for a code in our news broadcasts, since, even now, they are completely absorbed with its propaganda content. They are so obsessed and inflamed over our anti-German rhetoric we are confidant their attention will be diverted from our other purpose.*

Renee continued reading the dozen pages of instructions, starting with the BBC code. It was a simple system of scrambling letters whenever a key word combined with a grammatical error was given.

On the other hand, the code for transmitting from France was much more complicated, because the Germans would obviously be suspicious of any short-wave transmissions coming from occupied territory. The French code was based on page numbers and text of certain books common in France, starting with Balzac. Furthermore, the French reference book would be changed every fourth month. Only Renee would know about these changes. Every fourth month, she would need to pass along the change to the three designated transmitters. The second four-month period would be keyed to

Voltaire, and ten more authors were listed.

Renee stopped reading and stared into space. Good Lord, Sir Charles thinks the war could last as long as forty-eight months. She shook her head and read on.

The code contained a provision for alerting the English monitors if one of the French sources should be captured and forced to transmit false data. The transmitter should make a spelling error in the code at exactly every tenth word, but otherwise seem to be going along with his captors. Thus, he could appear to be a double agent cooperating with the Germans.

The letter ended with a remonstrance not to mention its existence to anyone, and a third reminder to burn it as soon as possible—that is, as soon as she had it committed to memory, and in no case longer than two weeks.

Charles would be looking for confirming messages in the new code from the three designated sources.

The letter was signed,

Most Affectionately,

Charles

> *Post script: As you know, I care for you very much, Renee, and I do not want you taking any undue risks. The Nazis can be exceedingly nasty. If they come nosing around, you must back out of this assignment. We will send word to our contacts some other way. I am assigning you the code name of CRICKET. If there is any trouble, use that name and contact us through one of the sources. Also you must listen to BBC yourself in case we need to warn you of any dangers.   C.A.*

Holding the letter as if it were a hot coal, Renee's hand shook. Her first reaction was to write Atwater and refuse, until she realized that such a letter would have no chance of getting through. And if the letter were intercepted, it would obviously compromise too many important things—for France, for England, for Charles. Also the long distance telephone lines had been cut, so there was no way to communicate, short of setting up the radio contacts Charles had requested.

What if she simply burned the letter and forgot the whole thing? Was there anyone she could talk it over with? No. Charles had warned against that. She decided to sleep on it.

She hid the letter again under the top cover of the farm's beehive. I'm the only person in the world who ever goes into the hive, she reasoned. Addressing a stray bee that landed on her arm, she asked the friendly little critter, "How could I have let myself get into this fix?"

The answer was clear enough. She sat down on the ground and went over in her mind the crazy circumstances that led up to this moment. It had started with the scholarship she had received from her village of St.-Pierre-du-Bois to attend one of the most prestigious girl's schools in England—a goodwill exchange program for outstanding students. She would take her senior year of secondary school, 1938-1939, at St. Anne's near London where she would board during the weekdays but spend weekends and holidays at the estate of Sir Charles Atwood, the youngest son of an Earl and a new Member of Parliament.

She had enjoyed the experience immensely and had quickly mastered the English language, having had a fair grounding at her native school in France. It soon became obvious that Sir Charles, a handsome man in his thirties, was unhappily married, and he began to flirt with his eighteen-year-old boarder.

Renee's older brother, Henri, had warned her about such things. "You may not realize it, *Mon Petite*, but you are an extraordinarily beautiful girl. Beware of smooth-talking men—especially married men. One other thing: watch the way you walk, the way you swing your hips. Oh well, I guess there's nothing you can do about it, but I'm afraid you're going to drive some men wild."

Going out of his way to be kind, Sir Charles had taken her on outings and started confiding feelings of fondness in a typical British starchy manner. At a Christmas party, he had become quite tipsy and kissed her full of the mouth when his wife wasn't looking. Renee had returned the kiss, but embarrassment had set in immediately. She had been flattered, liked the kiss, and liked him well enough, but managed to avoid his advances thereafter.

Subtly, Charles expressed his frustration with his wife's lack of interest in his political life and began using Renee as a sounding board for some of his ideas. Apparently finding the exchange of ideas stimulating, he confided to her the outlines of his role in Parliament, which included oversight of the newly rejuvenated British Intelligence Service. On the last day of her stay in England, in June of 1939, Sir Charles kissed her hard on the lips again as he bid farewell and handed her a large plain brown envelope. In a serious tone, he told her it was extremely important and must not be opened until and unless Germany invaded France, after which it must be memorized and destroyed. He had refused to elaborate.

Now, a year later, fear and indecision tormented her. Days went by, and she hardly slept, nor did she come any closer to a decision. In the meantime, like a flash flood, the Germans swept through Normandy on their way to Paris. Fortunately for the Brusards, the main fighting bypassed St.-Pierre, but to her horror, she could see the French army crumbling. Then the debacle of Dunkirk followed swiftly, and she heard tales of unbelievable German atrocities in Holland and Belgium.

Numbly, Renee pulled the letter from the beehive and began to memorize every word. *Madame Anice Roulen, 27 Rue de Marse* ... She went over and over the words in her mind as she worked in the fields, in bed at night, when she rode her bicycle to the village— every waking minute.

The specified two weeks flew by like a black cloud in a windstorm. Charles must be alarmed and dismayed, having heard nothing from Roulen, Etienne, or Pouilon. It would take another week of concentrated reading and re-reading before she could make her first contact. She decided it would be with Monsieur Etienne in St.-Lo, the closest to St.-Pierre.

Even then she couldn't bring herself to burn the letter and decided it would be safe enough hidden in the beehive—at least for a while. The codes were the hard part. She might have to refer to them one more time.

Since petrol for the farm's truck was impossibly scarce, Renee set out for St.-Lo on her bicycle, only an hour's ride.

German troops and an occasional command car passed on the road, eyeing her curiously. *What if they stop and quiz me? Would they be able to wring the truth out of me? And what about all the terrible stories of torture and rape? They can't be true, can they?* She was not accosted, but all manner of frightening thoughts loomed in her mind. In the future she vowed to wear a shawl and shapeless clothing.

Renee found Msr. Etienne with no difficulty. A small shopkeeper with very little business, he sat in front of his Tabac shop smoking a pipe and reading Le Figaro.

"*Bonjour Monsieur,*" Renee began tentatively, leaning her bicycle against the wall. "You are Monsieur Etienne?"

"*Oui, Madame.* What can I do for you?"

"I believe we have a mutual acquaintance, a Monsieur Charles Atwater, who has suggested I bring you greetings."

The sleepy Etienne instantly dropped his newspaper and sat at attention. His head popped around like a turtle, as he looked to see who might have seen them together. Knocking the ashes out of his pipe, he stared at Renee with dark, piercing eyes, then rose silently and beckoned her to come inside. Middle-aged with sallow cheeks and a neat black mustache, Etienne was a string bean. Renee looked at his long nose and elongated neck. He'd make a perfect Don Quixote, she mused.

Placing a *FERME* sign on the door, he pointed to the only chair. "Business has been slow today," he said quietly. "Yes, I know an Englishman by the name of Atwater." An awkward silence grew between them. "May I ask how you happen to know this Englishman?"

"I lived with the Atwaters for a year, and I..." Renee went on to explain the relationship in a near whisper.

"In the future, you must not be so open," Etienne cautioned. "You must not tell your name or even where you are from." He stared at her and finally continued, "Nevertheless, it is clear you are who you say you are. We must be very, very cautious." He tapped the stem of his pipe against his front teeth. "And you absolutely must not trust anyone unless you are very, very, *very* sure."

She nodded, frowning, as the dangers began to sink in. "I'm sure you're right, Monsieur."

"I was expecting someone to contact me," Etienne added, "but, to be quite frank, I had no idea it would be a young woman. I hate to see someone like you exposed to this. We could all be killed, you know."

Renee nodded slowly, paused, and went on to explain her mission, including the codes, in painstaking detail.

"You will, no doubt, need to write down all of this," she said, "but memorize it and burn it as soon as you can."

"Yes, of course," Etienne said, "but what about changes? Will there be any occasion to meet with you again?"

"Yes. I will bring you a revised code every fourth month."

"I see. And then ...?" He fiddled with his pipe.

"You must send a confirmation in code to London right away, saying I've made contact with you. Always refer to my code name, 'Cricket.'"

"All right, Cricket." Etienne jabbed the stem of his pipe in her direction. "But you must be seen with me as little as possible. If I sense any trouble, even the slightest whiff, I'll place a large white vase in the front window of the store. If it's there, you must not stop. You mustn't even slow down."

Renee nodded.

"Here, let me show you the vase and the window, so there can be no mistake."

Etienne re-lit his pipe, sat back and looked at Renee thoughtfully. "Let's pray we both get out of this alive. All I can say is, be careful— very, very careful," he repeated, "and if there's any doubt about anything, err on the side of caution."

"Yes, certainly." Renee nodded.

"We must both listen to BBC every night," he continued. "I will relay any suspicious activities and warnings to London using the code. They'll be passed back to both of us from London using your code name."

"Certainly. I understand." She nodded again, but the back of her neck began to feel prickly. She felt a sudden urgency to flee back to the familiar surroundings of the Brousard farm.

"Any day now," Etienne added, "the Boche will try to confiscate our radios, but, of course, we must keep ours. We must hide them. Hide them very, very well."

"I'm sure you're right. I'll do that," she responded slowly.

He rose and stared at her, his eyes misting perceptibly, then hugged her. "May God go with you," he murmured and turned away to hide his tears.

When Renee returned home, she removed the letter from the beehive and studied it late into the night—one last time. Now it was etched into her memory and could be burned.

In order to reach Mme. Roulen in Caen and Msr. Pouilon in Cherbourg, she would need to set aside a full day for each. A train ran daily to Cherbourg, but the Germans had started checking every traveler's identity and their reasons for travel. Bicycling would be safer.

She made weak excuses for her absences to her father and brother, but she could see that Henri was beginning to suspect something unusual was going on.

Pouilon's address had made Renee particularly nervous about making contact. She suspected the *hotel de ville*, city hall, in Cherbourg, would be occupied by the Germans. So, when she circled the building on her bicycle, sure enough, the first thing she saw was a row of German command cars parked in front.

With a shawl pulled over her head and slightly hunched over, she climbed the stairs, pulled open the heavy door and peered inside, not unlike a timid child playing hide-and-seek. A German soldier sat at the reception desk, and a French gendarme sat at a small table to one side. In French, she started to ask the German if she could see Monsieur Pouilon, but before the first words were out, the soldier pointed to the Gendarme. Apparently, the German either did not speak French or he did not wish to be bothered with an unimportant woman.

The Frenchman, in a strained voice, told her to wait to one side. He would summon Pouilon.

Minutes later, Pouilon strode into the entry hall and spoke to the German soldier in German. The latter nodded and pointed in the direction of Renee.

Poulion introduced himself brusquely to Renee, "I am Monsieur Pouilon. You wish to see me?"

"Yes, Monsieur," she spoke in low voice, "I would like to speak to you in private if possible."

He took her arm, and steered her out the door before she could say any more. "Who are you," he asked. "Please identify yourself."

"Monsieur Atwater asked me to bring you greetings."

"I was expecting you," he whispered as they walked down the stairs. "Let's walk down by the river. There are some benches."

When she was sure they were alone, Renee explained her mission as she had explained it to Etienne, except she did not give her real name or where she lived. Poulion confided to her that he was a minor official and had gone out of his way to ingratiate himself with the Germans. He also spoke German, acting as their interpreter, an indispensable service to the occupiers.

"I'm sorry I have only a few minutes to explain everything," she said. "I have a long ride home and must be back before dark." Talking fast, she told him the essentials. He took out a small scrap of paper and wrote down the codes as Renee dictated.

"You must burn that piece of paper as soon as you have it memorized, tomorrow at the latest."

"Yes, certainly," Pouilon nodded, "but we must agree on a place to meet again. We will need a different contact point."

First looking over shoulder, Renee fidgeted and nodded. "Yes, of course. You know Cherbourg. I don't."

In the end they agreed to meet on a different bench by the river. He would be there once a week on Fridays at lunch hour in case an emergency was signaled via a BBC coded message. However, if everything went well, he would not expect to see her for four months. If he suspected he was being watched, he would warn her by a newspaper rolled up and wedged under the armrest.

"If you see the newspaper, don't even go near the bench," he said.

Three days later, Renee visited Madame Roulen in Caen. A large woman, obviously in poor health, she was, nevertheless, eager to participate. Renee gave her the codes as before, but went away worried, peddling hard. The woman seemed to Renee to be a bit too eager.

The next evening, Renee gave a sigh of relief when she heard the confirmations to "Cricket" on the BBC news. The three sources had successfully contacted London.

*   *   *

Almost immediately, the Germans instituted systems of iron-fisted control over the northern half of France. Every Frenchman in the sector was required to register and be fingerprinted by the SS.

Renee stood in the long line of silent men and women. A black-shirted soldier stood at each side with a bayoneted rifle held at the ready. Three hours later, Renee finally reached the front of the line, a German barking questions at her in broken French, "Name. Address. Occupation. Age. Put fingerprint here." Renee smiled prettily at the German as she smudged her fingerprint. *Maybe it was intentional or was it a nervous twitch?*

Afterwards, a second soldier handed each person a list of regulations about the curfew, work requirements, ration cards, travel cards, identification cards—every imaginable rule and permit, printed in both French and German. The Germans liked to be thorough.

In spite of dire threats against it, Renee listened secretly to the BBC every night. She learned that the Germans were leaving the Southern portion of France under the control of the puppet Vichy Government for the time being. According to the British, this was because the Germans had barely enough manpower to control their nine occupied countries—Austria, Czechoslovakia, Poland, Denmark, Norway, Belgium, Holland, Luxembourg and half of France—plus mobilize for the next invasion.

Next she heard the warning on BBC. "Hide your radios immediately. Repeat, immediately. The SS is planning a raid tonight. Penalties are severe."

Her brother, Henri, had anticipated this edict and had already pried loose some boards in the floor of the cellar, exposing an ancient crawl space about a meter deep. Less than fifteen minutes after the warning on BBC, Renee heard heavy pounding on the front door. Without waiting to find out who was knocking, she grabbed the radio, ran to the cellar, jammed it into the hole, and loosely replaced the boards. Henri, hesitated as long as he dared, then opened the door. Three Gestapo blackshirts, carrying flashlights, pushed past him. One ran upstairs, one down to the cellar, and one stalked through the rooms on the main floor, pushing furniture aside and looking in closets. Only one, a corporal, spoke some French. "You listen English radio, Yes?" he snapped.

Renee lied, *"Nous n'avons pas un radio."*

The Corporal peered suspiciously at Renee. "You better tell truth," he said, pointing the flashlight into her face. But obviously he was in a hurry, no doubt with other houses to raid. "We come back again," he growled, with which he rushed out of the house, slamming the door.

As time went by, Renee discovered that the BBC reports were quite accurate, and she began to rely on them not only for warnings but also as the only source of factual news. According to the BBC, and also rumors traveling north from Vichy, the Petain puppet Government had become a willing lackey of the Nazis. They had set up a Gestapo-like police, using French nationals called *Milice*. Renee was appalled when she heard the details on good authority. Made up of French thugs and released criminals, the *Milice* were arresting, torturing, and killing thousands of their own people, Frenchmen suspected of aiding the Resistance.

In St.-Pierre, Renee watched with disgust as the Germans made clumsy efforts to control the French with their heavy-handed methods. On the other hand, their unfamiliarity with the French language and customs made it nearly impossible for them to tell the difference between real collaborators and French resisters.

As a result, the Germans increasingly resorted to the *Milice*, rewarding them with bounty payments. These thugs became masters at penetrating the Resistance, wrecking the cover of Allied agents, destroying safe houses, and even committing murder on demand.

Renee and Henri and the loyal French came to hate the *Milice* more than they hated the Germans. They were, after all, contemptible traitors, even worse than an oppressive conqueror.

Each Friday, Renee walked into the village to buy the few staples needed for the farm. With a shawl over her head, she practiced walking without swinging her hips. It wasn't easy, but the last thing she wanted to do was attract attention.

On the last Friday in September, when the air held the first nip of fall, she saw the large posters tacked on every tree and storefront.

ALL RADIOS SHALL BE TURNED INTO SS HEADQUARTERS IMMEDIATELY. ANY PERSON APPREHENDED WITH A RADIO (OTHER THAN AUTHORIZED MILITARY PERSONNEL) WILL BE PROSECUTED. THE PENALTY WILL BE A FINE OF 10,000 FRANCS AND IMPRISONMENT.

Renee hurried home to find Henri alone in the barn. "Did you hear about the radios?" she asked. "We're supposed to turn them in. There's a ten thousand-franc fine. And the notice says imprisonment too."

Henri stared at her and frowned. "So they finally made it official, but obviously we can't do that. We won't have any idea what's going on."

"I know. For one thing, we've got to be able to listen to de Gaulle."

"Father will insist on turning them in. I know he will. He'll say we haven't got 10,000 francs."

"Well, we're not going to do it," Renee said. "We'll just have to hide it and lie to father. I'll tell him it was stolen."

Renee couldn't tell Henri about her dealings with Atwater and her special need to listen to the BBC, but she could see that his suspicions were growing. Stoic by nature, Henri only stared at her and said nothing.

Renee felt as if she was being drawn deeper into a tar pit, stuck with no way out. She started going over contingencies in her mind—what to do or say if she was caught, escape paths, hiding places, maybe a hidden trap door into the crawl space under the kitchen or the root cellar. Maybe the secret entrance to the St.-Pierre caves?

The very thought brought a smile, replacing her frown, as

she recalled the happy day in her youth when she and Denis had discovered the entrance to the caves. She was eight years old, and Denis LeCoc, the stocky, red haired boy from the neighboring farm, was her only close childhood friend.

In the middle of the night, she heard the pebble hit her window. She sat up in bed, clutching her doll, and strained to hear. Another pebble. Silently slipping out of bed, she pushed open the window and peered into the yard where she made out a form dimly in the moonlight.

"Come on down," Denis whispered, waving his arms. "I've got to show you something."

"Are you crazy? Go away," Renee hissed. "My father'll kill me. And you too."

"I've got a secret camp. You gotta see it now, or you'll never get into my club."

With no idea what he was talking about, she said nothing.

"Hurry up, and bring a candle."

Curiosity got the better of her. She pulled a sweater over her nightclothes, put on shoes, picked up the stub of a candle, then climbed out the window onto the low roof, and shinnied down the apple tree that grew just close enough.

"Denis, this is stupid," she whispered, poking a finger at his middle.

"No, it's not. I'll show you. Did you bring the candle?"

"Un huh, but ..."

"Shhh, just follow me," he whispered.

Denis led the way for the better part of a kilometer, then pointed to a hole in the ground. "Look what I found."

Not more than a meter in diameter and partially covered with brush, it didn't look like much to Renee. "So what. It's just a hole," she said with exasperation.

"No. Look, it's a secret entrance to the St.-Pierre caves—from the backside. No one else knows about it. Just you and me." Without waiting for a response, Denis pushed the brush aside and started to squeeze, feet first, down into the hole. "Come on," he whispered.

Everyone in St.-Pierre-du-Bois knew about the caves. At one

time, a limestone quarry, it was now abandoned. The caves, which in ancient times had served as a refuge for the hunted, went down hundreds of feet and then horizontally for more than a mile in five different directions. Never completely explored, they were dangerous. Every child in the village grew up with a warning to stay away for fear of getting lost.

At the main entrance, tour conductors took visitors, for a fee, down the stairs cut into limestone walls and to cavernous galleries studded with stalactites and stalagmites. The guides would point out mystical ancient symbols carved in the stone walls, including depictions of woolly mammoths, and strange horned beasts. There were stories of medieval knights hiding in the cave and of poor folk seeking refuge from marauding crusaders.

Renee had heard rumors of other entrances or airshafts but had never believed they existed—until this day.

"I'll light the candles," Denis said, pulling out matches and lighting both candles at the same time.

They could now see the outline of a shaft going down at an angle with just enough bumps and crevices to provide a few handholds.

"Gee, Denis," Renee whispered, as if someone else might be listening. "We shouldn't go down. We could get lost."

"Come on. It's all right. I've already been down once."

At the end of the wet, slippery shaft, they came to a huge cathedral-like room. In the flickering candlelight, the huge stalactites created ghostly shadows. Shielding her candle, Renee looked around and shivered. Suddenly there was a rush of air and their candles blew out.

Renee grabbed Denis' arm. "I'm scared," she whispered. "Let's get out of here."

"Don't be a mouse," Denis said, re-lighting the candles. "Look. We can have a secret camp here. See these shelves. And look over there, a perfect fireplace."

"Un huh."

"Look. This is just like a big church. We can get married down here. We'll have a secret wedding, and Father Francois can marry us again after."

"Un huh."

"We'll hide the entrance with branches and stuff. No one will know about it, except you and me. Someday we'll explore the rest of the caves."

"Sure, Denis, it's terrif, but I've got to get back home before I get in real trouble."

Denis gripped her arm. "Someday we can make money and charge for tours, but only after they've sworn never to tell anyone."

"Denis, that sounds like ..." She didn't finish the thought. "We've got to get home before my father finds out."

Now, ten years later, she went over in her mind the pros and cons of using the caves as a hiding place for the radio and perhaps some other things the Germans might want to confiscate. But there were a few problems. The entrance was too far away from the farm for quick access. She might be seen, and it was dangerous to go out after dark because of the curfew. Besides, if she used the caves, she would have to tell Henri, and she'd promised Denis to keep the entrance a secret. Still, she needed to talk it over with someone.

The next Nazi edict hit the French like a thunderbolt.

ALL MALES, AGE 17 AND OLDER, RESIDING
IN FRANCE, REGARDLESS OF NATIONALITY,
SHALL REGISTER IMMEDIATELY AT THE
NEAREST SS HEADQUARTERS.

Claude Brousard, at age sixty, reported as required, but was excused to run the farm. The Germans needed food as much as they needed forced labor or unwilling soldiers. "I fear for Henri," he said to his wife, Annette, when he returned. "They're not letting any of the young men off for any reason. They're sending them off to Germany for God knows what."

Renee could see her mother near tears. "Didn't you explain to them," Annette protested. "We need Henri. The farm needs him."

"That excuse won't work," Claude said. "All the young men are being taken. The women will be expected to do the farm work."

After registering, Henri was told to report back in five days.

He should bring one small suitcase containing clothing and toilet articles—nothing else. An assignment would be made at that time. In one sense, he was fortunate. Some of the young men had been put on a train for Germany the same day they reported.

Walking home slowly, Henri fumed. He had watched his friends, neighbors, and old school chums, Denis, Anton, Jacques, Paul, and a dozen others standing in the same line. He would talk to them.

That night, in violation of the curfew, Henri crept over to Denis's house. "Damn the Bosch," Henri snapped at Denis. "They want to ship me off to Germany. What about you?"

"Yeah, me too. I've only got four days, but Anton and Jacques: they have to go Tuesday. Damn, damn, damn them. I can't believe the bastards."

"They're trying to tell us the pay'll be good and the working conditions just wonderful, but I've heard different."

Denis pulled on one earlobe and frowned. "Well, if the stories I've heard from Holland and Belgium are true, half the workers are starving, and a third of them have been forced into the Wehrmacht."

"The stories are true all right," Henri agreed angrily. "BBC's been reporting it, and everything they've said has proven to be absolutely accurate."

Henri was interrupted by a soft knock on the back door. "I think it's Anton and Jacques," Denis said. "I asked them to come over."

Anton and Jacques pushed their way in. "*Comment ce va?* Sure glad to see you, Henri," Anton said, out of breath. "We need to talk. I don't know what the hell to do."

"Denis tells me you have to go Tuesday. The bastards only gave you three days. Is that right?"

"Yeah, me too. How about you, Henri?"

"Five days. But I'm thinking maybe we shouldn't go."

"Chee-rist, they'll shoot us if we don't," Anton exclaimed.

They all looked at Henri. "I've been thinking," he said slowly. "We have choices. We can go to Germany and die of starvation or die fighting in the Wehrmacht, or we can go into hiding. We know the woods and the rivers around here ten times better than the Bosch. Then there's the St.-Pierre Caves. They'd never find us there."

The other three continued to stare at Henri. Anton broke the silence. "I don't know. We're liable to starve that way too."

"Maybe," Henri said, "but at least we won't be helping the damn Nazis win the war. We've all got guns, and we're all pretty good at hunting. Fishing too."

Jacques spoke up. "I'm with you, Henri. The four of us would make a pretty good team. We can survive. The Bosch'll never find us."

"Count me in too," Denis said. "I know a hidden entrance to the caves. Renee and I've been keeping it a secret, but I'll show you. They'll never find it."

Henri nodded. "We'll keep the caves in reserve in case we really get in trouble, but I think we'd be better off now in the woods where we can hunt and fish." He looked around for confirmation and saw them nod. Then he turned to Anton. "How about it Anton. We need you too."

"All right. I'm with you. But we haven't much time."

Henri could see they were all looking at him. "What the hell do we have to lose?" he growled. "This gives us something to live for. We're going to beat the bastards eventually, you know. It's going to be tough and damn dangerous, but we can do it. Let's shake on it. We're a team."

Solemnly they shook hands and embraced.

"Like Anton said," Henri continued, "we've got to move fast. We'd better clear out by Monday. Gives us two days to get our stuff together. We'll need clothes, blankets, guns, ammo, a lot of other things. We'll have to think hard about it."

"I know a couple of other guys who'd probably join us," Jacques said.

"Me too," Denis added. "I can think of four or five."

Henri scratched his left ear. "Good. But only good men. We don't want anyone who'll be a problem. Gotta be damn careful we don't get anyone who'd cave in and sell us out when the going gets tough."

Henri saw them nod. "Let's meet tomorrow night at the creek behind my house. It's a good hiding place, a good place to stash our gear. Bring your friends—only the ones you can really vouch for—and we'll firm up the plan. But don't say a word to anyone else, even your family."

At midnight Henri shook his sister awake. "I think it's time, *mon petite,* to talk." Renee gradually came awake, sat up and frowned.

"I'm leaving tonight with Denis," Henri paused to let the words sink in. "I don't want Papa, or even you, to know where we're going—in case the Nazis force you to talk. It's enough for you to know we're not going to work for the Nazis."

Renee tried to ask a question, but he cut her off, "Tell Papa I love him and not to worry. We know how to take care of ourselves."

They stared at each other. "Now, Renee, I know you've been up to something, and I suspect it would be safer if you don't tell me what it is. Just don't get too involved. The Nazis would just as soon shoot you as swat a fly."

Renee put her arms around her brother, and a tear ran down her cheek. "We've got to figure some way to stay in touch," she whispered.

"Our biggest problem'll be food," he said, ignoring her point and her tears. "We'll have to forage and even steal."

"Just from the Bosch I hope," Renee said, recovering her composure.

"I have my gun to shoot birds and rabbits, but I'd be shot if they catch me with it." He began to speak rapidly with urgency. "We have friends who'll help. I better not tell you who, but we'll have to be extra careful of collaborators. Never too sure who might turn on us to save their own hide."

"I'll save some potatoes and cabbages for you, but I'll have to hide them."

"The Bosch will probably come around looking for me," Henri said, "and they'll think it's suspicious if you have a pile of extra food in the house, so leave whatever you can spare out in the root cellar."

"All right. I can do that."

"Let's agree on a time when we can meet. There'll be a lot of things we haven't thought about."

"You'd better come at night."

"All right. To begin with, how about meeting next Friday at

midnight? I'll knock on the back door—three short knocks, then three more, repeated twice. *D'accord?*"

Renee hugged him fiercely. "All right, I'll go along with that for now, but we may want to change some things after we think about it. But for God's sake, Henri, be careful."

Armed with little more than their determination, Henri and twelve other young men took to the woods of western Normandy and Brittany. Rocky, forested, and hilly, the area was sparsely inhabited, but Henri and his childhood friends had hunted and tramped it since they were children. They knew it as well as a fox knows his own burrow.

At first, the majority of Frenchmen reported to their captors as ordered. But the stories began filtering back, confirming the earlier rumors, telling of atrocious treatment in Germany. The pay was nil, many were starving, and thousands were being forced to fight in the Wehrmacht. As a result, thousands more young Frenchmen, like Henri, went into hiding. Disappearing into the forests, mountains, swamps, and caves, they gradually organized themselves into the *Maquis*, which became the nucleus of the Resistance.

* * *

In the beginning, the Germans left Claude alone to run the farm. But as the war wore on, the shortage of food grew into a major crisis, and the Nazis began to confiscate increasing amounts of the produce with only token compensation.

Once a week, a truck would back up to the Brousard's barn. Silently, the soldiers would load precisely half of everything—the potatoes, cabbages, apples, beets—whatever was available. The Sergeant would address Claude in broken French. "I must have list, list of everything in storage, everything in fields."

With tight lips, Claude would hand over the requested piece of paper, knowing the frightful punishment if he held back anything or failed to have the inventory ready.

On the third visit, the Sergeant demanded, "We will require ten percent more next time," then turned on his heel, not waiting for a response. To Claude, this meant his half share of his own produce would be reduced to forty percent. He ground his teeth and spat on the ground.

GERMANY

Captain Otto Streikler was swept along with the tide of Nazi conquest. He listened with pride to the daily bursts of news from Propaganda Minister Goebbels as the Wehrmacht overran Poland in a matter of weeks in the fall of 1939, then feverishly built up its military strength during the winter.

In May of 1940, the Wehrmacht unleashed its Blitzkrieg on Holland and Belgium, while Hitler delivered impassioned speeches, exhorting their *"Deutsch bruders"* to serve their conquerors with zeal. They were ordered to contribute manpower and materials to the Nazi industrial war effort and fighting men to the Wehrmacht. Then Otto began to hear the rumors. When a German soldier walked into a Dutch restaurant, the Dutchmen would walk out. Telephone lines were cut. German flags disappeared in the middle of the night. Underground newspapers sprang up, denouncing the Nazis. But Herr Goebbels' propaganda failed to mention such news items, instead trumpeting how much the Dutch loved their new masters.

Nevertheless, within the German military, Hitler expressed his fury with the Dutch and decreed, in January of 1941, that the "criminals be taught a lesson, a lesson that will serve as a warning to the Belgians, the Danes, the French, and others yet to come." The lesson would involve turning the SS loose on them after the regular troops moved on.

*　　　*　　　*

Marshal Heidendorff, covered with medals, including the iron cross, was flushed and excited as he tapped on the large map spread across his desk. The Hitleresque mustache twitched as he spoke, and he sweated like a horse at Derby Day. Otto thought the man looked sick.

Heidendorff slurred his words. "I have recalled you from Austria, Kapitan Streikler, for another important project." The Marshal had put on another fifty pounds since their last meeting and now tipped the scales at almost three hundred pounds. He reminded Otto of a giant frog.

Heidendorff pounded the map with his massive fist to indicate where Austria used to be. "In many ways this assignment is similar to those you have carried out so successfully in Vienna."

Otto saluted and clicked his heels. "At your service, Herr Marshal." He was beginning to feel slightly more comfortable with the awesome Marshal.

The jowly face scowled. "The Fuehrer is rightfully incensed with the lack of cooperation of the Dutch. As you know, the Wehrmacht has moved on to Belgium and France." The fist pounded on the subject countries. "What we need now is a strong hand to bring the Dutch into line. The SS must step in and provide that strong hand—provide the necessary force to create proper order." The table shuddered as the fat man pounded his fist on the map again.

"You will have a full battalion of SS troops under your command, Kapitan. The Fuehrer wants this job done right—thoroughly—no loose ends, no half measures. You are to teach the Dutch a lesson—a hard lesson. It will send a message to the other occupied countries. They must cooperate or face the full fury of the German forces. There will be nothing left but smoke and rubble. You understand? Smoke and rubble. You must make them understand that."

"Yes, Herr Marshal, of course."

Eyes glittering and voice rising, the Marshal went on at length, making it clear that the Captain would have considerable discretion. He would not be held responsible for any necessary killings— 'atrocities' as the soft Allies might call them. The important thing was to get the job done thoroughly.

"All Jews are to be rounded up and shipped back to Germany for forced labor or to the concentration camps." Heidendorff was sweating profusely now. "You will route them to Ravensbrueck, and Herr Himmler will determine their dispensation from there. Do you have any questions about that part of the assignment?"

"No. It is quite clear."

"Then, all Jewish property, having any significant value, is to be confiscated and shipped to Germany in accordance with the written orders in this packet of instructions." The Marshal handed Otto a thick packet marked SECRET. "On this assignment you will report to General Schoenigburger in regard to all matters—except, of course, the artwork. The artwork is to be routed to my Bernau estate and will be handled from there."

"Yes, of course—like before in Austria."

"Yes, exactly. Except, in regard to the art, you will use Netherlands 'credits' to compensate any owner who can be found. The credits will give the appearance of legal purchase."

"I'm not sure I understand, Herr Marshal."

"It's all explained in your written instructions. Holland has been charged the cost of the invasion and, in payment, has issued credits in that amount.[2] Now we will use those credits to acquire certain items, including art masterpieces."

"I see."

"Anyone resisting, whether Jew or not, will be shot. You need not trouble yourself with legal proceedings. Is that clear?"

"Yes, Herr Marshal."

"Next, certain industrial materials, machinery, food, clothing, and vehicles needed for the German war effort are to be taken and shipped to Germany. The specific items are spelled out in your written instructions. For further orders, you will report immediately to General Schoenigburger in Amsterdam."

Heidendorff waved his fat hand, a signal of dismissal. "That will be all, Kapitan."

Transferred two days later to Amsterdam, Otto Streikler proceeded to carry out his assignments with commendable efficiency. General Schoenigburger made it clear. He was to show no mercy. He was ordered to assassinate two or three bankers and diamond merchants regardless of their guilt, preferably in public places so the general populace would get the message. It would set an example. The rest would fall in line.

Otto did not sleep for two nights. He had saluted and answered,

"Yes, Herr General," knowing his career—and probably his life—depended on following orders. But his stomach churned and his hands shook when he returned to his barracks.

Ordered to strike quickly, he rose at sunrise the next day, assembled a squad of SS, and set about visiting the business establishments known to deal in gold and diamonds. Transvaal de Meers, Ltd. headed a short list provided by the General.

President Roos van der Voort, being a particularly conscientious businessman, took pride in being the first employee to open the Transvaal bank in the morning. He had just opened for business, and the other clerks had assumed their duties, when Otto's troop marched up to the entrance. Otto stood ramrod straight, pressing his right hand hard against the pistol lodged in his belt to hide the shaking, and demanded to see the President. Half a dozen bank employees cowered silently against the back wall, while the SS squad held their guns at the ready, and a secretary went to fetch President van der Voort.

"We wish to inspect your vault," Otto ordered when the president emerged from his office, tentatively holding out his hand.

Otto refused the handshake. "You will open it at once," he growled.

Van der Voort, a small, balding man with thick gold-rimmed glasses, hesitated. "Of course, *Herr Kapitan*, but my assistant in charge of the vaults is not here and—"

Otto pulled his Walther out of its holster and shoved it hard into the small round belly. "I will not repeat myself. You will open it now."

"Certainly, *Kapitan*." Van der Voort's hands shook as he twirled the dials. Otto could hear the dials turning, but he could also see that the man was trying to obscure the combination by standing between him and the dials.

Otto lowered his voice and pushed the gun into the Dutchman's back, clutching it in a vise-grip with both hands. "You will write down the combination and turn the dials slowly."

"But, *Herr Kapitan*, this is highly—"

"NOW," Otto demanded, shoving a paper and pen into the man's shaking hands.

Van der Voort wrote six barely legible numbers on the paper, opened the vault, paled, and stepped aside. The vault stood empty. The reason was obvious to Otto. The Dutchman had cleaned out the vault and hidden everything. He had been warned.

"Where is your gold?" Otto demanded, pushing the gun harder into the Dutchman's belly.

"It is gone. We shipped it all out of the country."

"I don't believe you." Otto spat out the words. "Let me explain very simply. If you don't lead us to the gold now," he paused and stared at the Dutchman, "I will shoot you."

Van der Voort stood erect and stared back at Otto. "No. It is a sacred trust, more sacred than life itself to me. You will have to shoot me."

Otto glared at the Dutchman. "Sergeant, tie his hands. Take him out to the street."

In February, the trees were bare, and patches of ice covered the street in front of Transvaal de Meers. Heavily dressed women and businessmen, hurrying along the busy street, turned to stare, as a dozen black-shirted German SS propelled the small Dutchman out onto the sidewalk.

Two soldiers tied him a lamppost, while a small crowd gathered. Otto, first looking around to be sure there was a crowd to witness, barked the orders to his squad of twelve men. "Back off ten meters."

Van der Voort started to babble incoherently, and a low murmur of protest rippled through the crowd.

Otto raised his right arm, "Take aim." He brought his arm came down. "Fire."

At that close range, the twelve bullets ripped the man apart, spattering pieces of flesh against the far wall. A river of blood ran down the lamppost and into the gutter. A woman screamed and a dog howled, but the rest of the crowd fell silent, staring at Otto with undisguised hatred.

"Leave the body where it is," he said.

That night, Otto sat alone, sleepless, on the edge of his cot. He pressed his forehead with both hands, trying to make the nightmare go away—the rivers of blood, the globs of flesh, the screams, the hatred in a woman's face, the wide-eyed blank look of a child, the grin on General Schoenigburger's face as he delivered congratulations.

Not surprisingly, the hiding of gold and diamonds stopped. To stay one step ahead of the firing squads, the bankers, traders, and merchants began bringing their gold to SS headquarters in wheelbarrows. There was no petrol available for automobiles.

Otto managed to hide signs of weakness from his men by lowering his voice to a growl and keeping his shaky grip on his sidearm or hooking his thumbs into his belt. His men broke into every bank, demanding the vaults be opened, and Heidendorff sent auditors to check the books. If there was a discrepancy, or if a safe deposit box had recently been emptied, the missing valuables were tracked down and the offender shot forthwith.

The Marshal had ordered Otto to be particularly diligent about confiscating any gold or diamonds that had the slightest connection to a Jew. If a bank or an importer had only a single Jewish employee, it was enough to impound the entire business. If a man even looked Jewish—a swarthy complexion and hooked nose was enough—he was shipped to Ravensbreuck and his possessions confiscated. Hunted with Germanic efficiency, hardly a Jew, or anyone resembling a Jew, escaped Otto's net.

Otto watched stonily as the General underscored his authority by swaggering down the streets of Amsterdam, carrying a riding crop. He would snap it against his leg, as he walked and smiled when women and children cringed and ran inside. But Otto's shaking intensified, and an uncontrollable tic in one eye began dogging him day and night. He could not hide the tic.

ROOSEVELT NOMINATED FOR THIRD TERM
July 19, 1940

PRINCETON, NEW JERSEY

In September of 1940, Mitch Carter had begun his freshman year to study architecture at Princeton University, a world totally new to him, like Alice stepping through the looking glass.

On his first day, he had marveled at the neo-gothic architecture, mellowed by time and ivy. And the history—Woodrow Wilson, Aaron Burr, George Washington, the cannon balls still lodged in the walls of Nassau Hall from the battle of Princeton in 1777. His fingers itched to attack his sketchbook.

Every freshman was required to take history in depth, and this included a full measure of current history, playing out at the time. As well informed of world events as most Washington legislators, Mitch and his classmates followed the news and analyzed it in class. The conflict in Europe held them spellbound like a thriller movie.

Half a world away, the forces of Nazi Germany were sweeping through the low lands and into France like a hoard of locusts; and, hanging on by a thread, Britain had every reason to expect an invasion of their virtually defenseless island.

At Princeton, Professor Wardenbaker stirred the debate: "Who thinks we should help the British before it's too late?"

A dozen hands went up. He pointed to George Adams in the front row. "I think it would be a terrible waste of American money and lives," Adams said with conviction. "Let them fight their own battles. We'll just be drawn into it, and a lot of Americans will be killed."

"Anyone take the opposite view?" asked the Professor.

Only two hands went up. He pointed to Mitch Carter. "All right, Carter, what do you think?"

"I happen to think the survival of Western Civilization is at stake. If Hitler conquers all of Europe, does anyone doubt that Russia will be next? And if Italy conquers North Africa and Japan overruns Asia, where does that leave us? Hitler is a bloodthirsty madman. I say it would be one hell of a world. I think our only chance to stop them is now, before it's too late."

Mitch was in the minority. A Gallup poll showed that 80% of Americans were still solidly isolationist. In fact, many prominent people, such as Charles Lindberg and the American Ambassador to England, Joseph Kennedy, argued that Hitler wasn't such a bad fellow.

Wardenbaker asked the class, "What do you think of Roosevelt's lend-lease idea and the deal to give Britain fifty old U.S. destroyers?"

Most disagreed with it. Mitch and one other boy found themselves up against a dozen others with the debate becoming heated. Mitch argued, "England lost more than half its fleet of destroyers, sunk or severely damaged at Dunkirk, and eleven more were damaged the next month. Now their Merchant Marine is at the mercy of German U-boats. They're nothing but sitting ducks. Without the ships to import food and arms, England is completely defenseless. Germany will starve them out."

To Mitch and his classmates these events were unfolding like a fast-moving adventure story, in which the ending was likely to be a tragedy. Mitch thought a betting man would give ten-to-one odds on Hitler.

CHAPTER TWO
1942

American Forces Land In French Africa
British Naval, Air Units Assisting Them;
Effective Second Front, Roosevelt Says
<u>New York Times</u>, Nov. 8, 1942

ST.-PIERRE-DU-BOIS

Using the creek for cover, Henri came to the farm every Friday night at midnight without fail. Each time, he pleaded with Renee for more food—all this in addition to the increasing demands of the Germans. Terrified that the Germans would figure out the discrepancies in the food inventory, Renee told him she absolutely positively could not keep it up. It was too dangerous. But she could see her brother, near starvation, could not be denied. In the end, she would cave in.

On one nocturnal visit, her childhood friend, Denis, came in place of Henri. He explained that her brother was away on an important mission. Renee was shocked when she looked into Denis' eyes. They looked like hollow sockets.

"We have a frightful problem, Renee," Denis said in a hoarse whisper. "Our men are being persecuted by the damn *Milice*. Did you know they're being paid a bounty, as much as 5,000 francs for every one of us they turn over to the SS?"

Renee knew all about the *Milice*. Mostly criminals with twisted personalities, they relished revenge against their own society as much as they coveted the bounty money.

"Up until two weeks ago," Denis went on, "We've been able to dodge what they call 'rat hunts,' but now they're getting to us. Six of our best men have been caught. They've either been shot or dumped in the Rouen prison. They're as good as dead, I'm afraid."

"That's terrible," Renee whispered. "Is there anything we can do about it?"

Denis, looking much thinner than she remembered him, coughed and rasped, "As a matter of fact, there is something. That's why I'm here. You see, all six of these men have been captured just in the last two weeks—all because someone is feeding information to the Bosch."

"Do you have any idea who?"

"Yes, we're sure it's a young woman who works in the St.-Pierre brothel. As you can imagine, most of the customers are German officers, and she's feeding information to one of them."

"How do you know all this?" Renee asked.

"We have our own informant. Her name is...Well, it's probably safer if I don't tell you her name. She's working inside this *maison de tolerance*—an invaluable source of information by the way. Seems that men, whatever their nationality, talk too much when they're having sex."

Renee shuddered. "Horrible as it sounds, you're going to have to eliminate her."

"Normally we'd have killed her by now. After all, our men have been killed by her as surely as if she'd done it with her own hand. But this is a special case."

"Why?" Renee frowned. "I don't want you or Henri killed because of some whore."

"Here's the problem," Denis rubbed his chin thoughtfully. "*La demoiselle* is Jewish, hates the Germans every bit as much as we do, but she's very young, sixteen or seventeen I believe, very pretty, and very scared. According to our source, there's one high-ranking German officer who knows she's Jewish and threatens to send her to Auschwitz unless she cooperates. He demands information about every Frenchman who patronizes the establishment, and, incidentally, demands sexual favors for free."

"That's terrible, but you can't go on having your men killed because of her."

"You're right, of course," Denis replied after a long pause, "but, according to our source, she's known to be a high class young lady and she's there only because her father took her as a last resort. It was the only hiding place he could come up with—just before he was arrested and sent to Auschwitz."

"*Mon Dieu.* That's…Good God, what can we do?" Renee stared at Denis, pale and stony-faced. "You must do something. Get her out of there. There must be something."

"Of course, I'm worried about her, but I'm more worried about our own people." Denis rubbed his forehead. "On the other hand, I agree with you. We've got to get her out—and right away. We can't take the time to talk about it or with Henri when he gets back. We've got to decide right now, and get her out right now."

"I don't see what we — "

"We must get a message to her. Her name is Michelle LaRoth. Tell her to come here, to your house. She isn't locked up all the time. She's allowed to walk in the village and could find her way here easily enough without arousing suspicion."

Renee frowned. "I don't like the idea. It would be dangerous. Isn't there some other place she could go?"

Denis responded slowly, "It must be in a well-concealed place with a hidden path leading away. Your root cellar is the best choice. Definitely the best. Then there's the curfew to consider, but it would be too dangerous to take her out in daylight. I'll have to come here and take her away at night."

Renee and Henri had discussed the subject of access many times. Their farm had always come out the obvious choice for connecting with the Resistance because of the dense thickets running along the creek. But that didn't make it any less dangerous. If you were caught, you'd be shot.

"I still don't like it," Renee said. "We could jeopardize too many things."

"I understand what you are saying, Rene, but we can't afford to wait for our source to come to us. It might be another month before she makes her next report, and a dozen more of our men could die in the meantime. We must get a message to Michelle—now."

Renee hesitated, then responded slowly, "That shouldn't be too difficult. The Germans never raid brothels. It would embarrass too many of their own officers."

"That's what I'm thinking. It shouldn't be difficult—or dangerous.

You could do it real easy. Nobody would think twice about one more young woman in the place."

"Stop right there, Denis." Renee was livid. "I am not going to be seen in any brothel, and that's final."

"I know. I know. I understand." Denis' mouth formed a hard line. "But you're sealing her death warrant if you won't do it. We'll have to kill her."

"For God's sake, Denis, you can't kill her."

"Do you want to help the girl or not? Do you have a better idea?"

Renee stared angrily at Denis, who stared back at her without flinching. Finally she shook her head and murmured a barely audible, "All right."

The first rays of morning light were creeping across the frosty fields, and Denis had to leave, his pack loaded with squash and potatoes. "I'll be back for her tomorrow at midnight. She has to be here, or, like I said, we'll have to kill her."

Renee did not need another stress, contributing to her fragile state of mind, but she was too furious to be depressed. The damnable Nazi, taking advantage of a young, innocent girl, made her blood boil. She would tackle this in the morning. *But watch yourself. Slow down. This kind of thing can lead to total disaster. Be careful, careful, very careful.*

Renee didn't know anything about brothels, but she supposed the safest time to go was in the morning and wondered how early they would be open. At least there shouldn't be many customers.

Waiting until 10:00 a.m., she bicycled the kilometer and a half to the other side of the village, the seamy east side, and knocked on the door of the grandest house in the neighborhood. She did not have to be told which house. Everyone knew.

A large, round-faced, jolly-looking woman opened the door as far as it would go on the chain. Dressed in purple velvet and dripping with gold jewelry, she peered at Renee quizzically, then let her in without even asking her name.

Assailed by the overwhelming odor of cheap perfume, Renee said politely, "I hope this is not a bad time to call."

"To call!" the fat lady laughed uncontrollably. After a coughing spasm, she asked, "What's your name, child?"

"Regina, Madame," Renee thought it best to alter her name a bit. "If possible, I would like to visit one of your girls, Michelle LaRoth. I have an important message for her, which I'm sure she will want to receive."

There was a long pause. The jolly face tightened. "So you are not asking for employment? No, of course not." She answered her own question. "Wait here, I'll see if Mademoiselle is available."

Indeed, she had to wait more than half an hour, while she marveled at her surroundings. They were more opulent than anything she had ever seen before, even at Sir Charles' London estate. Velvet curtains, huge gilt-framed mirrors, carved cupids, a purple plush settee, and matching inch-thick carpets completed the image of grandeur.

Renee fidgeted, afraid some customer would come in and wonder what she was doing there. She hunkered down in a dark corner of the dimly lit room. *God help me if it is someone who knows me. But I suppose these ladies work all night and certainly won't get up at 10:00 a.m.*

Madame returned without Michelle. "I must know more about ..." she hesitated, "what it is you wish to tell my girl. You must know I try to look after them, and—well—I'm worried, very worried, about Michelle. These times are very difficult, you know."

"I'm afraid it's confidential," Renee responded slowly, "but it's important. I can assure you it is for her good—and her safety."

They studied each other without speaking for a full minute. Finally, Madame broke the silence. "Can you at least tell me whether your message has anything to do with her leaving here?"

"Possibly, but, of course, that's up to her."

Madame sighed and drew in a deep breath. "You look honest, my dear, and there comes a time when I must trust someone. We— you—someone—must get her away from here. You may or may not know the girl is Jewish. Yes, I make it my business to know everything about my girls. There's a horrible Nazi threatening her. He knows. Knows everything about her—and I'm afraid for her life."

Renee nodded slightly and smiled a little to indicate her understanding.

"I could be shot for telling you this, but I am old, and she is young. And she's a very special girl."

Renee hesitated, "I think that's all we should say to each other. I will, of course, keep our conversation absolutely confidential, and I must trust you to do the same. You'll have no idea where she went, but I assure you it will be to safety. When this terrible war is over, we'll come back and thank you. After all, if it weren't for you, she'd be dead by now."

"Bless you, my child. I think you should talk to Michelle upstairs. You must be seen by as few people as possible. Sometimes we get morning customers."

To Renee's embarrassment, Madame smothered her with a massive hug and then showed her the secret back door that she should use after talking with Michelle. Of course, Renee realized, every *maison de tolerance* in France has a discrete exit. Her parting words were, "We must not be seen talking any more."

*   *   *

The Nazi Colonel glared at Madame, his face a mottled red. "Madame Lazzard, you—you..." he sputtered, "let her go without telling me. You must be out of your mind. You knew she was very, very important."

Madame whined in a high pitch, "How could I know, she would ..." The German sent her sprawling with a blow from the back of his gloved hand.

He stood over her, as she wiped a trickle of blood from the corner of her mouth. "You will bring the girl back immediately, immediately, or you will find yourself on the next train—or perhaps I should say the next boxcar—to Ravensbrueck. You have two days, no more."

"But I swear to you, I have no idea where she—" Madame began, but the Colonel cut her off with a raised hand to strike her again.

"Madame Lazzard, I am not interested in excuses. And it is not of the least concern to me whether your fat body rots in Ravensbrueck or not. You will bring her back."

He turned and stormed out of the house, slamming the door.

The whole house shook.

Madame had not the slightest idea what to do. She could try to track down Regina, or whatever her real name was, but then, she would not bring the girl back even if she could find her. Besides, she was certain the Resistance would have taken her away by now.

Madame Lazzard picked her ponderous body off the floor and lumbered to her room. She pried up the loose floorboard under her bed and pulled out a small tin box. She removed the lid and counted the money—twenty-four thousand francs and a diamond pendant—her life savings.

Knowing the Colonel would carry out his threat, she had no choice. Ravensbrueck was as good as a death sentence. She would go into hiding.

BERLIN, GERMANY

Once again, Otto found himself face to face with Heidendorff. He snapped to attention with a polished Nazi salute and barked, "Heil Hitler!"

"Heil Hitler." The fat man grunted and brushed the air with a laconic wave.

"Reporting as ordered, Herr Marshal."

"At ease, Kapitan. Be seated."

Otto sat stiffly, like a large stump.

In awe, Otto took in the scene, while Heidendorff dismissed the guards. Everything was out-sized, including the man dressed in his favorite white uniform, sitting slightly elevated behind a huge desk. One could imagine Louis XIV looking down from his throne on a cowering subject. Two solid gold eagles, mounted on pedestals, flanked the desk. A giant portrait of Hitler with his arm outstretched in the Nazi salute graced the back wall. On the sidewall was a blown-up photograph, at least six feet high, of Heidendorff as a young soldier during the first World War, standing beside Corporal Schicklgruber-Hitler.

"I want you to know," the Marshal resumed, after assuring

himself there was no one else in the room, "your good work in Austria and Holland has come to the attention of the Fuehrer. You are to be congratulated."

"Thank you, Herr Marshal."

"Herr Kaptain, I have arranged to detach you from your regular command. You will be free to carry out a special assignment for me. Actually it's two assignments, both very important." Then Heidendorff began to ramble, and Otto wondered what was really on his mind. "The war drags on, and there is much to be done. Much indeed. We should have finished off England before we took on the Bolsheviks." His voice trailed off, and Otto could see his eyes go out of focus. "But I digress." His eyes snapped back and studied Otto long enough to make him uncomfortable. "Yes, yes, the assignment."

Grossly overweight, the Marshal had developed a nervous twitch in his left eye, which matched the twitch of his mustache. To Otto, he looked more like a candidate for an asylum than one of the most powerful men in the Third Reich. Nevertheless, he was not a man to be taken lightly. He could order your execution with a wave of his fat hand.

"Yes, Herr Marshal," Otto responded with emphasis.

"What I have in mind is a matter of extreme secrecy, and I repeat, extreme importance. I have chosen you to carry out this assignment—alone. No one else is to be involved. You have been trusted with some of our most difficult projects in the past, and you have carried them out with precision."

It seemed to Otto that Heidendorff liked to refer to the business of exterminating people as a project. His fat index finger waved in a circle and pointed at Otto. "Now if you can carry this one out successfully, I will see that you are promoted to Major. I believe it would make you the youngest Major in the SS. Am I not correct?"

"Yes, Herr Marshal," Otto replied, having no idea whether it was correct or not.

"You will report to my estate at Bernau January tenth at 1:00 a.m.," Heidendorff continued, his mustache twitching back and forth like a metronome as he talked. "I will have a truck and two Jewish prisoners to help you. When you have completed the assignment, you will eliminate the prisoners and report back to me in person—

to me and no one else." The eye twitched faster now. "I suggest you first promise the Jews some reward to insure their cooperation, but then eliminate them at the end. Is that clear?"

"Yes, Herr Marshal." Otto was glad he was not on the wrong side of the fat man's ledger.

"Only you and I are to know anything about this. That includes Himmler and even the Fuehrer. Absolutely no one."

"Yes, of course."

"I have here a map of France." Heidendorff heaved himself out of his chair and unrolled a large map on the oversized desk. With a shaky finger he pointed to a small dot designating the village of St.-Pierre-du-Bois in Normandy. "You will set up SS headquarters here." He made a small mark with a pencil about one kilometer west of the town. "You will be in charge of the entire province of Normandy. You must understand, this is probably the most important area in France."

"Yes, I understand."

The fat man plopped back down in his chair. "You will take over this farm owned by a French farmer, one Claude Brousard." He circled the dot he had just made. "We have checked it out. It's in the center of Normandy. It should be exactly right for our purpose. The farm has a large barn, which you will use as a temporary office and storage building during the construction."

"What will the construction entail?"

"I'll get to that in a minute."

"Will I be provided with a construction crew?"

"Certainly, but only after you have completed the first part of your assignment. Initially, you will be alone, except for your two Jewish helpers—temporary, of course. You will bury six sealed steel boxes, which I will personally deliver to you on January tenth at 1:00am. They must be buried here, in the Caves of St.-Pierre." The Marshal hoisted himself out of his chair again and put another dot on the map about half a kilometer from the first dot. He then slid a shaky hand under the large blotter on his desk and pulled out a hand-drawn sketch labeled THE CAVES.

"I've had these caves surveyed. Or, to be precise, I've had one particular section surveyed and mapped in detail." He ran his finger over the crude map to a large X. "The caverns run for many kilometers in at least five different directions. It seems nobody has ever mapped the whole thing, but we only need to be concerned with this one section."

Otto stood and leaned over the map. "You want the boxes buried in this section?"

"Yes. You can see plainly by the X. It's the deepest part."

"What kind of access—?" Otto began.

Heidendorff interrupted. "There are steps cut into the walls. At one time, the French took tours into the caves, but the entrance is boarded up now, and no one goes in."

"Should I bury them in any special way or just—?"

"You will pile limestone rocks over them until they are completely hidden. Actually, not a single person has entered the caves for years, so that is probably an unnecessary precaution. But I want you to do it anyway. We must be sure.

"Will I receive a copy of the map?" Otto was becoming nervous. *Have I asked enough questions? Or too many?*

"Yes, I have here a copy for you, but you will destroy it as soon as the mission is completed. You must be precise about the location. I must be able to find and recover the boxes at some future date regardless of what transpires in the interim."

"Yes Herr Marshal. You can rely on me."

"Now, after you have completed this assignment, you will set up a group-one, highest priority, SS headquarters at the Brousard farm in St.-Pierre-du-Bois. You will administer the area from Cherbourg to Caen, including the entire Normandy coastline. Your staff will, of course, be assigned by Herr Himmler."

As Heidendorff ran his finger over the area of the map and leaned on the desk for support, Otto could see the hand shaking more now.

"I must emphasize again this is an extremely important assignment." The fat man sank down into his chair. "The area is infested—infested like rats—with British spies and French resistance. They must be destroyed at all costs. They are becoming a serious detriment to our New Order in France."

Otto nodded.

"Also there is increasing British commando activity in Normandy. This must be stopped and stopped hard. Once and for all. When you catch them, I want them eliminated. Understood?"

"Yes, Herr Marshal, I understand. Eliminated. *Ja, Ja.*"

"Now, about that construction I spoke of, you will be assigned a construction team of French workers to build a proper headquarters and a radio transmission center and tower. This will become a radio communication center manned by the Wehrmacht, reporting to General von Kleister, but your SS Company will also billet there."

The fat man tapped the portion of the map designating Normandy and stared hard at Otto. "But first you will report back to me in person, to confirm our special project. Our project has number one, top priority. Understood?"

"Yes, Herr Marshal, and I am to report to you personally at 1:OO a.m. on January tenth."

Heidendorff leaned back in his chair, put the tips of his fingers together, and watched the backside of the blackshirt leaving the room. *There are still a few small details to consider,* he mused. *Perhaps it would be wise to eliminate the Captain—after we are sure the boxes are safely hidden. There will be no need to promote the big oaf. No need to have anyone, other than myself, knowing about it. Streikler may be crude, but he isn't altogether stupid. After all, he successfully carried out the looting of Austria and Holland and shipping the best of it to Bernau. The contents of the steel boxes must be obvious, even to an oaf.*

He went over the options in his mind one more time. It wasn't too late to make a change. He had carefully researched hiding places throughout Europe, trying to find a small, out-of-the-way place where he could recover his loot after the war without being noticed. When he had discovered the Caves of St.-Pierre, he knew he had found the perfect place.

Only the previous week, General von Kleister, Kommandant of the Wehrmacht in France, and Admiral Kreigsfelder, head of German Intelligence for the western sector, had been in his headquarters, badgering him to set up an SS headquarters in Normandy. The rigid von Kleister had been brief but emphatic, while the more articulate Kreigsfelder had made the case in detail. The French Resistance fighters were becoming a serious threat especially in the northern sector. Explosives, weapons, and supplies were getting through to them in increasing quantities. They had to be stopped.

"Why can't the Wehrmacht stop it?" Heidendorff asked. He could see Kreigsfelder struggling to hide his contempt. The Marshal knew that the Admiral had a complete file on him: his drug addiction, his expropriation of loot, his lavish personal life style, every one of his unsavory habits.

Expressionless, the Admiral replied that the Wehrmacht has its hands full on three fronts, and that the SS must pick up more of the load in the occupied countries.

Heidendorff had only nodded.

Kreigsfelder pointed out that most of the supplies were being air-dropped to secret rendezvous points, and it was obvious that some kind of radio communication was pin-pointing the drops—the nub of the problem. Pointedly, he made it clear that the SS should have been doing a better job of tracking down the Resistance and stamping it out.

"I see." Heidendorff looked the smaller man hard in the eye.

"In our opinion," the General pressed his point. "It is of the utmost urgency that a substantial SS headquarters be set up in Normandy. It must be equipped with radio-direction-finding *Funkspiel* vans to track down clandestine transmitters."

"Yes, of course."

"Also the Wehrmacht needs a communication center to provide radio contact with our divisions stationed in northern France. Sooner or later, the Allies will invade. Normandy or the Pas de Calais, one or the other, or both, are the most likely targets. A first rate communication system will be absolutely essential."

The meeting had ended without a commitment, but Heidendorff knew he had to act.

He smiled to himself. Getting these two pests off his back, and at the same time handling his personal project, was a masterstroke. He would kill three birds with one stone.

PRINCETON, NEW JERSEY

Addressed to Mitch Carter, 42 West Hall, Princeton University, Princeton, N.J., the letter came from his former roommate, Hank Welling, heavily censored as expected. Hank was not noted for decorum.

Nov. 23, 1942

Hi Tiger,

For Christ sake, Mitch, stay out of the army. (The next part was censored, no doubt because he had said something undignified about the U.S. military.)

We just landed two days ago in (blank) North Africa. There was a little token resistance from the Vichy French bunch, but you have probably heard all about that on the news. It's damn hot, sticky, dirty, and generally miserable, and there are no dames. At least if there are, the French have them all locked up—the bastards.

The French, at least the ones around here who are supposed to be fighting for the Axis, obviously don't like the Germans, but they don't seem to like us very much either. Up to now, they figured the Germans were winning for sure, and they had no choice but to make the best of it. Now they are all screwed up—I'd say they're between a rock and a hard place.

The Arabs aren't the friendliest bunch in the world either. They hate the Germans—and the French—and us. They just want everyone to go away. Guess I can't blame them. Looks like we are going to be in for some nasty fighting pronto. (the last part of the letter was completely blanked out.) Miss you, you old crumb. Don't do anything dumb and get patriotic. We need someone to hold down the fort at old P.U.

Signed,

Handsome Hank

Mitch had received a special congressionally mandated deferment from the draft, because he was in the top 10% of the class at one of certain selected universities—supposedly a great honor. The problem was he didn't feel honored. In fact, he had begun to feel downright guilty, not being in uniform—guilty and lonely and maybe even a little bit patriotic. Mitch thought it had become obvious—the war had to be won, or the Japs and the Krauts were going to have us for lunch. Studying architecture wasn't helping win it, no matter what the draft board said.

Tomorrow he would go down to the Naval office on campus and see Jerry Smithen, his Navy V-12 buddy. Maybe Jerry could come up with some words of wisdom about how to get into the Navy—anything to stay out of the foxholes.

In 1942, Mitch knew that anyone with a grain of sense tried to join the Navy or the Air Corps. But it was practically impossible to get in, unless you had some inside track—like maybe being the son of a senator. At the induction centers, they were sending twenty-five draftees to the Army for every one to the Navy.

Mitch got up early, cut his 8:30 a.m. class and sat in Jerry Smithen's office.

"How do you expect to win the war fighting all that paper?" Mitch teased.

Jerry grinned. "You're right, there's no way."

"Jerry, I've decided to join up. I can't sit on my butt watching you guys lose the war. Besides I can't even get a date without a uniform."

"Thought you had a congressional deferment."

"I do, but I can't stand it any more. You guys are having all the fun."

"It's no fun. Just looks that way sometimes."

"Sure does look that way. Anyway, I need your advice. Can you figure any way I can get into your picky-choosy navy? If I volunteer now, would I have a chance?"

"Maybe, if you're dumb enough to give up that deferment. Also you have a scholarship don't you? But, if you're really that stupid, you oughta go for the ET test. The Navy's desperate for ETs."

"What's an ET?"

"Electronic Technician. You ought to be able to eat up the test—no sweat. If you do, you're in, and they send you to electronic school for nine months—damn good training by the way."

"Okay, so where do I go to find out about the ET test?"

"Come back later and see Lieutenant Jacobs upstairs, but make an appointment with his Yeoman first. He's kind of sticky about protocol."

GREAT LAKES

A month later, Mitch found himself slogging his way through boot camp at Great Lakes. After that he would go on to the Navy's electronics school at Treasure Island, California. But suddenly his life was swept into a whirlpool of events, events he had not imagined. It all started when the C.O. called him into his office, which was startling, because commanding officers didn't speak to lowly seamen except when they were in trouble.

"It has come to my attention, Seaman Carter," he began officiously, "that you have an interesting background. This report says you were at the top of your class at Princeton, that you excelled at certain sports—swimming and baseball, I believe—that you had a full scholarship, and that you speak French fluently. Do I have the right Carter? Is that you?"

"Yes sir. I grew up in a French-speaking family, but I'm afraid my French may be a bit rusty."

"Hmm. In that case I have something here that may be of interest to you—and to the Navy. Are you familiar with the Special Forces?"

"No sir."

"For your information, Carter, the Special Forces are set up to gather intelligence, sometimes demolition work, sometimes commando raids—mostly in France, all kinds of unpredictable assignments. Never know what next, but I can say this much: it's all vitally important to the war effort."

Clearing his throat and shuffling the papers on the desk, he continued. "Now I have here a request for two competent men who might qualify for our Special Forces in England. They must speak French fluently and be exceptional men in every respect, physically and mentally. I have to warn you it could be dangerous, but there is an incentive. We can offer you a commission if you satisfactorily complete the rigorous training program in England."

"I don't know..." Mitch began.

"This is entirely voluntary, Carter. You can think it over, but I want you to see Commander Schwartz tomorrow morning, 7:00 a.m. sharp. He can fill you in on the details, and you can decide. But your decision will have to be made tomorrow, or I'll have to find another candidate."

"Is there anything more you can tell me about it, sir?"

"No. You will have to get the rest from Commander Swartz."

The C.O. dismissed him with an abrupt nod and turned back to his papers.

Mitch went through some mental gymnastics. *Wait a minute. Don't rush into this. You're likely to get yourself killed. A little glory and a commission aren't worth it. On the other hand, I'd be able to send home twice as much pay as an officer. And there's the overseas premium.*

In any event, he had no choice but to see Commander Schwartz in the morning.

Schwartz, who wore the military intelligence insignia on his sleeve, offered Mitch virtually no help toward making up his mind. Dour and brusque, he repeated the same information he had heard the day before. Special Forces' duty was dangerous but important. It was an opportunity to make a real difference, and fluent French-speaking men with the other qualifications were hard to find. The only information added was that there was a great urgency and that Mitch would have to make up his mind on the spot. After a long wait, during which Schwartz simply stared him down, Mitch finally gulped and nodded a weak affirmative.

Apparently anticipating acceptance, Schwartz had precise orders typed and ready, which he handed to Mitch with a terse admonishment, "Tell nobody about your assignment, not your present C.O., not your family, no one. You can tell your family you are shipping out, but nothing else, nothing about this assignment. You will leave day after tomorrow and follow these written orders precisely. That's all Carter. And good luck." Mitch had a feeling he was going to need it.

Back at his barracks, Mitch sat on his bunk and read the orders. Then he went in search of Mike Haines, the other candidate selected by Schwartz. Mike frowned and shook his papers at Mitch. "For Chris' sake, Mitch, they've only given us twenty-four hours to get our gear together. Must want us pretty bad."

They were to report to New York where they would board a troop ship for England after a one-day abandon-ship-and-survival drill.

Mitch and Haines were flown to New York, in itself extraordinary, because trains normally transported enlisted men. It was the first time either of them had been in an airplane.

Sailing from New York, they boarded a troop ship, part of a convoy headed for Liverpool. They knew the odds. German U-boats had been sinking more than thirty transport ships a month. That meant one a day, and almost every convoy lost at least one.

"Keep your fingers crossed and pray," Mike said, "and bring a rabbit's foot."

"And keep your life preserver handy." Mitch added.

In fact, every man on board slept fully clothed, even with their shoes.

"Jeez, Mitch, we sure got stuffed into this situation awful fast. They didn't even let us finish boot camp, and we're supposed to be ready to fight a war. I'm beginning to think I was stupid to volunteer. Sounded super patriotic at the time and, you know, exciting. But more 'n likely we're going to get ourselves killed before we can do any good. So, how'd you get into this?"

"Well, there were several things, Mike. First of all, I grew up in a French immigrant family, so I'm pretty fluent in French, and it seems they really need that in the Intelligence. Then I got a scholarship to Princeton. All of this never would have happened without a couple of years of college, and that wouldn't have happened if it hadn't been for a rich old geezer who paid my tuition. He didn't have any children to inherit his money and took a liking to me. He knew I had an interest in architecture and wanted me to be the architect he had never been. My family is poor, and I never had the faintest idea I would get to go to college, much less Princeton."

"You must've been real smart to get in."

"I had pretty good grades in high school, and Princeton was looking for what they like to call 'diversity,' not all preppies from New York and Boston."

"What did that have to do with getting into this business?"

"Well, as you know, the Special Forces are looking for certain things. I was captain of the swim team. That seemed to interest them. And good grades. You should know, Mike. You must have gone through something similar to get picked."

The Wolf Pack struck the second night out. Flanked by three destroyers and two sub-chasers, the blacked-out convoy had followed a zigzag course. But a bright moon silhouetted the ships like ducks in a shooting gallery.

An explosion, then sirens shook Mitch out of a fitful sleep. The loudspeaker blared, "All hands lay up to emergency stations on the double." Leaping out of bed, he grabbed his life vest and found himself jammed into a mass of bodies, all trying to climb the narrow ship's ladder at once.

Standing on deck, he saw the sky turn bright orange and seconds later inhaled the nauseous reek of burning oil. More explosions thundered across the water, and the shrill sirens of sub-chasers echoed against the steel of the ships. Then the whoomp whoomp whoomp of depth charges. His ship did not slow down or try to pick up survivors. Instead, it swerved violently from one course to another. Mitch slammed against the rail and held on for his life as the ship bucked like a bronco.

In only minutes, minutes that seemed like hours to Mitch, the flaring sky faded into the distance. The sounds of the sirens gradually quieted—and no one slept.

At the time, Mitch didn't know that his convoy marked a turning point in the battle against the U-boat Wolf Packs. For the first time, the broken German code, "Ultra-Enigma," had been used to track and kill U-boats. Allied Intelligence, the organization, which he was now joining, had unraveled this Nazi secret code through some incredibly brilliant detective work.

Arriving in Liverpool in a heavy fog, Mitch was assaulted by the acrid smell of coal smoke and the bleating of foghorns.

Great masses of khaki-clad humanity surged down the gangplank and lined up on the dock. The sounds of creaking hawsers and orders, shouted by the sergeants on the dock, were muffled in the fog. Mitch felt vaguely disconnected. Were they in the right place? Had the Navy forgotten about them?

His concern didn't last long. A loudspeaker blared, "Seaman Carter and Seaman Haines, report to the Port Captain's office on the double."

They shouldered their sea bags, elbowed their way through rows of soldiers and finally found the office. A British corporal with a yellow MP band on his arm met them with a curt "hello" and hurried them away to a waiting Jeep.

Try as they would to engage the driver in conversation and find out where they were going, all they could squeeze out of the Corporal was, "Sorry mate, orders are not to talk 'bout anything 'cept the weather. Even got to be a bit careful 'bout that".

"In that case, how about dames?" Mike asked. "Can you talk about dames?"

"What are dames, matey?"

"You know, skirts, dolls, the opposite sex, girls. Do any of these words translate?"

"Blimey, where you're going, forget it."

"Doesn't sound too encouraging," Mike muttered to Mitch.

"Wonder if we can get out of this whole thing."

"I think we're stuck with it now," Mitch said with a wry grin.

A light drizzle began to patter on the canvas top of the Jeep and blow into the open sides. Mitch had been warned. England could be raw and cold in winter. They were right, he thought as he pulled his pea jacket tighter around him and took in the scenery—the gray stone churches, the withered hawthorn hedges, and fields full of soggy sheep.

They sat in silence, musing about their fate, as the Jeep drove up the rocky coastline and finally turned into a backcountry dirt road.

Well hidden in a grove of trees, a group of dilapidated buildings suddenly emerged out of the fog like a mirage. They would soon realize the disheveled look was part of a disguise. Anything but dilapidated, these buildings housed some of the most sophisticated military facilities in England.

Met by a British sergeant and an American MP, then searched and checked for their ID, they were taken to see the Chief of Operations.

The three-striper seemed to be cut out of the same cloth as Schwartz. An American, he was wearing the insignia of the Intelligence Corps.

The commander did not return their salute. "Welcome to Dayton Cross." His manner was precise and his speech clipped. "I am Commander Ames." He picked up two small pieces of paper from his immaculate desk. "You are ...?" He looked at Mitch.

"Seaman Carter, sir."

"And you are Seaman Haines?" He scrutinized the young men.

"Yes sir."

Ames was a compact man. Lean and erect with precisely combed dark brown hair, he formed his mouth into a tight line and got straight to the point. "By now you are undoubtedly wondering what this is all about." He shot out the words, not waiting for a response. "But there is only a limited amount I can tell you at this time."

Mitch thought that was all he'd been hearing from the beginning.

"You have been selected after careful screening, along with thirty other Americans, to train as Special Forces which will have a specific focus on the eventual invasion of Europe. Obviously, I can't tell you where or when an invasion will occur or even what your assignment will be. But you can be certain the invasion will occur, and you will play an important part."

Ames stood, walked around the desk and sat on the front side, collecting his thoughts. "You will be attached to British Intelligence, but you will, of course, remain in American uniform. You will not wear any insignia or carry any identification connecting you with the Intelligence services. You will become expert in commando tactics, demolition, short wave radio, special codes, and specialized arms of various kinds. Am I correct in my understanding that you both speak French fluently?"

They both responded, "Yes, sir." Mitch hesitated, then added, "The dialect and pronunciation vary a good deal from place to place. That could present a problem, especially in Brittany."

Mike Haines tried to ask a question, but the Commander held up his hand. "You will attend an accelerated officer's training school, ten hours a day, six days a week, after which you'll go on to Special Forces training run by British Intelligence, MI-6. It'll be rough, and frankly I don't expect everyone to get through it. But if you do, you'll be commissioned an Ensign in the U.S. Navy."

"Why the British and not American Special Forces?" Mitch asked.

Commander Ames turned and looked out the window, "I'm not at liberty to say much about that, except to say our help has been requested on an urgent basis, especially with anyone who can speak French. It seems the British have run out of the right kind of manpower."

"Do we get any liberty?" asked Haines. "Can we go anywhere?"

"You'll have one half-day a week, but you'll have to take your chances on transportation. We have a truck going to Liverpool once in a while. Check with Chief Petty Officer Johansen about that. Or you can walk to the village—Drayton Crossing. Pretty good pub there."

"Is there—?" Haines tried to get in one more question, but Ames cut him off. "See Chief Johansen if you have any other questions. He'll take you to your quarters."

He started to dismiss them, then added, "One more thing. This is important." He tapped on the papers with his index finger. "Your training is extremely confidential. You are not to say anything about it to anyone outside this base. And don't get involved with any women at the pub. It's too easy to talk if you get involved. We'll have an MP there at all times to keep an eye on you."

Over the next few weeks, Mitch became aware of the reasons for the urgency of their training. British Special Forces had been carrying an impossible load with their commando raids and their SOE (Special Operations) agents. More than a thousand agents had been killed or captured by the Germans, and virtually all of those captured had been executed, even those in uniform—in flagrant violation of the Geneva Convention—a minor detail not mentioned when Mitch had been asked to volunteer.

At the end of thirty days of officer's training, Ames called Mitch and Mike into his office. "Normally we'd give you ninety days of O.C.S.," he began. "But our need for French-speaking agents is so urgent, we're going to cut it short and send you on to Special Forces training in Scotland."

"When do we go?" Mike asked.

"Right away. I want you to pack your gear and be ready to leave tomorrow morning."

"Can you tell us any more about the kind of duty we're getting into?" Mitch asked.

"Yes. I was getting to that. But first let me give you a little background. You're going to need to understand it when it comes to working with the French. There's an overwhelming need of aid for the Resistance, especially in Northern France where several thousand *Maquis* Resistance fighters are hiding out in the mountains and forests. They desperately need arms and training on how to use them—also food, clothing, radios, transmitters, and the codes to communicate with us. Many of them are starving or dying of exposure. They need just about everything you can think of."

Mike squirmed in his chair and frowned. "Where do we come in?" he asked.

"To begin with, you'll be trained in radio transmission, explosives, mines, mortars—all kinds of small arms. Later, when we can infiltrate you into France, you'll train the French."

"How do we make contact with the French?" Mitch asked.

"Frankly, that's our next biggest problem on several levels. There's a pressing need to set up radio contact with the Resistance, also with thousands of ordinary French citizens who are trying to feed us information. Some are providing safe houses for escaped prisoners. Others are trying to relay information on troop movements, railroad schedules, fortifications, armament factories, and other enemy activities. If these sources can be tapped, they'll potentially save thousands of Allied lives. We have to figure out ways to set up transmitters in France and train Frenchmen to use them."

"Sounds like we've got an awful lot to learn," Mitch said.

"That's just the beginning," Ames continued. "Special Forces are being used to take out key German installations—radar stations, radio towers, docks—you name it. By the way, you'll get a short course in German language. You may need it."

"Sounds like commando stuff," Mike said.

"That's right. At some point, you'll be assigned to a commando team under the auspices of British MI-6, good training before we send you in all the way."

Mitch felt his head swim. The MI-6 wish list obviously far exceeded its capabilities, and the frightful risks of his new assignment were beginning to sink in.

CHAPTER THREE

1943

AXIS ARMY ROUTED
Moscow Claims Victory
Over 43 Divisions In
Don-Volga Drives
New York Times, Jan. 1, 1943

ST.-PIERRE-DU-BOIS, FRANCE

When the German army truck pulled up to the house, Renee straightened up slowly and leaned on her shovel. Scanning the gray clods of soggy dirt and piles of potatoes dotting the half-dug rows, she frowned. She would never be able to finish today, especially with this interruption.

At the sight of the truck, she ran a sleeve across her sweaty forehead. It had been a grim year, and the sight of the German vehicle—no doubt with demands for more food—filled her with dread.

A German officer in a black uniform stepped out of the truck, marched up to the house and pounded on the front door with a heavy fist. Even from a distance Renee could hear the German demanding to speak with Herr Brousard. Her mother, Annette, who had been putting up preserves for the winter, apparently too frightened to speak, only pointed to the field. The officer then marched off in Claude Brousand's direction. She could see two other smaller men, not in uniform, standing by the truck.

The German looked over her dirt-covered father with obvious contempt and spoke in German, "I am Captain Streikler. You are Herr Brousard?"

Claude looked at the German without responding.

"Herr Brousard, the German Armed Forces will require the use of your barn."

"*Je ne comprend pas.*" Claude returned Otto's glare with a steady gaze.

Otto repeated his words louder and more slowly, mixing in a few mangled French words, and pointed to the barn with added arm motions. Renee knew that her father understood enough German, but he was apparently trying to see if it would do any good to play dumb. Finally he stabbed his shovel into the ground, glared at the German, and answered in French, "I am providing food for the German army, and I need the barn for my equipment and hay and—— "

Renee could see that the SS Captain did not fully understand. He interrupted Claude in broken French. "You have barn empty tomorrow night—empty—no hay—no nothing." He was speaking even louder now. "*Comprend?*"

"My tractor will be ruined," Claude spoke in flat monotone. "At least, let me—"

"Barn empty tomorrow night," Streikler growled. "That's an order. If no empty, I repeat, empty, no nothing. I burn everything. You will see, I mean exactly what I say."

Claude stared without flinching into the German's milk-blue eyes, but remained silent. He understood enough.

"One other thing." The Captain spoke slowly. "The German army make military building next to barn. You stay away from building— fifty meters—unless you ordered otherwise. Anyone not stay away be shot."

Renee tried to make herself inconspicuous and started to move toward the house. But the Captain turned to her, "Halt fraulein, I make list all people who live, work on farm." She halted but didn't understand the rest of it.

"I repeat," Otto spoke loudly and slowly in German, "I require the names. All who live or work on farm. You will write names and bring list to me tomorrow morning, at barn with identity cards." Claude shook his head, and Otto repeated his demands in fractured French.

"There are only the three of us. We—" Claude began.

Otto cut him short again, "I do not repeat myself." Then turning his attention to Renee, he stared at her, his eyes moving over her figure, which, because of the sweating, was obvious in spite of the sack-like smock.

"What your name?" he asked in a suddenly unctuous tone. Renee murmured something barely audible and tried to look away, which invited an irate look. "I deal with you later."

*   *   *

As he stalked away, Otto's thoughts turned to women. *It has been too long, he muttered to himself.* When in the *Jungvolk*, he had been accustomed to having his way with any woman he wanted. The *Jungmaedel* girls had been readily available. In accord with Hitler's unofficial encouragement of the procreation of the Aryan race, Otto had done his share.

Of course, intercourse with a Jewish woman was another matter. Hitler had declared it a vile crime, punishable by heavy fines and imprisonment. There was no worse crime than the tainting of Aryan blood by conceiving a half-Jewish child. But Otto knew the SS was essentially above the law. In the course of raping Jews in every other way, they raped them sexually too. They took whatever women they wanted, Jew or Gentile. And now, here is this beautiful blond French woman.

But at the moment, he had urgent business. He must complete Heidendorff's private project immediately and dispose of his helpers. Von Kleister would be arriving in the morning and wanted to start construction without delay.

Otto found himself strapped for time. He would not be able to bury the boxes in the cave before von Kleister arrived in the morning. But he knew he had to do something with them immediately. And get rid of his Jewish helpers. He would bury them by the barn—the boxes *and* the Jews. Later, he would have time to see about the caves.

Tonight, he would be busy digging—not just for the boxes. On second thought, his Jewish helpers would be doing the digging. He would have them dig two extra holes.

*   *   *

To Renee, it seemed as if the sky was falling. Her brother had been pressing her for more food than she could provide, and now this malignant SS Nazi had intruded. Everything had become infinitely more difficult. The Germans had also been escalating their demands for food, and she could see they were becoming increasingly belligerent, suspicious that farmers were hiding their produce—which, of course, they were.

On the Brousard farm, ever-larger amounts of foodstuff were unaccounted for, so, after the blackshirt Captain left, Renee decided she could no longer put off telling her father about the food she was hiding for Henri.

"I'm sorry, father," Renee shuffled her feet and looked at the ground. "We have to talk about Henri."

Claude's face clouded over. "What do you know about Henri? Your mother and I've been sick with worry."

"I haven't told you about the food. I'm sorry, father. I should have told you, but Henri asked me not to. He didn't want to upset mother, but of course, she's going to be even more upset, not knowing. Anyway, the truth is that he comes two or three times a month, always in the middle of the night. I've been giving him whatever we can spare."

"I suspected as much." Claude looked off into the distance and answered softly. "Of course, we can't let him starve." He sighed, and Renee could see an affectionate expression she had seldom seen in her father. "I'm afraid for both of you. If you're caught giving him food, we...Dear God, we'll all be dead before this war is over."

In a strange way, Renee was relieved by her father's pessimistic words—the most words she had wrung out of him since the invasion. But she still didn't tell him about the radio contacts. Charles had said not to tell a soul. *Oh, father,* she thought, *if only you knew your daughter was a spy.*

"We'll have to come up with a better hiding place for food, father," she said. "The Germans are checking up more closely on all the farmers now. As you well know, they're already demanding three-quarters of everything. We could be shot if they find out what we're doing."

Claude hesitated. "You're right, of course. I suspect you and Henri have already cooked up some ideas. So tell me."

Renee sidestepped the question. "What I haven't told you, father," she searched for the right words, "Henri's asking for more all the time now. He's trying to feed hundreds. He's scrounging, even stealing. They're desperate."

Resigned to the inevitable, Renee and her father talked it over for an hour and poked around in all the forgotten corners of the ancient farmhouse, finally deciding to dig out an extra space under the root cellar. It would be covered over with old weathered boards.

Now, on top of everything else, this ominous SS Nazi had intruded. She would have to warn her brother at their next meeting, which was every tenth day now.

Renee was shocked when she saw him. "I hate to say it, Henri, but you look terrible." She gave him a quick embrace, stood back and stared at him. His stubble-covered cheeks were gaunt, his hair disheveled, and his coat was torn. "I've never seen you so thin. Come on into the kitchen and warm up by the stove," she added and set to work heating some potato soup.

"The truth is I feel terrible," Henri said, slopping up his soup like a starving dog. "The nights are cold, and we don't have enough to eat. We don't even dare light fires."

Renee sat on a stool across from her brother and stared at him, damp-eyed with compassion. "I'm sorry, Henri, but we've already given you all the extra blankets and clothes, and all the food we can spare."

"I know. Believe me, we're grateful as hell. But we're starting to go on the offensive now. We need a lot of things besides food. We need rifles and ammunition and explosives and more blankets and clothes."

"Sounds like you want to get yourself killed. Also you talk as if I could do something about it."

"The truth is I think you can so something. I've been suspecting that you are in touch with some agents. My boys have their ears to the ground, you know."

"You told me it was safer if you didn't know."

"True, but we're desperate now."

"So, what are you talking about?"

"You've got these agents, don't you? And somehow they're in contact with London, aren't they?"

Renee just stared at her brother, but he knew her well enough to know by her expression that it was true.

"I've got a long list. It's urgent. We'll all be dead from starvation if the Brits don't come through with this. You've got to send this list off tomorrow."

Renee kneaded the crease on her forehead. "Well, It's supposed to be completely secret. I can't imagine how your men got wind of this, and I guess I don't want to know. It's dangerous as the hell, and I probably shouldn't…Oh, what the devil. We're all going to die in the end anyway, so I'll try to do what I can. Just pray my contact in Caen is still working—and, while you're at it, pray I don't get arrested, bicycling up there."

MAQUIS CAMP IN NORMANDY

Four days later, at precisely 1:45 a.m., Henri and a handpicked crew of six men waited silently, crouching behind a hedgerow alongside a secluded pasture.

Henri had given the plan a great deal of thought. He would choose a different location for each drop, always a field adjacent to dense woods, which would provide an avenue for escape if—and inevitably when—escape should be necessary.

They had taken sticks and chased the cows down to one end of the pasture, then dug two holes, which would be needed to bury the parachutes. With barely enough moonlight to make out an approaching airplane, all six men squinted anxiously toward the north. Henri shivered. *Was it fear or the cold?* He rubbed his hands together and checked his watch again. It was probably a little of both.

Then he saw the airplane, flying so low it barely cleared the trees, exactly on the time agreed, 1:55 a.m.

Shielded on the sides by a paper cone, Henri's flashlight sent the all-clear signal—five short flashes skyward. A few seconds later, ten black parachutes appeared, and the attached crates hurtled downward, hitting the ground with a violent thud. Unlike the standard personnel parachutes, these small black chutes only slowed the fall, but they had the advantage of being easier to disentangle and dispose of. While one of Henri's men stood watch at the edge of the field, the others quickly cut loose the chutes, folded them into a tight bundle, and buried them.

Luck was with them this time. The Germans had not spotted the plane, and they were able to carry away about a quarter of the new supplies. They hid the rest in the woods to be recovered later.

Henri's *Maquis* became a bit overconfident after two successful supply drops. On the third drop, just as the crew was burying the last parachute, Henri heard the warning signal from his lookout—a bird whistle and three narrow-beam flashes with a flashlight. Apparently the Germans had spotted the low-flying Lancaster coming in over the coast. Seconds later, he heard the rumble of a troop-carrier bumping along the dirt road, approaching at high speed.

Abandoning their supplies, the *Maquis* ran for cover. As the *Kubelwagen* (the jeep-like military vehicle) roared toward them, Henri hissed in a loud whisper, "Take cover behind the *bocage*. Wait 'til they're clear of the car. Hold your fire 'til I give the order."

The Germans weren't entirely obliging. They climbed out of their car two hundred yards away, spread out and came along the road slowly, crouching as they advanced. Henri waited until they were directly in front of them. "Fire," he yelled.

Two of the five Germans were hit instantly and lay motionless on the road. The remaining three dove into the ditch on the far side of the road and began firing back. Henri's group had the advantage for the moment—six to three—but he knew the Germans had more firepower and would have reinforcements in a matter of minutes.

"I'll cover you," Henri whispered to his men. "Stay low. Make for the woods on the north side. Don't wait for me. I'll join you later. GO!"

Raking the Germans with one last volley, the five men ran for the cover of the woods. A few seconds later, Henri emptied his rifle and pistol to make it sound like a small army, then ran, zigzagging toward the woods. Seconds after he scrambled away from the *bocage*, a grenade landed on the exact spot where he'd been crouching. Bullets flew around him, but he made good his escape.

However, the supplies were lost to the Germans.

This operation was repeated dozens of times with varying degrees of success. Henri knew they had to go through with it to survive, and he calculated that they were successful about ninety percent of the time, although the risks were frightful. Henri participated in most, but not all, of these operations. His own luck held, but over time, four of his men were lost. He was physically sick when the reports came back.

Late one night, Anton, limping, brushed aside the tent flap and stumbled over to the crude desk where Henri was working. "You look like something a dog dragged in," Henri said, frowning. "How'd the drop go this time?"

"A disaster. A total disaster. I was lucky, but we lost Patrice and Guillaume, and the Bosch got the entire drop—ten chutes. The bastards got 'em all."

"Damn, that makes six men we've lost now. They're getting on to us."

"Damn it, Henri, that's not the worst of it. The worst part's the torture. I hid in the trees. Couldn't see what they were doing, but I could hear the screams. They were trying to squeeze information out of them—about us, our camp, our radio contacts with the Brits, everything. Patrice talked. Gave 'em a lot of nonsense. Guillam wouldn't talk. Wouldn't say a word. Then the pigs shot 'em both. I tell you, Henri, it's better to shoot yourself than be captured."

"Damn the bastards." Henri pounded the rough planks of his desk. "One thing, though. This kind of brutality is backfiring on them. The more the word gets around, the more Frenchmen are joining up. The Goddam pigs are going to pay. We're starting to get what we need now, and we'll hit them hard."

In fact, Henri and his men began to fight back with equal brutality, killing scores of Germans, derailing trains, wrecking trucks, and cutting telephone lines. The stakes were escalating rapidly. In order to survive and also fight, Henri's *Maquis* needed, demanded, and received explosives, grenades, radios, machine guns, mines, blankets, clothing, tents, and food. They were beginning to hope, and some even to believe, that an Allied invasion might come soon.

In addition to parachute drops, the British began supplying the *Maquis,* using a short take-off version of the Lysander airplane, nicknamed the "Lizzy." It could land and take off on pastures as short as two hundred yards. Beginning in late 1942, the Lizzies managed to bring in SOE agents, as well as critical supplies. With the BBC code, they could schedule the landings with precision, landing and taking off in as little as two minutes. The *Maquis* learned how to unload them in less than a minute, then melt into the woods without a trace.

The British picked up reports of German frustration by deciphering occasional radio intercepts. These were passed on to the Resistance via BBC, knowing they would provide a much-needed morale boost. Increasingly frustrated and infuriated, the Nazis were pouring spiraling amounts of precious manpower into their efforts to thwart the *Maquis.* Hitler was reported to be apoplectic with rage over the diversion of troops from the Russian front. He replaced more than one general in charge of occupied France, hysterically berating them in front of their peers for their inability to destroy the *Maquis.*

Henri laughed aloud for the first time in a year when he heard the reports. Incredibly, the Germans had not yet figured out the simple BBC code, the key to the *Maquis'* survival and success—so far.

THE BROUSARD FARM

Renee was terrified when she remembered that Henri was scheduled to meet with her at 2:00a.m. tonight. She would have no way to warn him about the German SS officer.

With a knot forming in her stomach, she sat at the window in the middle of the night, watching the barn and the truck parked in front of it. Her worst fears were realized when she saw the black uniform and the two helpers emerge at midnight, unload six large boxes, and begin digging. The boxes must have been extremely heavy, judging from the bent-over, struggling efforts of the helpers.

How can I warn Henri? There is no way. I never even know which way he will come.

As the minutes ticked by, she realized the Germans were completely absorbed in their urgent project. She saw the Captain jerking around, obviously in a hurry, alternately pushing his helpers, pointing, then grabbing a shovel. She saw his mouth moving, apparently issuing orders, but the words must have been a near-whisper. She could not hear anything except the scraping sounds of the shovels. With mounting alarm, she watched this bizarre behavior as the time approached 2:00 a.m. They were still digging. There were no lights. Why were they digging in the middle of the night?

With just enough moonlight to see faintly through the October mist, Renee thought she could make out six large boxes being lowered into a large hole. They were, indeed, extremely heavy. Why else would it take all three men with ropes to lower them into the hole one at a time?

Next, she heard the *thunk thunk* of dirt, as they filled in the hole, followed by scraping noises. It seemed they were smoothing the surface with extraordinary care. *Are they trying to hide the evidence of digging? What on earth could be in those boxes? Surely they wouldn't be burying arms or military materials. The boxes aren't the right size or shape for rifles. Besides, what possible reason could there be for burying guns?*

In near panic, she realized it was two minutes before 2:00 a.m. She had to get to the root cellar and warn Henri. Silently, she crept out the back way.

Henri was already there. "What's going on?" he muttered before Renee could say anything, "That truck? Our men spotted it yesterday. What's it doing at our place?"

Choked with worry, she hugged her brother and whispered, "I have no idea what they're doing, Henri, but, for God's sake, keep your voice down and keep out of sight." In the moonlight, she saw how thin and haggard he looked. "You look awful," she whispered, still holding his arm.

Henri exhaled heavily and breathed close to her ear, "All hell's broken out lately. Eight of our men have been killed. We need medical supplies more than anything now. And food. You don't realize what's happening, but we are up to three hundred men now, and getting more every day—women too, and we can't feed them."

"Slow down, Henri. Come in the house and get warm. Keep low. We'll use the back door. I won't light any candles. There are three Germans, digging holes and burying things out by the barn, but I have no idea what it means."

"Never mind," Henri whispered. "I've got more important things to deal with."

In the dark kitchen, Renee knew her way well enough to fix some hot chicory, while Henri sidled up close to the warm stove. He continued to whisper with urgency, "We need someone to teach us how to use the explosives the Brits have been dropping—plastic stuff, detonators, mines, automatic weapons. We've been using some of it, but most of it is too complicated. We'll just blow ourselves up if we don't know what we're doing. Also they dropped a transmitter, but it's no good to us unless we know how to use it. And the code. We don't know the code. Besides, I'm afraid the Bosch will track us down with their *Funkspiel,* unless there is some special way to use it we don't know about."

"For God's sake, Henri, don't try. It's too risky."

The creases on his forehead deepened. "You're right, of course. That's why we're still depending on you to get our messages through."

Renee frowned. "I'm down to only one contact now, the one in Caen. I don't know what happened to the others, but they put out their warning signal, and I suspect the worst. Fortunately they don't know my name, so I don't think there's any way they can identify me."

"I wouldn't be too sure, sister, dear. Those Nazi fiends can squeeze the last drop of information out of anyone. I mean anyone."

"Yes, but I don't think—"

Henri gripped her shoulders. "The bravest man in the world

will talk when the Bosch get hold of him. Now, if your radioman was caught, you can be sure he's given an accurate description of you, because he'll live only if the information proves correct. You wouldn't believe the horrible stories we're hearing. I'm afraid your radioman will die a horrible death, unless they find you. And if they do...?" He didn't need to finish the sentence.

Renee shuddered and stared silently into the darkness. He put his arm around her, "I'm terribly proud of you, *"mon petite."* We all are. We really depend on you. And you know how much I love you. But you must be very, very careful."

"You too."

"You must change your appearance, cut your hair, wear an old woman's shawl, anything."

"I'll do something, especially to get that SS Blackshirt to stop leering at me."

"Has that bastard tried to make a pass at you?"

"No. Not really, but..." Renee shivered and decided to change the subject. "How about your list—all those things you say you need?"

Henri pulled five wadded up scraps of paper from his pocket. "Here, I've written it all down. There's an awful lot of stuff. We'll be lucky if the Brits can deliver half. Anyway, we've got to try."

Renee looked it over, frowned and pursed her lips. There was no point in telling him he was slightly demented.

Henri tapped his forefinger on the scraps of paper. "You must destroy these as soon as you have it in your head."

"I'll have to bicycle to Caen," Renee said, "but I can't get away until Sunday. Let's pray this contact's still working."

Henri moved closer to the stove, rubbed his hands, and sipped his chicory. Renee sensed he had something else on his mind. She knew him well enough to know it was something she wouldn't want to hear.

"There's one other thing, Renee. I really hate to stick you with this, but I don't know any other way. We have an RAF flyer. Shot down over Cherbourg. Farmer picked him up and turned him over to us just as the Germans came around looking for him."

"What's that got to do with me?"

Henri skirted the question. "Of course, it would have been easier

70

all around to let him be captured. But the damned Bosch have started shooting captured fliers lately—an outrageous violation of international law. It's a horrible crime to shoot prisoners. They're doing it to the Russians too, by the thousands."

"I still don't see wh — "

"Besides, the RAF is running out of pilots," Henri interrupted, still in whispers, "and if there's any way to get them back to England, it'd be *une grand chose* to help win this God-forsaken war."

"Of course, but what on earth can we do about it?"

"It happens I know exactly what we can do. It's called the 'Escape Line,' or sometimes it's called the 'Evasion Line.' It's already been tried in southern France—very successfully."

"Yes, I've heard of it, but I — "

"Here's how it works. We dress up our flyer to look like a Frenchman. Then we get him some identity papers. We have papers from our own men who've been killed. We teach him a few French words. The Bosch can't tell the difference, just so he sounds French. Then we pass him from one safe-house to another until he gets to the Pyrenees and Spain, then to Gibraltar."

"I still don't see what this has to do with me."

"We need someone to take him to the first safe-house in Vire. He'll have a good chance if we can take him that far and if he's with someone who knows the way, the back roads, the language, how to act. Otherwise he's dead."

"You're right, of course, but I —"

"The *Maquis* have set up the whole chain, but no one link in the chain knows the identity of any of the others. So there's no way the Bosch can torture one person and find out about the rest of the line. The links are mostly women, and even some children. We think they're less suspect."

"Why me? I'm already over my head in this code and message thing."

"There isn't anyone else I can trust to get it right. Please do it for us just this once. It'll only take you one day. We'll find someone else next time, but this time we're stuck. We need you. Besides, there's never been a hitch up to now. You'll never even meet the next link. All you'll see is a pot of begonias in the window. It's the signal that everything is..."

Henri never finished his sentence. Two shots rang out from the direction of the barn. Henri grabbed his sister by the shoulder and pulled her down onto the floor.

When they heard nothing more, they crept, crouching low, to the front window. They could hear a soft scraping sound as they peered into the mist through the imperfect leaded glass and strained to make out the distorted image. A muffled *thunk thunk* sound drifted across the yard from the direction of the barn. Then the indistinct vision of a black-shirted man, shoveling dirt into a large hole, came into focus.

Renee rubbed her eyes and squinted. *"Mon Dieu,"* she whispered, "what's he doing? Where are the other men? Those shots? Do you suppose he killed them?"

"Why would he kill his own men?"

"It's a mystery," Renee mumbled, "but right now we've got bigger problems. It's getting light outside, and you've got to get out of here. I'll try to send your message, but we'll have to talk about your flier later."

"A bientot. Be back next Monday, 2:00 a.m. Okay?" He gave his sister a parting hug. "Be careful, Renee."

The next morning a German general arrived with three command cars full of officers carrying rolls of blueprints. Trying to stay out of sight, Renee watched through a window as the General strode purposefully around the barn. He stabbed his riding crop at the blue prints, at the ground, at the men, and back to the blueprints. Pointing, waving his arms, and barking orders, it was obvious he was in a hurry to get something built.

Her heart ached, as she watched her father hard at work clearing out the barn. She saw him approach the General, arms outstretched in a gesture of appeal. Then the blackshirt Captain intervened. He was shouting, jabbing his hand at her father and pointing toward the barn. A German Corporal, who had come with the General, marched over to Claude. He spoke briefly and set to work with considerable energy hauling bales of hay out of the barn. Apparently the Germans were in such a hurry they were helping clear the barn.

Renee strained to listen to the foreign words. It must be terribly important, she thought. Why else would they bring a full general?

That night on BBC, she heard her code name, "Cricket," for the first time. At first, she thought it must be a mistake, but it was repeated three times, the signal of urgency. Disguised as news about a cricket match, it had the earmarks of a coded message.

She reached for a pencil and started writing. Decoded, it read, "All three sources blown. Do not attempt contact. Repeat. Do not make contact. Will send new agent, code name TROUT. Keep listening for timing, more details."

Henri showed up, as promised, at 2:00a.m. With him, a tall, gangly man stumbled into the back door with a dirty, bloody bandage covering one arm. Dressed in a turtleneck sweater and a black beret, neither of which fitted well, he appeared to Renee to be a poor simulation of a Frenchman. She had difficulty holding in her laughter. After her schooling in England for a year, she could tell this was an Englishman even before he opened his mouth.

Henri had a determined look. "I've brought you the English flyer I told you about."

"*Mon Dieu*, you're not asking me to take him out are you? I didn't say I'd do it. Damn it, Henri, I can't do it. I have too many other problems."

"Please, Renee, we really need you on this. It's important and ... What do you mean, 'other problems'?"

"All my sources are blown, and I have to be here to receive a new contact. But I shouldn't be talking about it in front of another person. I don't care who he is. He might be forced to talk."

"What are you trying to tell me? Sources blown? What about my messages?"

"Henri, your Englishman will have to go outside while we talk."

"All right, all right," Henri grumbled, "but let me at least introduce you. This is Captain Weatherby of the RAF. You can see he messed up his arm in the crash."

With his wry smile and under-fed look, Weatherby was the sort of fellow any woman would want to help without quite knowing why. They exchanged greetings in English, obviously a relief to the Englishman who didn't speak a word of French. Renee began to feel real empathy for the wounded flyer who was keeping a stiff upper lip in the best British tradition.

She touched his arm lightly. "I'll put a clean bandage on that hand," she said, "but first I must talk to Henri alone. Please step outside for a minute. But keep low and don't make any noise."

"Now, let's talk, Henri," she began in a no-nonsense tone. "Last night, I got a coded message on BBC. Said not to go near any of my contacts. They've all been shut down, probably tracked down by the *Funkspiel*. So I haven't been able to send your message. They said a new contact would be sent, and I have to stand by for more details."

"Have you heard any more?"

"No, but I obviously have to stay here for my new contact."

"*Sacre Bleu!* It could mean trouble, but I guess we'll have to find someone else for our flyer."

"Sorry, I'd sure like to help him."

"Damn. Anyway, how about giving us something hot to drink? And fix his bandage?"

LONDON, ENGLAND

"I don't like it," McDonald growled, pacing the floor of his office. "You're taking my best men."

"My dear fellow," replied Atwater. "We simply have no choice in the matter if we're going to succeed with the invasion. I've run out of trained men, and this operation absolutely must succeed. We must have the best men available, and MI-6 does not have them. Fortunately you do. The outcome of the war could well depend on it."

"Don't get melodramatic on me, Charles. Besides, why can't de Gaulle take this on?"

"Don't quote me on this, Bill, but Winston won't hear of it. He thinks de Gaulle would make a mess of it, and there is no margin for error here."

McDonald stared out the window, searching for the right

words. "It's probably a death sentence, you know. The record's been atrocious, and this one's going to be even tougher than the others."

* * *

Mitch saluted. "Lieutenant Carter reporting as ordered, sir." He was not quite sure whether he should stand at attention.

"Good morning, Lieutenant. Please be seated," General Charles Atwater tapped a pencil on his desk, then touched it to his forehead in a half salute. "Good of you to come. Had a devil of a time persuading your commanding officer. But I think, after you've heard what I have to say, you'll agree this meeting is most important."

Before the meeting, Mitch had been briefed about Sir Charles by his C.O., Captain Ames. In the year Mitch had been reporting to Ames, they had both been promoted one rank, and the two had developed a close friendship. Now the Captain had become concerned about the younger man. "I owe you as much of an explanation as I can give you, Mitch," he had said with a worried look. "You've volunteered for damned dangerous duty. You're an American who's being used by the Brits. They have a way of sounding real nice and gentlemanly, but they can be pretty ruthless."

Mitch had listened without comment. Ames had held up one hand as if fending off an attack. "For God's sake, Carter, don't quote me on that."

"Of course not, but I'd sure like to get the straight scoop, or as much of it as you can tell me."

"I'll tell you what I can, but keep it to yourself," Ames stopped to light a cigarette, apparently considering how much he should say. "When the war broke out in the fall of 1939, Atwater was made an instant brigadier in spite of his complete lack of military experience. He'd been the leading hawk in Parliament. Took a leave of absence from Parliament and was put in charge of some parts of British intelligence, sort of an oversight position. Now he has a tiger by the tail. Hundreds of the men, and even some women, who volunteered as MI-5 and MI-6 agents have disappeared—killed, captured, God knows what. There've been some successes to be sure, but far too many agents have died, largely because of lack of preparation and training. At least that's my opinion."

"What can you tell me about MI-6," Mitch asked. "I think that's where I'm headed."

"Umm. I'm afraid you're right. MI-6 has become a great deal more than an intelligence operation. Sir Charles has built up a corps of SOE, Special Operations Executive Agents, and infiltrated them into every one of the German-occupied countries. They're providing arms, supplies, training, and some semblance of organization for the Resistance, in addition to gathering intelligence."

"What do you know about the French? According to the training I've had so far, we're going to have to work with a crazy-quilt of Resistance people—Communists, Fascists, de Gaullists, and who knows?"

"Well," Ames blew smoke at the ceiling, "I've heard there's a lot of infighting, nasty bickering. Winning the cooperation of competing groups has turned out to be Sir Charles' most frustrating problem. More often than not, one group'll blow the cover of another. Even de Gaulle has been a pain, working at cross-purposes with British Intelligence. I once overheard Charles say, 'That damned Frenchman wants to run everything himself.' By the way, Churchill is in complete agreement with Atwater on that point. He's been publicly quoted as saying, 'Everyone has his cross to bear. Mine is the cross of Lorraine.' I have it on good authority that even Roosevelt has become so incensed with de Gaulle he once recommended to Churchill the Frenchman be arrested.[3] Of course, Churchill didn't act on the suggestion. In any event, I think you should know that Atwater has been instructed to run his own show and keep de Gaulle in the dark."

Sir Charles stood and pointed to a huge map of Europe on the wall. "We have a situation, Lieutenant—here." Mitch watched the pointer trace the coastline of Normandy. "A critical situation, indeed."

The General tapped on the map and cleared his throat. "I have asked your section head for his best man, someone who speaks French, with commando experience and trained in explosives. He tells me you're the best man for the job."

"I'm honored, sir," Mitch replied, "but I'd like to know. We're talking about SOE work aren't we?"

"Yes."

"The Germans consider it spying, don't they?" Mitch looked intently at the General. "And they shoot spies. So my question up front, is this assignment voluntary, or is it—?

Charles held up his hand. "Yes, of course it's voluntary, Lieutenant." He paused and cleared his throat again. "But we're in a frightful box at the moment. Don't want to overstate the case, but I happen to think victory or defeat may well hinge on what we do here."

Mitch shifted his gaze to the map and rubbed his chin.

"Unfortunately, we've lost a number of our best men," Charles continued, "and, as I was saying, you were picked as the most qualified man for this particular job. To be quite honest, you're the only qualified man available who's not already tied up."

Mitch didn't feel that well qualified. In the year he had been in England, he'd been put through intensive Special Operations training in Scotland—weapons, explosives, parachute training, secret devices. He'd learned how to kill silently, to operate short wave radio, to attach cyclonite plastic explosives, to parachute from a low-flying airplane, and how to handle a simulated Gestapo interrogation. There had been a brush-up course in French language, customs, dress, and behavior, even a short course in basic German. But he felt like a rank amateur, acutely aware he would need to learn a great deal more if he was to survive in this game.

In terms of real action, he'd been sent on two commando raids on northern coastal towns of Brittany. On the first raid, they had gone ashore in rubber boats from a submarine and demolished a radar installation. It had gone like clockwork. Silently killing the two German guards, the raiders had vanished in a matter of minutes, leaving the explosive charges to go off seconds later. Mitch had been only a minor participant.

Unnerved by the killing, he knew he was not cut out for that kind of work. But no turning back—kill or be killed. The die was cast. Orders were orders. Nevertheless, it made him physically sick.

The second raid had been more complicated. Trying to sneak across the English Channel in a motor torpedo boat, they'd been spotted and chased back to Southampton by a German E-boat. Luckily an RAF Spitfire had spotted the E-boat, strafed it and nearly sunk it. Taking advantage of the confusion, the commandos had slipped into their target near Cherbourg. This time, Mitch had been in charge of setting the explosives. Half a dozen loaded barges had been sent to the bottom, and an important dock put out of commission. But they had to fight their way out, and two of their men had been wounded.

Now, the General apparently thought Mitch was qualified for a critical mission behind enemy lines just because of two commando raids and his language background. Mitch thought that was absurd.

He had wondered why French Nationals weren't being used by MI-6 for this kind of assignment. The answer was supplied by Ames, explaining that de Gaulle had siphoned off all the qualified Frenchmen for his own teams. He was concentrating his efforts on building a fighting force to liberate Paris when the time came. His own political agenda revolved around taking control of Paris ahead of the Communists. Hence MI-6 was forced to train agents from scratch who had little knowledge of France or French customs.

"You may want a day to think this over," Sir Charles continued, "but first I'd like to tell you something about the mission." He folded his hands behind his back and stared out of the window. Mitch studied the General's anxious expression.

"We have two serious problems," Sir Charles waved the pointer at the map, "which can be resolved with an agent of your capabilities and with the help of a specially trained radioman. By the way, we have an excellent radioman who has volunteered for this assignment."

"Perhaps I had better at least hear what's involved, sir," Mitch said without conviction.

"Our most urgent needs are two-fold—first, to train the Resistance in the use of the weapons, which we are dropping by air; and second, to replace our radio transmission contacts. We had three contacts: one in Caen, one in Cherbourg, and one in St.-Lo. They were sending us valuable information about troop movements, coastal fortifications, railroad schedules, Luftwaffe activities, the things we will need if an Allied invasion of Europe is to succeed. Also they were pinpointing airdrop locations for us—different locations, timing, and signals. We simply can't supply the Resistance without exact drop points and exact timing. And we can't do that without radio contact."

Mitch nodded, drawn into the logic.

"You see," Atwater explained, "the Germans stake out known landing sites and shoot up our planes and the men on the ground— and, incidentally, make off with the arms and supplies needed by the Resistance."

"You have some solution in mind?"

Apparently Charles was bent on defining the problem further, not the solutions. "Our biggest problem is *Funkspiel,* the radio-direction-finder vans, which the Boche have running all over the place. They spot a transmission signal and hone in on it in less than a minute. If a message can be kept under thirty seconds, the vans can't get a fix. But invariably the sender starts taking chances, and, as I said, all of our contacts have been caught. We believe they have been tortured to tell what they know about the code and the Resistance, and then shot, even after they have told everything. Nasty bunch, the Gestapo—don't play by the rules at all."

"Sounds pretty hopeless," Mitch said, feeling his blood pressure rise.

"Actually, we've learned a lot, and I think we know, now, how to beat them at their own game."

Mitch wished he would not refer to it as a game.

"In any event, we absolutely must set up another radio contact. Absolutely must. And we know the place to do it. And how to do it."

Mitch looked skeptical but didn't say anything.

"Now here's the plan." Charles began pacing the floor and talking faster. "The Wehrmacht has set up a powerful transmission station in the small village of St.-Pierre-du-Bois in Normandy." He turned and pointed to a small dot on the large map of France on the wall. Colored pins protruded from the map like quills on a porcupine. Mitch assumed they denoted the whereabouts of various agents.

"This station is unusually busy, transmitting day and night—virtually all the time, mostly routine army orders as far as we can tell. Our idea is to set up our own transmission station right next to it—cheek-by-jowl you might say—in a farmhouse where we have an excellent contact. The *Funkspiel* won't waste their time tracking their own transmission signals. You see, our signals will appear to them to be part of theirs."

"Won't they be suspicious of the English content and won't they be on a different frequency than ours?" Mitch asked.

"Our code will be set up to sound like German to them. And for the most part, the only thing their vans detect is the direction of a signal, not its content. All the operator hears is a squeal. He usually has only a few seconds to get a bearing, and then they race toward it hoping to make an arrest. They'll never suspect us of having a station right under their noses, and they will assume the radio transmissions are their own. Our man will transmit only when they are also on the air, and, of course, it won't be in English."

Mitch shifted in his chair, increasingly aware that he was being sucked into Sir Charles' "game".

"Sounds like it might work, but — "

"It has to work. We know it will work. I've gone over this with our electronics and communications people. They are one hundred percent behind it. Besides, we'll get you in and out in a few weeks' time, so your risk will be minimal. It's our radioman who'll be taking the bigger risk, and he's convinced the plan is entirely first-rate. He'll have to stay with it for the duration."

"Why do you need me? It seems your radioman is the key."

"Two reasons: First, we think it will increase his chance of success if there are two of you, supporting each other in the set-up phase. There is more equipment to carry in than one man can handle, and you have the commando experience, which may be needed if you get into a tight spot. Second, and perhaps even more important, your mission will involve training the Resistance. I will get to that in a minute."

Beginning to feel a bit sheepish, Mitch nodded noncommittally. Sir Charles lowered his voice perceptibly and stared out the window. "Our contact in St.-Pierre happens to be someone I know personally, a very delightful, and I happen to think an extraordinarily attractive young woman. I don't want anything to happen to her. In fact, after you have set up our radioman, I want you to find some way to get her out."

"Doesn't that complicate the mission? The whole thing sounds pretty important. We wouldn't want any complication that might compromise it, would we?"

"I don't think so. The lady grew up in the area and can guide you to the Resistance, including their safe houses and eventually to an evacuation point, which we will arrange. And that gets me to the second part of your assignment."

Mitch could see that Charles was now ignoring the possibility that he might refuse to volunteer.

"As I said, we need you to train the Resistance, the *Maquis* as they are calling themselves now. Show them how to use plastic explosives and specialty mines—shouldn't take long. I understand you mastered those in your tour with Scotland MI-6."

Mitch had plenty of experience with Cyclonite plastic explosives, but the mines were another matter. They were tricky. One kind, disguised to look like a cow patty, would be placed in roadways used by German trucks and tanks. Another, made to resemble a loaf of bread, would be delivered to German mess halls. Still others, disguised as lumps of coal, were designed to explode when shoveled into a boiler.

"I can handle those, but they're touchy, and I'm no expert," said Mitch slowly.

"We'll give you a couple of days to brush up. And there are a few other small details that will need attention." Mitch was getting used to Charles' British understatement. "You'll need to equip yourself. You know the drill, essentially like your raids on the coast."

Mitch only nodded. Apparently this was no longer a volunteer situation.

Charles paced the floor faster and waved his map-pointer vigorously. "We are in somewhat of a quandary as to the best method of delivery."

"Delivery?"

"Yes. How best to deliver you and our radioman, Roger Smith, to the coast. Normally we would take you in by Lizzy, but we can't get a proper fix without our radio contacts. Of course, we could go in on the same field as last time, and give the *Maquis* the time and place via BBC, but I'm not comfortable without a cross-check response; and we can't get a cross-check until we have your transmission station going. More than likely, the Germans will be watching any field that has been used before, so that option is out."

"I suppose that leaves parachuting or by boat," Mitch said.

"Don't like parachutes very much. A bit too risky. You see, it's the same problem. We can't be certain about the drop-point unless we have a cross-check. This is too important. We can't afford to lose you."

Mitch was inclined to agree.

"Last time, you went in by Shelburne motor torpedo boat, but lately the E-boats[4] have been going after them. The Germans are getting a bit uppity about our commando raids in the last few months. So I think our best bet is by sub. Wouldn't you agree?"

Mitch nodded, knowing it was too late to debate any of this. Charles had obviously thought it all out ahead of time. He handed Mitch a folder of written orders with his code name, "Trout," on the cover. Inside were a host of instructions, a detailed map of Normandy and St.-Pierre-du-Bois, where to report next, and the particulars about his female contact, code-named "Cricket."

"You must destroy all of this after committing it to memory." Charles smiled, extended his hand, and dismissed Mitch with a jolly "Good Luck," as if he were being sent off to a cricket match.

ALLIES START INVASION OF SICILY
A 'LIBERATION' START, BUT EISENHOWER URGES
FRENCH BE CALM 'TILL THEIR HOUR STRIKES'
<u>New York Times</u>, July 10, 1943

ST.-PIERRE-DU-BOIS, FRANCE

Renee couldn't sleep. Worried about Etienne, Roulen, and Pouilon, she rose early and decided to bicycle to St.-Lo and have a look at Etienne's tobacco shop. Not slowing down, she cycled past the shop and saw that it stood dark and empty. She could make out the WANTED sign in large print, posted on the door, but she didn't dare stop to read it.

Her thoughts in turmoil, she pedaled hard for home. It had been stupid to go. She had just put herself and everybody else in danger. From now on she would believe the BBC.

She told herself to stop shaking and get control of herself.

Think. Think.

It's obvious Etienne has been caught, and I'll more than likely be next. I'll have to do something pretty drastic about changing my looks—cut my hair short, wear an old woman's shawl, anything to make myself ugly. Maybe it'll also get the blackshirt Captain to quit staring at me.

Two nights later her brother came for food. "Did you know," he said, "the Germans have issued a priority-one search warrant for a young woman, about twenty, height 160cm, weight 45kg, with long, light copper-blond hair, last seen riding a dark blue bicycle."

Renee stared at him in disbelief.

"The pigs tend to be pretty accurate about details, don't they?" Henri added with a twisted grin. Renee didn't think it was funny.

Of course, the bicycle didn't mean much. Almost every Frenchman rode one, and half were dark blue. Nevertheless, Renee carefully scraped the old paint off of hers and repainted it with the only paint available, barn red.

Next, she cut her hair still shorter. Sitting in front of her chipped mirror, she brushed her hair until it shone, then took the shears and chopped. She choked back the tears and sighed. No man will look at me twice now, she thought.

Over the next few days, Renee listened intently to the BBC, hoping for more information about her contacts. What was she supposed to do? Finally she heard, "TROUT coming to CRICKET Oct 28 or 29. Signal: four taps on north window 1:OO a.m." That would be nine or ten days off.

In the summer heat, the shapeless smock clung to her as she went about her chores, tending the chickens, the beehives, the eternal weeding. Acutely aware of the stares from the German soldiers across the yard, she tried to stay out of sight as much as possible, but without much success. The farm had to be attended.

On a particularly hot July day, the blackshirt Captain strode across the dusty courtyard to the field where she was stooped over a row of cabbages. Renee turned her back, pretending she had not seen him. Sweating from fear as well as the heat, she felt almost naked with the smock pressed against her body like a wet towel.

"Bonjour Mademoiselle", the Captain touched the rim of his hat in a half salute. "I wish speak you," he said in broken French.

Renee straightened up from her weeding, but refused to look at him and only mumbled a faint *"bonjour"*.

"My name Otto," the German continued in a conciliatory tone, "Captain Otto Streikler. You may call me Otto." He waited for a response, but receiving none, went on, "We make good relations with French, no? So we have party—music and dance in village. You come, yes"?

"Non", Renee responded, almost a whisper.

"I take you—with me—special—personal".

"Non." She turned her back and went on weeding. From the corner of her eye, she could see him raise his arm as if to strike her, then lower it. He stood staring at her for a moment but finally turned and marched away.

An hour after all three Brousards had retired for the night, Renee awoke to the sound of a thud coming from the direction of the front door. She sat up in bed. There was a second and a third thud, followed by a loud crash. Someone had broken down the ancient wooden entry door. Next, she heard footsteps, the tread of boots on the stairway.

Renee jumped out of bed, grabbed her bathrobe and peered into the hall. Catching a glimpse of the blackshirt Nazi, she rushed back into her room, and quick as a cat, threw open the window, climbed onto the low verandah roof, and scrambled down the apple tree to the ground. From below she heard the heavy footsteps enter her bedroom. She knew the moonlight would expose an empty, mussed bed and an open window.

Then she heard more footsteps running down the hall toward her bedroom and her father's voice shouting, "What's going on here." Then a crash and orders in a German voice. "Back to your room and stay there. Now. Or I shoot. Now!"

The German leaned out the open window and bellowed, "Return to your room!"

Renee pressed her body against the wall of the house, frozen in silence.

"NOW," he yelled.

More silence.

"I know what goes on here. You work for Resistance, *Ja*?"

More silence.

"I send you to Ravensbrueck, if you don't obey. NOW!"

Silence.

He fired two shots into the low roof.

Renee realized she had no way out. Without question he could carry out his threat, and where would that leave Henri and Charles? At Ravensbrueck she'd be tortured to tell everything, and then she would die one way or another.

Slowly she inched her way back through the broken door and up the stairway. A black-shirted hulking form loomed at the top, staring down at her. To Renee he looked like the Frankenstein Monster.

Stopping halfway, she gathered her robe around her and hunched over, staring at her feet. The German reached down, grabbed her arm, and pulled her up the stairway and into her bedroom.

"You be nice to Otto," he said quietly in fractured French, "or you'll be ... You know what they do to women in Ravensbrueck, don't you? If you don't talk, they tear you apart. You'll wish you had never been born. I save you from that if you nice to Otto. You very beautiful, Fraulein. Your name Renee, no? Yes, Renee. Your father give me list of names. "

Renee collapsed on the floor, and curled up in a fetal position. "Please. No," she whispered.

Otto reached down, pulled her up with one hand, and leaned over to kiss her. Renee wrenched her head from to the side and screamed. She had never screamed like that in her life before, but she screamed now, loudly enough to be heard for half a mile. When he tried to muffle her with both hands, she bit him—hard. She tasted the blood and saw him wince.

He raised his hand to beat her into submission, but something stopped him. She put up both arms, closed her eyes and stopped breathing. When the blow didn't fall she opened her eyes a crack. She could see the ice-blue eyes staring at her as if in a trance. Renee finally gasped for air. *Why did he stop? Why?*

Renee found her breath and began screaming again, while Otto tried to hold her still and kept staring at her.

Her screams echoed through the house, finally driving Claude to action. Through half-closed eyes, Renee saw her father rush into the room and charge at Otto with the fireplace poker raised above his head. Renee was able to pull free as Otto fended off the blow from the poker. She watched helplessly as the German reached for his gun and calmly shot his assailant. Still clutching the poker, Claude collapsed on the floor.

Annette, barefoot and hair streaming behind her, rushed into the room and flung herself on her husband. She screamed at Otto and cupped her hand under Claude's head. *"Mon Dieu. Mon Dieu"*, she kept repeating.

Otto left the room—and the house. Renee assumed it was the screaming of two women that had driven him away, but she thought she heard him whisper, "I'm sorry."

Back in his quarters, Otto paced the floor late into the night. *She should have talked to me—should have gone to the dance—she had no right to turn her back on me.* But his mind kept returning to Ilsa.

The eyes and the hair. Otto had suddenly seen Ilsa in the blue-green eyes and the golden hair, Ilsa, the one bright spot of his childhood. But Ilsa was dead now, killed in a terrible accident, which had destroyed the only joy in his youth. He wanted this Frenchwoman more than any woman since Ilsa. He wanted her to like him, but he didn't know how.

Finally recovering some sense of equilibrium, Renee pulled the torn robe around her, gently pushed her mother aside, and knelt over her father. He was breathing rapidly and groaning softly, but his pulse was strong. Taking off his nightshirt, she could see where the bullet had entered, just below the shoulder.

She tore off a strip from the bottom of her nightgown and pressed it on the wound to stop the bleeding. "Put a blanket over him," she told her mother. "Keep him warm but don't move him. I'll fetch Doctor Rouleau."

The farm had no telephone, and it was illegal to go out at night after curfew, but Renee had reached the point where she didn't care. Throwing an old coat around her, she bicycled furiously into the village and hammered on Dr. Rouleau's door. The doctor knew everyone in St.-Pierre and was accustomed to emergencies. Besides, he had permission to violate the curfew when there was a medical emergency.

Putting aside the book he had been reading by candlelight, he responded instantly to Renee's frantic knocking. And when he heard her tearful appeal, it took him only seconds to grab his coat and medical bag. He pulled his bicycle off the porch, and pedaled alongside Renee back to the Brousard farm as rapidly as their legs could propel them.

First, he had to calm Annette and comfort his old friend, Claude. Then he cleaned and bandaged the wound.

"How bad is it?" Renee asked.

"The bullet tore some tendons and cracked the shoulder bone. He's lost a lot of blood, but he'll recover in time."

"How long will it take, doctor?"

"At his age, it's hard to tell. If everything goes well, it'll be five or six months, probably a little more before he'll be able to work the farm."

Renee groaned inwardly. Somehow the farm had to be tended. Both the Germans and Henri were demanding more produce. Food had become the most important aspect of their lives.

"How in Heaven's name are we going to run this place?" Renee asked her mother after the doctor had left. "We don't know how to run the tractor or any of those things. The two of us can't possibly do it all."

Nevertheless, Renee and her mother immediately went to work in the fields, toiling like beasts of burden from dawn to dark. From the beginning, they knew it was an impossible task. The squash would rot on the vines, the apples and pears would go soft, and the potatoes would still be in the ground with winter approaching.

Renee answered a timid knock on the door. Her first reaction was panic when she saw the the gray Wehrmacht uniform with two small stripes of a corporal on the sleeve. But her consternation changed to incredulity as the Corporal saluted and tried to communicate in halting French, *"Je voudrais vous aider dans les paturages"*— I would like to help in the fields. Fresh-faced and shy, he appeared not more than seventeen, not at all the typical Nazi she had come to fear.

"I am called Hans." He bowed slightly. "I like to see tractor."

Renee stared at the young German silently, but with an expression that asked why?

"I come help with farming."

Renee pondered, *why would this soldier be helping me? If he has been ordered to help, I can't order him to go away, and I certainly need the help.*

Saying little and working hard, Hans soon had the tractor functioning and miraculously obtained some petrol to run it. The benefits were felt immediately. Towing a produce cart through the fields improved efficiency ten-fold compared to carrying everything in sacks and buckets.

Every day at mealtime, precisely noon and 6:00 p.m., Hans would disappear into the new barracks, which had been built next to the barn. But he would reappear after dinner to work some more. He would steal glances at Renee, then blush and quickly look away whenever she caught him staring at her.

*   *   *

Otto Streikler was having erotic dreams. *The French goddess stood naked in a field of blue flowers, the sun rising directly behind her, creating a halo effect and accenting her curves. Adolf Hitler entered the scene with his arm outstretched in a Nazi salute. Heidendorff, dressed in a gleaming white uniform, sat on a throne on Hitler's right. He leered at the Goddess who was holding a long-handled garden implement, which passed between her breasts. Her hands were on her breasts, pressing them around the upper part of the handle, and her lips touched the end.*

Hitler was speaking, and Otto strained to hear. "Streikler, you have sworn to give your life for me, have you not?"

"Of course, Mein Fuehrer."

In a hollow, God-like voice, Hitler intoned, "You must know, everything will be destroyed. You understand that, don't you?" Then a long pause. "But you must save the French girl. You must save the French gi ..."

Heidendorff turned slowly and pointed a gun at Otto's head. "You know what has to be done, don't you, Streikler? But it doesn't matter. I'm going to kill you anyway. Kill you. Kill you. Kill. Kill ..."

Otto woke up in a pool of sweat.

He couldn't get the French girl out of his mind, to the point where the distraction began interfering with his work. His men noticed him staring out the window, and his orders were confusing. Adding to his frustration, von Kleister was putting pressure on him to get on with his "Rat Hunts" and root out the pesky rats, the *Maquis*.

But the rats had eluded him every time. Each time the SOE brought in supplies by their "Lizzy," Otto's men were just minutes late. And when he had a firm fix on their camp, they always melted away into the forest just minutes before his men arrived.

It became obvious to Otto that the local populace was one gigantic information network. The slippery "rats" were being warned of their every move. He would fix that.

Certain that the locals knew where the rats were hiding, he tried a new tack. The logical solution was to arrest and torture a few of the squealers. He would get the answers in short order. So Otto arrested a dozen old men—the young ones having been shipped off for forced labor or the military—and threatened them with torture. If they didn't cooperate, it would be a firing squad.

The threat of torture had the desired effect. Quickly the twelve unlucky citizens told everything they knew, which was accurate enough. But Henri's *Maquis* had anticipated such a contingency. Using a simple system—a shirt hung on a clothesline, a flowerpot in a window—local patriots provided timely warnings. In a matter of minutes, the warnings found their way to Henri or one of his lieutenants. They would move their camp and change the warning signals. With a few exceptions, the rat hunts in Normandy were a failure—for the time being.

Captain Streikler heard rumors: General von Kleister was on the verge of being replaced by Hitler for his failure to control the Resistance. In turn, the General was incensed with him for the same reasons and wanted him replaced. He also soon found that Heidendorff would not allow it. Otto smiled to himself. *Von Kleister must be wondering why.*

Aside from his lack of sleep over the disturbing French girl, Otto had another distraction. He'd been ordered to report the results of Heidendorff's private project directly to the Marshal. Now, a curt reminder arrived by courier, marked TOP SECRET, demanding that he report immediately in person.

With the pressure from von Kleister, Otto had not found time to complete Heidendorff's assignment and move the boxes to the cave. Now he was forced to give up a night's sleep and take the time to explore them. Taking Heidendorff's crude map and a lantern, he set out alone to reconnoiter, knowing he couldn't let anyone else in on the Marshal's secret.

As Heidendorff had stated, the entrance was boarded up. A battered sign read:

ACHTUNG
DEFENSE D'ENTRER

Otto pushed the boards aside, lit the lantern, and groped his way down a long flight of slippery steps carved into the limestone. Twenty minutes later, he found himself in a huge gallery, studded with floor-to-ceiling stalactites and stalagmites. In the dim light of the lantern he consulted the map.

The next part was more difficult. Slick with running water, the steps were steep and poorly defined. As he worked his way down two more levels, he realized it would be impossible to move Heidendorff's heavy boxes down the treacherous shafts without help. He would need ropes and at least three men. Slowly inching his way down, he felt the shaft become steeper and the steps fainter. Half way down to the third level, he slipped and fell, sliding twenty feet before landing hard on a small projection. A sharp pain shot through his left ankle.

Otto grimaced, "Damn," he muttered out loud.

He'd sprained his ankle, but, gritting his teeth, he consulted the map again and managed to push ahead. "I shouldn't have eliminated those Jewish helpers so soon," he muttered aloud. With water running down the steps, Otto was getting soaked. Besides, his ankle hurt like fire. He would have to retreat and try again another time.

He scowled as he limped back to his headquarters. What would he tell Heidendorff? He couldn't delay any longer, and he didn't dare admit he hadn't carried out his orders. The Marshal would have him shot. He obviously couldn't use any of his own men to help. He'd just have to lie to Heidendorff and pray the fat man never found out.

Then there was the matter of the rat hunts. How the devil was he supposed to concentrate on rat hunts if he had to trot off to Berlin? It seemed to Otto a complete waste of time.

But a mere captain didn't argue with a marshal if he wished to survive.

BERLIN, GERMANY

Otto took the train to Berlin, a risky business, because the Americans had been bombing the rail lines daily. Nevertheless, he arrived safely at SS headquarters in Berlin and exchanged messages with Heidendorff's aide to the effect that he would visit Bernau the next afternoon.

He checked a car out of the SS car pool in Berlin and drove ninety kilometers east to Bernau, arriving at the massive bronze gates of the estate at 3:00p.m. He saluted the sentry, informing him he had an appointment with the Marshal.

Forced to wait, he stared at the stately mansion, the immense gold eagles perched atop the marble pillars, the grand terraced garden lined with Greek statues, the fountains, and the immaculately trimmed Cyprus trees. *I'll wager I could have an estate like this,* he mused, *if I had the contents of just one of those boxes.*

After waiting two hours for a summons and pacing nervously, he glared at the sentry and ordered him to try again. Another interminable wait, then a message came back that he was to report back later at 2:00 a.m. Otto shrugged. The fat man seemed to like to do things in the middle of the night.

At precisely 2:00 a.m., he once again approached the imposing gates. The sentry, apparently expecting him, saluted and directed him to a side door shrouded in trees. A sliver of moonlight lit the garden path dimly, but the unlit side entrance was totally obscured in dark shadows.

A prickly feeling assailed him as he groped his way up the path. Hearing a faint rustling noise from the shrubbery, he whirled around just as two shots were fired.

PORTSMOUTH, ENGLAND

Driving an American Jeep, Mitch and radio expert, Roger Smith, reported to the submarine base at Portsmouth loaded down with the special equipment they had been ordered to assemble—explosives, specially adapted bicycles, two rubber rafts, all the supplies and devices they would need for their operation.

"I don't see 'ow in the bloody 'ell we're ever goin' to get all this stuff to those French buggers," Roger ventured as they drove up to the gate, "assumin' we can get to the beach in the first place."

"You and I'll have to figure that out, Roger. I've got some orders here. Supposed to cover it, but we're going to be briefed by the sub Captain and the Special Forces Commandant."

Roger looked skeptical. " 'ope they know what in bloody 'ell they're talkin' about."

"They're supposed to have the answers. The Commandant has had all kinds of experience supplying the Resistance, commando raids, that sort of thing."

Mitch knew there was no time to lose. In order to meet the October 28th or 29th date at St.-Pierre-du-Bois, they would need to hit the beach in Normandy on the 26th or the 27th at the latest. It would take less than a day to cross the English Channel, but he knew the weather could be nasty in October. Going ashore in a rubber boat would be messy in a rough sea. If the weather socked in, they could expect an unpredictable wait off shore, submerged, of course.

The October 28th date had been chosen for several reasons. Backing up two days to the 26th, the tide would be right, the moon would be just a sliver, and most important, it would be a Sunday.

Commander Wainwright of Special Forces extended a leathery hand and greeted them with a tight smile. A naval officer, wearing a slouched hat and with four tarnished stripes on his sleeve, stood in the background, staring out the window. Mitch guessed this would be submarine Captain, Jamison. Wainwright had met Mitch before and knew everything about him. The two men had formed a good relationship. They respected each other.

The Commander's headquarters was nothing more than an ordinary house on the outskirts of Portsmouth. Mitch wondered whether it was some kind of disguise or just classic British austerity.

Mitch knew the Commander to be a man dedicated to precise

detail. He had personally led dozens of commando raids, and had survived longer than most because of careful planning. With weather-beaten, hawkish features, Wainwright stood erect and spoke with precision, while Captain Jamison slouched in a chair, looking like he would drop off from lack of sleep.

"Gentlemen," Wainwright began, holding up a sheath of papers. "General Atwater has sent these orders and impressed on me the extreme urgency of this mission. Everything else must assume a lower priority for the moment. He has insisted on our most reliable sub for the job, and asked that we provide the best possible support for this operation. First off, let me introduce you to Captain Jamison, skipper of HMS Dartmoor. He's one of our best, but I have to tell you, he's been at sea continuously for more than a year, so please make allowances."

"I'll be tip top by tomorrow, Commander," Jamison interjected. "No problem."

Wasting no time on the usual British niceties, Wainwright got down to business. "The crossing will be from Portsmouth to a beach near St.-Aubin." Wainwright pointed to the large map of the French coastline on the wall behind him. "This beach has been used several times before without arousing suspicion—as far as we can determine. It's sheltered by high bluffs and thick underbrush. The brush will provide a good hiding place for equipment as well as shelter for the two of you until you are ready to move out and up the bluff."

He paused, "Any questions so far."

"I have a bunch," Mitch said, "but I think we'd better hear you out first."

Wainwright pointed to the map again. "Our reconnaissance photographs show gun emplacements under construction at the top of the bluff." He spread half a dozen enlargements on the table.

"Let's have a look." Mitch got up and leaned over the table.

"Certainly. You can see the beach where you'll go ashore, here—and the bushes, here. The cliff is steep, but not too tough to climb. Your only problem will be hauling up your bikes and equipment. But I'm sure you can manage it."

"No problem," Roger murmured.

Wainwright nodded. "The German patrols are thin and spaced far apart. They don't have enough men to patrol the entire coast of France as well as fight the war in Russia and Italy."

He placed another blown-up aerial photo on the table, showing the beach at low tide. "That beach goes out nearly a mile at low tide," he explained. "You won't want to haul your equipment up that long stretch of beach, and we don't want you exposed any more than necessary, so you'll hit the beach at high tide. The landing will be timed for the darkest time of night, but a little moonlight will be needed, so you can see to load the rubber boats without using telltale flashlights. If the weather is socked in, and there's no light, we'll just have to wait. This is too important to take any chances."

Wainwright paused, searching the strained faces. "You'll be transferred to a rubber boat about a mile off shore, the closest the Dartmoor can come in the shallow waters."

He looked at Jamison for comment, but the sub Captain only nodded.

"To reduce the chance of detection by radar," Wainwright continued, "your paddles will be thin wood, and there'll be as little metal as possible in your other equipment. But, fortunately, from what we know, the Germans have very little radar. As you probably know, because you have been involved, our commandos and the RAF have taken out most of their coastal radar. They're relying on watch-towers manned by the French."

Jamison interrupted. "I'm confident there's no radar in the St.-Aubin area, but we'll proceed as if there is. We'll go in with minimum periscope and stay submerged until it's time to transfer you to the rubber rafts, but the transfer will have to go fast."

Wainwright removed his glasses, pulled a handkerchief from his pocket and wiped them. "Once on shore, you must deflate and bury your rafts in these bushes." He pointed to the photo. "There may be a few more items you can't manage to haul up the cliff. They can also be buried in the bushes and possibly recovered later by the *Maquis*. But the transmitter must be carried with you. You'll need it immediately when you get to St.-Pierre."

"Won't that look suspicious as hell if we're stopped?" Mitch asked.

"It'll be in pieces, disguised as telephone repair equipment. You'll reassemble it when you reach St.-Pierre. Roger shouldn't have any trouble with it. Other than the transmitter and the bicycles, you'll travel as lightly as possible."

Mitch listened intently. This was a lot to absorb. Too many things could go wrong.

"Some of the smaller parts of the transmitter will be hidden in the tubular frames of your bicycles." Wainright placed a sample on the table. "The bikes are a genuine French make. If you're stopped and inspected, you must be above suspicion. We'll remove the wheels to make them lighter to handle, and so you can get them in and out of the sub and up the cliff easier. Any other items that might be questioned will be folded inside of dirty sox and underwear— purposely dirty and smelly to discourage inspection. They will be placed in the bottom of your packs."

Roger pulled on one earlobe. "We'd better 'ave a go at those bikes before we leave," he said, "so we know 'ow to put 'em together, 'n get the tubes apart, 'n all that."

"Yes, certainly. We'll arrange that. The bicycles will be particularly important. Biking along back roads will be less noticeable than walking—and much faster."

The deadly serious planning got a moment of comic relief when Wainwright held up a couple of pictures of nude women. "You may think this is a joke," he said with a vestige of a smile, "but these may prove to be lifesavers."

"I gotta see those," Roger grinned and inspected them closely.

Wainwright kept a straight face, "These photos will be placed near the top of your packs. German soldiers are just as easily distracted by such things as soldiers everywhere. If you're stopped and interrogated, they'll probably confiscate the pictures and feel a bit guilty. We've had it happen before. More often than not, they forget to look at the stuff underneath."

Roger let out a low whistle. "Looks like you gents 'ave thought of everythin'."

Wainwright continued to lay out the details. They would each carry a small sidearm concealed in an inner vest. A few other refinements, with which Mitch was already familiar from his commando experience: the L-pill hidden in his belt buckle, a small hacksaw blade buried in the sole of his boot, and money hidden in a hollow heel. If captured and facing torture, the pill would bring instant death. The hacksaw was for escape if imprisoned. He chose not to think about either contingency.

"What about dress?" Mitch asked.

"Ah, that's a tough question, one you'll have to decide—whether to go ashore in uniform or dressed as Frenchmen. Of course, if you decide to go in uniform, it would only be for the landing. Once on shore, you would have to be disguised as Frenchmen in any event." Wainwright walked around the table and rubbed the back of his neck, seemingly to give Mitch and Roger a little time to mull over the choice. "An intruder in disguise is considered a spy and summarily executed. A soldier captured in uniform must be treated humanely according to the Geneva Convention. However, on Hitler's orders, commandos captured in uniform have been routinely executed since 1942. So, frankly, it seems to me there's not much point in going that route. Nevertheless, you have the option. It's your choice."

Mitch looked at Roger and grimaced. "I think we might as well be dressed as Frenchmen the whole way."

Roger returned the look. "I agree," he said quietly.

Wainright nodded and pointed to the map again. He ran the pointer over a shaded area along the north coastline of France. "The Germans have declared the entire Normandy coast to be what they call the 'verboten zone.' It's about ten miles deep. Basically it's the area where they're building their 'Atlantic Wall.' The French have been moved out except for those with special permits."

"Will you fix us up with permits?" Roger asked.

"Yes. We can do a good job of that, but be aware that the Zone will have patrols and roadblocks. Anyone caught without a good reason will be microscopically scrutinized, but you can handle that with good I.D. and a credible cover story. I'll get to that in a minute."

Mitch and Roger already knew about permits and I.D. from their commando experience, but Wainwright went over it anyway. Three different kinds of forged I.D. would be needed: a travel permit, a work permit, and a general I.D. with photograph. MI-6 had become proficient at forging these. Also, if you were circumcised, you would need a birth certificate to prove you were not Jewish. The Gestapo seemed to take special satisfaction in checking penises, then shipping the suspect off to Auschwitz if he was circumcised and looked Jewish—unless he had solid proof he was not Jewish. Birth certificates were the most difficult to forge. Fortunately Mitch and Roger did not need them.

One other forgery would be needed, not for I.D., but for food: a ration card.

"For a cover story," Wainwright continued, "you'll be essential workers for the telephone company on your way to Caen to fix downed lines urgently in need of repair."

Roger groaned, "Jeez, I don't know anythin' about telephone lines."

"Tomorrow morning, you'll be given a quick run-down of the essentials by a local telephone company employee. You'll carry pole-climbing cleats and straps and a few tools in a carryall box. The box'll have a large label printed on both sides, *TELEPHONIQUE DE FRANCE*. They'll be strapped to the rack on the back of the bikes."

"What about money?" Mitch asked. "We'll need French francs."

"You'll carry fifty thousand francs—real, not forged—for the Resistance as well as for your own use. To avoid detection, the francs will be hidden inside the frame of the bikes. In addition, you'll have a small sum in the hollow heel of your shoe."

Wainwright lit a cigarette and sat down. "One last thing," he said. "I have arranged for you to meet with Monsieur LeBeau tomorrow. He has lived in St.-Aubin all of his life and knows the area intimately. He'll give you a detailed description of the back roads leading to St.-Pierre. He even knows the location of the Brousard farm."

"How about a map?" Roger asked.

"Sorry. You'll have to memorize the details. You'll carry no maps or anything in writing."

As the weather turned fair and calm on the 25th of October,

Roger and Mitch were driven to the submarine pens, those dank underground concrete tunnels, designed to protect the subs from air attack. Assailed by the unpleasant odor of diesel oil, they scrambled to board the *Dartmoor and* stowed their gear. She was a small U-boat, crowded and a bit tired, like its crew. Not designed for passengers, the sub accommodated Roger and Mitch by wedging them into a corner of the galley.

Captain Jamison welcomed them on board with a brief tour of his boat and an abbreviated safety run-down in case of emergency. He was in a hurry. "We should get underway," he said. "The tide is right, and the weather is perfect. We'd better take advantage of it."

"How long will it take to cross the channel to St.-Aubin?" Mitch asked.

"Only three or four hours, but I want extra time to get our position exactly right."

"Frankly," the Captain added with a tired smile, "I'm not at all keen about operating in those shallow waters so close to German shore guns. The trick is to get you two ashore as quickly as possible and move out."

Roger grimaced. "Sure c'n understand that."

Jamison didn't like to waste words. "The tide will be full high at four-O-five hours. Gives us a window of time from three-O-five to five-O-five to surface and unload."

Leaning against their packs, Mitch and Roger were too keyed up to sleep, but it gave them a few hours to get to know each other. Mitch sized up Roger as a solid fellow, friendly, muscular, round-faced, the sort you could rely on, but not totally happy about their assignment.

"What in the bloody 'ell are we doin' 'ere anyway?" Roger had a crooked grin, which seemed to be his trademark.

"Atwater told me you were real happy with the idea."

" 'e told you that? 'orseshit. I was dragooned into this; 'e said I was the only one right for the job. Suppose it's 'cause I know French. Besides, I'm good at this kind of radio stuff. I c'n send real fast, 'n that's important if the Krauts are listening."

Mitch thought, *sounds to me like he is, indeed, the man for the job,* but instead, he asked, "How much weapons training have you had?"

"Plenty."

Mitch looked at him questioningly.

Roger shrugged and proceeded to tell Mitch about one particular experience. He had been a member of the Norwegian-British commando team that destroyed the Norsk hydroelectric plant in Norway, which had produced deuterium oxide, "heavy water." The raid had effectively shut down Germany's atomic energy research.

Trekking across mountainous wilderness in a blizzard, then scaling a precipitous cliff, which the Germans had assumed to be impassable, they had succeeded in blowing up the heavily guarded plant. One of the team had died and the rest had nearly frozen to death. Miraculously, they had escaped, in spite of a massive manhunt by the Germans. Roger's primary duty had been communications, but he had also helped set the explosives and shoot their way past the guards.

"What'd you do before the war?" Mitch asked.

Roger wrinkled his forehead and answered slowly. "I was a radioman on a British freighter, but in forty it was torpedoed in the North Atlantic. I was lucky. Weren't a lot of survivors. Then MI-6 got a'old of me 'n trained me for the commandos."

"Go on any raids?"

"Yup, six, 'n some'ow managed to come out in one piece."

No wonder Atwater picked him for this job, Mitch thought. "Are you married?"

"No, but ..." Roger went on to explain with relish his complicated love life. It seemed that he had lived off and on with a number of "doxies," all of whom wanted to marry him. "But now I've met a certain young lady. She's really somthin'. Gives me a reason to come out of this bloody war alive, 'n maybe be a little more careful. 'ow 'bout you, Mitch. You married?"

"No," Mitch admitted. "Truth is I never had enough money for women—even for a date. Seems like I was always too busy trying to help out at home. To be honest, I don't know a heck of a lot about women."

Mitch felt a bit sheepish as he watched Roger trying to control his laughter. "Looks like we've both got some livin' to do, mate, so we'd better try'n get out of this business with our 'ides."

Mitch grimaced. "Yeah, but I'd say the odds aren't just great."

"I'll say this much," Roger said in a serious tone, "seems to me like we'll make a good team. It's goin' to be just you and me against the ..." He didn't finish the thought.

"We ought to try to get a couple hour's sleep, Roger. I have a feeling we're going to need it."

But, try as they would, sleep eluded them. Instead they talked about the world they had known and the better world they hoped for, even religion.

"D'you believe in God?" Roger asked out of the blue.

"Honestly, I don't know." Mitch ran his fingers through his hair. "Times like this I wish I had a stronger faith. If we're killed, it'd be comforting to know there was an afterlife."

"Sorry, but I don't believe any more," Roger said. "I've seen too many men pray 'n then get blowed up. Seen the ones that didn't pray get saved. I figger prayin' doesn't work. But I've prayed a lot anyway. Guess it can't hurt."

Captain Jamison stuck his head into the galley and cut off their conversation. "Time to get ready, mates. You've got fifteen minutes."

The two men blackened their faces, pulled on the black stocking caps and moved their gear next to the hatch. Roger was calm and collected, but Mitch felt jumpy as a cat. "Who knows what's waiting out there, Roger?"

"We'll be okay. Jamison's had a good look around by now."

The submarine rocked gently, as Roger and the Boatswain's mate climbed the hatch ladder. Mitch handed up the packs, four waterproof duffels, the bike frames, then the wheels, and finally the two deflated rubber boats. He clambered up on deck and helped Roger spread out the rubber. The Boatswain brought up a compressed air hose and screwed it onto the valve. As the raft inflated, the hissing noise sounded like a factory whistle to Mitch.

"Ceeehrist," whispered Roger. "Keep the noise down. And don't bang the hull with any of this stuff. The sounds really carry on a night like this."

ST.-AUBIN, FRANCE

Other than a too-bright moon, everything went according to plan. Mitch and Roger climbed into one of the black rubber boats, each holding a small wooden paddle. The second raft, to be towed behind, was loaded with the extra gear.

The stillness was frightening, and the lapping of ripples against the hollow hull of the Dartmoor sounded like machine gun fire to Mitch. Surely the Germans could hear it only a mile away. Jamison came up on deck. "Good luck." He whispered and gave them the thumbs up. "And good hunting."

They pushed off and paddled, dipping the paddles in the water like surgeons to avoid any sound. Mitch squinted at the moon. *There's too much light,* he thought. *They're bound to see us. Everything's too quiet. They'll hear us for sure.* But he kept his thoughts to himself. Roger would think he was a wimp.

A faint buzzing sound in the distance obliterated the night stillness. It quickly grew louder. Mitch breathed a sigh of relief when he recognized the outline of a flight of Allied bombers crossing over the sliver of a moon. There was someone on their side after all, something comforting about the sound. It would drown out the deafening sound of their paddles in the water.

A mile of paddling their awkward craft exhausted them. It took the better part of an hour while the sub stood by at periscope depth and watched. After that, they would be cut off from any semblance of support, a frightening feeling.

Thoroughly soaked in the process of clambering out of their rafts in shallow water and dragging them up the beach, they collapsed at the base of the bluff and allowed themselves a two-minute breather. They'd been sweating from their exertions, but the temperature was barely above freezing, and now they were shivering.

Mitch became aware of a glimmer of light to the East. "We've got to get moving, Roger," he whispered. "It's starting to get light."

"Yeah, you're right. First we've gotta wipe the black off our faces 'n deflate these rafts 'n bury 'em in the bushes, or they'll stick out like a couple a sore thumbs."

As Wainwright had predicted, the thick brush at the base of the bluff made a perfect hiding place, but the cliff presented a nasty challenge. Two hundred feet high and nearly straight up, it appeared to Mitch like the wall of a giant fortress.

" 'ow in the bloody 'ell are we gonna get these bloody bikes up this thing?" Roger whispered with his usual grin.

Mitch didn't answer the question, knowing Roger well enough by now. He would know exactly how to climb the cliff and probably looked forward to it.

When they had finished hiding the rafts, they mounted the wheels on the bikes. "I think we're better off if we put 'em on down here," Roger whispered. "What the heck. It doesn't look all that tough. We'll haul the bikes up on our backs."

Mitch checked his watch—6:OO a.m. Plenty of daylight now. Time to tackle the cliff. The curfew would end at 7:OO a.m., and they planned to hit the top slightly after that. Their cover story would be useless if they were spotted during the curfew.

"We're goin' to have to climb this thing in two stages," Roger whispered and pointed to the route which had a few hand holds, "First, let's take up the bikes. We can leave them just under the lip at the top. I see a place where they won't slide." Mitch was not about to argue with Roger's experience. He scrutinized the sharp rocks at the base of the cliff and frowned. It was not a technical rock climb, but one slip and they would be goners.

"I'll go first," Roger whispered. "Watch me carefully, where I put my feet, and watch my hand-holds."

With the bikes strapped to their backs, they slowly worked their way up, holding onto small branches and rock outcroppings. Roger stopped half a dozen times, pulling out his hunting knife to cut footholds. He pointed to them by jabbing his knife at the spot two or three extra times to be sure Mitch saw them. All the while, Mitch prayed silently that no German patrol waited at the top.

Careful not to dislodge any rocks, they clawed their way to the top slowly and silently. Exhausted, they peered over the edge. Barely visible in the light fog, a farmhouse loomed two hundred yards straight ahead, and, to their right, a watchtower stood out in the haze about half a mile away.

They'd been told not to worry about the watchtowers. The lookouts only searched skyward for aircraft. According to Wainwright, American bombers kept them busy reporting numbers, directions, and altitudes to their anti-aircraft batteries and Luftwaffe fighters.

The second climb up the cliff wasn't much easier. Now they had to bring up their packs and the carryall boxes marked TELEPHONIQUE DE FRANCE.

Mitch checked his watch again—6:55. Staring intently into the mist, there spotted no patrols, but they'd been warned to expect them at half-hour intervals. Now they would sit tight, under the lip of the bluff, until a patrol passed, then make their move.

Stretching to their left, as far as the eye could see, huge piles of construction materials, concrete formwork, reinforcing bars, steel I-beams, pile drivers, and cement trucks, comprised the makings of fortifications and gun emplacements. The Germans had been working around the clock on their "Atlantic Wall" except for Sunday mornings. French workers, most of them devout Catholics, had been granted this half-day off to attend church.

Realizing this, Wainwright had insisted they time their approach for a Sunday.

ST.-PIERRE-DU-BOIS

Renee thrashed in her sleep. *The blackshirt Nazi pounded on the door, tramped on the stairs, leered at her. Henri yelled, "More food," and BBC radio repeated, "Confirmation, Trout to Cricket on schedule. Confirmation, Trout to Cricket."*

Shaking, she sat up with a start, stumbled out of bed and looked at herself in the mirror. The imperfect glass with its chipped reflective coating gave back an image of a wide-eyed, pale young lady, frightened and exhausted. Her thoughts ricocheted in all directions with no connecting threads. *Would she survive this war? Would the terrifying Nazi try to rape her again? Would France survive? Sir*

Charles? Henri? Denis? Dear God, she was still a virgin. Would she ever ...? She pulled a blanket around her and fell asleep in a chair, exhausted.

Hans provided the one bright spot, working tirelessly with a cheery countenance.

"Who sent you?" Renee asked, struggling to communicate through their language barrier.

"Der Capitaine" he responded in a mangled mixture of German and French. Surprised, she wondered if he was referring to the same noxious SS Captain who had tried to rape her. Of course, it couldn't be. But she thought it odd she hadn't seen him for more than a week.

"You are a good worker, Hans," Renee said. "I can't tell you how much we appreciate your help. And the tractor you fixed is making all the difference."

"Danke schon, Mademoiselle." Renee thought Hans' pink complexion turned a bit pinker as he stammered, "I like farming for you. I not like to be soldier. Please don't tell anybody I say that."

In subsequent short, stilted conversations, when they labored together in the fields, Hans made it clear that he was deathly afraid of being sent to the Russian front. "Maybe, I do special good farming here. Maybe they let me stay. Make food for them. Food for everybody."

One day, Renee saw Hans with a pad of paper and a pencil in his hand. "I don't know why I supposed to make lists," he said with a wrinkled forehead. "I supposed tell der Capitaine how much food we make." Startled, Renee stared at Hans with raised eyebrows. *Of course,* she realized, *Hans has been sent to spy on us, but he doesn't realize it. I always knew the Germans suspected us of hiding food and probably suspected us of supplying the Resistance. If the Captain can prove it, he'll send me to Ravensbrueck? Or will it just give him some kind of power over me? Then again, maybe I can give Hans some smaller numbers without arousing anyone's suspicions.*

Recovering slowly, Claude Brousard would not be strong enough to help on the farm for several more months. In the meantime, Renee and her mother, with help from Hans, worked in the fields, harvesting cabbages, potatoes, and squash. They started at daybreak and stopped only when they could bend over no longer. Too tired to talk, Renee and Annette would collapse in bed after a cold dinner.

BERLIN, GERMANY

Hearing the faint rustling sound from the bushes, Otto stopped abruptly and whirled around. The sudden movement had been just enough to save his life.

A bullet smashed into his left arm, and a second bullet nicked his right ear. Otto hit the ground, pulled his gun with his right arm, and fired in the direction of the shots, all in one motion, instinctive reactions, ingrained in him from years of military training. He then rolled into the nearest bush and waited.

Nothing.

Crawling back toward the entry under cover of the bushes, he waited again in the shadows. Still nothing.

Holding his bloody left arm with his right hand, he sprinted toward the gate with a zigzag motion. The sentry saluted as if nothing had happened.

Fumbling with his car keys, he became aware that his left arm was not functioning. Nonetheless, he managed to reach his car parked outside the gate, jerked open the door, climbed in, and sped down the forested road to *Schorfheide*.

Approaching Berlin, he slowed down to think. *Where to go? If Heidendorff wants me dead, I'm a dead man. I'm expected to return the car to the car pool, then return to St.-Pierre by train. Should I disappear? No, I can't desert. They shoot deserters. Damn. What to do? But first, I've got to get medical attention.*

Removing his shirt, he could see where the bullet had passed cleanly through some muscle and flesh, but luckily it had missed the bone. He couldn't stop the pain, but he managed to stop the bleeding by tying his shirt around the bloody arm. He knew there was a hospital in Potsdam only forty kilometers away and steeled himself to reach it.

The doctor inspected his arm. "The bullet passed through cleanly," he noted. "We'll clean it up, bandage it, and give you a shot of penicillin. You've lost quite a bit of blood, and you should lie flat for a day, but the arm will heal in a couple of weeks."

Otto ignored the doctor's advice, opting to leave Potsdam immediately. He ordered an SS private, who happened to be on leave, visiting a wounded comrade, to return the car to Berlin. Then he took a train to Paris.

In Paris he radioed a message to his Sergeant-at-arms in St.-Pierre-du-Bois. "Has anyone been looking for me? Have there been any orders from Berlin or any couriers?" Two days went by, and the answer came back the same—no one was looking for him.

He couldn't put it off any longer. He would have to report back to his post and pray that Heidendorff had better things to do than go after him in St.-Pierre.

Unknown to Otto, Heidendorff had been called out of town by the Fuehrer at the time of Otto's close encounter. Momentous events had diverted him. Catastrophic reverses on the Russian front had caused Hitler to convene an emergency meeting with his generals and field marshals at his "Wolf's Lair." The Fuehrer had ranted in a monologue for hours, accusing his generals of treason, demoting and replacing three of them. He finally turned to Heidendorff.

"Why haven't you destroyed the Resistance?" Hitler screamed inches from the fat man's face. "I have diverted too many forces from the Russian front to your western sector. Why have the Americans been allowed to bomb Berlin? What are you doing about it? You promised to destroy the RAF. You promised to ... You said ... You said ... I can't even find you half the time. If you don't do something about, I'll demote you to Private. You'll be cleaning latrines—latrines."

When the Fuehrer was forced to take a breath, the Marshal finally got a word in. "Mein Fuehrer, I am forced to work with old men and the dregs of the Wehrmacht, but I have a plan, a secret weapon. The Americans are nothing. We'll destroy them. I promise. You'll see. I promise, mein Feurher."

Between his drug addiction and Hitler's pressures, Heidendorff became befuddled. He had not been told that the assassination of Otto Streikler had misfired. Also his attention was now diverted to the faltering troops and building the "Atlantic Wall."

Otto received a reprieve—temporarily.

THE VERBOTEN ZONE

"Halte! Ausweis, Papiers!"—Halt! Papers!

The German sentry spotted Mitch and Roger just when they thought they had made it safely across the *Verboten Zone*. On Sundays, few people, military or civilian, frequented the small dirt road, and the sentry was alone.

"Certainement. Voila," Mitch said with a forced smile, handing over his papers.

Obviously reading with difficulty, the German Corporal studied their papers at length, then eyed the two of them suspiciously. Heavy set, with porcine features and small squinting eyes, he gave off an aura of stubborn stupidity.

"What is business in *Verboten Zone*?" he demanded, pointing his bayoneted rifle first at Mitch, then at Roger.

Trying to appear relaxed and friendly, Mitch went through their prepared explanation. They were telephone workers on an urgent assignment to repair downed lines near Caen, which no doubt had been severed by the damned Resistance.

"Open packs. Everything on ground," demanded the German, apparently unwilling to take his hands away from his rifle. "Bicycle baskets too."

They obliged, carefully placing the nude pictures in plain sight, then pointing out that their assignment was of enormous importance. "The *Kommandant* needs the lines fixed immediately," Roger said. "Anyone slowing it down will be in serious trouble."

"I take these," the German ordered, pointing his bayonet at the pictures, adding *"Schwarzmarkt—ja"*.

Making a small show of reluctance, Mitch handed them over with a shrug. "Go ahead, sell them on the blackmarket," Mitch said with a forced grin. The German stuffed them inside his coat and stared at Roger and Mitch. Finally he growled, "I must report this to *mein Kapitan. Komm mit."*

"We can't come with you. We are on an urgent assignment—*tres presse,*" Roger protested, gesticulating like a typical Frenchman.

Besides being a bit slow, the German was also stubborn and did not take kindly to an argument. He poked Roger with his bayonet and repeated, *"Komm mit."* Then he jerked his rifle in a beckoning motion.

Roger glanced at Mitch who nodded imperceptibly. They had practiced for this situation. Mitch pointed up the road and yelled, *"Pass Auf!"*—Look Out!. As the German looked up, Roger grabbed the rifle and, in one motion, swung it with all his strength into the fat midriff, sending the Corporal silently to the ground, his wind knocked out. Roger pulled out his knife to finish the job, but Mitch grabbed his arm. "Isn't there some other way?"

"No. We've got to kill him. 'e's seen us. There's no other way." The Corporal gasped for air, his neck wedged under Roger'foot. "They'll come after us, and the whole mission'll be shot." Feeling sick, Mitch turned away, while Roger finished the man.

Fortunately it was foggy. Their voices wouldn't carry far, and they had not been seen. The narrow dirt road had pastures and hedgerows on either side. Quickly, they dragged the body behind the nearest hedgerow, then went back to retrieve their bicycles and packs. The whole incident had taken less than five minutes.

A horse-drawn cart came by, as they picked up their gear, and the farmer looked at them quizzically. Roger smiled and gesticulated, *"un petit accident."* The farmer hurried on without a word.

"Let's get out of here *toute de suite,*" Roger said. "When that sentry doesn't report in, they'll go lookin', "and when they find the body, there'll be 'ell to pay. Just pray they don't line up ten villagers and shoot 'em."

"Let's try to hide the body. Put some branches over it or something," said Mitch.

"Okay, a few branches, but it won't do any good. They've got dogs, 'n they know 'is beat. I figure we've got four or five hours head start at best, so let's get out of here. We don't want to be seen in the area."

Pedaling hard, they tried to put as much distance behind them as possible before curfew.

"Keep your feet on the pedals," Roger said. "They'll try to track us with dogs, but that'll only work if you put your foot on the ground. We'll stop after a couple of miles 'n take a pee. The dogs'll lift their legs 'n pee too. Really confuses them. Wipes out the tracking smell you know."

They passed several locals and two French Gendarmes, but fortunately none stopped them. By dusk, they'd covered sixty kilometers, three quarters of the way to St.-Pierre-du-Bois. Rather than press their luck, they found a field with haystacks, buried their bikes and bedded down for the night.

Out of the Verboten zone now, they ate a few bites of bread and cheese, food that had been carefully selected to resemble typical French fare. Burrowing into the hay, they fell asleep, exhausted.

At first light, Roger shook Mitch awake. After a small bite of bread and sausage, Roger checked his watch. "Curfew's over in five minutes, time to get a move on. But I been thinkin', mate. We'd better split up. By now the Krauts'll have grilled everybody on the road, 'n they'll be lookin' for two chaps travelin' together on bikes. But there are thousands of Frenchmen ridin' these things. They can't stop 'em all. So what d'you think?"

"Splitting up sounds like a good idea to me, but let's agree on a time and place to meet."

Roger nodded.

"We'd better change our shirts," Mitch added, "something with a different color, and scrape the TELEPHONIQUE signs off the side of our boxes. There's bound to be someone who's noticed them."

"Okay," Roger agreed and dug into his pack for a shirt. "We can come back together at the 'ouse in St.-Pierre, in the thicket along the creek on the north side of the house. You remember that from the map?"

"Sure, but if we keep moving, we'll get there before 1:00 a.m. We'll just have to sit there for a few hours and try not to freeze."

"You take the road through Bayeaux," Roger said while scraping away the TELEPHONIQUE letters, "and I'll take the one through St.-Lo. Okay?"

"Sounds good. See you tonight."

Roger waved as he applied pressure to the pedal. "Good luck, Mitch. Stay out of the bars."

They took off at exactly 7:OO a.m., bicycling hard.

ST.-PIERRE-DU-BOIS

Von Kleister stormed past the sentry without saluting and burst into Captain Streikler's office. Purple veins pulsing on his forehead, he pointed his riding crop at Otto's chest and exploded, "Two British spies walked right through your zone and killed one of my men. And you do nothing. You and your SS are a joke, a disgrace."

Not intimidated, Otto glared at von Kleister. "May I remind you, General, it was your patrol, not ours, that was derelict, that allowed itself to be taken by surprise, that was grossly inadequate for the job. May I also remind you, my reports go directly to Heidendorff and from there to the Fuehrer." Otto was bluffing, of course, aware that Heidendorff was trying to get rid of him. But the bluff worked.

Sputtering, von Kleister backed off. "All right. All right. So what are you doing about it? We can't afford to let them get away."

"I've got my best men on it," Otto replied, coolly staring down the General. "And dogs. They've picked up the scent. We are combing every village between St.-Lo and Caen, interrogating everybody. We have descriptions."

Otto could see von Kleister struggling to control his anger and contempt. He knew the General had always despised the SS. Otto smiled faintly. *The officious bastard has no choice. He's stuck with us.*

"You realize, Captain, that the damnable Resistance is tying up thirty of our divisions in France, divisions which ought to be fighting in Russia. It's all because the British are getting through with supplies, and that's because you and your stupid SS are not doing your job."

After a long pause, while they glared at each other, von Kleister snapped, "The sabotage is getting out of hand. We've lost twenty barges on the Orne just in the last month. You've got to stop them— stop them NOW."

"You don't have to tell me that, General. I know what's going on. For your information we caught and executed six of them last week."

Von Klug turned on his heel and stalked out without saluting. Otto noticed the lack of the obligatory Heil Hitler.

NORMANDY

Splitting up had been a stroke of genius.

Major Schmidt watched his prize bloodhounds running in circles on the dirt road. He scratched his head. "What the hell's going on?" he yelled at his Corporal.

"Damned if I know, *Herr Kapitan.*" The dog-handler grabbed a large stick and began striking and screaming at the dogs. They yelped and cringed, then began running in circles again.

The Major, red in the face, reared back and kicked the lead dog with his heavy boot. The yelping became louder, and the dogs split up, heading off in two directions. They kept raising their legs to pee.

On the outskirts of Bayeux, a pair of French Gendarmes stopped Mitch and scrutinized his papers.

"What's your business," the Gendarme asked civilly. "Your papers only say you're a repairman."

"You know how it is these days." Mitch gave a practiced shrug, which he hoped looked like a Frenchman. "I repair lots of things—like bicycles."

The Gendarmes looked at each other, then at Mitch. "*Quelle bonne chance.* It happens we have several bicycles at *le Poste de Police* which need repair. It's a terrible problem for us."

The second Gendarme chimed in, "*S'il vous plaît, Monsieur,* would you come to the station and see if you can fix them. It would be a great service to us."

"I'm sorry." Mitch waved his arm in the direction of his carryall box. "You know how it is with the war—an impossible shortage of spare parts."

"*Mais oui*." The Gendarme said with a friendly gesture, "but we insist you come and see if there's anything you can do." Trapped, Mitch followed them to the *Poste de Police*, while the Gendarmes chatted happily, congratulating themselves on their luck at finding a repairman.

Fortunately, Mitch had some tools as part of his original cover story. To make it look convincing, he set to work dismantling one of the Gendarme's bikes. He stared at the pile of parts with dismay, then studied a second bike and noticed a broken sprocket. He picked through the loose parts and said a silent prayer. Please God, let this sprocket fit. His prayer was answered. It fit, and he actually succeeded in fixing the second bike.

Mitch shrugged and pointed to the pile of parts. "Sorry, I can only fix this one."

The German supervisor in the gray uniform of a Wehrmacht sergeant sat at a desk in the corner of the station and eyed him suspiciously, but the Gendarmes were so pleased, they smiled and saluted and gave him a cup of tea. Sweating like a horse on derby day, Mitch gulped down the tea. "*Merci, merci tres bien pour le te,*" he returned their smiles and pushed his own bike toward the door. "I have to move on before curfew."

Now running late, he wouldn't be able to reach St.-Pierre by dark, and Roger would be worried. Peddling like a steam engine at full throttle, Mitch found himself within four kilometers of his destination at 6:00 p.m., curfew time. Cursing himself for not having made a late-arrival contingency plan with Roger, he decided to take a chance. It should only take another fifteen minutes to reach the farm—if he didn't collapse from exhaustion.

At five minutes after six he heard the German patrol car coming up the road. Chugging along, running on gasogene, the wood-derivative ersatz fuel, the car ran at a maximum speed of 45 kilometers per hour. The loud sputtering noise gave Mitch enough warning, time to scramble behind a hedgerow.

Peering through the leaves, he could see the German driver peering from side to side, then straight at him. As the patrol chugged slowly past, he froze and held his breath. The car finally disappeared over the next rise. Mitch resumed breathing.

With darkness settling over the countryside, Mitch climbed out of his hiding place. He said another silent prayer. His heart beating like a jackhammer and his legs wobbling, he once again began peddling hard toward St.-Pierre, now only two kilometers away.

"For Chris' sake," Roger whispered when the bedraggled figure crawled into the bushes. "What took you so long?"

"Just stopped for a spot of tea," Mitch grinned, happy to see a friendly face.

Completely exhausted, he collapsed and slept for an hour before Roger shook him awake and demanded an explanation. "Fer Chrise sake," Roger grumbled, "whatever it was you were doin', it'll 'ave somethin' to do with whether the Krauts track us down—or not."

THE BROUSARD FARM

Renee couldn't sleep.

She knew they would be coming either tonight or tomorrow night—supposed to be at 1:00 a.m. Sitting tight up against the kitchen stove in the old wood rocker, she stared at the north window. From time to time, she added a small piece of wood to the cast iron stove.

The kitchen had always been her favorite room. Dried herbs hung from the low wood beams and copper pots hung neatly from iron hooks. The massive wood table had been the family meeting place ever since she was a child.

When the knock on the north window came exactly on the stroke of 1:00, she jumped out of the chair like a scared rabbit.

"Who is it?" she asked in an urgent whisper through the window, which she had left slightly ajar.

"Trout," came the muffled reply.

She went around to the back door and opened it gingerly.

"You must be Cricket, *n'est-ce pas*?" the taller man said between his chattering teeth, shaking and beating his arms together.

She looked them over critically. They looked awful—dirty, unshaven, and half frozen. "Yes, I'm Cricket. And you?" she asked, nodding at the second man.

"I'm Smith," he muttered. "Can you get us a couple of blankets 'n somethin' 'ot to drink? We're freezin.'"

"Of course. Come in the kitchen where it's warmer."

Renee got two blankets and bustled around in the kitchen to stir up the fire in the wood stove, then fixed a hot chicory drink. "Sorry," she said in a near whisper, "it's all we've got."

The only light came from a single candle on the wood table. "We must be very quiet and not attract attention," she said. "You know they're right over there," she pointed across the yard, "and they post a guard."

Hardly able to keep his eyes open from lack of sleep and exhaustion, Mitch explained the bare essentials of their situation. "I don't think we've been followed, but can't say for sure."

"Come. I'll show you where you can hide." Renee led them to the back of the house and lifted the door to the root cellar and the secret panel to the hollowed-out place underneath.

Roger inspected the dark interior and rubbed the back of his neck. "There's not 'nough room for us *and* our bikes."

Renee bit her lip. "Well, at least we can hide the bikes and your gear in there. We'll just have to take our chances with you until morning."

She led them to Henri's room. Mitch staggered behind and instantly collapsed on the bed. In ten seconds he was asleep. Renee pulled off his shoes, put a blanket over him and tucked it in around the edges.

"Roger, it looks like you'll have to sleep on the floor. Sorry, I can only give you one blanket." The ancient wool blanket was full of moth holes. "It's all the bedding that's left." Renee apologized. "I'm afraid all the extras have gone to my brother, Henri, and his *Maquis.*"

Unable to sleep, Renee wrapped herself in a heavy coat and sat in the stiff bedroom chair. How was she supposed to know whether they'd been followed? It would be the end of everything if the SS tracked them here.

She studied the two men who were sleeping like hibernating bears. In spite of their dirty, disheveled appearance, she liked what she saw. Smith looked solid—the competent type, square jaw, solid body, the kind you could depend on. The one called Trout looked more complicated, a few contradictions showing, a strong but gentle face, young but showing a few creases around the eyes.

She fell asleep in the chair, thinking she wanted to know more.

Mitch woke up with a start. He hadn't slept long while his mind had been racing with wild dreams about German soldiers and dogs. Then he saw Renee asleep in the chair.

For a moment he thought he was still dreaming. The vision that slowly came into focus was an angel. He didn't know much about angels, but he was sure this must be one. A single ray of sunlight slanted through the window and shone on the light copper-gold hair.

Mitch didn't move, not daring to destroy the illusion. He held his breath and examined the angel, at least the small part showing above the bulky threadbare coat. The lips, which were slightly parted, looked full, warm and friendly. Definitely kissable, Mitch thought. She had four faint freckles. He counted them. And a pert nose. And rosy cheeks. *She would never make a Vogue model with those freckles*, he mused. *But I hate the Vogue model look. This girl has the most beautiful face I—*

Renee shifted in her chair and one eye opened slightly. He winced. She'd caught him staring at her.

He jumped out of the bed. *What's wrong with me? Likely as not, I'll be caught and face a German firing squad, and here I am, staring at this girl.*

"Where's Roger?" he asked.

"Ummm, I don't know," the angel mumbled sleepily. "He was sleeping right there." She pointed to the floor and shook herself upright.

Mitch looked at his watch. It was 5:00 a.m. "What about your parents?" Mitch asked. "Do they know what's going on?"

"No. I'm going to have to explain to my mother, but my father's bedridden. I don't want to worry him with all this."

Roger had already gone to work in the kitchen, assembling the transmitter when Mitch and Renee came down the stairs. Without looking up, Roger said, "We'll 'ave to find a 'idin' place for this. D'you 'ave a place in the attic? Transmission's better from there."

Renee looked him over critically. "We'll get to that in a minute. But right now, looks like you need to wash up. Come on, I'll show you."

Ten minutes later, the two men returned, looking halfway civilized. Mitch could see that Renee had stirred up the fire in the stove, and was now fixing some griddlecakes. Each time she flipped one over, Mitch saw her turn and examine her new boarders. He found himself hoping he looked presentable. At least he no longer looked like a tramp. He wanted to smile and be jovial, but on this particular morning he had to be deadly serious.

Mitch studied her as she bustled about in the kitchen. His thoughts wandered. *This girl doesn't belong here, risking her life. She should be the belle of the ball somewhere. Having fun, or getting married and raising kids.* She caught him staring at her again and gave him a hint of a smile. *With even a little smile she can light up the room*, he thought.

Mitch shook his head to get his mind on other things. "We have a lot to talk about—and not much time. You see, I have to move on right away."

With a skillet in her hand, Renee turned abruptly and gave him an anxious look. "Why's that?"

"My part of the mission is to get to your *Maquis* and train them in weapons and explosives. According to Charles Atwater, you can get me in touch with them—or take me to them. That's up to you."

"I can do that." The reply was barely audible.

"Then Charles wants me to take you out of here. I can understand why. This is too dangerous for you."

"I *can't* do that," she answered without hesitation. "I have to take care of my father who was shot by the Germans. He's very weak and still bed-ridden. And I have to keep the farm going if for no other reason than to help feed Henri's *Maquis*. They're practically starving as it is."

"If I don't bring you back, Charles'll have my hide. He was pretty insistent about it."

"Sorry, but that's final. I'm staying." Her lips were pressed in a tight line, her eyes narrowed. Mitch realized this girl had gumption. Maybe she was not just the belle-of-the-ball type after all.

"Okay. We'll talk about it later—next time when I come back—if I come back."

Renee stared at him. Her look conveyed her meaning. She wanted him to come back, but her words said something different. "You shouldn't come here again. It's too dangerous."

Roger broke in. "We can discuss that later folks. But first, I'd better tell you 'ow this transmitter's goin' to work." He nudged the metal box he'd been working on. "If we do this right, there'll be no danger of the Germans tracin' my signal. I'll send only when the Germans are sendin' from next door. The *Funkspiel* won't pick it up."

Renee frowned. "You sure about that?"

"Yeah. I'm sure. But, right now, I need some boards and a 'ammer and nails to board up a good 'idin' place in the attic, just in case the 'ouse is searched."

"I think I've got what you need," Renee said. "I've been planning for this—up in the attic, under the eaves. We'll have to tear off some of the wallboards, save the nails, and rebuild it. It'll take a bit of work."

"I'll help with that," put in Mitch, "but let's go at it right away. I've got to get moving. In the meantime, Cricket—or should I call you Renee—I have some money to leave with you. Five thousand francs. I'll have to get them out of my bike."

"Five thousand! That's a lot of money."

Careful to avoid suspicious movements at the still-dark hour of 5:30 a.m., Mitch and Renee stumbled out to the root cellar in the darkness and pulled out the bikes. Back in the kitchen, Mitch removed the rubber handlebar grips and pried the rolls of French francs out with his pocketknife. He pressed the money into her hand. Her eyes went wide, and she stared at it as if it would bite. It was more money than she had ever seen at one time.

Mitch went on, talking faster now, "I know there aren't a lot of things you can buy any more, but there's still the Thursday market, isn't there? Roger will be here for quite a while, and there'll be things he'll need, things both of you'll need. Besides, we know there are many things your brother and his *Maquis* need. That's the main purpose of this mission—to find ways to supply his men. I realize that you can't do a great deal without arousing suspicion, but every little bit will help. Actually, I am carrying more money to deliver directly to your brother assuming I am successful in getting there with your help."

"Yes, but is the money real?" Renee asked, "The Germans are on the lookout for counterfeit. It must be old and dirty. New money looks suspicious."

"It's real all right, but you'll want to scuff it up a bit."

Mitch started to ask, "Where's a hammer, so we can ..." when Renee's mother, Annette, suddenly walked into the kitchen. The gentle woman stared wide-eyed at the two men and stammered, "Who are these people?"

Renee put a finger to her lips. "Please, mother, don't ask any questions right now. I'll explain later."

THE MAQUIS CAMP IN NORMANDY

Henri Brousard, only twenty-four years old, found himself the leader of a band of *Maquis*, which had grown to three hundred men and women and was adding dozens more every day.

Every member had a price on his or her head. The *Milice* were being paid a bounty for every *Maquisard* they turned over to the Germans—four of Henri' men so far—and each had been executed.

Henri's biggest problem was food. While each member had sympathetic friends or family on the outside, making contact with them was dangerous, and food was short for everyone. All food in the markets was rationed and required ration cards, which the *Maquis* did not have, unless they were forged, which Henri would not allow. It was too risky. Up until Renee's radio contacts had gone dead, food for the Resistance had been supplied by British airdrops along with a few arms and other supplies, but now these had dried up. Henri was acutely aware that the British were stymied. They had no way of knowing where or when to make their drops. In desperation, one of the *Maquis* had tried to use a homemade transmitter but had been tracked down almost immediately by the *Funkspeil* and summarily executed.

Henri grimaced when Anton limped into camp, caked with mud, a dead dog slung over his shoulder. "Looks kind of scrawny, Anton."

"Hate to say it, Henri, but this critter may be the last dog in France."

"We'll cut him up real fine and cook him with a couple of potatoes."

"Geezy's got a mess of frogs," Anton continued. "We'll eat pretty good tonight."

Most of Henri's men had rifles, smuggled from their homes or supplied by the British before the airdrops had stopped. Now these were used more for hunting food than for hunting Nazis. Shooting and eating any small animal that came in sight, they survived on dogs, birds, squirrels, frogs, insects, mice, even rats. Also fish became a staple. A fish farm on the backwaters of the Orne River not only provided food but also became one of their favorite hiding places. They rounded out their diet with cooked ferns and nettle soup.

Henri's *Maquis* constantly moved their camp to avoid the "rat hunts" and were forced to improvise a new makeshift shelter each time. At times, they had been able to crowd into farmer's barns in isolated backcountry areas, but more often they slept under trees with tarps and old blankets strung up to keep the rain off.

"Damn it all, Henri," Denis exploded. "We ought to be doing something worthwhile—like blowing up a few Germans."

"Patience, Denis," Henri answered. "We'll get to that, but we can't afford to expose ourselves just yet."

"Well, seems to me, all we're doing is hiding a bunch of Commies 'n Gypsies 'n weirdos."

"Patience, Denis," Henri repeated. "They're here for a lot of good reasons. Most of them would be dead if it wasn't for us, especially the Jews. Don't forget, they'll fight to the death when the time comes."

"Yeah, you're right, of course. But some of those Gypsies give me the creeps. You know, discipline is damn near impossible, 'n any one of these guys could get us all killed if he goes off half cocked."

Henri struggled to sit up straight and sighed when three new men straggled into his makeshift headquarters. He sat under a tattered tarp on a crude bench and studied the newcomers. Denis pointed to the log in front of the plank, which served as a table, and told the men to sit.

"What's your name and where are you from?" Henri asked the thin, dark waif who looked as if he hadn't eaten in a week. Henri didn't waste time on niceties. He had to screen half a dozen new men every day.

"Sam Frankel from Paris," answered the waif in a barely audible voice.

"You're Jewish?"

"Yes."

"How'd you escape the Nazis? How'd you get here?"

"I hid in a coal bin under a neighbor's house. I've walked for five days, always at night."

"Do you have any contacts on the outside? Any family?"

"No. They were all taken. They're all dead now."

"If we take you, do you swear, by all that's holy, to be loyal and true to the *Maquis,* obeying all orders from me or my lieutenants—Denis, Anton, Paul, Jocko, and Geezi—who you see here? Put your hand over your heart and swear."

"I swear."

"The penalty for betrayal is death. No matter what the circumstances. No excuses. Understand?"

At times, Henri was forced to function as judge and jury in life-and-death situations. More than once, there had been outright betrayal, leaving no choice but to execute the traitor. Often the traitor was someone whose family or wife or lover had been taken by the SS and tortured. If he wanted to see them alive again, his only chance was to tell everything he knew to the Gestapo—where the *Maquis* were hiding, who their contacts were on the outside, where they got their supplies, everything. Of course, this was devastating to the *Maquis*. It could result in wholesale slaughter and obviously could not be tolerated, no matter what the excuse.

The *Maquis'* first significant action against the Germans was the bombing of an army barracks in the small village of St. Marat on the edge of the Verboten zone. After a protracted argument, Denis finally won the debate, arguing that morale would degenerate and discipline become impossible, unless the rag-tag band did something dramatic, something to carry the fight to the Germans. He had volunteered to conduct the raid himself, single-handed.

Disguised as a wine supplier, Denis drove the horse-drawn wagon, containing two cases of red wine, to the main gate of the Wehrmacht army base. He saluted the sentry and said slowly in French, "I have orders to deliver these cases of wine to the mess kitchen."

The sentry apparently understood only a fraction of the Denis' words, but it was enough. He carefully inspected the contents of the wagon, including the wine, but he failed to uncork any of the bottles, some of which contained gasoline and others nitroglycerin. He also failed to discover the igniter cap and fuse line wound around Denis' right leg under his long stocking.

The assistant quartermaster, a corporal in charge of food supplies, expressed surprise when the wagon pulled up in front of the mess kitchen. "I do not have authorization to pay for this," he asserted, but his tone implied he would like to have the wine nonetheless.

"I have already been paid," Denis replied with a depreciative wave.

"Humph," the Corporal scratched his ear. "Put them in the scullery." He pointed to a storeroom. "Over there."

"Oui, Herr Sergent," Denis flattered the Corporal with a salute, opened the door to the storeroom and began to carry in the boxes. The Corporal stood watching, still scratching his ear. Denis looked up and smiled at the German, *"S'il vous plait, Herr Sergent,* could you please check on my horse to be sure he's tied up? *Merci, merci*

beaucoup."

As soon as the Corporal turned his back, Denis attached the igniter caps and fuse line. With a silent prayer, he lit the fuse, closed the door and strode rapidly back to the wagon. He figured he had four minutes. As Denis drove off, he again saluted the Corporal who was still trying to subdue an itch on his left ear.

The one-man raid succeeded in blowing up the entire mess hall, killing two Germans and wounding half a dozen. When Denis returned to camp and told his story, he was greeted with cheers and hugs. Henri's *Maquis* were energized.

But in the end, the French suffered far worse than the Germans. Responding like rabid dogs, the SS lined up one hundred old men from the village of St. Marat, and shot every tenth man. Then they hung the bodies from trees in the town square.

From that time on, the *Maquis* only carried out sabotage that could not be tied to any one town or village. A favorite tactic was to put sand in the fuel tanks of German trucks and silica in the oil of locomotives and rail cars. Derailing of trains was another successful form of sabotage, but always in isolated areas well away from any village.

On October 30th, Henri received two different reports from his network of informants. A German sentry had been killed in the Verboten zone, and the SS had every man in their sector—and their dogs—combing the area between St.-Lo and Caen. They had been looking for two men on bicycles and searching every house.

Alarm bells went off in his head. It must be the British agent and the radioman, the ones Renee had told him about. It fit the time and place.

According to his sources, the Germans were working their way south and would probably reach St.-Pierre within twenty-four hours. He had to warn Renee. Not trusting anyone else with the message, he decided to go himself.

ST.-PIERRE-DU-BOIS

When she heard the knock on the back door at an unusual late hour, Renee, who had been jumpy as a cat all day, whispered to Mitch and Roger, "Hurry. Hide in the attic."

The two of them ran for the stairway. Renee, her heart racing, delayed a full minute before unlocking the door.

Henri pushed his way past her. "You scared me out of my wits, Henri. You forgot the coded knock," she hissed.

"Sorry, *mon petite*. I haven't time to explain. You've got those Brits haven't you?"

"Yes. How did you know?"

He ignored her question. "You've got to get 'em out of here *toute de suite*. The Bosch are searching every house, and they're liable to be here any minute."

Renee called Roger and Mitch down from the attic and introduced them briefly to her brother. Henri looked them over with a cold stare and said nothing.

Renee broke the awkward silence. "You'd better take them with you," she said, "and bring them back here later when the coast clears."

Henri frowned. "Are you crazy? I can't do that. The dogs will just follow them to our camp." He stuck his hands in his pockets and continued to glare at the two men.

Renee retorted angrily. "See here, Henri, these *confreres* are very, very important to us. Smith is setting up a transmitter to get through to London—primarily for *your* benefit. And Trout is here to train your men. This is the break you've been waiting for."

"That's all very well, but we can't have the Bosch tracking them to our camp. We could be wiped out."

Mitch broke in, "Obviously we don't have a lot of choices—or a lot of the time to argue about it. Roger and I have alternate safe houses where we can hole up for a few days. But I think it's best if we split up."

"I go along with that," Roger said.

"We may get caught," Mitch was talking faster now, "but at least we won't destroy your whole operation. When the smoke clears, we'll come back here."

"I don't like it," Henri muttered, "but I can't think of any other—"

"Roger is the most important part of this," Mitch broke in, talking rapidly. "He should use the best safe house, which happens to be the St.-Pierre brothel—at least according to our briefing. Do you agree?"

They all stared at Mitch. Finally Henri nodded. "You'd better tell us where the other safe house is," he said, "where you're going. We might have to help at some point."

"It's the home of Dr. Rouleau. I believe you know where it is."

"Umm, I know it well," Henri acknowledged. "A good choice. Anyway, you've got to get moving. And so do I. Sorry if I growled at you. Renee's right. We're going to need you, and I wish you good luck. You'll need it. I'll check back here in two days, around midnight."

"We'll have to tackle the transmitter later," Roger said, "when I come back."

"I'll hide your equipment in the root cellar," Renee said, "but you'd better get a move on right now. I assume you'll want to take your bikes."

As they hurriedly parted, Mitch reached out and touched Renee's hand, looking into her eyes a few extra seconds. She returned the look, her eyes a bit misty.

"*Bonne chance*," she whispered.

Mitch and Roger would be fully exposed in broad daylight, but fortunately the streets of St.-Pierre-du-Bois would not be patrolled, because Otto's entire SS company had left their home base, searching door-to-door over half of Normandy. Also, fortunately, both safe houses were less than a kilometer from the Brousard farm.

Mitch reached Doctor Rouleau's house without incident, but convincing the doctor to let him in was another matter.

The doctor was thorough. He grilled his visitor with test questions about baseball and Roosevelt, which Mitch answered to the doctor's satisfaction. Finally the doctor smiled and shook Mitch's hand. "Of course, I can tell you're a Yank by the accent, but you'd better not tell me any more than necessary about what you're doing here. By the way, what should I call you?"

"Trout. It's my code name."

"I see. You must understand I have to be very careful. The Germans have been using bogus British agents and fake RAF airmen to trap us. If I'm caught, I'd be shot on the spot. But fortunately, the Boche have been rather clumsy. A German pretending to be Brit or a Yank stands out like a pig in a parlor. I've spent quite a bit of time in England and America. I can spot a fake easily enough."

"I can tell you this much," Mitch said. "I'm here to help the Resistance, but the Germans are looking for me. I've heard they're searching every house between St.-Lo and Caen, and I'm afraid they'll search here too in a few hours."

To Mitch's surprise, the doctor replied affably, "That's all right. I'm used to it."

"In England, I was given your name and address as a safe house of last resort."

The doctor smiled, "Indeed? Well, you came to the right place. I'm glad to do what I can for you—and for France." Rouleau sat down behind his cluttered desk and pointed to a chair. "I've been able to get away with this up to now because I'm essential to the Nazis— as well as to the locals. As you can imagine, there's a shortage of doctors, so the Germans give me quite a bit of freedom. So far, I've avoided any suspicion."

"How do you manage to hide someone if the Krauts come around asking questions?" Mitch asked.

"Usually I disguise them by bandaging them up so they're unrecognizable. Works every time."

Mitch fidgeted. "There may be an extra problem in my case." Mitch wore a worried frown. "They may be using dogs."

Rouleau chuckled, "No problem. We've had that situation before too. What we do is pour a little iodine on the dressings. You may not like the stink, but I guarantee you the dogs won't like it either. Now we'd better get busy and doctor you up a bit, eh?"

Three hours later, four black-shirted Gestapo and two dogs burst in without knocking. Smelling of iodine and wrapped in bandages, Mitch lay on a cot in the back room.

"We search for British spy," the Sergeant in charge announced without preamble. "We search house, interrogate everyone."

"I have only one patient. He's had a bad accident," the doctor replied, adding some obscure medical terms.

Staring at the doctor suspiciously, the Sergeant signaled to his men to begin the search. Next, he went into the back room to interrogate the patient, but the dogs backed off and showed a distinct lack of interest.

The Gestapo always began an interrogation with the presumption the suspect was guilty of something, even if it wasn't the particular something they were looking for. Before starting, the Sergeant stared silently at his subject for a full minute, then began firing questions.

"Who are you? What is business here? I must see papers," the Sergeant demanded—all the standard questions.

With his bandaged arm, Mitch pointed to his coat and mumbled, *"Papiers."* He had well-rehearsed answers to the questions. The Sergeant studied the papers and grunted, apparently satisfied. He returned the papers to Mitch's coat pocket and headed for the door. Halfway across the room he stopped, turned, and studied Mitch a second time.

"Tell me about accident," he said slowly. "Exactly what happened?"

Mitch stumbled over the unexpected question. "Er—accident. Yes, accident. Bicycle. I was riding my bicycle when a truck hit me. I was thrown in the ditch."

The Sergeant's eyes narrowed. "Where is bicycle now?"

Mitch hesitated again. "I ... I don't know. I don't know what happened to it. I was knocked out and brought here. I suppose it's still in the ditch."

"We check story. Exactly where did accident occur?"

Starting to sweat under his bandages, Mitch tried to describe a place on the road, which he vaguely remembered.

"We check story," the Sergeant repeated. "Your papers say you a repairman from Rouen. We check that too. One of my men look for bicycle. I stay here. Keep eye on you."

Across town, Roger fared better. The Gestapo broke into the brothel with their dogs, stormed past the madam, and immediately began searching the rooms. The first room they entered happened to contain a German Colonel on top of a French girl, panting hard.

Without disengaging, the Colonel croaked between pants, "Get the hell out of here. NOW, or I'll have you shot."

They hesitated while the Colonel glared at them. But it was cold and getting late. There was a lot of ground to cover. They slammed the door and moved on.

Not so lucky, Mitch sweated and squirmed in his tight bandages. Returning to the doctor's house half an hour after he had been sent in search of evidence, the SS Corporal displayed a wide grin like a cat that had just caught a fat bird. Saluting, he reported to the Sergeant, speaking in German, "As you ordered, *Herr Feldwebel*, we have searched the area where the bicycle is supposed to have been. We found no trace of a bicycle and no trace of an accident. We interrogated everyone in the vicinity, and no one saw an accident."

"And did you contact Rouen?"

"*Ya, Herr Feldwebel.* They can find no record of our bicycle repairman or anyone registered at the address."

"Thank you Herr Corporal. Good work. I think we have something very suspicious here. Arrest this man. We will take him to headquarters."

Rouleau understood the words, but decided his best tactic was to remain silent and pretend he did not understand German. Anything he said would incriminate him. Mitch made out the gist of it and started to protest, but the Sergeant growled some orders and the two of them summarily man-handled him out the door and into their truck.

When the Blackshirts had left with the still-bandaged suspect, Dr. Rouleau rushed to the telephone and called the *Maire de Chabeaux*.

The doctor and the *Mayor* were among the few Frenchmen allowed to have telephones. Occasionally, their phone lines were tapped and monitored, but the doctor would take a chance tonight. The Mayor was his only pipeline to the Resistance.

"I have an emergency," the doctor began. "An American agent came to me on the run from the Gestapo[5]. He's been caught—unfortunately in my house."

"Do they suspect you of anything, or just the American?" the Mayor asked.

"I don't think it's occurred to them yet that I might be involved in the deception. But they'll find out soon enough when they remove the bandages. Let's face it, my days are numbered. I have to go into hiding or join the Resistance. But first we've got to try to save the American."

"What's so important about the American?"

"He's here to train the *Maquis* in weapons and arrange to restart the air-drops."

"Sounds important."

"Yes, but the way it looks, I'm in as much trouble as he is. I'll have to go underground."

There was a long silence on the other end of the line. "Are you sure?" the Mayor asked. "We need you on the outside."

"No, I'm not absolutely sure. I'm sorry if I sound like a coward, but I don't relish the idea of facing a firing squad. So I'm going under. But first, I'd like to help save this American if there's any way. He could be very important to the Resistance."

"So what can we do about it?" The Mayor sounded doubtful.

"Get a message to Henri right away. I think he might have time to do something—if you can get to him immediately. Tell him they're taking the American to Rouen for interrogation. But I heard them say they'd first take him to the St.-Pierre headquarters, and then to Rouen in the morning. Henri's men just might be able to intercept them on the road tomorrow—ambush them."

"Did you say ambush?"

"Yes, that's what I said. You know, they've done it before. There's only one road to Rouen. They're bound to be on it in the morning."

"Why Rouen?"

"From what I overheard," the doctor hesitated, trying hard to recall exactly what he'd heard, "the American is claiming to be a bicycle repairman from Rouen, and his story wasn't checking out. These particular Gestapo were from Rouen, and they want the credit with their boss. You know it isn't every day these pigs catch a spy."

"*D'accord*, I'll get this to Henri right away. But what about you?"

"Don't worry about me. I've got a few things lined up. I'll get in touch with you as soon as I can, but get to Henri tonight. There may be time to do something."

THE MAQUIS CAMP

The messenger woke Henri at midnight. Even in his groggy state, Henri immediately realized it was "Trout" who had been caught. *No question,* he muttered to himself, *We have to do something about it. We need the American.*

Henri roused Denis and his trusted lieutenants, now eight in number. In less than three minutes, the lieutenants had squeezed into his makeshift headquarters. Henri sat on a log, studying a ragged map, illuminated by a single candle. His rifle leaned against a bedroll in one corner of the tent, and a small ammunition box served as the table. He indicated two logs for the men to sit on, then explained the situation. "*C'est tres, tres important, mes amis.* The future of our operation will depend on this link to London. This may be our only chance."

Anton objected. "Slow down, Henri. Are you sure about this American? It could be a trap."

"It's no trap. I met this man and the radioman at the farm. He's a real pro. I saw the transmitter, and he had the right introduction to Renee. You know about her year in England. She knew the headman of MI-6. This is direct from the top."

Denis rubbed his eyes, finished buttoning his coat, and added his endorsement. "You can count on Renee. She knows what she's talking about. Anyway, we're not going to beat the pigs with our ratty collection of old rifles," he said with conviction. "There's no argument. We gotta save this guy."

There were murmurs of approval from the circle of lieutenants.

"We don't have a lot of time," Henri emphasized. "If the SS decides to leave St.-Pierre with their prisoner first thing in the morning, we've got about three hours to figure out what to do—and then do it."

They discussed the options. Jacques argued that it would be best to do nothing. Any rescue operation would be too dangerous. But Henri was adamant. Trout had to be saved.

Henri took charge. "We haven't got time to debate it any more," he said. "Here's what we're going to do. We'll ambush the SS car in the most isolated stretch of the road between St.-Pierre and Rouen. There's only one logical route, and here's the place." He pushed the map up close to the candle and pointed to the intersection of two roads. Pausing to look around the circle of men, he could see they were all with him. "We'll do this well away from St.-Pierre. Don't want the Bosch shooting a hundred villagers."

Geezy started to argue, but Henri shut him off. "We can't discuss it any more. Shut up and listen. This is the plan. I need five volunteers. Five plus myself." Henri was talking faster now. "We can't afford to lose all our lieutenants if anything should go wrong."

Denis spoke up first. "I'll go."

"No, Denis, I want you to stay behind. You are my replacement if anything should happen to me."

When all the others volunteered, Henri selected five.

As they hashed over the plan, they began to get excited about it. "It just might work!" Denis declared.

"I'm going to assign numbers to the six of us," said Henri. It'll be easier for me to lay out the action and the timing, that way. "Anton, you're number one. Jocko, you're number two. Paul's number three. I'm number four. Ricco's five, and Geezie, you're number six. This must be done with precision—exact timing." He paused once again and looked over the faces in the flickering candle light to be sure they were following him. Satisfied, he continued.

Henri turned to his number one man. "Anton, I want you to round up a "DETOUR" sign, even if you have to steal it off the roadway. You've only got half an hour. You won't have any problem. The Bosch have been putting up road blocks and detour signs all over the place."

"No problem," Anton agreed.

Henri hurriedly laid out the rest of the plan by the numbers. "I'll carry the talkies," he said. The walkie-talkie was a small American-made radio, almost a toy, but a necessary tool of their trade, which Jacques had brought along when they first defected. "The rest of you bring an ax and your rifles."

"Be real careful, Henri," Denis said, "and for Christ sake, don't get yourself killed. If anything even starts to go wrong, I say back off."

In the pre-dawn half-light, the six men with charcoal-blackened faces and stocking caps pulled down low, pushed off on their bicycles. Henri had warned them, "We don't want anyone identifying us later when the Gestapo starts asking questions."

The curfew was still in effect, but the *Maquis* used the back-woods trails, which they knew intimately.

Half an hour later, they emerged from a narrow path in the pine forest. Henri held up his hand. "Stay out of sight," he whispered. He squeezed the arm of his number one man. "This is the spot. It's almost exactly half a kilometer from here to our detour turn-off. When you see the Bosch car, radio to number two. Give him its speed and description. That'll give number two about three minutes to place the DETOUR sign. Is that clear?"

Anton nodded. "Yeah, no problem."

"Good. Here's your talkie. Take care. Everything depends on you starting this off right. Remember, stay out of sight in the trees the whole time."

Anton smiled. Henri clasped his arm and whispered, "Be careful." He rejoined the others on the path and checked his watch—6:02 a.m. He prayed the Germans would not start for Rouen this early.

Five minutes later, they came to the turn-off onto a side road, marked by a small green sign with faded letters, RD-234. Shrouded in a stand of pine trees, the turn could easily be overlooked by a passing car.

*   *   *

As the doctor had surmised, Mitch had been taken to the SS headquarters in St.-Pierre, then bound to a chair and interrogated by the Sergeant in an effort to shake his story.

Sweating rivers and starting to shake, Mitch watched the

Sergeant wrinkle up his nose when he looked at the iodine-soaked bandages. Incredibly, his captors never removed the bandages to find out whether his injuries were faked. *Maybe there is an outside chance they will leave them alone and believe my story.* Mitch knew he was grasping at straws. There wasn't a damn thing he could do, except pray, so he prayed and thought about home. Then he found the French girl invading his thoughts. He wanted to survive if for no other reason than to see her again.

Pretending to be on the verge of collapse, he stalled for time, groaning and babbling incoherently in French. He didn't know if it was doing any good, but he couldn't think of anything else to do.

Mitch heard the Sergeant gloating in German. He understood the gist of it. "We're going to get a commendation out of this," the Sergeant declared. "Maybe even an iron cross. Catching a spy is big."

"*Ja, Ja,* for sure."

The Sergeant smiled. "I'm glad Streikler's not here. No need for him to get the credit. We're the ones that captured this spy."

"*Ja,* of course."

" We'll take him to Rouen in the morning, early. Just hope Streikler doesn't show. He can be a real sour bitch. We'll have a good excuse for moving the interrogation to Rouen if he's not back."

*   *   *

At 6:30 a.m. the German car startled Henri's number-one man, Anton. It was the first traffic of the morning. He fumbled for the buttons on the talkie. "Number two. This is number one. It's the car, an open-top SS command car with three Blackshirts and a man all bandaged up. I'm sure it's our American. They're going about forty kilometers per. Figure they'll reach you in a little less than three minutes. No other cars in sight. I'll let you know if anything else comes along."

Number two jumped out of the trees onto the road and placed the DETOUR sign in the middle of the intersection with the arrow pointing left. He then ducked back into the grove of pines. Two minutes later, the German car approached and slowed to a stop.

The driver, a burly SS Sergeant, got out, inspected the road ahead, removed his cap, and scratched his head. He squinted at the fine print at the bottom of the DETOUR sign. *Actung! by order of the Kommandant 3rd Army. Compliance subject to fine and imprisonment.*

"Ach. Idiots," he muttered.

He inspected the weather-beaten sign with faded green letters that marked the dirt side-road, RD-234. Consulting his map, and obviously hesitant, he finally decided to take the detour.

The number-two man immediately radioed ahead to Henri and removed the DETOUR sign. There must be no extra traffic diverted to the detour.

Henri rubbed his forehead. *Up to this point, everything's gone exactly according plan. But something's bound to go wrong. There's always something. Think, damn it. The car should reach the attack point in ten minutes, plenty of time to cut down the trees.* Aloud, he turned to his men. "This is it. We've got about nine minutes. Geezi, you go ahead another half kilometer and fell a good-size tree across the road." Henri made a circle with his arms. "About this size—like so. We'll stop any traffic from coming from the other way. Then come back here quick as you can. That'll give us four men to ambush the car—ought to be enough. Remember, surprise is the key. Don't want them to smell a rat."

It all sounded simple, but the men started to sweat. The prospect of killing always made them sweat. They waited in silence. Nine minutes began to seem like an eternity.

Five minutes later, they felled a large tree at the main ambush point. But no sooner had the tree crashed into position than a farm wagon came rattling up the road loaded with hay, approaching from the same direction as the Germans. Henri rushed up to the farmer. "Go back. Back!" He yelled, waving his arms, palms pushing the air backwards. "Turn off the road for God's sake."

The farmer scowled. "What's going on here? Get out of my

way." He edged his wagon further forward. "Move that damn tree. I need to get through."

"Move back. Now!" Henri ordered, pointing his gun at the man. "If you don't, you'll get hurt."

The farmer continued to glare at Henri and crossed his arms over his chest.

Henri felt the sweat running down his shirt. "Move your Goddamn cart NOW, or I'll shoot your horse." He shifted his rifle to the horse's head.

The farmer stood his ground. "Go ahead and shoot. I'd still be in your way, wouldn't I? You'd be hell of a lot better off if you just moved that tree."

At this point, Henri's number-six man, Geezi, returned.

Calculating they still had three or four minutes until the Gestapo car arrived, Henri growled at his men, "We've got to move the damn tree. Help me grab the end and move it around enough to let this blasted cart get through."

They tried mightily, but it wouldn't budge. "We'll have to cut it in half," Geezi groaned.

With three minutes left—then two—they chopped the tree in half, shoved it aside, slapped the horse on its rear and sent the cart careening down the road. Grasping the reins frantically in one hand, the farmer managed to turn and shake his fist at them. *"Fils de cochons,"*— sons of pigs—he shouted.

Returning the log to its road-blocking position, they took cover in the trees, just in time to see the German command car come over a small rise.

Henri whispered, "Hold your fire 'til I give the signal, 'n careful you don't hit the American."

Letting out a Teutonic oath, the German driver jammed on the brakes, skidded to a stop, and got out to inspect the roadblock. "Help me move this," were his last words, as he beckoned to the other two Blackshirts.

It was all over in seconds. Leaning over to lift the tree, the Germans were sitting ducks. Mitch, still in the car, was well out of the line of fire.

While Henri went back to check out the command car

and Mitch, his men quickly stripped the bodies of uniforms, weapons and papers. Henri found a key in the Sergeant's pocket and removed the handcuffs. "You all right, Trout?"

Shaking, Mitch could barely get out the words. "I'm okay, but thank God for you guys. I thought I was a goner."

"Were you tortured?"

"No. Just grilled, but I sure wish you'd get me out of these smelly bandages."

*   *   *

Renee couldn't sleep. She sat up all night watching out the window, expecting the countrywide search to reach the Brousard house. Would the dogs pick up telltale scents? Would they find Smith's transmission gear hidden in the attic? Would they find her radio? Would they discover that she'd been hiding food?

In a state of near panic, she waited, first one day and then two. Nothing happened. She could see every other house in the neighborhood being searched, but the Brousard farm was skipped over. Why?

SS HEADQUARTERS IN ST.-PIERRE-DU-BOIS

Like a tiger with a toothache, Otto lashed out at everyone in sight. "How could you let those stupid idiots take him to Rouen?" he screamed at the Wehrmacht Corporal who had been on duty the night before.

"Sorry, *Herr Kapitan,* but I had no authority to— "

Otto cut him short. "I'll have you court-martialed," he yelled, knowing full well he had no authority to carry out his threat. Turning to his own Sergeant, he yelled, "Get me through to Rouen."

The Lieutenant in Rouen and Otto shouted obscenities at each other. Yes, they would capture the infernal *Maquisards* and chop them up in small pieces, preferably in the town square with the entire populace forced to watch.

But Otto wouldn't let it go at that. He yelled at the telephone, "How could your men be so stupid as to fall for such a crude ruse? What's the matter with your training? Are they *all* that stupid? You know this makes you responsible. Himmler is going to hear about this. What do you think he'll do to someone stupid enough to let a dangerous British spy escape?"

Otto found himself talking to a dead telephone. His face had turned an ugly shade of purple, and his gut started to hurt again. His left eye twitched, and both hands shook. *Damn, I'll have to see a doctor*, he muttered to himself.

Next, the Captain turned his wrath on the farmer who'd been driving a hay wagon and had been arrested, trying to remove a tree from the road. After repeated attempts to force a confession out of the tough old man, Otto finally gave up. He did get descriptions of the attackers, but only of men with blackened faces and hats pulled down low. Some were tall and some were short, and in his opinion, they all should be shot. This only added to Otto's fury.

Pacing the floor like a wild man, he screamed at his men. "We're going to scour every inch of this country, and every house. We'll kill them all. They'll wish they'd never been born before we're through with them."

His men stood at attention and said nothing.

THE MAQUIS CAMP

Hiding out with the *Maquis*, Mitch began the process of familiarizing himself with their people and equipment, such as it was. The motley collection of humanity hated the Nazis with a white-hot passion. They were fearless and willing to take any risk, but Mitch discovered most of them to be completely undisciplined and untrained in the use of any kind of weapon. Many had never handled a rifle before, and ironically, their enthusiasm tended to cause more harm than good. Getting too aggressive at the wrong moment could get them all killed. Henri found himself forced to clamp down hard. "You are not to do anything outside of our camp without direct orders from me or my lieutenants," he decreed. "Anyone disobeying will be shot. Is that clearly understood?"

Mitch intervened. "We've got to talk this out, Henri. We need discipline and some organization for where we go from here, Henri," Mitch said.

"You're right, of course. I know it's a mess. I'd better call a meeting of the Council."

The eight Lieutenants gathered around Henri's table and stared at the American. Mitch knew he had to inspire the respect of these *Maquisards* if he was going to accomplish anything. "First off, I want to thank you men for saving my hide. That was a very courageous thing, very courageous. You could have all been killed. Also I want to say, it was a brilliant plan—that ambush. I'd be in front of a firing squad right now if it hadn't been for you. Well, I'm going to make it up to you. I'm going to help get you some decent weapons and then teach you how to use them. We'll get food and supplies coming too if we do this right."

There were some low growls from the group, which sounded like approval to Mitch.

Henri spoke up. "This can be a real turning point for us, men. Thanks to Trout here, we've got a radio contact in the works. It's secret, and I can't tell you about it yet. But it's what we've been praying for. As you very well know, the most important thing is to get through to London and start the air drops again."

"How soon will they start?" Denis asked. "We're damn near starving."

"We can get them going right away if we're lucky," Mitch responded, "but Henri and I've got to get to our new radio contact *tout de suite*. We'll give it a try tomorrow."

"One thing I want to emphasize," Henri warned. "When we get our new weapons we've got to be cautious, real cautious using them. Some of them will be downright dangerous and sometimes tricky. And we have to be extra careful about when and where we use them. A loused-up attack will just give away our position, or worse yet, get a whole village destroyed. We know now that Hitler has issued orders to kill one hundred Frenchmen for every German killed. I don't need to remind you about Lidice."

Mitch frowned. "What about Lidice?"

"You haven't heard? The SS slaughtered an entire village, more than a thousand Czechs, mostly women and children, in retaliation for one Nazi killed."

"God, that's horrible," Mitch said softly.

"There are dozens of other cases, villagers tortured and hung from trees in the village square, in Italy, in Poland, and now France. It's so gruesome, we sometimes wonder if the Resistance can keep going."

A melancholy silence settled over the ragged gathering of angry men. Mitch got up from his stool and walked around the table. "You *Maquisards* have shown tremendous courage to come this far, but, for God's sake, don't give up now. It's going to get better."

A savage murmur erupted from the group.

Mitch turned to Henri. "You and your lieutenants are going to have a devil of a time keeping the lid on your people—until we're ready. That's going to be your problem. My problem's going to be to train them. There'll be more than a dozen kinds of weapons— explosives, mines, grenades, automatic weapons, mortars. And that's just the beginning. They're going to learn something about hand-to-hand combat, how to set bugs, how to rig timer wires—a lot of other things."

"Bugs?" Henri queried.

"Yeah. Hidden listening devices.

"It's going to be messy," Denis cautioned. "I don't envy you, Mitch."

Mitch looked around the circle. "I'm afraid you're right, but we'll do the best we can, and I'll need your help—a lot of it."

"Sure," Denis agreed, and the others nodded their assent.

"Of course, we won't be able to do any of this, until we make radio contact with London," Mitch continued, "and start the air drops. Henri and I will get to our radioman right away, but I don't want anyone else to know who or where he is located."

"Tomorrow," Henri inserted. "We'll go tomorrow."

"We'll divide the camp into eight training groups," Mitch continued, "one for each of you lieutenants. I'll work on the assignments. We'll reconvene and start the training as soon as we get the first drop."

As soon as the meeting broke up, Henri took Mitch aside. "That was a good meeting, Trout. We've got 'em with us. Now let's go to work on the list for London."

"First, we've got to figure out the coordinates for the air drop," Mitch added.

"Yeah, sure, but it's too dangerous for you to go to the farm. I'd better go alone."

But Mitch persisted. "It's not just Roger and the list. I have to talk with your sister. Sir Charles ordered me to bring her back to England."

"You won't get anywhere with her. She's stubborn as a mule. But come along if you insist. We'll just have to be damn careful."

"Thank God," Renee whispered, when she opened the door to their coded knock at 2:OO a.m. "I was afraid ..."

Henri hugged his sister, and Mitch gave her a wry grin. "I told you I'd be back." They talked softly so as not to wake Claude and Annette.

"There are WANTED posters for you everywhere," Renee said. "A ten-thousand franc reward for each of you—and descriptions. The description of you, Trout, means nothing, but the one of Henri is pretty accurate."

"So far they've only seen me all bandaged up," Mitch noted.

Henri shrugged. "You can see he's growing a beard and letting his hair grow. He'll look like a Frenchman pretty soon."

"By the way," Renee asked, "isn't it time you told us your real name? You don't look much like a trout to me. Besides, we're not going to tell anyone, and if we did, I can't see it would make any difference."

Mitch decided he was more than happy to oblige. Some day I'd like to tell her lots of things, he thought. "It's Mitch Carter, or if you prefer, Lieutenant Mitchel Carter, United States Navy. At your service, Mademoiselle," he added with a chuckle.

"Okay, okay. We've got work to do," Henri said impatiently. "Where is Smith? We've got to start the ball rolling with London."

"He's hidden in the attic," Renee said. "I'll call him down."

Roger had been busy the last few days. He had finished the job of hiding his transmitter behind a false wall against the eaves of the attic. The antenna was a wire pushed into a crack between the rafters and the roofing. After setting up his equipment and studying the German transmissions, he had made contact with London, and the signals had been confirmed through the BBC.

"So, tell me honestly, Roger. How does it look to you?" Henri asked in a skeptical tone. "Are you going to be safe here? I don't want anything happening to my sister, no matter how important the messages."

Mitch broke in. "That's why Sir Charles wants me to take her out of here. And I agree."

With her hands on her hips, Renee bristled. "I'm staying, period."

"Le'me answer 'enri's question," Roger said. "It's safe all right. At least my transmissions won't be a problem. I's more worried 'bout *your* comin's and goin's, 'enri."

Henri stared at Roger. "I'll keep the visits to a minimum. You'll be okay on that count, but right now, we've got to talk about getting our messages to London. It's a matter of survival. As it stands, you are our only hope."

Roger returned the look steadily and nodded.

"I've got a list here," Henri continued, "and Trout—I mean Mitch—has an even longer list. Of course, London will object, but we'll ask for all of it and see what they can do."

"I don't like long transmissions," Roger cautioned," but I can send it in pieces."

"Make it clear, food's our number one priority." Henri was emphatic. "Followed by Mitch's list of weapons. Now, let me give you the coordinates for the drop. They'll choose the time, we'll choose the place, and we'll live with whatever they come up with for timing."

"I can word the messages so you won't 'ave to come back 'ere for the answers. You'll get 'em on BBC, and I'll be 'earin' them too. If anythin's unclear, I'll ask for clarification."

"Sounds good." Henri turned to Renee. "How about something to eat. We're starving."

While they munched on boiled potatoes, she filled them in on the local news. "Did you know the Blackshirts are swarming all over the place looking for you? Seems you're both public enemy number one."

Mitch smiled. In a way, he was pleased they were causing the Nazis that much trouble. His eyes followed Renee as she bustled around the kitchen. *I didn't realize how much I liked a few freckles,* he mused. *Or is it the golden hair—or the way she moves—or? Darn it all, it's everything.*

Henri asked Renee about their parents, and they talked in near-whispers for an hour, but he kept coming back to his number one concern—food. "We'll need to take back whatever you can give us, Sis. Potatoes are best, if you have them."

They left before dawn. Renee hugged both of them but it seemed to Mitch that she clung to him a few seconds longer than necessary. Her eyes glistened with moisture as she handed Henri a large sack of potatoes and Mitch a bag containing a bottle of wine and a piece of cheese. "You can open it later," she whispered, "Dear God, please be careful. I don't want to lose you."

Mitch felt himself starting to choke up. "I—we—don't want to lose you either. I still wish you'd let me take you out of here. At least think about it and give me an answer next time."

She shook her head and murmured, *"a bientot."*

*   *   *

In the fall of 1943, Henri's *Maquis* were on the run. In addition to Otto Streikler's SS, a full company of Wehrmacht was scouring the countryside.

Henri had heard the rumors. "You know what I've been hearing," He confided to Mitch. "Von Kleister's issued orders to go all-out to drive us out of Normandy." Henri scowled and spat out the words. "And the Goddamn SS has recruited the rotten, stinking *Milice.*

They're a lot better at finding us than the stupid Bosch."

Mitch groaned. "Moving your camp every other day is killing us."

"There's another thing going on," Henri added. "The Gestapo has a favorite trick. They purposely let one of their prisoners escape, one they think might have some connection with us. Then they follow him. We've got to watch out for that. It's liable to work."

But the *Maquis* had their own network of informants, and up to now, they had been warned in time to move on to the next hiding place. It had become a terrorizing game of cat and mouse, a game where the mouse would be devoured if he lost.

"You know, Mitch, there's one thing we can do," Henri said, poking the American in the ribs, "We can't kill Germans because of what they do to the villagers, but we can track down and eliminate as many of the damned *Milice* informers as possible."

"I sure agree. How about going after Gazari? You've been complaining about him ever since I arrived. He sounds like the worst of the bunch."

A particularly malignant French traitor, Pierre Gazari had been a convicted rapist and murderer. Released from prison and reprieved from a life sentence by the Nazis in 1940, he now collected bounties for every *Maquis* he delivered, dead or alive. Henri agreed the time had come to do something. But first, he would find out everything he could about the damnable collaborator. He sent for Anton.

In a sour mood, Henri snapped at his lieutenant. "Anton, we need someone to follow Gazari. I'm damn near certain he's the bastard that's been squealing on us but I want to be sure. We need to know more. What he's up to? Where does he go? How can we get at him? I think you're the man to do a little investigating."

"You want me to follow him?" Anton asked.

"Yeah, I think you're the best man for the job for several reasons."

Anton looked skeptical but didn't say anything.

"Gazari spends a lot of time in the Blue Boar," Henri explained. "You're not known there like most of us, and you're good at disguise. I kind of like that paste-on mustache and black sailor hat you've been using. Looks good on you, by the way."

Anton grimaced and scratched the back of his head. "It'll be dangerous. "The Bosch spend a lot of time in there."

"You'll be okay if you just listen and keep your mouth shut. Gazari blabs a lot. Just listen and follow him."

Anton shrugged. Henri gave orders, not requests.

A week later, Anton reported back to Henri. "You're right about that bastard, Henri. Gazari talks a lot when he's had a few cognacs. He even brags about his new wealth."

"Is he collecting bounties?"

"He sure is. And getting rich. According to his own boasts, he's collected on a couple dozen Frenchmen—five to ten thousand francs apiece, depending on their importance. Now he's living in the LaMonde estate. You know, the big villa on Monk hill."

"Unhuh, I know it well."

"It belonged to the wealthy LaMonde family. He even laughed about putting the fat-cat businessman in jail, while he lives the life of a tycoon."

"The filthy pig!"

"That's just the beginning. He even managed to get rid of his wife by accusing her of aiding the Resistance, which happens to be the truth. Now she's in Ravensbreuck. Then he installed a young mistress, a whore he imported from Marseilles, along with a house full of bodyguards who double as servants."

"Did you find out anything about his information sources?"

"Yeah, sure. He meets with two of his *Milice* buddies in the Blue Boar almost every night. They listen for clues all over the countryside, and invariably hear something. A fisherman'll talk about some men he's seen on the backwaters of the Orne, or a woodcutter will say something about seeing men in the forest. Then they go and check it out. More often than not, they find something they can report to Gazari, who reports it to the SS. Gazari gives them a cut of the bounty, so they keep working at it. "

As he listened, Henri's eyes narrowed and his countenance darkened. "You know, Anton, we've lost three of our men and at least a dozen of our best info sources because of that son-of-a-bitch. It's time to get rid of the bastard."

"Yeah, the sooner the better."

Henri pounded him on the back. "Good work, *mon ami*."

Henri called a council-of-war. "The time has come to eliminate this cancer," he snapped. His fist hammered the crude table. "Besides, we're going to make an example of him—show those traitors treason doesn't pay."

"Damn right," Denis agreed, and the rest of the council chimed in with a chorus of ideas for how to best kill, murder, eviscerate, or chop the man into small pieces.

"All right, all right," Dennis interrupted. "First, we have to get to him. We know the bastard spends half his time in the Blue Boar, but we can't kill him there. It's too risky. Too many witnesses. Too many Bosch."

"I think we should nail him in his villa," Henri countered. "We could take out his bodyguards at the same time."

The council murmured their general agreement.

"Any special ideas?" Henri asked.

Denis spoke up, "Two or three of us can hide out in the garden. Shoot him when he comes out. Simple as that."

Anton shook his head. "I don't like it. He's pretty careful when he goes out."

Henri scratched his head. "It must be something where we don't have to wait around like sitting ducks, something where we can get in and out fast."

After an hour, they had exhausted all the possibilities and agreed on a plan.

At 1:OO a.m., Henri, Denis, Anton, and Geezi, wearing black, hid in the bushes and watched the last light turn off inside the LaMonde villa. They each carried a liter of kerosene.

"Coordinate your watches," Henri whispered. "Denis, you take the north side. Anton, the west. Geezi, the east. I'll take the south. At exactly 1:1O, douse your side and light it."

The four checked their watches and nodded. Henri continued,

"Then back off and be ready to shoot anyone that runs out. Make your shots count. We don't want to get into a firefight. We want to beat it out of here real quick—five minutes at the most. If anything goes wrong, run for it. We'll meet back at the creek."

At precisely 1:1O, Henri threw his kerosene against a wooden lattice, struck a match and held it. He watched the flames take hold, then retreated to the bushes. The flames rushed up the lattice, and seconds later he saw a bright glow flashing on the east and west sides.

Henri crouched, motionless, holding his breath—first an eerie silence, then screams and the crash of breaking glass. The figure of a large man appeared in a second story window. Henri took aim, fired, and the figure fell twenty feet onto a rockery. Seconds later, a totally naked woman appeared, outlined against the flames. She climbed out the same window and slid down a drainpipe. Henri held his fire and grinned as he watched her run into the garden, breasts bouncing like cannonballs.

Three more shots rang out from the far side of the house.

Henri checked his watch—1:14. No more people appeared on the south side. Then he caught sight of Geezi running. Time to beat a retreat.

Half an hour later, the four men straggled into their camp, each having taken a different route through the woods. "I got him." Anton grinned and slapped Henri on the shoulder. "It was Gazari."

Henri discovered that the Nazis didn't seem to care how many French collaborators his *Maquis* killed, so they tracked down and eliminated two more. The results were dramatic. The Nazis found themselves unable to recruit more informants in Normandy.

The game was improving for the mice. No longer did they have to move their camp every few weeks. Even more important, Roger's transmissions were getting through to London, and the flow of food and weapons started almost immediately. The RAF came through in fine style, air-dropping mostly American-made weapons and supplies.

Now Mitch went to work training the ragtag *Maquis*. Rifles, mines, mortars, machine guns, grenades poured down from the sky.

As Mitch had requested, Henri divided his people into groups based on competence, designating his eight lieutenants as team captains. Mitch began training them first in the simpler weapons. Only the most proficient would be trained in mines and plastic explosives. The others would learn to use automatic weapons, mortars, and the essentials of hand-to-hand combat. The frustrating and dangerous undertaking resulted in accidents, but gradually the scruffy band molded into a marginally respectable fighting force.

ST.-PIERRE-DU-BOIS

The proprietor of *Les Trois Maggots* had always claimed that the famous *Deux Maggots* cafe in Paris had stolen its name. In St.-Pierre, the cafe had been called *Les Trois Maggots* ever since anyone could remember. The only cafe in the village, it was St.-Pierre's meeting place, social center, a place to barter goods, and like a second home to Renee.

With faded blue, checkered oilcloth table covers and large umbrellas shading outdoor tables, *Les Trois Maggots* served beer, wine, French bread and cheese. The Germans, who patronized the café in large numbers, made sure it had the proper ration cards, especially for beer, which they regarded as a war-time essential.

Renee's lifelong friend, Lucie, was the sole waitress, pert, buxom, and jolly, hardly the type the Nazis would suspect of subterfuge. And the German customers seemed to appreciate the view when she leaned over to serve the beer in her low-cut peasant blouse with a gold crucifix hanging in the cleavage. Besides, she made an effort to be especially friendly with the Germans who would pat her ample bottom when she served their tables. They would usually leave a nice tip, never suspecting she understood German and had become one of the Allies' best information sources.

It was not just the bits of chatter she was able to collect and piece together. It was also the first rate information she picked up from Louis "The Clam."

Lucie told Renee all about Louis' shady past. Before the war, he had been a small-time underworld con-man. His specialty had been fencing stolen goods, and the war had furthered his career nicely. Now he drove a beer truck from a brewery in Amiens to restaurants in Caen, Cherbourg, and towns in between; also to certain German garrisons, where he was one of the few Frenchmen allowed to enter. After all, Germans considered beer a top priority item.

Like most French underworld characters, Louis had a colorful moniker. He had acquired the name, "The Clam", partly because of his taciturnity, but also because of his habit of pursing his wide lips like a tightly shut clamshell. Short, fat, and bald, he was constantly the butt of crude jokes from his cronies. Louis would grin. The jokes were a mark of acceptance.

Lucie knew exactly how he operated. He drove a beer truck, which provided the perfect cover. Aside from delivering beer and taking mental notes on everything he saw at the German bases, he had established a pipeline to the morgue in Amiens, which had become increasingly busy of late.

Louis had an accomplice, a talented pickpocket, now an orderly in the morgue, who had turned his formidable talents to lifting watches, rings, cigarettes, and other items from bodies brought in daily by the truckload. The wallets and papers had usually been removed before he received a corpse, but occasionally he managed to get his hands on them too. Identification papers were unquestionably the most valuable of black market commodities.

Louis the Clam served as the outlet for this talented orderly, and, even though Louis received only a pittance for driving the beer truck, he was becoming wealthy, fencing black-market items. Part of his success was due to his generosity with cigarettes, which he gave to German gate guards and to local gendarmes who turned a blind eye to his black-market dealings.

The French had never been uptight about petty underworld affairs and had a laissez-faire attitude about the black market. In fact, the more astute Frenchmen were inclined to feel the black-market served a useful purpose, especially when it came to I.D. papers.

One day each week, without fail, Louis could be found sitting at a corner table near the back of *Les Trois Maggots*. And Lucie, who knew every Frenchman in the village, had a habit of sitting with her customers when the cafe was not busy, chatting about the affairs of the day, sometimes sipping a small glass of wine. She would always find a brief moment to sit with Louis, just long enough to pick up his latest observations of German troop movements along with a tally of tanks, artillery, planes, and trucks observed on his delivery route. With remarkable accuracy, Louis could estimate the size of troop concentrations by the amount of beer consumed.

Early in the day, always a Friday morning and, more often than not, before any of the other customers arrived at the cafe, Renee would make her once-a-week visit to the village and to *Les Trois Maggots*. The farm always needed a few staples, and this shopping trip provided her one contact with the outside world. Since the Germans never patronized the cafe in the morning, she felt less conspicuous sitting with Lucie and less threatened, walking through the village at that early hour.

Lucie would anticipate Renee's visit and have a cup of herb tea ready, real tea being unavailable. First making sure there were no Gestapo in sight, she would sit with Renee just long enough to relay everything she had gleaned from Louis and from listening to her German customers. Some weeks, there would be nothing significant, but even the small bits and pieces added up to useful information when London patched it together with reports from other sources.

Before returning to pass this information on to Roger, Renee would stop and read the posters, announcing the latest German edicts and lists of WANTED CRIMINALS. These invariably included a description of a young woman with long blonde hair, riding a blue bicycle. Now her hair was shorn to three inches in length, the bicycle was barn red, and she always wore a shawl.

THE RESISTANCE

Le Maire de Chabeaux sat behind the large battered desk with a ten-foot high swastika flag behind him. On the sidewall hung a huge picture of Adolf Hitler. The desk was cluttered with papers. In this Normandy village of less than one hundred souls, he was not just the Mayor. He doubled as the keeper of records, the issuer of licenses, and even janitor at the one-room city hall.

"Oui, oui, ja, ja, Herr Kapitan," he said to the rigid figure in the black uniform. "Of course, of course. We will take care of it right away—immediately." The florid cheeks smiled, the round head bobbed up and down, and the mutton-chop whiskers quivered like a frightened mouse.

"See to it at once," the SS Captain said with a steely look. He turned on his heel and strode out of the room. As he reached the door, a diminutive Frenchman in a greasy smock passed him. The Frenchman avoided eye contact with the German but touched a finger to the rim of his beret in a half salute.

The Mayor put his right index finger vertically across his lips and waited until the Captain had shut the door behind him. He then rose from his chair, keeping his finger over his lips. With his left hand he beckoned the Frenchman to the far corner of the room.

"There's a bug, a listening device, in my desk," he whispered. "Now let's go back and say something nice about the Nazis. Tell me how happy you are to make good sausage for them. Then we'll come back over here, and you can tell me what's on your mind, *n'est-ce pas?"*

Jacques Donnay was a sausage-maker, and a good one. The Germans made extra allowances for anyone who could make decent sausage. Although Jacques was careful to appear cooperative with his new masters, he was, in fact, one of the most fervent Resistance workers. His sausage-making establishment, an attachment to his home, doubled as a safehouse for Jews and escapees. Also he had become adept at collecting bits of information about train schedules, the location of German military installations, troop movements, and whatever he could glean about the new coastal fortifications.

Transmitting such information to the Allies had become an almost insurmountable problem, and even communicating among his friends and neighbors was extremely dangerous. Recently, two of Donnay's compatriots had been captured and executed because someone talked inadvertently. Never completely sure whom to trust, he depended on the Mayor for help and reassurance.

"You and I know perfectly well what the problem is," Donnay had said to the Mayor on more than one occasion. "Frenchmen talk too much. We like our wine too much, and the Bosch listen in on our chatter."

"I know. I've got that problem myself," the Mayor admitted. "It's an impossible habit to break."

Patriots like Jacques Donnay did have one trusted point of contact, *le Maire de Chabeaux*, whose underground function was to act as a go-between, to make contact between these information sources and elements of the Resistance that could transmit the information to London.

"I've come across something of the greatest importance," Jacques whispered. "You must look into it immediately."

"Of course, of course, Jacques. You exaggerate, no doubt, but what you got?"

"A Flemish house painter sent me a message. He says he's stolen a complete set of German blueprints of Hitler's Atlantic Wall. But he doesn't know what to do next."

"Holy Moses! That could be the biggest thing since de Gaulle," the Mayor whispered. "Did your painter tell you any more than that?"

"No. Just that he has a secret meeting place, a safe house in Rouen where you can contact him."

The Mayor frowned. "Is your messenger reliable? This could be a trap."

"It's no trap. I know the messenger well. I can vouch for him."

"All right, you've never messed up yet. So where is this safe house? Of course, I'll have to check it out. Yes, indeed, if these plans actually exist, as you say, I know exactly what to do next. So tell me, how can I find him?"

Two days later, the Mayor made up a plausible excuse for visiting Rouen and requisitioned the town's only vehicle from the water commissioner. He found the house painter after a convoluted search, which eventually brought him to a shack on the outskirts of town—the apparent safe-house.

The two fenced for half an hour, finally deciding to trust each other. "You realize we would be shot—both of us—if the Bosch find out," the Mayor warned. The painter never flinched, just nodded and proceeded to pull a large packet of folded blueprints out from behind a heavy curtain.

The Mayor listened with growing astonishment as the painter's story unfolded. "Ten days ago I was hired by the German *Kommandant* to repaint his headquarters," he explained. "I pretended to be a bit slow and talked with a lisp, so the Germans would think I wasn't very smart. I always do that around the Bosch."

The Mayor smiled. "Sure, I do that too."

"As it turned out, it was the *Kommandant* who wasn't very smart. He left me alone with my paint and brushes and left this set of blueprints on a table in plain sight. Here, see for yourself." He unfolded five blueprints. "See, they're a detailed set of plans of Hitler's Wall. They may not be complete, but they show the essentials."

The Mayor thumbed through the sheets and let out a low whistle. "Good God. Look at the detail."

"I knew I'd be shot on the spot," the painter continued, "if I was caught with the plans, so I picked them up and slid them behind a picture on the wall, a huge picture of Bismarck. Then I waited three days while I finished the painting project. I still can't believe my luck, but the *Kommandant* never noticed the plans were missing. In fact, the next day, another set appeared in their place. I figured it was simply one of many sets. Believe it or not, the one I picked up had not even been missed."[6]

"That's the bravest, most incredible story I've ever heard—and the bravest too," the Mayor exclaimed, bussing the man on both cheeks. "Do you realize what this means? It could mean the difference between victory and defeat for the Allies. After the war you will get a medal. I'll see to it personally. In the meantime, we have to get these blueprints to London, and I know exactly how to go about it."

The painter shrugged and looked a bit skeptical. "Frankly, I'm glad to have them off my back. I haven't slept for days, worrying. Anyway you've got the problem now, and I'll pray for your success.

Anything to help get rid of the goddam pigs."

The Mayor tucked the plans inside his baggy winter coat, bussed the painter one more time, and rushed out the door. He knew he had to get to Henri Brousard as quickly as possible. Henri would know what to do.

The Germans believed the Mayor to be a reliable collaborator and allowed him the freedom to move about and communicate with his constituents. The gregarious Mayor knew nearly everyone in central Normandy, and was one of the few who knew how to contact Henri and his *Maquis.* Nevertheless, it wasn't easy, usually involving secretive travel to rugged backwoods areas or swamps or even caves. As a result, he had begun using Renee as an intermediary to reach Henri. He knew she made contact with her brother, although he was unaware of her other activities. He had found it a great deal easier and safer to contact Renee, who was not under suspicion, than to try and track down Henri in his latest hiding place.

Renee was in the kitchen when she heard the knock on the front door. She peered out the window in time to see the Mayor waving and smiling at two Germans who were leaving their headquarters.

Out of breath, he pushed his way into the house.

"*Bon jour*, Renee," he began, flushed and panting like an overheated hound. "You won't believe this, Renee. You really won't. Frankly, it's almost too good to be true." He took a deep breath and sat down on the edge of a chair.

"Slow down, Mayor," Renee said. "You'll have a heart attack."

"Yes. Yes, of course, but this won't wait." Shaking, he unbuttoned his floppy overcoat, pulled out the blueprints, and spread them on the kitchen table. "Look at this, Renee. What we have here is unquestionably the most important intelligence coup of the war. It's incredible, absolutely incredible. It's a set of plans of Hitler's Atlantic Wall—you know, the coastal defenses they've been building like madmen lately.

"Good Lord, that *is* incredible. How did you get—"

"I'll tell you the whole story later, but right now I'm in a hurry, and I shouldn't be seen here any more than necessary. In any event, you've got to deliver them to Henri as soon as possible. He'll know how to get them to London."

"I don't know where Henri is right now," Renee protested, "and I'm not sure when he's coming. He hasn't been here for three weeks."

"*Tiens.* This can't wait." The Mayor wiped his sweaty forehead. "I suppose I could take it to Henri myself, but it's dangerous, and I really can't afford to be seen with him again. I've been seen on the Orne too many times lately, and it's starting to attract attention."

"In that case ..." Renee started to say something about Roger's radio, but changed her mind. She had never told anyone about Roger and thought better of confiding in the garrulous Mayor. "I can't tell you the details, Mayor, but I have a way to get word to him. When he hears what we've got, he'll come soon enough, and he'll know what to do."

"Good. It's in your hands then, Renee." The Mayor edged toward the door. "Be careful and keep them well hidden in the meantime," he cautioned with a parting wave.

As soon as the Mayor had left, Renee rushed up to the attic with the plans and tapped Roger on the shoulder. He was hunched over his transmitter.

"I've got something to show you." Renee said, breathing hard. "It's important."

Roger held up his left hand as his right hand continued to tap out a message. A minute later, he twisted around, frowning. "This 'ad better be good," he grumbled.

"It is. Look at this," she said simply as she spread the plans on the floor. The two of them got down on their hands and knees and studied the precise white lines on the blue sheet—silently at first.

" 'oly cow," Roger gasped. "D'you realize what we've got 'ere?"

After studying them for an hour, they worked out a message for London. "First let's tell them as much as we can about the details," Renee said. "Then tell them to alert Henri on BBC."

Henri never failed to monitor the BBC. The message came on the 6:OO p.m. news. "Extreme urgency, H.B. report to Cricket for intell."

Henri snapped at Denis, "For Christ sake, we're freezing to death, and all they care about is their bloody intelligence."

It was now mid-December, and living in the open had been miserable. They knew smoke from outdoor fires would attract the Germans, so they didn't dare light them—except for tiny smokeless cooking fires. Mitch had shown them the technique, learned from his training in Scotland. By punching holes in the bottom of a tin can and lighting dry twigs, one could produce an invisible cooking fire. It worked well enough for cooking but didn't do much for warming cold bodies.

At the moment, warming himself interested Henri more than some message about an intelligence breakthrough. Nevertheless, two days later, he made his way to the farmhouse, looking grim, cold, and ragged.

"Good God, Renee, you've got London all in a twit," he said with irritation. "This'd better be damn good."

"It is, but first you need to get warm. You look awful."

"You're right about that. I feel awful. What have you got that's hot to drink?"

"Sit up close by the stove while I fix something."

While Henri gulped the hot chicory, Renee pried up the floorboards of the root cellar where the plans were hidden, then summoned Roger.

Henri finished his chicory and grumbled, "All right, Renee, let's not waste time. Show me what you've got."

"We've got something here that'll knock your eyes out, Henri. Could save thousands of Allied lives, maybe even shorten the war."

Henri's forehead creased as he studied the blueprints. "*Mon Dieu*, you're right, *mon petite*. This is incredible. I can't read all these German notes, but..." He let out a soft whistle. "Truly incredible. You don't suppose it could be a fake, could it?"

"No. The Mayor was absolutely convinced the painter is the genuine article. Besides, we don't have to make that judgment. London can judge for themselves. They can see how it checks out with their aerial photography as the construction goes along."

"Okay. So we've got to find a way to get these to London right away."

The three of them stared at each other. Frowning, Henri broke the silence. "Getting them there is not going to be easy, and we can't

155

take any chances. We've got to find a safe way out."

Roger broke in, "Mitch, is 'bout ready to go back, isn't he? 'e must've bloody well finished your trainin' program by now. Told me 'imself 'e's s'pposed to get back to London soon as possible. Besides, 'e'd obviously the best man for the job—*if* you c'n figger a way out of 'ere."

"You may be right," Henri answered slowly, "but I've got to think this out carefully. It's too important to mess up."

"How about the RAF Lizzies?" Renee suggested. "Now that we can pin-point landing fields, but I know there are problems."

There was a long silence, while the three of them stared at the plans.

"I don't like it," Henri said slowly, "Half the Lizzies are shot up by the Luftwaffe, and some of them get stuck in the mud, especially this time of year. They never get back off the ground. Then the Bosch get them. I think we'd better go with a Shelburne torpedo boat."

"That's plenty risky too," Roger ventured.

"I know, but can you think of anything better?"

Another awkward silence while they looked at each other.

"I guess that answers the question," Henri concluded. "Roger, you get on the wire and ask London if they can send a Shelburne. Suggest the beach at St.-Aubin. That's worked pretty well up to now. See what they think. We'll have to wait 'til tomorrow for an answer."

Roger stroked his chin, "You don't 'ave to stick around 'ere. You can get your answer on BBC."

"You're right, Roger. I'd like to have an excuse to stick around here where it's warm, but I'd better get back to camp and talk to Mitch. We'll monitor the BBC like always. I want you to repeat the questions twice about time and place, so we get an absolutely clear confirmation—at least twice. Okay?"

Reluctant to leave the warm kitchen, Henri folded the plans inside his shirt, picked up the sack of vegetables, kissed his sister, and left with his usual warning. "Be very, very careful. Don't take any chances."

THE MAQUIS CAMP

Troubled by the plan, Mitch protested, "I'd rather go back the way I came—by submarine."

But Henri insisted, "The Shelburne's safer and faster. Getting yourself to the beach will be your only real problem, Mitch."

"Seems to me it'd be just as tough either way, sub or Shelburne."

"Subs are no good," Henri grumbled. "They have to lie a mile off shore. Leaves you with a long, exposed row. The Shelburne can come right up to the beach."

"Okay, okay. You know best."

Predictably, London reacted like a foxhound on the scent. They were willing to send the entire Royal navy if necessary to get their hands on the blueprints. Whatever transport Henri thought best was all right with them. They knew the French had the best knowledge of the beaches, so they had no reservations about St.-Aubin, and they bought off on the Shelburne idea. The date and time were set for December 20, 1:OO a.m., which coincided with a high tide and a new moon.

"I'm not real happy about crossing the Zone—after what happened last time," Mitch confided to Henri, "but I guess there's no other way."

"We'll fix you up with a guide who'll get you to the beach. His name's Gaston. Grew up in the area and knows the lay of the land, all the back roads and trails."

Henri laid out the plan. They would bicycle to the edge of the Verboten Zone during daylight hours, hide their bikes in a haystack, and wait until 11:OO p.m., then walk the rest of the way to the beach at night. "You'll be crossing the Zone through fields, and orchards, mostly on wooded trails," he explained. "Should be safe enough. The Bosch can't patrol everything."

"How wide is the Zone at that point?'

"About twelve kilometers. You should be able to cover that in less than two hours if everything goes well. Let me show you on this map." Henri pointed to a ragged piece of paper. "I can't give this because I don't have a copy, but you won't need it with Gaston along."

"Sounds like the timing is going to be dicey. We don't want to get there early and be standing around on the beach, and the Shelburne won't want to be sitting around on the beach waiting for us either."

"Actually, you should get there first. You can hide in bushes at the base of the cliff. There should be a bit if moonlight, but we never know this time of year, do we?"

"I'm darn well going to need some light to work my way down that cliff."

"We'll give you a torch, but I hope you don't have to use it."

Mitch and his guide, Gaston, a hearty, jovial Frenchman, left in a cold rain. Along with the plans, folded under his shirt, Mitch carried a small container of kerosene and some matches. Should they be captured, or even be in danger of capture, he was supposed to burn the plans; although Mitch couldn't see how he'd have time to do it.

Before they left, one of Henri's men, a draftsman in private life, had painstakingly copied the plans, using bits of paper, which could be fitted together later if the originals were lost.

Everything went according to plan until Mitch and his guide were half way across the Verboten zone, almost in sight of the coast. Then, as if Dante's Inferno had sprung to life, hell broke loose.

Gaston, walking twenty feet ahead of Mitch, suddenly erupted in flames. Instantly incinerated, he did not even have time to cry out. Mitch leapt backward and flattened himself against the wet ground. He felt the searing heat. In that instant, his mind raced— *What? Who? Why? Why was there was no explosion?*

His brain finally cleared. These were unmanned flame-throwers, triggered by an electric eye. There would be no explosion. He'd heard about these diabolical devices, but he'd understood they were experimental and rarely used.

In a state of panic, he ran back the way he had come. *Would a German patrol see the flames and come after him?* He stumbled onto the same haystack where he and Gaston had been hiding only two hours before, and vomited.

He burrowed into the hay, shaking violently, seeing the horror over and over in his mind like a slow-motion movie. Now he had no choice but to abort the mission. He could never find his way to the beach at St.-Aubin without his guide, and now he was hopelessly behind schedule. He'd missed the rendezvous with the Shelburne.

He could not sleep but he did not dare to move until the curfew ended. At the first light of day, he peered out through the strands of hay and found no human activity or German patrol in sight. *Would the Krauts inspect the charred remains of Gaston and conclude that he was alone? Either way, I've got to take my chances and get going.*

*   *   *

Although Henri had become hardened to tragedy, he was appalled when Mitch staggered into camp, looking like a ghost. After wrapping him in blankets and plying him with a sip of precious brandy, he finally extracted the story.

Mitch sounded totally shattered. "Dear God, Henri, I can't go on. I ..." He put his arms around Henri and cried like a child.

Henri tried to snap him out of it. "A lot of people get killed in this business, Mitch," he said quietly. "We can't let it destroy us. We just can't. We've got to go on. At least, you've still got the plans. That's what's really important."

"I'm not cut out for this," Mitch muttered. "Even when we kill a Kraut, I hurt all over."

"You'll get over it. I did. It wasn't easy. Besides, we don't have any choice. We've got to keep going. If we don't kill them, they'll kill us. It's that simple."

Stripped of the capacity to speak, Mitch nodded weakly.

Henri shifted gears from sympathy to hard-nosed reality. "While you were gone, Mitch, a message came through on BBC. They already know you didn't show up to meet the Shelburne, so they've ordered you to try again—as if it were that easy. Of course, they don't know what happened, but we'll have Roger tell them. In any event, we absolutely must get those plans to London," he poked his forefinger in Mitch's chest. "And you're still the man for the job. You need to get back anyway, *n'est-ce pas?*"

Henri saw the blank look on Mitch's face. "It's too risky to try to get through to the coast again, and the same goes for the Lizzy," Henri continued softly. "As I see it, that leaves the Escape Line as our only other option. I don't need to tell you about it. I'm sure you've been briefed, and you're the best man to do it."

Henri could see that Mitch wasn't registering and obviously didn't feel like the best man for anything. The American rubbed his forehead. "Let me get some sleep," he mumbled. "We can talk in the morning."

A few hours of sleep didn't change anything for Mitch, but Henri wasn't going to let him off the hook. "This needs to be done, Mitch, and there's no one else to do it. Renee will get you started. She knows the first leg of the Line like her own kitchen."

When Henri mentioned Renee, Mitch suddenly showed more interest. "Fill me in," he said.

Henri looked at him quizzically, aware of Mitch's interest in his sister and smiled inwardly. He liked Mitch.

"Frankly, I can't tell you a hell of a lot about the Line, except that it's a way out. I can tell you this much: it's been very successful up to now. More than a thousand RAF and American airmen have been evacuated. That's been confirmed to us on the BBC.

"What about Renee?"

"She knows nothing about the other legs of the Line, only her part. Each leg will be revealed as you go along. As you know, there's a good reason for that. The Bosch can't squeeze the information out of someone who doesn't have it. One other thing, though: don't pass yourself off as an American. Some of the French are fighting mad at the high altitude bombing that's killed a lot of French civilians. The British have been doing it with low level bombing, much more accurate, but not nearly as destructive as the Americans."

"Any suggestions for a cover?" Mitch asked. "So far I've been a telephone lineman and a bicycle repairman. Worked pretty well for a while."

"You'd better be something different," Henri replied. "The Bosch may be alerted to both those covers. We've got a couple of German uniforms, the ones we took off the SS when we rescued you. But I don't think you can get away with that, unless you speak German, which you don't. A monk's habit might work or a doctor's medical bag."

"I don't know anything about medicine or telephones or monks."

Henri scratched his head. "We'd better choose an occupation where you can pass yourself off as the real thing if you get in trouble. Carpentry's probably the safest."

"Yeah, I like the sound of that, Henri. Actually I'm pretty good at building things. Can you fix me up with some equipment—a carpenter's apron and a bag of hand tools?"

"Sure, no problem. And that'll give you a good excuse for travel. With all the bombing and destruction, there's always something that needs repair."

"Now let's talk about papers. I still have the old papers I got back after the rescue. The only Germans that saw them are dead."

"I'm not sure it's such a good idea." Henri ran his fingers through his hair. "For one thing, your picture's wrong, now that you have longer hair and a beard."

"Unh huh. You're right about that."

"Besides, the SS have a fairly accurate description of the old you. You can bet they talked to their headquarters in Rouen before we took them out. Your old papers say you're a telephone lineman from Rouen. We'll have to change all that."

"Okay, so what can we do about it?"

"We can fix you up with new papers. We're getting pretty good at it, but first we have to decide on a home town for you and an excuse to travel."

They finally came up with St. Flour, because it was about half way to the Spanish border and not well known by the Germans. An address in Paris or Marseilles would be too easy to check up on.

"So how do I go about getting the new papers and a new photo?"

"I can arrange that. There's an expert forger in Chabeaux. I'll give you a note. You take it to the Mayor, and he'll pass it on to my forger friend, the best printer in Normandy before the war. Then you'll need a new photo. We can take it here. The Mayor will deliver the finished papers to Renee in two or three days, and you can pick 'em up there."

CHRISTMAS AT ST.-PIERRE-DU-BOIS

Renee's farm helper, Hans, was unhappy. He had always celebrated Christmas in his hometown of Bad Munter with a Christmas tree, a roasted goose dinner, and a Christmas Eve church service. Visions of the Saint Nicholas traditions of his youth played in his head—the wooden shoe put out at night and miraculously filled with candy by morning, the mistletoe, the presents. Now there was nothing. When he approached Captain Streikler about putting up a small tree or perhaps a small wreath, the answer was an angry, "*Nein*, we have more important things to do."

Like a small boy, he looked wistfully across the yard at the Brousard house. Through the window he could see Christmas decorations, and on the front door a wreath with red and green ribbons.

Hans was not part of the SS and did not report directly to Otto, rather to a sergeant of the Wehrmacht. But the Sergeant, like the rest of the Wehrmacht, knew only too well the frightful power wielded by the SS. While the Sergeant dared not cross Otto with a show of Christmas spirit, he did grant his men the traditional time off on Christmas Eve and Christmas day.

A few days earlier, on one of their endless manhunts for the *Maquis*, Hans had spotted a gaggle of wild geese settling onto a pond near St.-Pierre. He did not have a shotgun, but a goose is a big bird, and he knew he could bag one with his rifle if he could catch it on the water.

On the day before Christmas, he rose early and hurried off to find the birds were sitting right where he had seen them earlier, obligingly in the middle of the shallow pond. Hans bagged one with a single shot, but he had to wade in freezing water up to his chest to retrieve his prey. It was a fine, fat bird, well worth the effort.

Fearful that Otto would see him, he stuffed the large bird inside his greatcoat and slogged, soaking wet, half a kilometer to the Brousard farmhouse. Teeth chattering, he knocked on the front door, at the same time admiring the beautiful holly wreath in spite of the cold.

Hans could see the worried look on Renee's face when she peered out the window, and then saw it turn to a smile. He knew she always jumped whenever she saw a German uniform, but not when she knew it was he.

She greeted him with a smile. "Won't you come in, Hans? It's cold out there, and it looks like you are soaked. You must be freezing."

"Sorry, Mademoiselle Fraulein, I can't come in. I mean, I really like come in, but I can't," Hans said, shivering. "I have Christmas gift for you." He pulled the bird out from under his greatcoat. "Here. It's goose for your Christmas."

Speechless for a moment, Renee reached out to hold the heavy bird, "God bless you, Hans," she said, embracing the bird with one arm and the embarrassed Corporal with the other. "This is the best Christmas present I've ever had. Thank you. Thank you very much. Are you sure you can't come in? We have a bit of brandy we've been saving for Christmas. You really should have a small drink to get warm."

Awkwardly thrusting the goose the rest of the way into her arms, he said, "Sorry, I not allowed. I must get back. I mean say Happy Christmas." He was afraid she might see the tear in his eye as he hastily retreated down the path.

"A very happy Christmas to you too, Hans!" she called after him.

No sooner had Hans left than Renee was jolted by a knock on the back door. She jumped. Henri never came at this time of day. But it wasn't her brother. It was Mitch, looking haggard, wet and cold, nevertheless managing a smile. She was so happy to see him that, without thinking, she threw her arms around him and started to cry.

"I'm sorry," she said, wiping away the tears. "That was foolish of me, but I've been so worried about you. It must be Christmas doing this to me."

"Thank God for Christmas," Mitch laughed, backing off enough to look into her eyes. He cupped her face in his hands and kissed her wet face lightly. Renee felt her heart racing, then disorientation, like being lost in a misty dream. She pulled back, put both hands over her face, and stared at him. "Oh, Mitch, I didn't mean ..."

"Renee, I hope you meant it," he said, pulling her into his arms again, "I've been in love with you from the first minute I saw you, even though you were all bundled up in that huge coat, and there wasn't much to see. I've been thinking about you ever since. You knew, didn't you?"

She collected herself but didn't push away. "Mitch, is it ... is it the war? Or Christmas? Maybe it's only the Christmas spirit."

"No, Renee, I'd have fallen in love with you anywhere, any time. But Christmas is a wonderful time, isn't it? Love. Peace. Good will. Christmas says it all, doesn't it? Right now, I'm in love, and I could love and forgive everyone, maybe even the Germans. It's like a wonderful dream, but I'm terrified I'll wake up and find out it's an illusion, that you aren't really there, that you don't return my love after all."

"Shhh, don't talk like that," Renee looked into his eyes. She felt dazed and confused, but her heart wouldn't stop. What to say? Finally, she managed to murmur, "Yes, yes, Mitch, but there are so many things... In the last few weeks I've lost a lot of sleep worrying about you—and Henri." She clung to him. "I don't want to lose you."

She didn't know why Mitch had come, but was afraid to ask, for fear of breaking the spell. She shivered against his wet coat. "Goodness, you're freezing. We've got to get you warmed up and dried off." She hustled into the bedroom and returned with a wool blanket, then brought a chair up close by the kitchen stove, gently pushed Mitch into it, and wrapped the blanket around him. She stirred the wood fire back to life. "It'll take half an hour to heat up enough hot water for a bath," she said, putting her arms around him for added warmth.

Renee called to her mother. "Come downstairs," she shouted a little too loudly. "We have a wonderful surprise guest for Christmas." Like a child who still believed in Santa Claus, Renee flushed and avoided her mother's gaze when she entered the kitchen and looked searchingly from one to the other. *"Bienvenue, Monsieur Lieutenant,"*

Annette offered politely, "It would be our great pleasure if you will have Christmas Eve dinner with us."

While they waited for the water to heat, Roger came down from the attic, and Renee told everyone about the goose. "It'll need plucking, Roger. Can you pluck a goose?"

"Of course. Fix me a little boilin' water, 'n I'll 'ave it for ya in a jif."

"I'll heat up plenty of boiling water, enough for plucking the goose and two more pots for a bath," Renee said. "Mitch is half frozen. He deserves a hot bath. Then I'll start cooking. We'll have a grand Christmas dinner."

"Don't forget the bottle of brandy," Annette chimed in, "saved all year just for Christmas. We'll forget the war for one night and drink to peace."

Renee took Mitch upstairs, showed him to the old tin-lined wooden bathtub, and handed him a warm towel. "Give me a few minutes and I'll fetch the hot water." She fidgeted, not wanting to leave. But the dinner needed attention, so she gave him a quick kiss and hurried back to the kitchen.

While Mitch soaked in the tub, Roger plucked the goose, and Renee busied herself in the kitchen, cooking squash, setting dishes, candles, and utensils on the table, arranging and rearranging napkins and chairs.

Annette stared at her daughter. "My goodness, Renee, I've never seen you bustle so."

By the time Mitch had dried off, the aroma of cooking goose permeated the house.

Roger and Mitch carried Claude downstairs to the dinner table. Obviously sick, Claude had dark circles underlining his eyes, deep furrows marking his forehead, and a voice that quavered like a dry rustling leaf. Renee's countenance showed the strain of her concern about him. *Would he survive the winter?* But Renee set aside all such thoughts and worries for the occasion. She wanted this to be a festive Christmas.

A little brandy cheered everyone, and they talked of happier days before the war—fishing, hunting, Renee's scholarship to England, country dances, market days.

Renee wanted to hear as much as possible about America and plied Mitch with questions. He told about his scholarship to Princeton and his benefactor, Bradstreet Meyer. Roger told of his adventures in the Merchant Marine. He'd seen more of the world than any of them.

Renee wondered why Mitch said nothing about his plans. *Will he try to talk me into leaving? Of course, I can't leave my mother and father behind. They wouldn't survive without me. And Henri needs me more than ever.* She closed her mind to such thoughts. She desperately wanted to keep the magic of Christmas working as long as possible.

Renee looked at Mitch. "I'd like to go to the late Mass tonight," she said quietly.

"I'd like to go too," Mitch answered with a slight hesitation, "but do you think it's safe?"

"Yes. The Germans have called off the curfew for Christmas Eve, but you should probably wear a hat and a scarf. Of course, the hat will have to come off at the door, but we'll find a dark corner in the back. There won't be any problem."

Renee could see that Mitch was still worried. "Well, if you're really sure," he said after some thought.

"I'm sure. Last Christmas, the Bosch left us alone. Of course, we'll have to walk right past a dozen WANTED posters with your description—and mine—on them, but it'll be dark, and you look entirely different now with your beard and the long hair. For that matter, I don't look anything like my description either."

Her mother broke in quietly, "I would like to go with you."

"Of course, Mamma," Renee agreed. She could see her mother looking at her strangely. *I probably look too excited, flushed*, she realized. Fidgeting, she looked away and busied herself with her coat and scarf.

Renee had put on her best print dress, a fine British tweed given to her by the Atwaters. Mitch smiled, "You look wonderful, Renee. I'm sorry I can't change into anything better." He was dressed in the same black sweater he'd come with. He had washed it a dozen times, so it was clean enough but badly frayed.

Purposely arriving late, they sat in the back row of pews. After the processional and the reading one lesson, their hands touched lightly. Mitch whispered, "Will you marry me?"

After a long pause, he looked at her sideways with an anxious expression. Renee was having trouble controlling her voice. "Oh Mitch," she whispered. Then an interminable silence while the priest droned on in Latin. "Yes, of course, I will marry you," she said loudly enough for the people in the next pew to hear. But her mother, who was hard of hearing, continued to look straight ahead.

Mitch leaned over close to her ear and whispered, "Before God, I promise to love, cherish, honor, and protect you."

"Before God, I promise to love, cherish, honor, and make you the best possible wife." Renee leaned as close as she could, so the rest of the people in the pew could not hear. "Does this mean we're actually married—in the sight of God?"

"Yes, but we will have a priest and friends and a proper wedding and all the other things when the war is over."

Renee had known the parish priest, Father Francois, all her life. He had been like a second father to her. Now she could tell he was tortured by his conscience, trying to give a sermon of hope, without becoming the next victim of the Nazis. Everyone in the church was acutely aware of what had happened in Poland and Czechoslovakia. Hundreds of priests had been murdered and thousands imprisoned for refusing to preach the Nazi dogma.

"Render unto Caesar that which is Caesar's, but render unto God that which is God's," Father Francois began. Renee thought that would be acceptable to the Germans. But he went on, "The righteous shall inherit the earth," and another biblical quote, "The Philistines shall be destroyed." Then he made it quite clear who were the righteous and who were the Philistines. Some in the congregation looked around at their neighbors with alarm, but the service continued without pause.

Side by side, Renee and Mitch took Communion at the altar. When the priest came to them with the bread and wine, Mitch said in a low voice, "Father, would you bless us together."

Having a full church and a long line of communicants, the priest faltered for a second, but after only the slightest hesitation, he put his free hand first on Renee's head, then on Mitch's and said, "Bless you my children."

That night, long after every soul in the Brousard house had retired, Renee came to Henri's bedroom where Mitch slept fitfully. She dropped the flannel nightgown on the floor and slid in beside him. "I want to be your wife in truth, without reservations," she said quietly.

On Christmas morning, first thing, Mitch went to Renee's father and formally ask for his daughter's hand in marriage.

"I am old and may not see the end of this war," Claude said in a weak voice, "and it would give me great happiness to see my daughter married before I die. Of course, I was hoping for a Frenchman, a Frenchman who loved farming, but you fight for France, yes? And it is what she wants, yes?"

"Yes, sir. I fight for France, and yes, it is what she wants. We love each other, so it will be good. You will be proud of your grandchildren."

"Ah, so many things are different now, different from what I would wish, but I feel it is good—good, as you say. So you have my blessing, young man. Please be good to her. She is very, very special."

Mitch leaned down and kissed the old man, feeling the tears on his cheek. "Yes, sir. She is very special, and I promise with all my heart to be good to her."

Next, Mitch and Renee went together and told her mother, who stared at them for an uncomfortable two minutes. "You know about the history of this farm, young man, do you not?"

"Yes, ma'am," Mitch replied politely. "Renee has told me."

"You know it must remain in the Brousard family, don't you?"

"Yes, ma'am. I—we—respect that, but we assume Henri will fill the role."

After an hour of questions and admonitions, Annette finally sighed and accepted the inevitable, but when Christmas dinner arrived, Claude put a positive note on the event. "My prayers have been answered. This is the best Christmas present anyone could have. You give us new hope and something to live for." Even Roger waxed eloquent, reciting a Welsh sonnet and embraced them all, one at a time, like a bear-wrestler.

"I have a present for you, my love," Renee said with a smile, holding out a small package wrapped in tissue paper. Mitch held the package with reverence. then tore away the paper to find a silver Saint Christopher medal on a thin chain.

"Thank you, thank you, Renee." He kissed her and held the charm up to the candlelight. "It's beautiful. Will you hang it around my neck? It will even more that way. It's a good-luck charm, isn't it? I have a feeling I'll need it."

"It's an old family piece," Renee said, "passed down from my grandfather."

"It's wonderful," Mitch murmured, and kissed her again. "I'll wear it always and treasure it."

At mid-afternoon on Christmas day, Renee heard the knock on the door.

She froze and whispered to Mitch and Roger, "Quick, hide in the attic." Only then did she peer out the window to see who was knocking. With a sigh of relief, she recognized the Mayor of Chabeaux. The Mayor presented himself with a friendly flourish and a jovial "Merry Christmas." It seemed to Renee that this large, florid man must have his mind on the next election, as he shook hands vigorously with Renee and her parents. He chatted about the weather as if there was no war while Mitch and Roger remained out of sight.

Only as he was leaving, did he finally get around to the real purpose of the visit. "Oh, by the way, I have a package for Trout."

"I'll see that he gets it." Renee edged the talkative man toward the door, relieved to see him leave.

She called Mitch down from the attic. "I have something for you. It's from the Mayor."

The package contained Mitch's new identity papers. He inspected the picture and laughed, "Good Lord, do I really look like that now?"

THE ESCAPE LINE

Roger looked worried. "London told me 'bout your orders, Mitch, two days before Christmas. But I didn't want to spoil your Christmas talkin' 'bout it."

Mitch nodded. "Thanks, Rog. I appreciate that." He knew it was time to get down to business and tell Renee and Roger about his new plan. "I already know about my orders from London. Henri and I heard them on BBC. I'm supposed to return to London with the blueprints as quickly as possible. It's an order. They didn't say how I'm supposed to get there—as if all I needed to do was buy a ticket on the next boat. But Henri thinks the only way is the Escape Line."

Renee nodded, "Henri's right. It's probably the safest way."

"I sure hope so, after what happened last time. In the meantime, Roger, can I assume your transmissions are still going through okay?" Mitch asked.

"Yeah, sure. Without a 'itch. I'll tap through to London and tell 'em you've got your orders."

"Tell them I'll be leaving tomorrow with the blueprints, going out by the Escape Line. I should reach Gibraltar in approximately two weeks if everything goes well. At least that's what Henri said to tell them."

With all that had transpired, Mitch almost forgot he was an officer of the U.S. Navy. He had no choice but to follow orders, but he didn't have a great deal of optimism about the ultimate outcome. Without conviction, he added, "Be sure and tell them we made a crude copy of the plans. If anything happens to me, someone else can try. I hope London realizes the Line is a slow process. Personally I think it will take longer than two weeks but don't tell them that."

"Yeah, they know all about the Line, but I'll remind 'em of a few things."

Mitch turned to Renee, "Henri tells me you can get me started, Renee. Says you've done it several times before."

Renee nodded. "Yes, my love. I'll get you started, and you'll make it just fine. I know you will. But the first leg is all I know anything about. It'll get you as far as Vire and then Le Mans, about one hundred kilometers south."

After his experience with Gaston, Mitch was still jumpy. "Do you run into a lot of Germans on the road?"

"No. We stay away from big cities, use back roads and trails, work our way to the south and west where there aren't a lot of Germans. In the past I've taken my fliers on bicycles as far as Vire, posing as man and wife. I've never had a problem."

"We ought to make a believable couple." Mitch smiled. "How long does it take to Vire?"

"About three hours. I have to get back to St.-Pierre the same day—in daylight."

"Yes, of course. What happens when we get to Vire?"

"At Vire we have a bread truck driver who delivers bread every day to Le Mans."

"Is he reliable?" asked Mitch.

"Yes, he always leaves Vire at exactly 11:OO a.m. I try to time our arrival so we don't have to wait around and arouse suspicion.

"Why do we have to expose you to the trip to Vire? Can't I go alone?"

"Because the driver will only accept a charge from me. He's scared to death of being trapped by a fake escapee or a fake RAF flyer. It's happened, you know. I know of two drivers who've been caught and executed, and there are others."

"Should I try to hide in the back of the truck or just ride up front and rely on my cover story?" Mitch asked.

"That's up to the driver. Sometimes he does it one way and sometimes the other. He'll brief you on that and about the next leg and a lot of other things."

They talked late into the night and agreed to start early the next morning. "It'll be a good day to start the trip," Renee explained, "because the Germans usually take the day after Christmas as an extra holiday. They won't officially recognize the extra day, but they'll let their guard down a bit."

December 26 turned out to be a cold but sparkling sunny day.

171

Mitch and Renee said tearful good byes, climbed on their bicycles, and headed south along wooded trails and small rutted roads used only by farmers. With his carpentry kit strapped on the carrier rack, food stuffed in his pockets, five thousand francs hidden in his shoe, and a pistol strapped to his ankle, Mitch felt reasonably well prepared for the trip.

They worked their way through fields, orchards, and wooded paths, and talked of the future as if there was no war. "Renee, this is the most beautiful country," Mitch said with feeling, "even in winter. What a wonderful place to live." As he said it, he realized with a start he might have to make a decision on that score some day.

Chatting like happy children on a Sunday outing, Renee told him about the people of Normandy. "They're independent and friendly to a fault," she explained, "quite different from the Parisians. Did you know we're descended from Viking Norsemen? That's why we're called Normans, and why so many of us are blonde."

Mitch grinned. Bicycling alongside, he reached out with one hand and touched her hair. "It's lovely," he said. "Thank God for the Vikings."

Renee laughed and went on like a schoolteacher, "Did you know about Rollo? He was the Norseman who conquered Normandy in 911, and William The Conqueror was his direct descendant. So the English are mostly Norse too, though they don't like to admit it."

"Fascinating," Mitch said, "but I wouldn't care if you came from Mars. I'd love you anyway."

They were running short of time together, so Renee started talking faster. "I never told you—didn't want to worry you—but I think you should know. That horrible Gestapo Captain tried to rape me and shot my father."

Mitch nearly fell off his bicycle. "So that's why your father... You should have told me."

"Father managed to hit him with a fireplace poker before he was shot, and drove him away that time. But I'm afraid. The damn German still stares at me a lot."

"You should have told me sooner," Mitch said angrily. "I'd have killed the bastard."

"I was afraid you might try something and get yourself killed.

That's why I didn't say anything. There's nothing we can do about him as long as the Gestapo runs everything, except just avoid him. After the war he'll get what's coming."

"Damn. I still think you should come out with me. We could make it together on the Line."

"Oh, Mitch. You know I'd give anything to do that. But I can't. I just can't leave my parents—or Henri."

"Damn. No matter what, you must stay away from that Nazi. Stay out of sight."

"I have a little surprise," Renee said. Mitch could tell she was desperate to change the subject. "I brought a small picnic. There's a nice secluded spot up ahead. I'll show you."

"Do we have time?"

"Yes. We're only about fifteen minutes from Vire. That gives us half an hour extra, and it's better if we don't get there too early."

Renee led the way to a shaded place on top of a knoll with a view of the fields and farmhouses in the distance. She reached into the bicycle's carrying box and pulled out a blue cloth, two slices of bread, a piece of cheese, and a small bottle of wine.

"You're amazing, Renee," Mitch exclaimed. "How'd you come up with all this?" He knew wine and cheese were as scarce as real coffee.

"I have to confess. I bought them at the market with a little bit of the money you left with me. War or no war, the French always have their wine and cheese, and they aren't requiring ration coupons for the wine. My excuse is I have to feed Roger, don't I? Actually, he seems to be rather fond of the French diet."

Mitch laughed. "Well, I think I might very easily get to like it too."

While they nibbled on their picnic, Renee told him about Sir Charles' flirting and about his letter and about the mysterious buried steel boxes. "I'd almost forgotten about them," she said thoughtfully, "but they've certainly piqued my curiosity."

Time was running out, and Mitch wondered when he would see her again. Where would the war take him? He pulled her close, her head resting hard on his shoulder and stroked her hair. "I don't care where the war takes me, Renee. I'll come back to you. That's a promise. This blasted war isn't going to last forever." They kissed without words, and she clung to him. Mitch reached up and wiped the tear from her cheek. "I'm afraid we've got to get moving."

With so many things still unsaid, they arrived in Vire on schedule. There would be no time for more conversation. Besides, they would need to move quickly so as not to arouse suspicion.

Renee left Mitch on a street corner one block from the bakery. She pointed to a dark entryway. "You stand in there, out of sight. I'll circle the town and check for Germans."

Five minutes later she returned. "The coast is clear," she whispered. "Let's go. Try to look relaxed."

A fat lady answered Renee's knock on the back door of the bakery. *"Bonjour, Madame. Ou est Maurice?"* Renee asked politely.

"He's not here." The fat lady glared at Renee and stalked away, leaving them standing in the entry.

"She doesn't like me," Renee whispered to Mitch. "She thinks her husband is in love with me. But she's harmless. It's really kind of funny."

Renee found a clerk and tried again.

"Maurice will be back from his local deliveries any minute now," the clerk responded to Renee's inquiry. "Then he'll leave for Le Mans right on schedule." Even as he spoke, the bread truck rattled up to the loading dock.

Maurice clambered out of the cab and smiled broadly when he spotted Renee. "Ah Renee, Renee, I see you have another Englishman. He kissed her on both cheeks. Next time, maybe you'll run away with me instead, eh?" Renee laughed and poked him in the ribs.

"Yes, Maurice, I have another Englishman for you. But tell me, how's the Line working?"

"My leg's still working fine. I can't tell you any more than that. As for your Englishman—of course, I'll be happy to take him, but only as far as Le Mans." Renee had cautioned Mitch to pass himself off as an Englishman, not an American. Most Frenchmen were not aware of the difference in accent.

Maurice knew the routine about the extra bicycle. He would hide it until one of Henri's men could pick it up later. She would need it for the next Englishman.

Renee couldn't stand long good byes, so she kissed Mitch hard, turned abruptly, and bicycled away, pedaling like a Grand Prix racer.

"Lucky fellow," Maurice observed with a smile, as he watched her disappear around the corner. "Well, let's get going. I've got a schedule. It's about two and a half hours to Le Mans, and I must be back before dark."

"Okay." Mitch nodded. "Where do you want me? Up front or in back?"

"You'd better ride in back," Maurice pointed, "behind the bread racks. I've never been stopped, but some of the other drivers have been checked lately. You never know."

"Anything I should do if we are stopped?"

"No, just pray and don't make any noise. I'll knock three times on the back of the cab if there's a checkpoint ahead, but I'm sure we'll be all right. Incidentally, if by any chance we're searched, I'll say I had no idea you were there. So don't give me away."

That's comforting, Mitch thought. He looked at Maurice with a wry smile, but said nothing.

"One other thing." Maurice scratched his ear. "When we get to Le Mans, I'll leave you off at the back door of *Le Chat Rouge*. I won't be talking to you again. You'll ask for Lily. Say 'Renoir sent me'—Renoir, like the painter, but don't mention my name. I won't go in or even get out of the truck—don't want to be seen there. I'll knock four times on the back of the cab, and you can get out with the door handle from the inside. Understood?"

"Yes. Understood."

"In case you're wondering," Maurice said with a grin, "*Le Chat* is a *maison de tolerance*. I don't even know what Lily looks like— presumably a code name—but she'll take care of you for the next leg of the Line. I'll circle the block to be sure there are no Boche. I'll stop only if the flower pot's in the window."

"Flower pot?" Mitch was puzzled.

"Yes, it's our signal that the coast is clear. I don't stop unless there's a flower pot."

After scanning the surroundings one more time, Maurice wrenched open the rusty back doors. "Climb in. Up there behind the racks," he ordered. Almost suffocating from the overwhelming odor of freshly baked bread, Mitch squeezed into the far corner. Then Maurice shoved the racks firmly into place, forcing Mitch into standing position. Apparently Maurice liked to make sure he had a full load.

The road to Le Mans had more than its share of bumps and potholes, and seemingly the bread truck had been manufactured without shocks or springs. After two tortuous hours, Mitch swore he'd never look at another loaf of bread. Then he felt the truck slowing and heard three knocks from the cab. He stiffened. Damn the luck.

"*Halte, Auschweis, Papiers.*" The accent was German. A second German voice asked questions in halting French. The patrol seemed to know Maurice. They complained about the cold and were obviously unhappy being on duty the day after Christmas.

After asking the routine questions, one of the German voices said, "We inspect inside—new orders."

Mitch silently removed the pistol from the strap on his leg and cocked it.

Maurice sounded jovial and asked if they had enjoyed their Christmas. Then he opened the back doors and said, "By the way, I have some extra Christmas tarts. Would you like some?"

Mitch heard, "*Danke, Danke, Frohlich Weihnachten*—Thank you, Thank you, Merry Christmas." It seemed the Germans forgot everything else when they smelled the odor of fresh-baked bread.

The back doors slammed shut. "All right. Move on."

Mitch resumed breathing and kissed the Christopher medal that hung around his neck.

Half an hour later, the truck ground to a halt, and Mitch heard four knocks on the back of the cab. Apparently the flowerpot was in its place with no Germans in sight. Carpentry bag in hand, Mitch gingerly opened the back door, climbed out, and thanked Maurice silently with a wave. He hurried up a short flight of stairs, peered at a faded sign, LE CHAT ROUGE, and rapped on the door. A buxom middle-aged lady, who showed remnants of bygone beauty, answered the door and looked him over critically. When he asked for Lily, she hesitated a moment, and finally let him in. Mitch had the feeling she was an expert at judging people. I'd better not try to fool her, he thought.

"Who sent you?"

"Renoir."

"Follow me," she said without expression and led him to a small, empty room upstairs. She closed the door behind her, leaving him alone. Mitch thought he heard a key rattle in the door. He felt the knob and found it locked.

Equipped with bottles of perfumed oil, a feather duster, and a mirror on the ceiling, the room had only one piece of furniture, a bed. Sitting on the bed, Mitch waited.

An hour later, a key turned in the lock, the door opened, and a pretty, young girl entered. "I'm Lily," she said in a musical voice, "and you are ...?"

Not yet sure of anything, Mitch fenced. "Trout," he offered.

"That's an unusual name. I shall call you *La Truite*," she said with a lyrical laugh and an open smile, "but that really doesn't sound like a real name, does it? You will have to tell me more."

"Renoir sent me."

"*Madame* told me that already, but..."

"I was told that was all I was supposed to say."

"You know how dangerous everything is. We have to trust each other or I cannot help you. We must be completely honest. You will have to tell me exactly who you are and convince me you are telling the truth."

It was obvious to Mitch that this lovely girl did not belong in a brothel. Fresh and innocent-looking, she had pink cheeks and wide eyes that crinkled around the edges when she smiled. Mitch could see the trace of a smile even when she was asking a deadly serious question.

"Can't you just take me on the next leg without all that?" Mitch asked.

"No." Lily was emphatic. "They've been sending fake RAF flyers—trying to trap us. I've already said too much, but you came with the right code word, and *Madame* thinks you look all right. I'm taking a chance on you, exposing myself you might say, so now you'll have to trust me and open up."

"I'm an American, and I have to get back to England. It's terribly important."

"You speak very good French for an American. How'd you learn that if you're an American?"

"My parents came from Marseilles and speak French most of the time."

"I want to go to America some time," Lily had a far-away look. "Tell me about New York."

Mitch had to admit he'd never been to New York, except to board a troop ship, but he found himself enjoying talking to this pretty lady and told her about other parts of America.

Continuing to fence verbally for half an hour, he finally convinced her he was, indeed, an American, in spite of speaking French so well. She told him she'd never met an American before and wanted to "talk some more American—maybe later." Lily apologized, "I have to go back to work, but I'll be back. Don't leave the room under any circumstances, unless you have to use *les toilettes*. They're down the hall. But check very very carefully first to be sure there's no one in the hall."

Mitch thought he'd better get some sleep. He'd need it.

CHAPTER FOUR

1944

HITLER SEES CRISIS IN 1944; WARNING TO GERMANS GRIM

New York Times – Jan. 1, 1944

LE MANS, FRANCE

New Year's day, 1944, found Mitch following Lily to the Le Mans railroad station, carrying her traveling bag in one hand and his carpenter's bag in the other.

"Relax," Lily said softly. "Everything will be fine if you just show your papers and don't look nervous."

"Yeah, sure. I'm about as relaxed as a mouse in a house full of hungry cats."

"Remember, *Truite*, for the sake of appearances, we're not traveling together. I'll board the train right behind you, but we must sit in the same compartment."

"What do I say if they question my papers?"

"Just stick to your story. The fisherman's wharf in La Rochelle needs repair. No one will question that."

Boarding the train, they showed their papers to the French official with studied nonchalance. As Lily had predicted, boarding was not a problem. "The only serious inspection will be made by a *Milice* or a German when the train gets going," she had said. "Actually the inspections get to be less of a problem the further we travel from the war zone."

They found a second-class compartment with room for both of them, then sat opposite and tried not to look at each other.

Trains ran full in wartime France, and the other six seats in the compartment filled quickly with three German soldiers, an old Frenchman, and two middle-aged women.

Lily held her suitcase protectively in her lap, the only passenger who did not put their luggage on the overhead rack. Smiling faintly and staring steadfastly out the window, she managed to ignore the German soldier who attempted to strike up a conversation. When he failed to obtain a response, he flashed a toothy grin and offered a Gauloise cigarette. Lily shook her head.

Squeezed into a low-cut blouse and a short skirt, Lily could not fail to attract the attention of any man under eighty. In the full bloom of youth, she was not only pretty but also well endowed. Studiously cultivating her attributes, she gave the impression of being about to fall out of the top of her blouse.

As the compartment filled with smoke and the train lurched forward, the door slid open, and the German inspector gave the eight people a rapid, fishy-eyed glance. *"Ausweis! Papiers!"* he demanded.

For the most part, the papers seemed to be in order. But when he squinted at Mitch's and hesitated, Lily dropped her suitcase off her lap and asked in a plaintive voice, *"Monsieur, pouvez-vous m'aider avec mon bagage, s'il vous plaît?"*

The response was most gratifying. The inspector's fisheyes changed to a smile as he leaned over—unnecessarily far, it seemed to Mitch—for a better view of Lily's assets, and hoisted her bag onto the rack. Saluting, he collected himself and moved on to the next compartment. Mitch put a hand over his face and struggled to control his laughter.

German occupation had one salutary effect: the trains now ran on time, and the train from Le Mans to La Rochelle was no exception. Arriving at noon, they stepped onto the platform, and Lily put her arm around Mitch. "It doesn't hurt to have them think we're lovers."

"Sure." Mitch smiled and happily reciprocated, putting his arm around her waist.

"I have exactly two hours before the return train. There's a cozy little cafe on the waterfront. Would you like to join me, *Truite*, for a glass of wine?"

"Is it safe?" Mitch asked, surprised at the suggestion.

"Yes, no problem. The Germans won't bother us there. Besides, you have good papers, and if they should come around, I'll pull my blouse a little lower, and—well, you know—it's amazing. It always works."

Mitch burst out laughing as they walked to the waterfront a few blocks away. He could feel the coiled spring in his gut begin to unwind. Feeling a good deal more comfortable about the future, he was looking forward to a friendly chat with this cheerful, pretty girl. Picking out a table in a quiet corner, they ordered two cassis, touched their glasses, and talked as if there were no war.

The inevitable question. "What's a nice—and beautiful—girl like you doing in a place like Le Chat Rouge?" Mitch asked respectfully.

Lily's cheerful countenance clouded over. "My father was killed for helping the Resistance." She stared at her glass and hesitated. "My brother was sent off to a forced labor camp in Germany. I haven't heard from him for two years. I'm afraid he's dead too."

"I'm sorry. I ... I shouldn't have asked."

"That's all right. I hate the Germans, not just for what they've done to my family, but for what they're doing to France and the whole world. They're the worst plague the world has ever known. So I want to do something to help, and I'm afraid the only thing I can do is ... Well, you've seen what I do. The Escape Line has been busy lately."

"Bless you, Lily," Mitch said, raising his glass to her. "You don't know how much good you're doing. I promise to come back after the war and explain. In my case, you may be helping to save thousands of lives. But I can't explain now."

After two more cassis, Lily's tone became serious, "I wish I could come with you, *Truite*, but..."

Mitch reached across the table and put his hand on hers. "I'd like to t—"

She cut him off. "Of course, I can't. Too many people like you are depending on me."

"I'm sorry."

"Me too. Ah well, the war will end some day. Right now I have to catch my train, but first I must tell you what to do next."

Mitch ran a finger around the rim of his glass and nodded.

"I don't know much of anything about the next leg of the Line," Lily explained, "except you're supposed to go to the pier marked *Quai des Poissons*. There's a big sign on the end, just two blocks that way." She pointed toward the row of docks. "You can't miss it. Ask for Antonio. He's a huge, black-haired Italian. Say, Renoir sent you, and don't mention my name—*d'accord*?"

"We will meet again," Mitch promised and leaned over to give her a goodbye kiss. She clung to him with a fierce grip, and her voice went husky. "Goodbye, *Truite*. Don't go and get yourself killed. For God's sake, be careful—and good luck."

She had to catch her train.

As he walked the two blocks to Antonio's, Mitch could still feel the tingle of the kiss.

At the *Quai des Poissons*, an old man, chipping paint on his barnacle-encrusted boat, looked up from his labors and eyed the stranger suspiciously. In response to Mitch's inquiry, he muttered, "Antonio's not here."

Since three words seemed to be the sum total of the information extractable from old man, Mitch decided he would have to wait. Antonio was, no doubt, busy catching fish. Mitch moved out to the end of the dock and sat on a piling, staring out to sea. *What if he doesn't show? I don't have any place to go. I can't sit out here exposed all night.* Twilight began to settle over the docks, curfew time approached, and Mitch began to fidget. The old man disappeared and the feeling of being totally alone made the back of his neck prickle.

Almost total darkness had descended on the dock, when Mitch discerned a small boat chugging noisily toward him. He looked at his watch and realized the short days in January had made it seem later than it was. Ten minutes still remained before the curfew would start.

Antonio's battered fishing boat finally pulled up to the pier, and the fisherman threw a mooring line to Mitch. Without introducing himself, he called out, "Give me a hand with these fish."

"Sure," Mitch replied, first tying the mooring line around a piling and then taking one end of a heavy crate full of fish. After they had set it down on the dock, the fisherman said only one word, "Thanks," his eyes boring hard into his visitor.

"I'm looking for Antonio," Mitch said.

The big man finished tying up lines, then examined Mitch slowly and finally answered, "I'm Antonio. And who may you be?"

Mitch avoided the direct question. "Renoir sent me."

"I see," Antonio straightened up. "We'd better go inside, but first help me get these fish in the ice house."

After twenty minutes of fencing, Antonio grunted, "All right, I'll take a chance on you. Do you know anything about fishing?"

Mitch shook his head.

"Well, you're going to be a fisherman for a few days. We'll head out in the morning—early. If we have any luck, we'll sell our fish in Arcachon. That's where I let you off."

"Have you ever been searched by the Germans?" Mitch asked.

"Sometimes. They make random checks, but you have good papers. You shouldn't have any trouble."

"If we're stopped, is there anything I should do?"

"Just act normal. The Krauts need the fish, and they know I need a helper."

"Have you worked the Escape Line before?" Mitch persisted, remembering the close call on the bread truck. "Have you ever had any really bad trouble?"

"I've made dozens of trips for the Line, but no, I've never had any serious trouble. A couple of the other boats have had problems, but not mine. One of them was caught trying to make contact with a British sub. That was a disaster. The bastards shot the whole crew on the spot. We won't try that again."

At 5:00 a.m. Mitch woke to a vigorous shake. "Time to get going," Antonio said and added a nudge with his boot. "I've got some breakfast for you. You're going to need it. Fishing's hard work, and, believe it or not, you're going to earn your passage."

ST.-PIERRE-DU-BOIS, FRANCE

On the same day Mitch was boarding the fishing boat in La Rochelle, Otto Streikler was pacing the floor at SS headquarters like a caged animal. Von Kleister, now a Field Marshal, had told him this was his last chance. Heidendorff be damned.

The day before, he had stormed into Streikler's office. "Whether you like it or not, Captain, your SS company is hereby ordered to coordinate an operation with the Wehrmacht."

"Jawohl, Herr Marshal." Otto could argue with a general but not with a field marshal.

Von Kleister glared at the Captain. "The Wehrmacht will mount a paratroop attack on the *Maquis.* Simultaneously, you will attack from the ground."

"Jawohl, Herr Marshal."

Otto actually liked the plan. They would set a trap and attack in force from two sides. This time the pesky rats would not escape.

"But first," Otto told von Kleister, "I'll need to get an up-to-date report from my informant, the Weasel. He's a genius at sniffing out the latest *Maquis* moves. He'll pinpoint their location for us."

The weasel-faced ex-pimp had increased his price to five thousand francs, claiming the information business had become more dangerous. He did not need to remind Otto that the *Maquis* had shot the last two informers.

"Sorry I'm late," the shifty-eyed Weasel wheezed, out of breath. "They've been moving their base a lot lately, but I've got it nailed down now."

"You'd better be right this time, or you're ..." Otto did not need to finish the sentence.

"I give you the right stuff every time." The Weasel sounded exasperated. "But you move too slow. Now where's my money?"

After the usual haggling, Otto gave him half. "You'll get the other half when the *Maquis* are found and exterminated."

"No deal. I want my money when they're found. I don't have any faith in the part about exterminated."

Otto glared at his informer and grunted a response, which the Weasel took to be acceptance.

THE MAQUIS STRONGHOLD

The roar of low-flying airplanes shook the ground. In the midst of a meeting with his lieutenants, Henri leapt up and dove out of the tent in time to see white puffs. *What the hell is going on? Oh my God. Parachutes. German parachutes.*

The attack confirmed his worst fears. His *Maquis* had been expecting some kind of attack because of their recent successes. Had they been too bold? Had the sinking of six barges on the Orne been the last straw? The thoughts raced through his mind in an instant. *Now we have no choice except to fight. No time to run. Besides, the time has come. The Germans don't know how strong we've become. We can beat the bastards this time.*

Shouting orders, Henri grabbed his rifle, yelled at his lieutenants and alerted the camp.

Buried in deep woods, the *Maquis* camp should not have been visible from the air. But a large field ran alongside. *Damn,* Henri cursed under his breath. *Someone must've squealed. We made a horrible mistake, camping too close to that field.* He shouted orders, "Fire, men. Fire with everything you've got. No holding back."

A murderous barrage of rifle fire greeted the paratroops, and Henri watched at least two dozen paratroopers crumple up and hit the ground lifeless. Some fifty others hit the ground running. Firing from behind trees, the *Maquis* killed or wounded another ten and pinned down the remaining attackers, who flattened themselves on the ground. *We've got 'em,* Henri thought. *They don't have a chance.*

But just when Henri had convinced himself they were winning, warning shots rang out from his sentry on the west flank. With lightening speed, a full company of SS troops charged up the hill from their blind side. Henri gave the orders to take cover in the trees. Now half the defenders faced the ground attack and the other half faced the paratroopers. Suddenly, everything had changed. They were not prepared for a dual attack like this, especially against elite SS troops.

The Germans set up mortars and began lobbing shells into the camp. Casualties started to mount. Now outnumbered and outgunned, Henri realized it had become a hopeless fight. He shouted the order to evacuate.

After two years of hard lessons, his *Maquis* had a thoroughly rehearsed contingency plan for this kind of emergency. Each person had been equipped with an emergency pack, provided by the airdrops after considerable prodding by Henri. Now the plan was to scatter into the forests, hills, and swamps, then reassemble several days later at a predetermined hiding place.

Initially, the Germans took heavy casualties, heavy enough to slow them down and prevent them from following up on their advantage. The extra minutes gave Henri's *Maquis* time to grab their emergency packs and scatter into the woods. The French had the advantage of knowing the terrain and trails through the woods intimately, having occupied the same camp for more than a month. Unfortunately, the bulk of their arms and supplies had to be abandoned, but in their packs, they each had a small supply of food, survival gear, and ammunition.

The SS troops finally took up the chase and began scouring the woods.

Henri had known this day would come and had planned for it. The caves of St.-Pierre had been designated the prearranged reassembly point, but his scattered *Maquis* would assemble only after three days. He hoped the Germans would not be able to trace the movements of his scattered people and would not find their new hiding place, but he knew in his heart that was wishful thinking.

Serving as a hiding place for the oppressed and the hunted since the time of the caveman, the caves would now serve again. Because of the endless passages and different levels, Henri was confident the Germans would never be able to find them, much less dislodge them.

Also the caves would provide shelter.

Over the course of the previous three months, after the airdrops had restarted, Henri and Denis had scouted the more accessible parts of the caves and stocked them with a few emergency stores, including kerosene lanterns, candles, and dried food. They had known from the beginning that this refuge would be needed eventually. Together, they had scouted dozens of passages and caverns, carrying lanterns high above their heads and leaving a paper trail to avoid being lost. They argued at length about the choices. Would it be defendable? Would it have drinking water? What about toilets? Space for up to two hundred people? Would it have access to the air hole, their emergency escape hatch, which Denis and Renee had discovered fourteen years earlier? Finally settling on a large cavern two levels down, they went to work digging out and slightly enlarging the air hole.

"Anyone trying to attack will be sitting ducks," Denis had said a little too smugly in Henri's opinion. He grunted his skepticism. "The Bosch aren't stupid. When they start throwing grenades around, we'll probably have to retreat. Our best defense will be to hide and hope they get lost."

Henri sat on the limestone outcropping, out of breath. He had clambered down the slippery shaft with the help of the flashlight he had used in the past to signal Lizzies. Fortunately, some of his troop also had flashlights, supplied by the airdrops in the last year. Relieved to find that the kerosene lanterns still worked, Henri looked around at the gathering of worried faces, reflected in the flickering light.

"Any idea how many we lost?" he asked Denis.

"The Krauts caught three in the woods, Bernstein, Kaminsky, and a woman. I can't recall her name. Shot 'em on the spot. That's all I know about."

When the remnants of the *Maquis* straggled into the cave, Henri took stock. "Can you get a count?" he asked Denis. "How many have come in?"

"About a hundred. Looks like fifty or sixty are still missing, but more are coming in all the time."

"Any signs the Krauts followed us?"

"Don't think so, but I've posted sentries."

"What about wounded?"

"We've got two real bad ones, Lamar and Gignone, and about a dozen others that are minor. Rouleau's taking care of them as best he can."

Henri stood on a limestone shelf in the shadowy light and called the ragged crowd together around him. He felt the cool, clammy air moving slowly across the grotto-like chamber and heard his voice echoing eerily off the walls as he called for quiet. "*Attention, mes amis.* I don't need to tell you we're in a tight spot here. If you want to survive, you—we—will all have to pull together and follow my orders to the letter." He stood with his feet apart, hands on his hips, and looked around slowly to be sure everyone was listening. When the echoes died down, total silence greeted him, except for the faint sound of a drip from a stalactite.

He continued in a slow, clipped voice to overcome the echoes, "You must obey my orders precisely and those of Lieutenants, Denis, Jaques, Anton, Paul, Jocko, and Geezi. You all know the penalty for disobedience. If you don't like my orders, I'm sorry. That's too bad. You don't have any choice at this point. We can't let anyone leave. If the Bosch catch you, they would torture you and you'd talk."

He paused and listened to the silence. "Now, about food. Denis and I put a few provisions here some months ago—smoked meat and a few tins, enough for a couple of days. And you have some food in your packs. All, I repeat *all*, of this food will be pooled in one place. No hoarding. Anyone caught hoarding will go without. You know what that means. Anton will be in charge of food and in charge of rationing it. Today, as soon as this meeting ends, Anton will collect all the food. I repeat *all*. We will, of course, start scavenging on the outside right away. Denis will be in charge of a three-man team for that. No more than three men. That's important. We don't want any extra people wandering around and the Krauts finding us. Is that understood?"

After the murmurs died down, Henri went on, "We have a secret back door to the cave, and it must be kept a secret at all costs, so I won't allow any extra people using it. I will use it and personally take the responsibility of getting through to London and attempt to restart the airdrops. I know how to do that, but I don't want anyone else to know—except Denis—for fear of leakage. Paul will be in charge of water and toilets and will tell you where to sleep. There's clean water over there." Henri pointed to a small puddle with seepage running down the wall. "I've tested it. It tastes of lime, but it's clean and safe to drink. We must be careful not to dirty it, so don't even go near it except to fill your pots and flasks. Any questions so far?"

A jumble of voices reverberated through the grotto. Henri picked up the words, "fires and toilets."

"Toilets? Yes. Paul will show you. There is running water one level down. You will have to climb down this shaft." Henri pointed to the far end of the chamber. "And fires. Jocko will be in charge of fires. He'll have a three-man team to collect firewood, but only at night. Of course, we have to be careful about smoke. You can feel the air movement, right? From this direction." Henri pointed to the right and swept his arm to the left. "The fires will be in the next room with the smoke moving that way." He pointed to his left. "And as soon as we can, we'll set up a field kitchen in the same room but away from the smoke. Geezi will be in charge of that."

Henri shut off the meeting. "That's all for now. You've all got a lot of work to do. We'll meet back here at O-eight-hundred sharp. That means everyone. I won't tolerate any no-shows."

SS HEADQUARTERS, ST.-PIERRE-DU-BOIS

Otto Streikler exaggerated his victory. He knew his survival depended on convincing von Kleister that the "filthy rats" had been eliminated. The Wehrmacht could not afford to repeat such a costly operation. They'd lost over one hundred men.

But Otto knew very well they had only made small dent in the Resistance. If serious sabotage started up again, von Kleister would have his hide. And he was terrified that his true relationship to Heidendorff would be discovered. No question about it. He'd have to find the *Maquis'* new hiding place and flush them out—without help from the *Wehrmacht*.

He sent for the Weasel again.

ST.-PIERRE CAVES

For Henri, the first order of business was to get a message to Roger and contact London.

He called an emergency meeting of his lieutenants. "I'll go myself," he announced without leaving room for discussion. "I know the access to the house better than anyone."

Denis objected. "I know it just as well as you."

"No, Denis. You stay here. In charge. Everyone stays in the cave, except for Jocko's three-man team. No exceptions."

Henri knew Renee and Roger would be worried. They would have heard about the parachute attack and would be wondering whether he'd survived. So when he showed up at the back door and gave the secret knock, he wasn't surprised at the exclamations and hugs from his sister. Roger grinned, "Sure good to see you ol' buddy—in one piece."

"You too." Henri managed a tired smile. "How're the transmissions going, Rog?"

"Without an 'itch."

"Sure glad to hear it." Henri sat down and let the air out of his lungs. "We're in trouble, Rog. We need a food-drop *tout de suite*. There are nearly a hundred and fifty of us that are going to starve if we don't get food in the next five or six days. Here, I've got the coordinates written down—and the time—1:00am. It's got to be real precise this time. And it's not just food. Tell them we need medical supplies, blankets, batteries, candles, and kerosene—lots of kerosene."

"Can you carry all that? The food alone will weigh several hundred pounds."

"There'll be three of us. We have good packs. But you're right. We'll have to stash a lot of it in the bushes and make two or three trips. The coordinates I gave you are for a place I know well—a small clearing with a lot of bushes."

"I'll get on it right away—soon as the Krauts are sending."

*   *   *

Henri decided to allow only two of his strongest and most trusted men out of the cave to go with him. He needed men who could shoulder sixty-pound packs and keep their mouths shut.

Inside the cave, at fifteen minutes before midnight, the three men clambered over slippery limestone projections and climbed up and down steep shafts, a trek of nearly a kilometer to get from their new camp to the "back door."

Henri checked his watch. At exactly 12:30am, he poked his head out of the hole and felt the spatter of cold rain. In the inky darkness, they listened for any sound before moving. He wanted to arrive at the clearing only two or three minutes before the designated drop time. He calculated they would have just the right amount of time to reach the drop point slightly more than one kilometer distant. The cave was only half a kilometer from the Brousard farm and the SS building, too close for a safe airdrop, so Henri had called for the drop to be made in the small field one kilometer in the opposite direction.

"I'll go first," Henri whispered. "I know every inch of this ground. Keep low and, for God's sake, don't made any noise." He went ahead slowly, stopping every few minutes to listen. He checked his watch again and cursed the rain under his breath. The Lizzy would have a devil of a time finding them.

As soon as they reached the clearing, Henri started tiny flashes skyward with his flashlight. Two minutes later, they heard a faint whir in the distance. It grew louder for a long minute, but then slowly droned past, not more than half a kilometer off the mark. Henri shivered and cursed in a whisper. "*Merde*, they've missed us."

But two minutes later they heard the whir again. Henri frantically flashed the signal, and the whir grew louder. Then suddenly a dozen black parachutes hurtled down out of the mist. "Ceee-rist, they damn near hit us on the head," Henri whispered.

Back in the cave, morale had deteriorated badly before the airdrop. Some wanted to return to their homes and take their chances. Others just grumbled and made life miserable for their compatriots. Even Henri's temper grew short. When a contingent of women descended on him, demanding to be allowed to go home, he had hissed at them, "The answer is no! Don't bother me now."

But the next day, when the three men returned from the airdrop, their packs loaded with supplies, a cheer went up, and, when the drops were repeated, life in the cave began to take on an uneasy air of normalcy. The new camp became a small village with a kitchen, an infirmary, sleeping quarters, a mess hall, and meeting room. Toilets were set up in a lower shaft where water ran constantly. During the next few weeks, the "scrounging team" managed to smuggle in firewood, boards for tables, boxes for chairs, and straw for mattresses.

Anton offered with a smile, "It's not the Ritz, but it's better than any of the other camps we've had."

FISHING NEAR ARCACHON

Mitch discovered that fishing was, indeed, hard work. Sore and slightly seasick, he decided he would never choose it as a lifetime occupation if he had any choice in the matter.

Antonio confided to Mitch, "Normally I like to work alone, but your help is sure welcome."

Mitch quickly developed a deep respect for the big, muscular man who could handle the nets and lines that normally took two men.

"You're Italian, aren't you?" Mitch asked.

"*Si*, I escaped from Italy to France with my boat when Mussolini joined up with the Nazis in 1940. I knew it would be a disaster. You might as well know, I can't stand Germans—any of them."

On their second day at sea, when they had made a fine catch of cod and flounder, Mitch saw a gray shape emerge out of the fog, coming straight toward them at high speed. He looked up from the net full of fish flopping at his feet and squinted at the fast-approaching boat. He made out a swastika flag and a German officer directing his field glasses at him. Mitch felt his pulse quicken and sweat start to run down his chest.

With surprising agility for his large bulk, Antonio tossed a rubber apron to Mitch and handed him a sharp, long-bladed knife. "Start cleaning those cod and spread some fish guts on your apron—*vite*."

The motor-patrol boat pulled along side and snagged the gunwale of Antonio's boat with a grappling hook. The German officer stepped across and stood with one foot on the gunwale of Antonio's boat. He scrutinized Mitch and methodically surveyed the fishing boat, seemingly absorbing every detail. Mitch could see that he knew Antonio. After a brusque greeting, the German wanted to know about the helper.

"*Qui est?*" The German squinted at Mitch, struggling with his French. "*Expliquer, Monsieur.*"

"*Certainement, Herr Capitaine.*" Antonio wiped his hands on his rubber apron. "He's a carpenter. Doing repair work on my dock at La Rochelle, but the fishing is good, and—you know how it is— we need the fish, *n'est-ce pas.*"

The German, hands on his hips, stared at Mitch. "We must see papers."

Mitch managed a forced smile. "Of course." He pointed at his chest, his hands covered with fish guts. "They're right here, in the inside pocket." Liberally smeared with guts, the rubber apron covered his front from neck to knee.

The German wrinkled up his nose. "All right, all right, we'll check you next time." He turned to go, but then turned back, standing on the gunwale, straddling the two boats. He continued to look hard at Mitch as if debating whether to ask more questions. He finally grunted something about "dirty Frenchmen," signaled to his coxswain, and pushed away with the grappling hook. Mitch wiped the sweat from his forehead. He knew he must have looked guilty as sin with all that sweat running down his face.

On the third day they docked at Arcachon with a full load of cod and flounder. Having plenty of time to talk, Antonio had told

Mitch why he hated the Germans. "They took over my village, Gittorio—the entire town—for a military base. They ordered us out of our homes and stole our wine. The wine, you know, was our livelihood."

"Didn't they pay anything for it? They were supposed to be your allies, weren't they?"

"No, they promised but in the end they paid nothing. They're liars. That's what they are. And murderers. They shipped my best friend to Auschwitz, because he's half Jewish. I'm afraid he's dead now." The big man looked like he might cry.

Mitch felt the man's sorrow. "The Nazis are spawning hate wherever they go," Mitch said quietly. "I'm afraid the world will never forgive them."

Antonio went on to explain everything he knew about the next leg of the Escape Line, which wasn't much. "You must go to the Abbey of Saint Laurent. You can't miss it. It's on the hill only six blocks from the dock. Ask for Friar Gregoire. There should be a flower pot of geraniums in the window, right by the main door, which will mean the coast is clear."

"What if it's not there?"

"If it's not there, come back here, and I'll sort things out. You mustn't say my name. Don't forget and let it slip. That's important. Like before, you say, 'Renoir sent me.'"

Like a ray of sunlight, the Abbey of Saint Laurent looked down on the town of Arcachon from the top of a rocky hill. The cream-yellow stucco walls and bell tower stood in marked contrast to the cluster of gray stone houses below.

Out of breath from the climb, Mitch noted the flowerpot with faded pansies in the small window. He pulled on the chain, hanging along side the massive carved wooden portal and heard the deep-throated clang of a bell echoing from a cavernous interior. While he waited, he admired the exquisite weathered carvings on the doors, which were finally opened by a short man in a brown robe. Jolly, rotund, and bald, except for a carrot-colored fringe, Friar Gregoire looked like a character out of Robin Hood. He greeted Mitch with a kiss on both cheeks. "Come in. Come in. It's a pleasure to—"

Mitch thought he'd better give the password before this went any further. "Renoir sent me," he interrupted.

"Yes. Yes. Of course." The Friar waved his hand as if to dismiss any concern. Apparently he had already identified the visitor as an American. "Ah, *Monsieur l'Americain*, tell me the news of America. And the war. I hear so little." Mitch wondered how the Friar could tell he was an American. Was he psychic?

Before he could answer, the Friar went on, "Please consider yourself my honored guest. I insist you stay for a few days. I shall just call you *L'American*. It is safer if I don't know your real name."

"Yes. Yes, of course. But I'm sorry," Mitch replied, "I have to move on as soon as possible."

"You must understand," the Friar explained, his disappointment showing, "hospitality and refuge are the traditional roles of our brotherhood. I would not want to send you away too quickly, at least until I can provide some proper hospitality."

"That's most kind of you, Father, but I'm afraid my journey is urgent, extremely urgent. So I must ask, how soon can I move on?"

"Ah, yes, of course, you impatient Americans. Such a pity. We shall see what we can do. You see, we must wait for the next funeral procession. I regret to say there are an inordinate number of funerals these days. I'm afraid hardly a day goes by without one."

"Funeral procession?" Mitch asked, puzzled.

"Yes, you will join the next procession on its way to Lourdes. That's our system. I'm told not to vary from it. But since you are in such a hurry, I'll look into it in the morning."

Muttering something about the mad world we live in, the jovial Friar brought out two bottles of fine claret. He poured a generous amount for himself and his guest, raised his goblet and toasted, "To France, to peace, to America."

Mitch smiled and returned the toast, *"Vive La France,"*

"I must hear the news. We hear so little, and the Germans tell us nothing but lies." And so they talked late into the night.

After four glasses of claret and an hour of rambling conversation, Friar Gregoire finally got around to explaining the essentials. "The next leg of the Line will take you to Lourdes," he said with a slight slur to his voice. "I'm sure you know of it, the famous place of miracles. Your journey from here to Lourdes will proceed in three segments."

Mitch nodded, and Gregoire poured another goblet of wine. "I'll dress you in a black robe, and you will attach yourself to the next funeral leaving Arcachon. It will take you to the mission of Saint Mary, then to the mission's gravesite five kilometers from town on the road to Lourdes. There you must deliver the robe to Friar Jacques and say, 'Renoir and Gregoire sent me.' The robe will serve as evidence of your authenticity, and he knows how to return it to me for the next traveler."

At 5:OO a.m. the next morning, Friar Gregoire shook Mitch awake. *"Monsieur l'Americain,* it's time to talk. There is, indeed, a procession leaving this morning, but, *mon ami,* you must stay one more day. I enjoy your conversation. There'll be another funeral tomorrow, and—"

Mitch interrupted the Friar with a groan. His head throbbed from too much of the Friar's wine but he managed to mumble, *"Bonjour,* Father, *bonj ... oui, oui,* of course, funeral procession. Certainly, I must go today. How soon does it leave?"

Obviously disappointed at Mitch's apparent lack of appreciation for his hospitality, Friar Gregoire sighed and scratched his bald head. "I will see to it that you have something to eat before you go but we haven't much time. The procession will leave at six."

The gregarious Friar had one parting request. "If the worthy American could find it in his heart to make a small monetary contribution to the mission, prayers will be said to insure God's protection and see you safely to your destination."

Two one-hundred-franc notes produced the requisite prayers and a parting blessing. The Friar kissed him on both cheeks, made the sign of the cross, and added, *"God go with you."*

Frustratingly slow, the funeral procession marched like a herd of snails. Nevertheless, late in the day, they finally arrived at the Mission of Saint Mary without sighting any Germans. Like a stone statue, Friar Jacques greeted the gloomy marchers at the gravesite with a silent nod and immediately proceeded to officiate at the multiple burials with a mechanical drone. Mitch waited patiently at the back of the assembly of mourners and fidgeted. *I suppose there have been too many deaths these days. The Friar must be either bored or depressed.*

After the services, he introduced himself to the dour monk who, quite the opposite of Friar Gregoire, did not seem the least interested in extending hospitality. Friar Jacques snapped, "Who are you?"

"Renoir and Gregoire sent me."

"I see."

Mitch pulled off the oversized black robe he had worn over his other clothes. "I was asked to return this to you."

The Friar took the robe without comment.

Impatient to move on, Mitch would have preferred to find a friendlier place to stay, but it was getting late. "Can you provide me with lodging for the night, Father?" he asked. "And can you, perhaps, arrange transportation for me to Lourdes in the morning?"

Friar Jacques nodded without expression, turned on his heel, and walked to the Mission. Not sure whether this was an invitation, Mitch shrugged and followed. Fed a morsel of bread and a few grapes, he bedded down for the night on a straw mat.

The next morning, the Friar led Mitch silently to the rear door of the abbey and pointed to a wagon filled with hay. A farmer sat on the front seat, his head tilted to one side, apparently asleep. "Wake up, Andre," Friar Jaques barked. "I have a passenger for you." He then turned on his heel and shut the door behind him without looking back.

Andre sat up and examined Mitch, expressionless. "So, you need a ride?"

"Oui, s'il vous plait. A Lourdes."

Andre pointed to the seat beside him. "I can take you there, but ..."

Since that seemed to be the end of the conversation, and Andre showed no signs of moving, Mitch decided to try the password, "Renoir sent me."

Andre looked sidewise at his passenger. "You'll have to tell me more," he queried. Nevertheless, without waiting for a response, he snapped the reins and started the wagon moving. The two men fenced for half an hour as the wagon bumped along the gravel road in a southerly direction.

"Tell me more about yourself. Who are you? Where are you from? You don't look like a flier to me."

"It's better if I don't tell you too much. But I can tell you it is important that I get to the next leg of the line."

"I suppose you're right about saying too much. Safer that way. At least, I can tell you're not Bosch. Your French is too good."

"What I can tell you is that I'm an American, but my family is French. So I grew up learning good French. Anyway, I can assure you we are on the same team."

Andre looked at Mitch with a twisted grin. "You Yanks have a droll way of saying things—team—all right, I guess I know what you mean. So you want to go to Lourdes. Of course, that's where they all want to go. But I can only take you to the outskirts of the town. There you can join a procession of pilgrims."

"I've heard about the pilgrims. They're all sick people, aren't they?"

"Yeah. They believe in all that miracle stuff. You know—the water."

"Won't I stick out like a sore thumb? I don't look very sick, and pilgrims wear rags or something special, don't they?"

"Nah. They all wear something different. I don't think you'll have any trouble with the Boche if you're careful."

"How about *Milice*?"

Andre spat on the floorboards. "Those filthy bastards. They concentrate on Marseilles and Toulon where they can make a lot more money for their dirty business."

"What can you tell me about the next leg of the Line?" Mitch asked after he had listened to a dozen stories about the "filthy bastards."

"I'm afraid I can't tell you much. We've lost the safe-house in Lourdes."

"Lost it?"

"Yeah. Last two trips. No flowerpot in the window. Looks like it's blown. I don't dare go near it again. The Krauts'll have it staked out for sure."

"Anyone else can help me?"

"Sorry, *mon ami*. You're on your own from here."

Mitch bit his lip and muttered, "I've got to get to Spain."

"I wouldn't try it this time of year. The Pyrenees are rough. You'd better figure some way to hole up for three or four months."

"I can't do that. It's important that I get through right away. It can't wait."

"That's up to you, my friend. I sure wouldn't advise it, but if you insist on trying, you'll have to go west where the mountains aren't so high. Don't go near the coast. The Boche have that closed off, and don't try any of the main routes."

Andre slowed his pace, waiting for a procession of pilgrims approaching from behind, then left Mitch off at the tail end of the procession within sight of Lourdes. "Just blend in at the end," Andre said. "Keep your head down, and you'll be all right. Good luck. You'll need it. And God go with you."

Now Mitch must fend for himself. There would be no more safe-houses or friendly contacts. All he could do was stay out of sight as much as possible and follow the road signs to the Spanish border.

At the edge of the town square, he dropped off of the procession, moved unobtrusively against a shaded wall, and watched the mass of pilgrims streaming toward the Grotto of Saint Bernadette. Andre had told him the story. In 1858, a fourteen-year-old girl, Bernadette Soubirous, claimed to have seen a vision of the Virgin Mary, and the Pope had made her a saint. Ever since, millions of pilgrims had visited the shrine every year in the belief that the holy waters would cure their infirmities.

I'm afraid I'm not a believer in miracles, Mitch mused. But I'll probably need one if I'm going to get back to London in one piece.

Up ahead, Mitch spotted two German soldiers inspecting the stream of pilgrims. When he saw one of the marchers stopped and pulled aside, he ducked into the doorway of small shop. He waited until the soldiers were facing the other way, then moved quickly into a side street.

Now he could see the snow-covered Pyrenees in the distance and shivered involuntarily. He was going to need heavy clothes, boots, and a store of food before he could tackle those massifs. He moved further down the side street looking for a store that was not as exposed as those in the main square.

His thoughts were diverted by some enticing odors drifting from a *boulangerie*, a tiny hole in the wall. And the next hole in the wall was a *charcuterie*, well stocked with meats, olives, and cheeses. Fortunately these basic foods were not rationed in Lourdes, but they were expensive. At the moment, cost was the least of Mitch's concerns, so he set about loading up his pack with bread, cheese, sausage, and sliced ham. Next, he found a small clothing shop and bought a heavy wool coat, a wool hat, wool gloves, extra wool socks, and boots.

Two thirds of his money was gone now, but his primary objective, to get out of German-occupied France as fast as possible, crowded out all other thoughts. He would worry about money later.

Careful to avoid the center of town and the main roads, Mitch set out on foot toward the mountainous Spanish border, so near— actually within sight—but yet so far. He pushed on along a little-traveled dirt road in a southerly direction through groves of nut trees, which were unfamiliar to him.

Climbing steadily now, he felt ice patches crunching under his feet. A light snow dusted the fields, and the Pyrenees stared down at him like malevolent monsters. Mitch desperately wanted the most direct route out of France, but it was obvious the frozen peaks ahead of him would present an impossible barrier in winter. As Andre had said, his only chance was to work his way west where the mountains were lower.

He had come to an intersection, which had no signpost and hesitated, when an old man, leading a donkey, passed him in the opposite direction. Mitch touched his hat, "*Monsieur, s'il vous plait,* can you help me? There seems to be no sign." Mitch waved his arm in two directions.

The old man nodded and mumbled something indiscernible.

Mitch persisted, "Can you tell me where it is possible to cross the mountains into Spain?"

The man looked Mitch up and down and finally spoke, "You're not Boche are you?"

Mitch shook his head.

"No, I think not?" The old man answered his own question. "You know it's not safe to ask such questions. No one crosses those mountains in the winter, unless—"

"I assure you, you are safe with me."

The old man continued to study Mitch, finally answering, "Hmm, all right, all right. I tell you, but don't get me in trouble. You must go to the village of St. Jean Pied-de-Port. There's a low pass, but you will find much snow. Do not go into the town. Too many Boche. You must go around." He pointed to the road, which turned right.

"Is there a sign? How will I tell the road to St. Jean?"

"Yes. There is a sign. The road is about twenty-five kilometers from here."

Merci beaucoup, Monsieur." Mitch touched his hat again.

"It is forbidden, you know. Be very careful."

Mitch repeated his thanks. The old man nodded but continued to stand motionless and stare at him as he trudged off in a westerly direction.

Realizing he had not seen a single German since the two soldiers in Lourdes, he became bolder and waved down a farmer, driving a horse-drawn wagon. The farmer grinned at him and, with a looping motion of his arm, invited Mitch to climb aboard. He reached down and gave Mitch a hand up onto the seat, then, friendly and gregarious, he inquired about Mitch's business.

Mitch stuck to his cover story. "I'm a carpenter."

The farmer winked. "Sure, I know how it is."

Talking in riddles as the wagon rattled its way westward, the farmer made it obvious he knew Mitch was trying to escape to Spain. But neither of them wanted to admit the truth.

When they parted, the farmer looked at Mitch with concern, "Good luck. Hope you get back safely. I'd better leave you off short of St. Jean. The place is full of Bosche." He stopped with a shrug. Mitch winced. He might fool a German but not a Frenchman. He prayed he didn't meet the *Milice.*

Without a guide, Mitch would need to find his way through the hills around the town, giving it a wide berth. As he stopped and studied the surrounding hills, which were covered with a thin, white

201

blanket of snow, a smattering of flakes began to blow horizontally into his face. He pulled his new coat tightly around him, beat his arms together, and started climbing. Late in the day, the weather turned colder, and prudence dictated he turn back, find shelter, and try to cross the border in the morning. But freedom beckoned only a few kilometers away.

He had heard that the Pyrenees were crisscrossed with trails and inhabited by fiercely independent sheepherders. Known to hate fascists, the Basques had no use for their own leader, Generalissimo Franco, and virtually anyone else in authority. Mitch knew he would need help at some point, and the idea of appealing for help from Basques sounded a great deal better to him than *Milice* or Nazis.

Now he could see the town of St. Jean in the distance and the latticework of beaten sheep trails the hills. He picked a trail leading up a steep hill, which led due south and appeared to circumvent the town by about a mile. For more than an hour he climbed steadily while the air turned bitterly cold, and the snow blew harder into his face. Putting his head down, he continued to trudge up the steep incline. *I'm so close to freedom now, I've got to keep going.*

The climb became steeper, the snow deeper, and he began to stagger in the heavy snow. He could feel his energy draining, and his feet starting to freeze, as the snow seeped over the top of the boots. Exhausted, he stopped and sat in the snow, wondering dimly if he would get up again. At that moment, in the peaceful white, it didn't seem to matter very much.

Like a kaleidoscope, he watched the flakes swirl around him, reflecting tiny glimmers of light. His mind played tricks. *It's a fairyland. I'm not really here, am I? Is it a dream? I don't even feel the cold any more. I want to sleep. I'll just lie down for a little while. I don't care any more. But where is Renee? Yes. Renee. I care about Renee. So I do care. What is that square thing? It's there and then it's gone.*

But there it was, the faint outline of a large square object on a post not ten feet away. Struggling to his feet, he staggered over to the object and found it to be real, not a mirage, a weather-beaten sign. He strained to focus on the words carved deeply into the wood, ESPAGNE on one side, FRANCE on the other. The light was fading now, and the snow was blowing harder. There were no haystacks or barns in sight. Besides, he would have to find something better than a haystack if he didn't want to freeze to death. Squinting into the white gloom, he struggled to see ahead as the snow piled up on his eyelashes.

It was almost too dark to see anything, when he spotted a tiny stone hut with smoke pouring from its chimney. At least there would be some heat. Surely none but the poorest peasant would live in such a house—surely no Nazis. He staggered up to the heavy, weatherworn wooden door, pulled off one frozen glove, and rapped as hard as he could. His hand had lost any feeling, but the knuckle hurt like fire.

A large, round-eyed woman opened the door a crack and spoke some words in a dialect Mitch didn't understand. Then she opened it further, revealing a shaggy black and white sheepdog, which lay flat against the floor, emitting a low growl, its pink eyes riveted on him.

Keeping one eye on the dog, Mitch explained in French, as politely as he could manage between chattering teeth, "I am very cold, madam. May I come in" The woman opened the door the rest of the way and spoke to the dog, seemingly a strange command known only to sheepdogs. *"Entrez, Senor,"* she said in an odd combination of Spanish and French, and reached out to help him in. The dog stopped growling, but the eyes followed him like glue. Mitch could see its legs coiled, ready to spring.

Cold as he was, Mitch involuntarily wrinkled up his nose at the sour odor of old sheepskins as he took in the woman's homespun wool dress, which reminded him of a gunnysack. Her black hair, tied back in a greasy knot, and her shapeless body gave off the rancid odor of unwashed wool.

Speaking in a Basque dialect, the woman made it clear that Mitch was welcome. Without asking, she fixed him an unidentifiable hot drink and indicated a chair by the stove. Then, helping him take off his snow-covered coat, she managed to get across the gist of two questions. "Where are you from? Where are you going?"

Mitch avoided the first question. "To Madrid, Signora."

A kindly concern illuminated her weathered face. "You'll never get across the mountains dressed like that."

"I really don't know how I ..." Mitch rubbed his cold hands together. "I'm going to need help, but I have money and can pay—if I can find someone to guide me."

Without responding to the point, she turned and shouted toward the back of the hut. Mitch couldn't make out the words, except the name Carlos.

If the friendly woman had not been present, Mitch would have run away in fright. The man who shuffled into the room reminded him of a monster from a B movie. With thick, dark eyebrows, coal black eyes, and long black hair hanging below his shoulders, he looked like the legendary Sasquatch to Mitch. When he smiled and held out his hairy hand, it was evident he had never seen a dentist in his life. He towered over the tall American by a good six inches.

Mitch need not have been concerned. He soon realized these were the gentlest of people and passionately anti-Nazi. Carlos launched into a monologue about the terrible things the Fascists had done in Spain without even finding out which side his visitor was on.

Waving his huge arms like a windmill, he proclaimed, "Our Generalissimo is evil fascist, but he never control us. Never. Never will. He's just as bad as Hitler. My Basque friends and I do anything—anything—to help anti-fascists."

"I certainly agree with you about fascists," Mitch said with feeling, "and I'm most grateful for your saving me from freezing, but I must talk about continuing my journey."

"Of course," Carlos replied. "You are French? English? Doesn't matter. We help you."

"I'd be glad to pay you to guide me through the mountains," Mitch said, holding up a thousand-franc note. "Would you accept French money?"

"*Si. Certainement,*" the sheepherder replied with obvious enthusiasm. He reached out and felt the franc note and grinned. He turned it over, examining both sides carefully. It occurred to Mitch that the man had probably never seen a note that large and might not believe it was genuine. He handed it back tentatively, but Mitch pushed it the rest of the way into his hand.

"It is real, Senor," Mitch offered.

Not only would Carlos be happy to be a guide, he would throw in a sheepskin coat and homemade sheepskin boots, which would "absolutely, absolutely be needed."

Even though his sense of smell had been eradicated, Mitch found himself enjoying a fine mutton dinner, some good wine of indeterminate origin, and the strange conversation. But completely exhausted, he could barely sit upright at the table, and immediately after eating, he explained to his host that he must sleep. Carlos showed him to a pile of sheepskins, where he collapsed, instantly asleep, his nose now wholly anesthetized. Carlos had agreed to set out with him in the morning.

Carlos' wife, whose name sounded like Marka to Mitch when her husband spoke to her, prepared a breakfast of corn bread and lamb chops. Afterwards, she busied herself in the kitchen assembling mysterious items of food in a large sling-like bundle. Carlos fitted Mitch out with a heavy sheepskin coat and a sheepskin cover for his boots, which covered his legs up to the knees. Both were too large, no doubt originally having been sized for Carlos.

When they were ready, Marka gave Mitch a suffocating hug, crossed herself, and said, "Go with God." Then she sent them off into the cold and snow with the sling of food and a wide smile. Carlos shouldered the bundle and beckoned to Mitch. "Follow me," he said. He whistled and called out, "Gooch." The border collie bounded out into the snow as if it had been shot from a cannon, attaching himself to his master's heel like a magnet.

In spite of the guide and the warm coat, crossing the snow-covered Pyrenees in mid-winter tested Mitch as he had never been tested before. While nothing seemed to bother Carlos, Mitch could not keep up with the long strides of the friendly giant who would stop and wait every few minutes with a toothy grin.

Seemingly kin to everyone in the mountains, Carlos guided Mitch from one farmhouse to the next where he had either a cousin or an uncle or a nephew. But Mitch soon realized the most important relationship was that of their dog, Hooch. It seemed that Hooch was related to all the other sheepdogs in the mountains, and their welfare was the primary subject of conversation.

On the second day, a violent snowstorm forced them to wait out the day and a night in the cabin of one of Carlos' kin. But the weather turned clear and bright the next day, and they moved on, slogging slowly through the deep new snow. Carlos explained that the mountains in this western portion of the Pyrenees were only about forty kilometers wide and nine hundred meters high at the highest part of their trail. "With good luck," he said, "we'll be out of high country in two—maybe three—more days."

But the going became painfully slow in the heavy snow, and Mitch was forced to stop and rest at increasingly short intervals. Carlos would grin broadly and pull him up when he collapsed in a snowdrift. The two or three days turned into four. On the morning of the fourth day, Carlos stopped and pointed to the faint outline of a village in the distance, far below to the southwest.

"Elizondo," he said. "You get bus there."

Now out of the deep snow and cold, Mitch decided he could make it the rest of the way without help. "You have been a life-saver," he said, holding out his hand and five hundred-franc notes. "I want you to have this extra. I never could have made it without you."

Carlos shook his head and gave Mitch one of his toothy grins. "No. You give too much already. You my friend now. I cannot take." He put his long arm around his new friend, giving him a bone-jarring bear hug. "You come back after war—after bad fascisti gone away."

Mitch promised he would, and meant it. The friendly giant apparently did not like long goodbyes. He turned and walked away without another word. As Mitch watched the sheepskin-covered figure disappear back into the snowy mountains, he fished in his pack and checked his pockets. He found enough bread and cheese for a couple of days and seven hundred francs—just as well that Carlos refused his offer. He looked out over the high plains of northern Spain and let out a sigh of relief. *At least I'm free of Nazi control—or am I?* A light blanket of snow covered the landscape, but the sun shone brightly. Now he could now see the small village of Elizondo clearly, not more than an hour's walk away.

When Mitch stumbled into the town, the locals looked him over as if he carried the plague. *It's probably this smelly sheepskin outfit,* he thought. *I'll have to get rid of it, and I've got to be careful not to attract too much attention.* Carlos had warned him to watch out for German sympathizers who would turn in escapees for a price. With cooperation from Spanish officials, many French and British refugees had been returned to the Germans at the border.

So Mitch avoided any person in uniform, keeping his head down. He slowly wound his way along cobblestone streets into the center of the village, cautiously asking directions to the bus station, addressing only older, less threatening-looking people. Trying every word he knew for "bus" in French, he finally found an old woman who pointed down the main street and said something that sounded like "ootoobooz."

Nothing resembling a bus station came into view, but the bus stop was evident from a line of waiting people. Mitch attached himself to the end of the line. He had only a few minutes to wait, when a rickety vehicle, which could be mistaken for a bus, rattled up to the stop. A sign at the top said PAMPLOMA. Mitch had heard of Pamploma, a town famous for the running of the bulls, and guessed it was somewhere in the general direction of Madrid. For the hundredth time, he ran his fingers over the precious blueprints stuffed under his shirt and grimaced. *God help me find the British embassy. This is one hell of a lousy way to run a war.*

At first, the bus driver refused the French money—a one hundred-franc note—but he finally took it after all the other passengers were seated. He stuffed it in his pocket rather than the fare box, grunted, and shoved the gearshift into position with a frightening grinding noise. The bus lurched forward.

At the bus station in Pamploma, Mitch found an Arab moneychanger who happily changed his remaining six hundred francs into pesetas. He had no idea what the exchange rate should have been, but the wad of pesetas seemed rather puny to him. From Pamploma, he had little difficulty finding transportation to Madrid, paying his way on buses and eventually on a train, which took his last peseta. Within minutes of boarding the train, he collapsed onto a hard wooden seat and fell into a deep sleep. The next thing he knew, the conductor was shaking him. Mitch caught the gist of the angry words. "Madrid. Last stop. Out. Off bus."

"Can you tell me, Senor, how I can find the British Embassy?" he asked in French.

"Huh? No. Off bus." He nudged Mitch toward the door.

Sticking to non-uniformed, elderly folks in the bus station, he inquired in both French and English and finally succeeded in obtaining directions. His feet ached and he felt more like sleeping than walking, but he summoned up a last erg of energy and walked the last mile to the embassy. Filthy and unshaven, he stumbled up to the gate guards. "I am Lieutenant Mitchel Carter, U.S. Navy," he announced with as much dignity as he could muster. "I must see the British Ambassador on urgent business."

At first, he thought the guards were going to arrest him. He knew he must look like a bum and smell like a skunk. Besides, he had no identification except his fake French papers. The guard wrinkled up his nose, told him to wait, and disappeared into the guardhouse. Exhausted, Mitch sat on a cold stone stair step and waited a full hour while inquiries were radioed to London. Finally the guard returned, looking chagrined. "We apologize for the delay, Lieutenant. London has instructed us to assist you in every possible way."

Cleaned up and shaven, Mitch was invited to a private meeting with the Ambassador, His Britannic Majesty's Ambassador Extraordinary, Sir Hugh Montgomery Effington-Peugh, Knight Commander of the Most Distinguished Order of St. George and St. Michael.[7] Kept waiting for another half hour, Mitch was at last ushered into the ambassador's office, carrying the all-important packet of rumpled blueprints under his arm.

Piles of unprocessed papers loaded down the Ambassador's desk and two adjoining tables. In startling contrast to Sir Hugh's grandiose title, the office was anything but grand. Nor was the Ambassador. Dressed in baggy tweeds, the balding, rotund Ambassador Extraordinary rose from his chair and pumped the American's hand vigorously.

"My dear fellow." Sir Hugh exuded friendliness. "I'm so sorry you were kept waiting. I understand you've completed a most extraordinary journey. You must tell me all about it. But first we must have a spot of tea."

Mitch, surprised at his own irriability, tried to cut short the niceties. He began to wonder if the Ambassador knew there was a war going on. But Sir Hugh had a captive audience and felt it his duty to be congenial. He launched into a long explanation of Spain's complicated relationship with Britain and Germany.

Mitch squirmed uncomfortably while his host leaned back in his chair, steepled his fingers together, and lectured. "You may not know that Hitler had only one meeting with Generalissimo Franco. But in that meeting he made a colossal blunder—indeed, quite an incredible blunder. He insulted Franco, who could have been an important ally. As a result, Germany lost the opportunity to control the gateway to the Mediterranean. After all, Gibraltar has been a sore point between Spain and England for hundreds of years. And Spain is a fascist country. You'd think Spain would have lined up on the side of the Axis."

"Interesting, sir, but—" Mitch was unable to break in.

"As a result of Hitler's faux-pas, these natural bedfellows never got together, and Franco has never made the slightest effort to aid the Axis. In fact, he's allowed our embassy to actively assist agents— like yourself—working their way in and out of the war zone."

Mitch was having trouble staying awake, but Sir Hugh had just begun. A schoolteacher at heart, he liked to pontificate. "In 1940, Franco propositioned Hitler. He offered to declare war against the Allies, but there had to be a little quid-pro-quo. Spain's reward should be the post-war prizes of Gibraltar and Algeria. Hitler haggled and insisted that Franco already owed Germany a debt of gratitude for her support in the Spanish Civil War. He insisted Spain should declare war without any strings attached. But Franco was a tough negotiator and stuck to his demands. Hitler, not accustomed to being argued with, broke up the meeting in a fit of rage and never pursued the matter again."

"That's fascinating, sir, but—"

Sir Hugh again ignored the interruption. "Hitler's ego could not tolerate negotiating with the Spanish upstart. Now the whole subject is moot. Franco can see the tide of war turning against the Axis and is wise enough to stay out of it."

Without disguising his irritation, Mitch finally succeeded in breaking in. "Sir, I have an extremely urgent matter to get on with." In a minimum of words, he outlined his MI-6 activities of the last few months, then stood up, unfolded the packet of rumpled blueprints, and spread them on the Ambassador's desk.

The Ambassador blinked several times, sat forward in his chair, and leafed through the pages. "Yes, yes, of course. Quite right. By Jove, it seems you have something rather consequential here. These plans must be photographed—as back-up." Sipping his tea, which Mitch refused, Sir Hugh summoned the Sergeant-at-arms and issued instructions to have the American turned over to the First Council. "See to it, Sergeant, that these documents are photographed and the originals returned to Lieutenant Carter at once." He reached for the telephone on his cluttered desk. "I will arrange for your passage to England immediately, Lieutenant. If I'm not mistaken, the Halifax is sailing for Portsmouth tomorrow."

Radio contact was made with London, informing them that Lieutenant Carter had arrived safely in Madrid with the German plans in his possession. They could expect delivery in person approximately six days hence if the Halifax sailed according to plan. Also would they please put a coded message on BBC letting "Cricket" know that he was alive and well.

The next day, treated with the pomp and circumstance normally afforded to visiting dignitaries, Mitch was driven in the Ambassador's personal limousine to Gibraltar, two small British flags fluttering on the front fenders. Piped aboard the British cruiser HMS Halifax, a ship famous for earlier feats in the battle of the Atlantic, the ship's Captain saluted at the gangway. "Honored to have you aboard, Lieutenant. The Ambassador has filled me in.

ST.-PIERRE-DU-BOIS AND CAEN

Otto Streikler was ecstatic. He had captured *"Le Lapin,"* The Rabbit, who had been on the Nazi's most-wanted list for more than two years.

Le Lapin had fallen into Otto's net quite by accident. In fact, the SS Captain had not recognized the man, who had been caught out after curfew, until his sergeant identified him from the WANTED posters that were nailed to half the trees in France.

Otto immediately radioed Abwehr headquarters.

The response was overwhelming. None other than the head of German Intelligence, Admiral Kreigsfelder, flew to Caen and drove to St.-Pierre the same day. Otto, expecting some sort of extraordinary commendation, was deflated when Kreigsfelder simply ordered him to escort the prisoner to Colonel Baummann's SS headquarters in Caen immediately, but without comment.

Le Lapin's reputation was familiar to every German Intelligence agent and to every SS officer, including Otto. Known to be the architect of the Escape Line, *Lapin* was the only Frenchman who had control of the entire Line. In fact, he had expanded the operations to three entirely separate Escape Lines. If he could be persuaded to talk, scores of partisans, who had been couriers or had managed safe houses, would be caught, tortured, and executed. Their capture would lead to hundreds more, who would be forced to talk, and would, in time, lead to the virtual destruction of the French Resistance.

Otto knew the Gestapo's tortures would inevitably extract every scrap of information from his victim—names, dates, places, secret plans, codes—everything. SS Colonel Baummann was famous for his methods.

To prevent any possible slip-up, Otto decided to escort *Le Lapin* to Caen with a force of thirty SS men and three armored trucks. He would not make the same mistake a second time, where the SS had been highjacked and had stupidly allowed a British agent to escape.

Lapin, a small, wiry man with a neat mustache and a thick head of reddish-brown hair, had dark eyes that never missed anything. At the moment, he was handcuffed and held by two Blackshirts, one on each side. Otto stepped forward and gave a smart Nazi salute to the Admiral. His black boots shone like a mirror. His uniform was starched, pressed, and immaculate. "Heil Hitler," Otto barked, "Captain Streikler, reporting as ordered, Herr Admiral."

Kreigsfelder nodded. "At ease, *Kapitan*." Otto noticed the

Admiral failed to return the salute. "That is all, *Kapitan*. You are dismissed. Colonel Baummann will take over from here."

Otto, hiding his chagrin, clicked his heels, pivoted, and strode from the room, but found an excuse to stay at the SS station long enough to follow what was going on.

Le Lapin would not talk. He would not even cry out under Baummann's most extreme torture. Otto could not help but admire the man's bravery, but he knew—and he knew the Frenchman knew—that he would be kept alive only as long as he held back information they needed.

That night, after Kreigsfelder left, Otto returned to Baummann's office. "I see you're having trouble with this rat," he noted. "You'll have to be careful not to kill him."

"We'll get him yet," Baummann grumbled. "We never fail. At night we'll throw him, naked, in our coldest dungeon full of real rats. Tomorrow, we'll drag him out by the balls and increase the torture. He won't hold out much longer."

But as the days went by and the torture increased, *Le Lapin* gradually turned into a near-vegetable, numb to his torture. Baummann became increasingly infuriated and began ranting and shouting at his victim.

"Herr Colonel," Otto offered, "If I may be permitted." He waited, while Baummann glared at him silently. "I suggest we try a new tack. We must nurse our captive back to health and then inject him with sodium pentathol. This method never fails to extract the truth."

"Leave *Lapin* to me, Streikler. I'll get to the truth," Baummann snapped. "I suggest you get busy with *your* job. You're supposed to be out arresting more of these rats. They're running free all over Normandy."

Smarting from the criticism, Otto took out his frustration on the local populace. He began roving the countryside like a loose cannon, arresting scores of Frenchmen on the faintest suspicions of dealing with the Resistance. He obtained long lists of suspects from the Weasel, who had found it extremely lucrative to supply lists of "traitors" whether there was any evidence against them or not. Soon the Caen prison was filled to overflowing.

Unfortunately for the *Maquis*, two key members of the Resistance fell into Otto's net along with the innocent. In addition to *Le Lapin*, there was the Mayor of Chabeaux and Dr. Rouleau, who had made the mistake of venturing from the caves to tend a sick friend.

*   *   *

All of Normandy was in a state of shock, and Henri quickly heard the news. Alarmed, he knew that, under torture, the Mayor would talk in a minute, implicating dozens of his contacts. And he doubted the doctor could hold out for long. Half a dozen others, who had been supplying food to Henri's Resistance, had also fallen into Otto's net. They would end up in front of a firing squad. And, most important, was *Le Lapin* who could bring on the destruction of a large part of the Resistance if he was made to talk.

Henri knew there was no alternative. No matter how dangerous, they must engineer a prison break, and do it quickly.

Henri called a council of war. "*Mes camarades*, you all know what has happened." Henri scrutinized the circle of grave faces. "We have no choice. If we don't get them out, the entire *Maquis* will be destroyed. The Escape Line will be gone, and all of us are as good as dead, so there is no point in arguing about whether we do it or not—just *how* we do it. Now let's get down to business and figure out how to break them out."

After an eerie silence, Anton spoke up. "The Caen prison is a fortress. There's no way to break in, or for that matter, to break out. It's hopeless—suicidal. I say it's suicidal."

"Damn it all, Anton. You didn't hear me. I don't want to hear any more negatives. I want to hear ideas about how to do it. There's always a way. We just have to find it. Now, let's talk about the possibilities. I'm sure we've all been in the building at one time or another, haven't we?"

The prison was an ancient castle. They knew it well from pre-war visits, when it had been a tourist attraction. Complete with medieval dungeons, it was made to order for the Germans who had taken it over to incarcerate the ever-growing prison population.

Henri pounded on the table and glared at his lieutenants. "Let's start with what we know. We know exactly where the gates are located and where the German guards sleep and eat. There's only one decent section—on the second level. You can bet they're keeping it for themselves. We also know, from the few ex-prisoners who've been released, the guards eat lunch at exactly noon, and the prisoners always walk in the north yard at precisely that time. They're allowed an hour of fresh air before being locked up again."

The lieutenants stared at Henri in the silence. He could read their minds. *It should be obvious to them I've given this a lot of thought. They think I'm nuts, but at least I have their attention, and, damn it, they know I've been right nine out of ten times.*

Henri continued, "All right, so let's take a look at access—or egress if you prefer. As you know, there are two massive wooden gates, one on the north side and the other on the west. They provide the only access. And two watchtowers, one at each gate. They're manned all the time, but only by a single guard."

A bitter debate broke out, but Henri shut it off. Finally they stopped talking about the obvious dangers and got down to the business of hammering out a plan. When the options were exhausted, Henri declared, "All right, that's it. We have a plan. We know what we are going to do, so let's get on with it. It has to be done. We have no choice. We'll blow the north gate at exactly noon when the guards are at lunch. Then we'll keep the two sentries on the watchtowers pinned down with rifle fire. This whole business must take place with lightning speed before the rest of the guards realize what hit them."

They went over every detail a dozen times. "It's a good plan," Henri said, "except for one thing. We have to get word to *Le Lapin*, Rouleau, and the Mayor ahead of time. They must be up close to the gate in the north yard at exactly the right time, ready to run."

"How on earth are we gonna do that?" Denis asked.

"We need a volunteer to get himself arrested—on some minor charge. You know, it's been done before. He'll get let out in a day or two, because they're short of prison space."

Denis rubbed his chin. "Makes sense, but none of us can volunteer. The Nazis know we're missing from their registration roles. They'd put two and two together. They'd figure we've been hiding out with the Resistance."

Henri's youngest lieutenant, Cazzey, spoke up. "I never did register. I was too young. They don't know I exist. I can still claim I'm under seventeen and get away with it. I don't mind volunteering."

Henri put his hand on the boy's shoulder. "Sounds good, Cazzey. Can't tell you how important this is. You're on."

Cazzey smiled weakly.

"Now we need to invent a minor crime. What d'you think? You could steal someone's cow—or maybe a chicken?"

"Yeah, but ..." Cazzey scratched his head.

"You're right. There's a problem with that," Henri agreed. "It would take too long to be arrested. We need to do this right away."

"I could just walk up to the prison, act drunk, shake my fist at the guard 'n yell at him," Cazzey offered. "Call him a dirty rotten pig. That'll get me arrested on the spot—unless they decide to shoot me."

"They may *be* a bunch of pigs, but they're not going to shoot you for *calling* them pigs. Anyway I like it." Henri laughed and clapped Cazzey on the back.

It worked only too well. Cazzey drank a whole bottle of wine to work up his courage. Then acting drunker than he was, he staggered up to the north gate and shook his fist at the sentry on the watchtower. "Pigs. Dirty pigs. You damn Nazis are dirty pigs."

"Go away," The sentry called out, pointing his gun at Cazzey.

The young man staggered, jumped up and down and yelled more epithets in French, "*couchons, couchons Nazi couchons.*"

The sentry raised his rifle to his shoulder and shot into the ground a foot from the boy and yelled, "Go away" again. But when he wasn't getting arrested Cazzey kept it up until the infuriated sentry decided to shoot the drunken boy in the arm. Cazzey yelped with pain, clutched his left arm, and fell to one knee. The German called for another guard to help him, pushed open the gate, and dragged the wounded boy inside.

Interrogated briefly, Cazzey was written off as a minor nuisance and placed in minimum security to sober up. Fortunately, the bullet had passed cleanly through his arm without hitting a bone. His captors did not offer to bandage it, so Cazzey tore a strip from his shirt to stop the bleeding. He would need his strength to get to Rouleau, the Mayor, and *Le Lapin*.

Two days later, Henri and Paul hid under the back canopy of a horse-drawn meat wagon, as Jacques drove the rickety conveyance to the prison. Jacques sat up front on the high seat, snapped the reins, and calmly maneuvered the wagon up to wooden north gate. A second farmer's wagon, driven by Anton with Geezi at his side, was stationed around the corner. Anton would listen for the explosion, which would tell him when to spring into action.

Jacques, semi-exposed, sitting under a small front seat canopy, called to the sentry, "I have meat to deliver."

"You'll have to come back later," the sentry barked. "You should know this is not the time for deliveries."

Waving his arms like an impassioned orator, Jacques pulled the wagon tight up against the gate and argued with the sentry. "You do not understand, Monsieur. You do not comprehend. The meat will spoil. It will go bad if I do not deliver it now. Right away, Monsieur. Right away. I must deliver it now. This is most important, Monsieur."

Meanwhile, Henri and Paul, sheltered from view by the side of the wagon, silently attached the plastic explosives to the gate, lit the short fuse, climbed back in the wagon, and hissed, "NOW." With only thirty seconds to get away, the driver waved affably at the sentry, whipped the horse, and drove briskly around the corner.

Henri could feel his heart pound and his breathing stop. *Jesus. Thirty seconds is a long time.*

The explosion rocked the town, and even from his side of the prison, Henri could see the splinters of the gate flying a hundred meters into the air. Timed to coincide with the north gate explosion, and to create a diversion, Henri threw two hand grenades at the far side of the prison. The wagon picked up speed. In seconds they were out of town and into the countryside. They had chosen a little-traveled dirt road that led to a deserted cemetery.

Henri, Jacques, and Paul jumped from the wagon, each holding a bundled-up smock and a slouch hat, then kicked the horse into a full gallop. As the wagon careened into the distance, they pulled the black smocks over their clothes and stuffed the hats on their heads. Now, like doddering old men, they walked slowly through the cemetery along a path leading into a heavily wooded area.

Anton heard the explosions followed by shouts from inside the prison in both French and German. The three explosions had created the desired chaos. He snapped the reins smartly on the horse's rump and prayed that Cazzy had prepped the key prisoners. Everything depended on their being ready at the north gate. He shouted at his horse, raced the wagon around the corner, and pulled up to the shattered gate as hundreds of prisoners began pouring out like water from a broken water main.

For the moment, only one German soldier manned the watchtower to the north gate. Three sharpshooter partisans started firing and kept him pinned down while Anton and Geezi searched for *Le Lapin*, the Mayor, and the doctor. The other escapees would have to run for it and take their chances.

Minutes went by while Anton screamed the three names. More German guards sprouted on the watchtowers like mushrooms and started exchanging fire with the partisans. Anton nearly abandoned the rescue effort when he spotted Cazzey and the doctor clambering over the debris of the shattered gate, dragging a third man.

One of the partisan sharpshooters was shot, and more German guards surged onto the upper walls. Anton and Geezi threw the three men into the back of the wagon, jumped onto the driver's seat, and whipped the horse into a gallop. Amidst rifle fire and shouting, the wagon careened off in the opposite direction from Henri's wagon. A hail of bullets began peppering the road and the wagon. One bullet caught Geezi in the shoulder, knocking him off the seat, but he managed to hold on long enough to get out of range of fire.

Before the Germans could regroup and start the chase, the farm wagon had disappeared down a forest road with Anton at the reins, Geezi crumpled on the floorboards. By then, Henri, Paul, and Jacques had found refuge in the woods beyond the graveyard.

Now hundreds of escapees were running in all directions, and the Germans could be heard starting up their noisy command cars. Anton knew the command cars could move faster than his horse, but not much faster with their gasogene fuel. He calculated he had enough of a head start. The Bosch would never catch him.

Only when they were sure of not being followed, would they reassemble at the Caves of St.-Pierre.

ST.-PIERRE CAVES

Two days later, back in the relative comfort of the cave, Henri assessed the results.

They had succeeded in freeing *Le Lapin* and the doctor but not the Mayor. Cazzey had told the Mayor to stay next to him during the escape, but somehow the portly politician had slipped behind. Knowing the Mayor had scores of partisan friends in Caen, Henri entertained a reasonable expectation that he had escaped and found someone willing to hide him.

Hiding an escapee was dangerous business. In the past, hundreds of Frenchmen had been executed for providing sanctuary, and the escapee could expect the same fate. Nevertheless, after the prison break, hundreds of homes in and around Caen suddenly became hiding places. The Germans could not begin to check them all, and the local populace had become skilled at disguises and secret hiding places. Men suddenly became women with wigs and dresses. Blank walls acquired hidden access panels. Attics found themselves filled with old trunks having false bottoms. Hollow pits mysteriously appeared under basement floorboards.

The German guards were short-handed, but they had their *Milice* collaborators and dogs. Unfortunately for the escaped prisoners who chose to run into the open fields, there was a light dusting of snow on the ground, enough to leave tracks. Besides, it was miserably cold. Some gave themselves up rather than freeze to death. Others took to the forests with more success. Some even managed to catch a train out of town before the Germans collected themselves and started checking.

The Gestapo went through the town with loud speakers mounted on command cars, blaring, "Give yourself up immediately. Those who do not will be executed."

Word filtered back to Henri. About a third of the escapees had been recaptured and at least twenty others killed. But almost two hundred had made good on their escapes. The *Maquis* had lost only one of their men killed and three wounded. Geezy's shoulder would heal with doctor Rouleau's treatment. "We're damned lucky," Henri observed. "The Bosch would've caught a lot more of us if the tracking dogs hadn't been completely befuddled by so many scents. You could hear 'em yapping in circles."

Henri was unable to take pleasure in their extraordinary success because of the lives lost, but he knew far more had been saved. Many of those who died had been destined to die in any event—in front of an SS firing squad after first being tortured.

If nothing else, the all-important Escape Line would not be destroyed. But Henri continued to fret about the Mayor, a soft man who would talk too easily and say too much. He prayed the garrulous official had made good his escape. They had out-foxed the Germans more than a dozen times now, and he worried that their luck could not last indefinitely. Perhaps they had used up more than their share.

LONDON, ENGLAND

The thirty days since he had left Le Mans seemed like a year to Mitch. On February 1st, 1944, he found himself facing a haggard Charles Atwater and a starchy American General, Ian McDonald. Tales of "Mad Mac" McDonald were legendary. The nickname was one of admiration and respect, concocted by those who worked with him in the shadowy world of espionage and intrigue. But Mitch had never heard of him.

To fill in the gaps, Ames, now a captain, had briefed Mitch before the meeting. "If McDonald wants to take the time to talk, you can be sure it's important."

"Anything I should know?" Mitch asked.

"Yes, I think you should be aware of a few things. If I know McDonald, he'll ask you to volunteer again—probably for dangerous duty."

Mitch rubbed his forehead. "I'm beginning to think I should quit volunteering. Anyway, I'd sure appreciate it if you'd fill me in on what you know about the man."

"He was appointed by Eisenhower to head up the OSS in England. It was, and still is, a damn near impossible job. Until 1942, the U.S. had virtually no experience with international intelligence. We depended on the FBI, whose only real expertise was in domestic crime. Now McDonald is stuck in a brutal game of catch-up. He still reports directly to Eisenhover, who's given him the authority to recruit men from just about anywhere. He was only a colonel when appointed, but he probably has just as much clout as any top general."

Mitch scratched his head. "Any idea why he'd pick on me?"

"Yes. It fits. He has the reputation for recruiting younger men in preference to more experienced and regimented senior officers. He likes independent thinkers, who have the guts to disagree with their bosses."

"Welcome back, Commander," McDonald began. "You've had quite a trip."

Not wanting to correct the General, Mitch hesitated, "Yes sir, but—"

McDonald interrupted, "I've seen to your promotion—to lieutenant commander—richly deserved I might add."

Taken by surprise, Mitch responded quietly. "Thank you, sir. I'm honored."

He felt uncomfortable as McDonald leaned back in his chair and studied him. Was he being set up again? Sacrificed? "I'll admit it may seem a bit unusual," the General continued, "for the U.S. Navy to be doing business with British Intelligence and the American Army, but the fact is we need you. We're short-handed, and, as you probably know, the OSS and MI-6 are working as a team."

Sir Charles broke in, "I would like to add, Commander, MI-6 regards your accomplishments as most exemplary."

Looking slightly irritated at the interruption, McDonald continued, "Whether you're aware of it or not, Carter, you have become one of our most valuable assets with your knowledge of Northern France and the Resistance in Normandy. Further, I might add that Northern France is now our number one priority area."

"With all due respect, sir," Mitch replied, "I'm flattered, but I hope you aren't sending me back right away. I barely got out in one piece this time."

"No, we have a more important assignment for you at the moment. We—General Atwater and I—are assigning you to a special task force ordered by General Eisenhower. It's comprised of British and American officers who are planning the Allied invasion of Europe."

"The French will not be represented on this particular task force," Sir Charles inserted, "and we must insist on absolute discretion. The French—and anyone else for that matter—must be kept in the dark about its very existence."

McDonald continued, "Most of the task force will consist of high ranking officers, but the OSS and MI-6 have each been asked to contribute one representative. You will represent the OSS." It was an order, not a question. After an uncomfortable silence, he added, "I'll be quite frank with you. I would have chosen "D" for the job, but he is on a vital assignment and not available. You're the next best man for it."

Mitch stared at McDonald trying to think of some appropriate reply. Sir Charles saved him the trouble. "You will be briefed by my people on a number of details so that you are fully up to speed on matters that might have a bearing on the invasion strategy."

"Both General Atwater and I will brief you on our ideas," McDonald added. "Although you will be encouraged to do your own creative thinking. I don't want you to be intimidated by older, higher-ranking members of the task force. Nothing will be held against you if you speak your mind. Go ahead and argue your point of view. By the way, in all candor, one of the reasons for your promotion is to give you a little more stature in that crowd."

Sir Charles interposed, "You should be aware that your task force will be only one of several preparing ideas for the invasion. SHAEF[8] will sort them out. Also Churchill has had a highly secret special group working for more than a year on ways of deceiving the Germans. MI-6 has, of course, been a major player in this, and these ideas will be made known to the task force in due time."

"I presume there must be some extraordinary secrecy and

security connected with this?" Mitch asked.

"Yes, indeed," Atwater replied, "You will live here at MI-6 headquarters and be escorted to and from the meetings by two MPs for your protection. It's hard to imagine German intelligence infiltrating this. But the invasion of Europe will, no doubt, determine the outcome of the war, and they must be plotting every imaginable scheme to uncover our plan. I'm afraid your private life will be quite limited."

McDonald abruptly excused himself from the meeting. "Good luck, Carter. Give it your best shot. It's important." Atwater was left to fill in the details.

In spite of the momentous turn of events, Mitch had one other matter uppermost on his mind. "Have you had any word from Smith and Cricket?"

"Yes, we've been getting through to Smith almost every day. He's our primary contact with the Resistance and functioning perfectly."

"What about Cricket?"

"I haven't heard anything from Cricket. I was hoping you could give me some word."

"She was fine when I saw her last, but it's been over a month. I'm sorry to report, sir, I was unable to persuade her to come out with me, though she was the one who organized my escape through the Escape Line."

Charles frowned. "We did pick up one thing. Claude Brousard died. I believe he was her father."

"I'm sorry about Brousard," Mitch replied, "but I'm not surprised. He looked very weak when I last saw him. Did you know he was shot by the Gestapo?"

"No, I didn't know anything about that." Charles stared at Mitch, his forehead wrinkled. "Do you know what happened? Have the Germans been in their house? Is Ren ... Cricket in danger?"

Not wanting to reveal his closeness to Renee, Mitch equivocated. "Yes sir. An officer of the SS garrison next door got into the house, and Brousard tried to stop him. He was shot for his trouble—typical senseless Gestapo brutality."

"Does the Gestapo suspect anything—their connection to the

Resistance?"

"I don't think so, or they would have arrested everyone long since. As you know, they've been arresting thousands of Frenchmen on the faintest pretext. There've been house-to-house searches, but they've always left the Brousard house alone. Probably think it's too close to SS headquarters for anyone to be crazy enough to get involved."

Atwater paced the floor. "I don't like it. We should get her out of there. It's too dangerous."

"I emphatically agree with you, but she won't budge, and we can't order her. She's a lot more determined than you would think for a beau ..." Mitch corrected himself, "for a young lady who has everything to live for."

Pounding on his desk, Atwater snapped, "Let's pray we get this invasion started soon before the Nazis slaughter a few million more French men and women the way they did in Poland and the Ukraine."

Atwater's warning to Mitch that "his private life would be quite limited" turned out to be a gross understatement. The next six weeks, twelve hours a day, were spent under guard, entirely engrossed with the task force. General McDonald personally introduced Lieutenant Commander Carter to the task force, explaining his reasons for the assignment of the young man. He emphasized the need to keep an open mind to new ideas and creative thinking, and stressed his conviction that the task force should have a balance of young, fresh minds along with the experience of more seasoned officers.

The senior officer, General Smythe, opened the meeting with a review of the background and the ground rules, the starting point for planning. He explained that Churchill, Roosevelt, and SHAEF had already set the wheels in motion in the broadest terms. Millions of men and countless ship-loads of war materials were pouring into England even as the task force sat down to its task. These were destined for a massive invasion of Europe, but the exact time and place and a thousand details were still open to debate.

The General went on to lay out a few other prerequisites that were not open to debate. First, the invasion must take place soon, in the spring or early summer at the latest. The other overriding premise was the composition of the unified command, a decision that would later prove to be crucial—the assignment of a single supreme command. In stark contrast, Hitler had fragmented his command, not trusting any general to make key decisions. Rommel, von Rundstedt, and Hitler would all have to agree before any decisive action could be taken in battle. Intelligence reports from MI-6 and the underground had dovetailed on that point. The Task Force should consider ways to exploit this in terms of deception— perhaps find ways to leak conflicting signals to different areas of the German command.

How to deceive the Nazis was a key concern. McDonald had expressed his conviction the Intelligence Services were the best equipped to provide ideas on the subject, and Mitch found himself in the middle of heated debates. How to best use the *Maquis*? How reliable were they? What were the beaches like in Normandy? How well patrolled was the Verboten Zone? What about radio communications in and out of France? How effective was their radar? What ideas did MI-6 and the OSS wish to bring to the table?

Of course, there were many inputs, and Mitch did not pretend to have more than a few pieces of the puzzle. But as the planning progressed, the higher brass began listening to his ideas with increasing respect. Nevertheless, he was careful to acknowledge that most of them originated with McDonald and Atwater.

Timing of the invasion occupied nearly a week of their discussions. British Naval Captain Williamson argued that the weather in the North Sea was too unpredictable and stormy to even consider March, April, or May for the operation. He brought in reports from the British weather service and several experts to substantiate his position. June first would be the first possible date in his opinion. Both the British Brigadier and the American Army Colonel on the team concurred.

Asked if he had an input on the subject of timing, Lt. Commander Mitch Carter suggested they study the tide charts and the moon cycles. "Logically, the invasion should take place at full low tide when the obstacles on the beach are exposed, so the Underwater Demolition crews can blow them and clear a path for the main force. Further, I think we would all agree the initial landing should take place at the first light of dawn, so the invasion force can cross the channel under cover of darkness. After June 1st, the first date where full low tide and first light coincide is June 5th. Besides, June dates give us the longest daylight, which will be important to the second and third waves of attack."

Captain Williamson spoke up. "Yes, but we must have minimum moonlight for the crossing. As you know, our commandos and air strikes have pretty well neutralized their radar, so they will be depending on visual sightings from their watchtowers. Moonlight will be a major factor."

Mitch had an answer ready. "It so happens, General Atwater and I have studied both the tide charts and the moon cycles and, by good luck, the night of June 5th is moonless, the so-called dark-of-the-moon."

The only objection to this line of thinking came from the Brigadier, "Let's hope Rommel doesn't think of this too. Is it so logical that it is almost obvious?" After further debate, the group overruled the objection and agreed it was the best way to proceed. There would be other ways to deceive the Germans about the timing and location.

Among the hundreds of other ideas placed on the table and discussed, a few specific areas involved input from Lt. Commander Carter. The proposals boiled down to:

- The French Resistance must be mobilized to disrupt German communications and transportation. Mitch argued they could be relied on for the task if supplied with certain arms and properly instructed. But to avoid leakage, they must not be informed of the location or the date of the invasion ahead of time.

- Commando raids on radar installations in March, April, and May should be widely scattered with a slight emphasis on the Pas de Calais area to deceive the Germans into believing the invasion would be at Calais.

- Our own agents should be told the attack will come in the Pas de Calais area. If any one of them is captured, the only information extracted will reinforce our deception.

- The Resistance should be called upon to prevent the opening of the floodgates of the Cotinen Peninsula on D-Day. MI-6 had uncovered such a plan as part of Rommel's defense strategy.

At the end of six weeks, the task force proposals were firmed up and in the hands of SHAEF. Most of the group felt confident they had hammered out a good set of recommendations, but it was obvious to Mitch, whatever the final plan, MI-6, the OSS, and the Resistance were going to play an important role.

CAEN, FRANCE

The prison escape was the last straw, and Heinrich Himmler had warned them to expect a visit from his right hand man, SS Colonel Strassermann, known as the "executioner" by his many enemies.

Captain Streikler and Colonel Baummann sat silently in Baummann's office, waiting for the ax to fall. At exactly 9:OO a.m., the appointed hour, Strassermann strode into the office unannounced and glared at Baummann. "Please explain, Herr Colonel," he began with his usual deceptively mild tone, "How could a hundred and fifty prisoners escape and simply disappear?" Baummann momentarily looked away in silence. When he finally started to answer, Strassermann interrupted, "And you allowed *Lapin* to escape—the most important prisoner we've ever caught."

"I used every precaut—"

"I'm ordering you back to Berlin, Baummann. There will be an inquiry. You will be demoted." He turned to Otto. "Captain Streikler, you will spend no more money on informants. They are an expensive waste." With no further words, Strassermann stalked from the room.

Otto Streikler let out a sigh of relief. He knew he was as good as dead if he was sent back to Berlin. But the recall was for Baummann only.

Lately, Otto's twitching eye and shaking hands had been getting worse. They were twitching and shaking now. As he left Baummann's office, he thrust his hands in his pockets to hide his affliction. Along with every other embarrassment, he'd spent a king's ransom on the

Weasel, and now his main source of intelligence was being shut down.

Furthermore, Otto worried about the puzzling lack of news of Heidendorff. Was the Marshal still trying to kill him? In the past, Goebbels' news bulletins had never failed to glorify Hitler's marshals. But lately his name had not been mentioned.

At the moment, Otto was even more worried about von Kleister. Now a Field Marshal, von Klug would have the authority to ship him back to Berlin if he didn't succeed in cleaning out the *Maquis*. And then what? Heidendorff would eliminate him.

With all these worries piled on top of him, Streikler was desperate. Since he could no longer finance the Weasel, he decided to try a new strategy. He would turn to certain French ex-criminals who could be coerced to work with him. If they refused, they would find themselves back in jail. He would dress them in prison clothes, pretend they were escapees, then follow them and arrest any Frenchman who tried to hide them—but only after the scum had found out a few things.

The strategy worked better than he dared hope. In a matter of days, the prison was filled again, this time with homeowners who had offered to hide the bogus escaped prisoners. More important, the scum discovered a well-beaten path to the hiding place of Henri's *Maquis*—the Caves of St.-Pierre.

Otto's twitching stopped for a whole day while he issued orders like a boot-camp sergeant and rushed to inspect the entrance to the caves. By the next day, he had rounded up a small army of SS plus a squad of Wehrmacht soldiers and set out for the caves.

He knew the *Maquis* would be prepared. He'd been out-foxed too many times. This time he would be more careful. Scouts, sent ahead, reported back, "*Herr Kapitan*, we've spotted *Maquis* lookouts stationed along the path. They're hidden in the trees. We think they're carrying signal flares."

"Can we take them out?"

"Possibly, but they will alert everyone in the cave with their flares and more than likely disappear into the woods."

"Is there any other way in?"

"No, *Herr Kapitan*. There is only one access."

"All right, we'll move in fast and catch them off guard."

Otto saw the signal flares. "*Ach*," he muttered. "At least they'll only have a couple of minutes to react." He'd been warned the slippery rats would probably move deeper into the cave. If he tried to follow them, he could easily get lost, while the damned *Maquis* would be on familiar ground. The rats would have the advantage. But there was no going back now. He had to attack.

So Otto ordered the SS troop to advance single file down the narrow shaft, picking their way carefully on the slippery steps. They had brought flashlights, but hardly enough to penetrate the total blackness, and the progress was painfully slow.

A shot rang out, and their lead man crumpled and fell two hundred feet down a stalactite-roofed shaft. Echoes reverberated eerily off the dank walls of the limestone caverns. With no idea how to return the fire, the Germans pressed their bodies against the walls of the shaft and halted to talk in whispers.

Another shot and another kill. Firing wildly, they retreated in panic, at the same time pulling the pins on half a dozen grenades and tossing them blindly down the shaft.

Otto called off the attack. He would try again another day. *Next time, we'll come equipped with tear gas and more light. But will the rats fly the coop? I know how to fix that. I'll mount a guard at the entrance and starve 'em into submission.*

There was one small problem he didn't know about—the air hole, the secret back door. One other thing he didn't know. The grenades had bounced at random off the limestone projections, and one of them had exploded directly on top of Henri.

LONDON, ENGLAND

Mitch shifted uncomfortably in his chair as Sir Charles looked at him with a piercing stare. "You no doubt realize, Commander, you are one of only a handful of people who know important elements of the Allied plan for D-Day."

"Yes, sir. That's downright scary, isn't it?" Mitch replied.

"Yes, indeed. Now our problem is this: we need someone, who knows the ins and outs of the *Maquis,* someone to be on the ground in France, to coordinate and inform the Resistance. We must bring to bear their forces, ragtag though they may be, without revealing the time and place of the invasion."

Mitch was skeptical. "I think you'll find them better than ragtag if we give them the right marching orders, but it'll be difficult to push them into the action unless they know what's going on."

"Yes, but that's where you come in. They can make a tremendous difference if they can sabotage the right things at the right time and feed us critical information. As you know, we have other agents in the area, but they've all been purposely misled—in case they're compromised by the Germans."

Mitch knew that "compromised" was a euphemism for being captured, tortured, forced to talk, and executed.

"So far as we know," Charles continued, "our BBC system of communicating with the Resistance is still working. We could use it to signal the time and place of the invasion, but that option has been ruled out on orders from SHAEF—at least until after the invasion actually starts. It would be taking too much of a risk of leakage. That leaves us with only one alternative."

Mitch frowned. "Let me guess. You want me to go back in."

"Yes, but not quite yet. To minimize your risk, and to minimize the risk of your instructions falling into the wrong hands, we've settled on May 21st, two weeks from now and fourteen days before D-Day."

"Am I the only one going in?"

"No, "D" will go in from Switzerland. He's done it several times now, and we're comfortable with that. He'll relay instructions to the key *Maquis* in the south-central sectors, as you will in the Normandy. And we have two other key players going into Brittany and Belgium. Then on D-Day-minus-1, we plan to send in a thousand agents trained in sabotage. But they'll work independently with other scattered groups of the Resistance."

"What if I get caught, God forbid?"

"If that happens, we'll obviously have to send in someone else, but I'm confident it won't happen. We'll expect a message from Smith confirming that you've made contact. In any event, if you should be caught, you'll have a most convincing story. You will offer to become a double agent. Tell them all about the First Army under the command of General Patton, poised to strike at the Pas de Calais. They'll probably make you a national hero and hang an iron cross around your neck."

Mitch wished Charles wouldn't talk about hanging something around his neck. "And when they find out I'm lying?"

Sidestepping the question, Charles went on, "By the way, we've turned two Abwehr agents we discovered in London and persuaded them—in return for their necks—to turn double agent. They're busily telling Berlin all about the First Army at Dover and General Patton. As far as we can tell, Hitler is buying it hook, line, and sinker."

Mitch nodded, acutely aware that Charles was dodging his question.

Charles walked around the desk and stared out the window. "Incidentally, Patton doesn't like this very much. He'd rather be running the invasion, but the Germans regard him as our best field general after the way he handled the Sicily campaign. Having him sitting there with our mythical First Army makes the whole thing look entirely credible."

"I presume you have some details figured out on my assignment—aside from having me get caught and supporting your fake army idea?"

"I assure you, we don't want you caught." Charles ran a finger over the creases on his forehead. "We have an extremely important assignment for you—or more accurately a list of several assignments. In fact, it's written out. I want you to study it carefully and meet with me again tomorrow. I'll be interested in your ideas."

Handing Mitch a sheaf of papers, Charles added, "This is the only copy. It's top secret, of course. I want it burned as soon as you have read it."

That night Mitch had two papers to read. In addition to the MI-6 assignment, a letter arrived from home, written by his mother. The scrawled address was barely legible. Sensing something wrong,

Mitch opened the letter with trepidation.

April 30, 1944

Dear Son,

> *How we miss you and your brothers. We pray for you every day and count the days until you can come home again.*
>
> *Your last letter spoke of a promotion, but did not say to what rank or what sort of duty. Anyway Congratulations! I hope you can tell us about it in your next letter.*
>
> *With all your concerns, I hate to write to you of bad news, but I have to tell you that your father has had a stroke. The good news is he will live, and he is able to move around, but he cannot work. The stroke has affected his speech, and it is almost impossible to understand him, but his mind is all right, and he can write out messages. The worst part is the medical bills have taken all our money, and I cannot make the mortgage payments. I don't know what to do.*
>
> *As you know, I have never worked for an income, but now I must pull myself together and find some work. With the war, there are jobs out there, but I don't have any skills. Nonetheless, I'm trying to find something.*
>
> *I miss you very, very much. Whatever you are doing, please be careful and come home safely.*
>
>
> *Your Loving Mother*

Mitch's put his head in his hands and fought back tears. *Dear God, she didn't even ask for money. She's absolutely helpless. And father. It makes me want to cry. Of course, I'll help. She should have asked. I'll send everything I have in my savings by wire in the morning.*

He had almost a thousand dollars in his account. It would pay the mortgage for a year and leave a little something for his mother to live on. Mitch knew his brothers would not be able to help. One was a private in the army and the other a corporal. But he would write to them. Perhaps one or the other would be granted leave to go home for a few days. He could not hope for any leave for himself.

Mitch shook his head and tried to refocus his thoughts on the assignment from Sir Charles.

He read and re-read the MI-6 wish list. It was obvious to him that the high command expected too much from the rag-tag Resistance. Henri's *Maquis* was fighting for survival. How could they be expected to seriously disrupt German transportation and communications? The plan seemed unrealistically ambitious to Mitch. Furthermore, Atwater was depending too much on four or five people to set everything in motion.

The document was neatly set off with numbers and headings, apparently in the order of priority:

D-DAY ASSIGNMENTS, FRENCH RESISTANCE, NORTHERN SECTOR:

1) Telephone Communications.
On D-Day-minus-1, cut all telephone lines between St.-Lo, Caen, Cherbourg, and La Roche-Guyon (Rommel's headquarters).
2) Power lines.
  Same as 1).

3) Bridges.
  Blow all bridges over the Caen canal, the Orne river at Caen, and the Seine at Rouen. Panzer divisions based at Rouen and Chartres must be slowed from reaching the front.

4) Mines.
  Place "cow-pie" mines on roads north of Chartres.

5) Flooding.
  Floodgates in the Merderet area of the Cotentin Peninsula must be protected to prevent the opening of the gates. When the invasion commences, it is expected that the Germans will try to open these gates. They must be stopped.

6) <u>Deception.</u>

Every opportunity to reinforce the deception of "Operation Fortitude" must be pursued, leaking the information to anyone suspected of being a German informant. Even the Resistance must be made to believe it.

7) <u>General.</u>

Every opportunity to create distractions and confusion behind German lines should be pursued.

Tight-lipped, Mitch sat in the general's office. "What do you think?" Atwater asked. "Do you have anything to add?"

"I'd like to subtract a good deal," Mitch replied with conviction, "but I suppose we can only do our best, and, of course, I can only work with Henri's *Maquis* and the forces in the Somme. To answer your question, I certainly don't want to add anything. It seems to be well thought out in spite of being too much."

"SHAEF realizes this is a tall order, but every piece of it that can be accomplished will save Allied lives and shorten the war. Now let's go over these maps and aerial photos. You must study them—commit them to memory. You have forty-eight hours."

"I'll give it my best, sir. By the way, have you had any reports lately on the strength of Henri's *Maquis* in Normandy?"

"Yes, it doesn't look too encouraging. The latest report from Smith says their main force is holed up in the St.-Pierre caves and is being attacked by the SS. Also he reports that Henri has been seriously wounded, and his lieutenant, Denis LeCoc, has taken command."

"That's terrible," Mitch replied. "Henri's been the brains behind the whole thing. Renee must be worried sick. First her father, and now her brother."

"The only good part of it," Charles said, "is they've managed to inflict heavy casualties on the SS and the SS hasn't been able to pry them loose. Those caves go for miles in all directions and down several levels. It's virtually impossible to root them out—unless the Germans resort to poison gas. Thank God they haven't done that yet."

"What about tear gas?" Mitch asked.

"Smith says they've tried tear gas, but there's a constant air movement that blows the gas back toward the attackers. The caves are so immense the defenders just move back and wait for the gas to clear. Incidentally, we've dropped some gas masks in case they need them."

"How do the *Maquis* get out of the caves and pick up our airdrops—or, for that matter, get messages to Smith?"

"Apparently there's more than one entrance—some kind of air shaft—and the SS haven't figured that out yet."

"Are we getting our supplies through to them? And weapons? Can I count on some firepower? We'll need it if we're going to accomplish any of this list of yours."

"Yes, to all your questions, and you should know their cadre has grown to nearly two thousand, counting the *Somme Maquis*. That's partly because of the successful prison break and partly because the SS has been threatening to arrest everybody in sight. It's stupid of them. They're turning the whole province into a support-the-Resistance army."

"The SS aren't going to take it lying down," Mitch pointed out. "They'll line up the villagers and start shooting them."

"I know, but the invasion is only one month away now, and the Resistance is going to play an important part. The French in Normandy are so bitter now that nothing will stop them. You'll have plenty of cooperation."

"I certainly hope you're right. So how do you propose I get in this time? I can tell you I don't like the beach route by either Shelburne or sub."

"McDonald and I have discussed that. You're a key player. We don't want to lose you."

"I'm certainly pleased to hear that."

Ignoring the trace of sarcasm, Charles went on, "The remaining options boil down to Lizzy or parachute. We think parachute is best. Do you have a preference?"

"Parachute sounds okay. There are plenty of open fields in Normandy, but I'd like to be met. I assume you can arrange it."

NORMANDY

On May 21st, 1944, 1:OO a.m., Mitch found himself floating down onto a Normandy cornfield. By the faint light of a new moon, he could see the soft finger-high corn shoots rising up toward him— just right for a comfortable landing.

He spotted the all-clear signal, five pinpoint flashes repeated twice, from the partisans waiting for him in the copse at the edge of the field. The rendezvous was going according to plan.

Two men, dressed in black, waited until Mitch hit the ground, then ran to meet him. With their help, the chute was disentangled and buried in a matter of seconds, the ground smoothed over, and a few corn plants pushed back upright. Not until they reached the cover of the trees did they introduce themselves, shake hands, and hug French style. "We've got to move out of here *vite*," the tall one said. "The Krauts have been tracking parachutes lately, sometimes with dogs."

"In that case, I think I'll take a pee," Mitch said, briefly explaining the theory. They nodded in agreement.

The men had specific instructions. They were to escort "Trout" to the caves by the "back door" about two kilometers distant. Walking silently around the edges of the fields to avoid exposure, Mitch started to recognize the familiar countryside in the faint moonlight. Despite the dangers, he found himself enjoying the beautiful spring night. The wild flowers, twinkling in the moonlight, caused his mind to wander, and visions of strolling through these fields with Renee invaded his thoughts.

His reveries were broken when three short light flashes in the distance were answered by his escort, who explained in a whisper, "Three means all clear. Two means stay away."

A man in black stepped out of the shadows. "This way. Hurry. Keep low. Follow me." The voice was barely audible. He took Mitch's arm and stepped back into the shadows, in reality a dense bramble bush, then slid sideways and wriggled down into a hole about the diameter of a garbage can. "Follow me," he repeated and shone his flashlight on crude steps cut into the wall of a limestone shaft.

Thirty feet down, they reached a wide chamber where they stopped and stared at each other. Mitch recognized the man in black, Denis LeCoc. Denis greeted Mitch like a long-lost brother, hugging him, but speaking in whispers. He handed Mitch a flashlight. "Welcome to our home-sweet-home, Mitch. First off, we've got a ways to go. Then we can talk. Watch your step—your head too. You'll have to duck around a lot of these stone daggers hanging down all over the place," he said, pointing to a dozen stalactites, "and it's slippery." He led Mitch down a long, wet shaft, cautiously picking his way down the steps cut into the walls, then along a slippery corridor and through one cavern after another. Half an hour later, they came to an immense cathedral-like room full of boxes, bags, bottles, and crates.

Wide-eyed, Mitch took in the rows of mortars, rifles, mines, gas masks, and stacks of canned goods, all neatly stacked. Next, Denis led the way to a regular field kitchen where the odors reminded him of home cooking. "Believe it or not," Denis declared with a broad smile, "we can offer you tea and all the fixin's."

"Sounds good to me, Denis. Looks like you've got everything in pretty good shape here."

"Like a cigarette?" Denis extended a pack of Parliaments.

"No thanks. Never liked the things."

It was now 3:OO a.m., and Mitch knew he should be catching up on his sleep, but he had too many things on his mind. While the others slept, the two men sat down at a makeshift table and parlayed.

Denis lit a Parliament and blew smoke at the ceiling.

"First of all, how's Henri," Mitch asked. "Can I see him?"

Denis' face hardened. "He's in terrible shape—completely torn apart by a grenade when the SS tried to storm the cave. I'm afraid he's not going to make it."

"Shouldn't we get him to a doctor?"

"Actually we have one of the best doctors in the province right here. You remember Doctor Rouleau, don't you? Helped you escape from the SS. After that, he had to go underground. Now, with the supplies dropped by the British, he's set up a regular hospital, right here in the caves."

"I'd still like to see Henri," Mitch insisted.

"You can if you wish, but he's unconscious, all doped up with morphine. At least he's not in pain. Even if he lives, which I doubt, he'll be a paraplegic. I hate to say it, but it'd be better if he dies."

Mitch scrutinized Denis as if he were seeing him for the first time. Now the leader of a small army, on which so much would depend, he would need to demonstrate extraordinary leadership. It would be an enormous challenge to hold this rag-tag group together and carry out the assignments that were about to be piled on him. Mitch saw a medium-sized man with a medium-sized intellect. But the open expression, the square features, and the firm jaw told of loyalty, honesty, and reliability. Perhaps these traits were just as important as brilliance at this point.

"What about Renee and Smith?" Mitch asked.

"They're okay. We've been contacting them regularly. You knew Claude died, didn't you?"

"Yes, it's God awful," Mitch said with emotion. "Renee's lost both her father and now her brother. She must be a wreck."

"True, but she's strong. And when you think about it, half the families in France have suffered as much or worse."

Short on time, Mitch changed the subject. "Denis, the reason I'm here is to lay out a mission—an extremely important mission— for you and your men. You will have a key role in the coming invasion."

For the next hour Mitch outlined the mission, covering the cardinal points and emphasizing the importance of secrecy. Exhausted, he cut short the conversation. "We'll go over the details in the morning, Denis. Right now, I want to see Henri."

Denis sighed, nodded, and led Mitch to another cavern where four men lay on cots in bandages and splints. The first was Henri, almost unrecognizable. Mitch tried to speak to him, but there was no response, his mouth agape, the eyes staring into space. Denis shook his head, "We've got to get some sleep, Mitch. You look beat. We'll call together the Council in the morning—and talk."

Remembering most of the lieutenants from his previous training sessions, Mitch was relieved to find that none, besides Henri, had been killed in either the attack on the cave or the battle with the paratroopers.

Denis explained with obvious satisfaction, "Our forces have grown to almost eight hundred. Now we outnumber the SS about two to one and we are pretty well armed, thanks to the airdrops and your training. The Bosch'll think twice about attacking again unless the Wehrmacht can be brought into it in force." Denis puffed on his cigarette and consulted the ceiling. "Of course, that's a possibility, but we've heard the talk in the village. The Wehrmacht detests the SS. There's no doubt they both want to get rid of us, but they just can't work together."

"In that case," Mitch said, "we'd better not stir up that particular hornet's nest until the invasion starts. We want them to leave you alone for now. You must be at full force for the really important action on D-Day."

"We have a million questions," Denis said. "Can't you give us any idea of when or where the invasion will be."

"Sorry. I can't tell you that, because everything depends on secrecy. There's always a chance of a leak, even from the most loyal partisan."

Jacques spoke up. "How are we supposed to know when or where to attack, if we're kept in the dark?"

"The reason I'm here is not to tell you *when or where*, but rather to tell you *how to know* when the time comes. Also I'm here to give you an understanding of where we need your help when it comes. I can tell you this much, "It's coming soon. There will be a signal on BBC twenty-four hours before the landings, but the shape of the signal will be given only to Denis, which you, Denis, must guard with your life. I can't talk about the time and place of the invasion, but I can go over your targets worked out by London. Again, I am only authorized to give the specific targets to Denis at this juncture. The rest of you will be queued in by Denis at the right time."

"Why don't they trust us?" Jacques grumbled. "We're the ones putting our lives on the line."

"The exact time and place of the invasion is one of the most tightly held secrets of all time. Even a lot of Allied generals don't know it yet. The Allied high command is putting a lot of faith and trust in you, and they want you to be full-fledged partners when the time comes, but I'm sure you can see why it has to be secret. Let me say this: for God's sake, Denis, don't take any special risks for a while. Everything depends on you being healthy and in command."

"Of course. I—we understand," Denis murmured.

"I'll tell you the signal and go over the details one more time when we're alone," Mitch said, "just before I leave for the Somme."

Denis looked puzzled. "Why the Somme?"

"As soon as I've gone over this with you, I've got to move on to the *Maquis* in the Somme and give them instructions for sabotage in the Calais area."

Mitch knew this was simply a deception of his own people, but the Somme *Maquis* did, indeed, represent a considerable force. He had to follow through with the ruse.

Denis led Mitch to an empty cavern where they could talk in complete secrecy.

"The first order of business for you," Mitch said, "is to assign a few men to the flood gates at Merderet. If the Germans succeed in opening them, it'll cause more trouble for the Allies than a division of Panzers."

Denis nodded. "Yes, we know all about them. We've been worried about that."

"Good. Our Intelligence has learned the Germans plan to flood the Cotentin Peninsula when the invasion begins," Mitch explained, "but we believe they'll send only a few men, crank open the gate valves, and go away. They won't want to get half drowned. So the way I see it, your men can wait until they've gone and then crank them closed again—if you're quick about it. They won't realize what's happened for several hours. By then our paratroops will have landed."

Denis stared into space and blew half a dozen smoke rings. "I think ..." he began, then shrugged, "I guess you're right. We should be able to handle it."

"If they come back and do it again or try to blow them up," Mitch continued, "you'll have to put up a fight. But I don't think it'll come to that. The odds are they won't touch the gates until they're convinced the invasion has actually started. After all, it would make a mess of their own operations. But our intelligence intercepts tell us it's definitely one of their plans—after the invasion gets under way."

Going over the other assignments item by item, Mitch emphasized, "Most of your actions will start only when the invasion actually begins. You mustn't tip off the Germans. That's important."

"We ought to be able to make some of the preparations ahead of time, like hiding mines and explosives near the targets."

"Okay, but remember, you won't know yourself when it's coming until twenty-four beforehand, so don't start anything suspicious until then."

"One other thing we could start early," Denis offered. "We can mess up their telephones. A lot of the connection boxes are scattered around outdoors, and we've become quite expert at crossing wires, so they get a lot of wrong numbers."

"Sounds good, but the Allied command wants you to wait until the day before the invasion, so they don't have time to straighten them out. And concentrate on the ones near La Roche-Guyon and Caen."

"We've discovered that cut wires are usually repaired in a few hours," Denis observed, "but it takes them days or even weeks to realign the scrambled wires. They're never sure whether it's sabotage or just a bad installation in the first place."

The list of assignments was growing long and complicated, but Mitch could see that Denis and his lieutenants were not at all dismayed. In fact, they were obviously excited. The idea that the invasion was finally coming, and that they would be important players, was intoxicating to those who had waited so long.

"Will you be making contact with Smith?" Mitch asked.

Denis nodded. "Yes, of course. We contact him regularly—once a week. In fact, our next contact will be in three days."

"Try to get to him tomorrow. It's important, but send one of your lieutenants. Like I said, we don't want you taking any risks right now. Tell Roger to radio London that I've successfully passed instructions on to you and that I'm on my way to the Somme."

After reviewing everything one more time, Mitch asked for a guide. He would need to leave tomorrow and try to reach the Somme *Maquis* in no more than three days. After that, he needed to make contact with the *Maire de Chabeaux* if anyone knew his whereabouts.

Denis tapped his forehead. "I have just the man you want."

"Does he know the Somme?"

"Yeah, for sure. His name is Raoul, the perfect guide for you. Grew up in the backwaters. Knows the lay of the land, but more important, he knows the vegetable barges."

"Vegetable barges?"

"Yes, that's how you get to the Somme *Maquis*. The Germans need the vegetables. They have no reason to suspect the barges of working for the Resistance, and, so far, they've ignored them. Besides, with hundreds of waterways connecting the main river, there's no way the Germans can patrol them."

Bidding Denis *adieu and bonne chance*, Mitch revealed the secret signal for D-Day—listen for the strains of the "Autumn Song" on BBC. "Don't fail to listen absolutely every night at 6:00pm and 9:00pm Twenty-four hours after it is broadcast, the invasion will begin. Now, hang in there, Denis. France is going to be free soon."

THE SOMME

Still in possession of the travel papers, which identified him as a carpenter, Mitch shouldered a small knapsack filled with tools and tied on a carpenter's apron. Similarly equipped, Raoul led the way. Bicycling the back roads, wooded trails, and farmers' fields, Mitch felt reasonably secure. He'd been told the Germans were concentrating their limited manpower on the *Verboten* Zone, which Mitch and Raoul would circumvent, staying to the south.

Their route took them through Beauvais and on to the Somme just south of Amiens, a hard two-day ride. The first night they bedded down in a haystack after eating their sandwiches and getting acquainted, talking in whispers.

"I actually was a carpenter before the war," Raoul explained, "but really more a jack-of-all-trades."

"What's it like in the Somme?"

"Life's hard in the marshes. Everyone has to pitch in and work at a little of everything, especially at harvest time. Everything depends on the crops—potatoes, beets, corn, cabbage. It's all connected to the rest of the world by barges, hundreds of them. We use the rivers like highways, same way the Vikings did a thousand years ago."

"Did you ever work on a barge?"

"Yeah, I worked on most of them at one time or another."

Toward dusk on the second day, they arrived on a deserted stretch of the Somme and hunkered down in the bushes along the bank. As Raoul had predicted, they did not have to wait long before they heard the chug chug chug of a one-lung engine. Against the swollen current, the barge was fighting its way slowly upstream.

"*Tiens*, I know that barge." Raoul smiled at Mitch and stepped out of the bushes. He waved both arms and shouted, "Alooo. Aloo. Guillaume. It's Raoul."

The man at the wheel waved back. "Alooo. Want a ride?"

"*Oui, Capitaine.*"

The Captain threw the craft into reverse and pulled over to the bank with the aid of a long pole.

"How far up-river you going?" Raoul asked.

"To Ebey's landing. I can give you a ride that far."

"Wanted to go up farther—to Pieri's slough, but Ebey's will give us a good start. Yeah, we'd like a ride. Can we bring our bikes?"

"Sure, come aboard," the Captain answered, as he lowered a wide plank, rigged by pulleys, onto the bank. He extended a long, weathered arm and helped them hoist the bikes on board.

Raoul had explained to Mitch, "There's no need to tell him what we're doing. He knows well enough. All the barge captains are sympathizers, but they know they can be most helpful to the cause by staying out of trouble. As long as they deliver the vegetables, the Germans will leave them alone. So it's best if we don't say anything."

In spite of this deceptively peaceful place, Guillaume told Raoul and Mitch to go below and stay out of sight. "It's safer for him not to know what his passengers are up to," Raoul said. "He won't ask us any questions." Raoul introduced Mitch to Guillaume who inspected the American with a non-committal stare and just nodded, but greeted Raoul with a hug and a grin.

When the barge pulled over at a small *auberge* for dinner, Raoul and Mitch stayed below and dined on cold smoked catfish, bread, and wine offered by the Captain.

Raoul chatted with his old friend, Guillaume, exchanging news of their narrow worlds—the worlds of Henri's cave and the Somme river. "You sure eat pretty good," Raoul said. "Best eats I've had a long time."

Ebey's landing would not be reached until morning, but Mitch was more than happy to spend the night on Guillaume's barge. He set his pack on the bunk and examined the cabin. It had all the accouterments of a small house—a kitchen, washroom, bedroom, a wood stove. This was Guillaume's home. "The life of a bargeman looks pretty good," he commented to Raoul. "A lot better than our *Maquis* friends."

Pushing on upstream in the early morning, they reached Ebey's landing, thanked Guillaume and immediately hooked up with another barge. This second barge reached Pieri's landing in the mid-afternoon. Shrouded in a thick overlay of deciduous trees, the marshy area appeared to Mitch to be the ideal place to hide almost anything.

As the barge approached the makeshift landing, Raoul pointed to a short figure in a blue uniform, standing at rigid attention. "That's the General," he said. "Some folks think he has delusions of being a descendant of Napoleon. He even came up with a name—kind of mixed the Bonaparte letters around and came up with Bartonne.

Charles Bartonne, or *Le General,* as he liked to be called, greeted Raoul with a smart salute and Mitch with a formal handshake. A life-long friend of Raoul, he wasted no time on niceties after a brief introduction. Without preamble, he said, "Follow me," and immediately proceeded to show off stacks of supplies, tents, crates of rifles, land mines, explosives, mortars. Then, with obvious pride, he showed them around his establishment, lecturing as he went. A regular arsenal, Pieri's farm, surrounded by a dense forest, obscured a small town, which housed a sizable army of more than seven hundred partisans.

A wiry, energetic man, Bartonne talked and walked like a steam engine. He tapped Mitch on the chest. "We can take on a whole division of the Bosch and kill every one of them. Just a matter of time. The right time. We can do it. We will do it. But the townspeople downriver keep pleading with me to wait for the right time, to refrain from rash action. We've got the weapons to attack now, but they keep telling me they've seen too many innocent villagers murdered when there's an attack. Well, I've about run out of patience."

Mitch and Raoul could hardly get a word in edgewise.

"Incroyable," Raoul exclaimed, wide eyed, as he took in the armament.

Mitch tried to figure out a way to cool Bartonne's impetuous inclinations without creating animosity. "I really admire what you have done here, General, and when I tell you the overall plan, I think you will very happy with it. You will be a major player. And the time is coming soon. You will strike and strike hard—with the element of surprise. So you won't want to tip your hand."

Bartonne looked Mitch hard in the eye. "That sounds like the news I've been waiting for. We can stay out of sight if they don't make us wait too long. My whole operation is undetectable from the air," he added with a knowing smile. "If the Germans ever decide to come up river and nose around, we'll have plenty of warning from our barge friends—time to pack up and move deeper into the forest. So, no matter what happens, we will be ready."

Mitch nodded, "Looks like you could beat up on them all right."

"You're right. If London will just let us know when the invasion is coming, we'll punish the bastards."

"That's why I'm here, General. We will talk about that."

After an introduction to Bartonne's lieutenants and a fine dinner, including some excellent wine, Mitch got down to business. "Your hospitality's wonderful," Mitch said, "I'm truly impressed with what you've done here, and I would certainly like to stay longer, but I'm running out of time. The invasion is coming soon, and I must relay vital messages to some other key people. So I have to finish up here and head back down river in the morning. The timing of the invasion is obviously a matter of extreme secrecy, so I must talk to General Bartonne alone on the timing question—in utmost confidence. But on the matter of targets to attack, I am instructed to include all of you."

Mitch proceeded to outline the instructions, which were almost the same as those given to Denis, except for the emphasis on the Calais area. They should lie low until the secret signal came for the invasion, then hit them with everything they've got. The Germans would be too busy on the beaches to come after them in the swamps.

Communications, bridges, radar stations, telephones lines, and rail lines in the Pas de Calais would be the prime targets. They would have only twenty-four hours advance notice, so everything needed for the attack should be cached ahead of time in readiness.

Mitch took *Le General* aside. "I'm instructed to tell you, and only you, I repeat, in utmost secrecy, the signal for the invasion. You must not give even a hint of this to anyone until the time comes."

"Yes, of course. I understand," Bartonne responded gravely.

"You must listen every night, without fail, to the BBC at 6:OO p.m. and 9:OO p.m. When you hear the strains of the Autumn Song, you'll know the invasion will begin twenty-four hours later. You know the song—the lyrics?"

"Yes, certainly."

Mitch embraced the Frenchman. "Good luck and good hunting."

"You too, *mon ami*." Bartonne saluted smartly.

Mitch returned the salute. "I'm afraid that Raoul and I are running behind schedule. We must hurry if we're going to reach certain other important players in time."

Raoul told Mitch he was reluctant to leave his old friends and begged to stay behind, but Mitch persisted. "Sorry, Raoul, but you've got to stick with me for a few more days. I need you not just for a guide but also to help me find *Le Maire*."

Raoul looked dejected. "That won't be easy—dangerous too."

"Look Raoul, you know as well as I that those contacts in Caen won't speak to me without a personal introduction from you. I need you."

What could be more peaceful, Mitch wondered, as they floated back down the Somme? The faint hissing and gurgling of river, blended with the rhythmic chugging of the engine, almost put him to sleep. But on the second day, as they approached the outskirts of Amiens, the peaceful spell was broken by the sound of artillery in the distance, followed by the thud of bombs. Mitch surmised that he was hearing German artillery in Calais shelling the fake "First Army" in Dover. It was such a short distance across the channel that their biggest guns could reach it. Mitch smiled, visualizing the vast quantities of plywood and cardboard, designed by England's foremost movie studio to resemble fortifications, being demolished. He could also hear the distinctive sounds of bombs falling on Calais, presumably dropped by the RAF to convince the Germans that Calais was, indeed, the intended invasion site.

Raoul and Mitch disembarked with their bicycles on the same riverbank where they had first boarded the up-river barge. Retracing their steps took another two days and brought them to within two kilometers of Caen on the edge of the *Verboten* zone. From this point on, any movement would be much more dangerous.

Now, with only four or possibly five days left until the invasion, Mitch worried—*will I be able to reach Smith and Renee in time? More than likely, St.-Pierre will be a battlefield. I've got to warn them. But what are their options even if I do get there in time? Should they evacuate, or dig a bomb shelter, or find shelter in the caves?*

CAEN, FRANCE

Raoul led the way as they approached the outskirts of Caen.

"We're going to visit Millie," Raoul said with a smile. "You'll like her. She's a mousy little old lady, the sort the Germans would never suspect."

Mitch frowned. "How safe is this little lady?"

"Safe as they come. Actually she's tougher than nails. Runs the best safe-house in Caen. Ever since the Germans killed her husband and her son, she hasn't cared what happens to her. She just wants to exact some kind of revenge."

"Can we approach her house without arousing suspicion?"

"Yeah, I think it's safe enough, but the best time to approach is about nine o'clock in the morning. The Bosch are usually busy in the morning. Besides her house is on the east edge of town. We'll be okay."

The two men found Millie hanging up laundry in her tiny back yard, fortunately screened from view by a high wooden fence. She jerked up from her basket of wet laundry with fright at the first sight of the two scruffy looking men, but her countenance instantly changed to a wrinkled smile when she recognized Raoul. She greeted him silently with an urgent hug, and beckoned them to come inside through the back door.

Introduced to Mitch as Madame Millie, she reminded him of a prim schoolmarm he'd known as a child. The starched white collar, the neatly ironed print dress, and the carefully brushed hair, tied up in a bun, made a stark contrast to Mitch's and Raoul's grimy appearance. Neither of them had shaved for a week. Streaks of mud smeared their faces and strands of hay protruded from their hair and clothes. Raoul asked if they might wash up.

Cleaned up and shaven, they sat on comfortable chairs for the first time in weeks—and talked. "How've you been getting along with the Boche?" Raoul asked.

Millie bristled. "The pigs never give me a thought. I give them nasty looks ever time one of them goes by, but, they ignore me, and at my age, it doesn't matter what happens to me."

"Millie, you look just as fit and feisty as ever," Raoul said with a wide grin. "Anyway, you may not have to put up with your pigs much longer. This war won't last forever. But right now I have to try and find the Mayor of Chabeaux for my friend, Mitch here. You know him, don't you? I'm hoping you might help us find him.

"Yes, of course I know him, but he's been hiding, and I haven't seen him for almost a year. Sorry, I can't help you."

"All right. I have other sources. I'll have to leave you now with

Mitch while I go looking. You be nice to him, *d'accord?*"

While Mitch sat tight, having ersatz tea with the little lady as if there was no war, Raoul went off looking for the Mayor. "We don't have nice visitors very often," she said in a genteel tone while she set out two lace doilies. "I make the tea, you know, of blackberry and nettle leaves. It just doesn't taste right, does it? But we must make do, mustn't we?" She chattered on non-stop while Mitch listened. "Do tell me the news from London."

Mitch struggled to make polite conversation, as he became increasingly worried about Raoul. Hours went by, then nightfall, and no sign of his guide. Finally Mitch fell asleep fitfully on an old, lumpy sofa. With excrutiating uncertainty and anxiety, Mitch waited out another day. He was about ready to abandon this part of the mission, when a disheveled Raoul staggered in the door.

"You look terrible," Mitch said. "What happened?"

"The Bosch spotted me," Raoul responded, out of breath. "Been on the run ever since. Gave 'em the slip, though, 'n I spent the night in a ditch. Sure lucky they didn't have dogs."

Mitch was worried. "Are you sure you weren't followed?"

"I'm sure. I was real careful."

"You'd better have something to eat," Millie offered.

"Yeah, I'm hungry as a bear, but I hope we're not eating up the last of your food."

"You're welcome to it," she said. "I don't eat much any more."

Deciding it might be a small opportunity to spread the deception about the Pas de Calais, Mitch said, "It won't be long now, *Madame*, before we'll be rid of the Boche and eating properly again. Just listen for the guns of Calais."

Turning to Raoul, Mitch asked, "Find out anything about our Mayor?"

"Yup, believe it or not, he's back in his own town of Chabeaux. He's got a lot of nerve, even if he hasn't much sense."

"Do you have any idea how to find him? I presume he'll be disguised."

"Sure enough. He's teaching at the grade school." Raoul devoured the last crumb of a biscuit. "We should be able to get there tomorrow if we leave early. But we'll have to be careful. The place is crawling with Bosch."

"What about you? Are they looking for you?"

"Yes, but I can fix that if Madame'll let me trade my outfit for one of those she keeps for us rascals. And I'll shave off my beard. Damn, I hate to lose it—better than losing my neck though."

Thanking Madame Millie profusely, they slipped out early the next morning. Staying well away from Caen, they circled to the southwest, then looped back northward toward Chabeaux.

Raoul was correct. German troops were everywhere, apparently energized by Field Marshal Rommel, who had been newly appointed to command the German defenses. However, under his command, it seemed to Mitch they were more intent on maneuvers and military preparedness than on harassing the local populace.

"Chabeaux's been turned into an armed camp," Raoul observed. "The locals are beginning to worry more about Allied bombing than about the Bosch. You can tell. They're digging bomb shelters in their basements."

Raoul led the way to a school where small children were skipping rope and playing hopscotch. With Mitch following a few steps behind, he made discrete inquiries. Inside, several teachers were correcting papers and preparing for the next class, except for one male who had mutton-chop whiskers, a florid face, and was arguing noisily with one of the women. Mitch could hardly keep from laughing. The Mayor of Chabeaux, poorly disguised, had managed to pass himself off as a schoolteacher.

Mitch's main purpose in meeting with the Mayor was to implant the rumor of a Pas de Calais invasion. If there was anyone in all of France who could spread a rumor, it was the talkative, outgoing Mayor.

Mitch could see that the portly politician failed to recognize him at first, but then a glimmer of recognition spread across the friendly face. Mitch put out his hand in greeting. *"Bonjour, Monsieur*, it is a pleasure to meet you again."

"Certainement," recognition gradually dawning. "It was at the farm house of the beautiful young lady. *Certainement*, now I remember. Who could forget such a lady."

With the pressure of time weighing heavily, Mitch decided he'd better get down to business without any of the niceties the Mayor would normally expect. "Your honor," he began, not quite sure of the proper address, "I have been sent by the High Command in London to alert certain prominent—that is to say, key—people in the French Resistance of the imminent Allied invasion of France."

"Yes, of course. We've been expecting some word, but who knows. We just get one rumor after another."

"This time, you can rest assured the rumor is fact," Mitch replied. "It is, of course, extremely confidential. You have been selected as one of a special few to be informed. But you must guard the secret with your life—except, of course, for a few of your most trusted lieutenants, who should be informed in order to carry out the needed sabotage."

The Mayor drew himself up to his full stature. Even the muttonchops seemed to elongate. "Of course, you can have absolute trust in my discretion."

"What I can tell you is this, your honor: the invasion will begin soon—very soon. I cannot give you an exact date, but you will be able to tell easily enough by the intense bombing, which will precede the landings. There may be deceptive actions in many areas, but the real invasion will be in the Pas de Calais."

His honor nodded.

Mitch, trying his best to look sincere, put a hand on the Mayor's shoulder. "You can make a great contribution to the Allied cause, your honor. You must create great confusion in the Calais area. Get the civilian refugees to clog the roads. That will bottle up German reinforcements moving up to the front just as effectively as Allied bombing."

"But of course," the Mayor responded, as if he were addressing a political rally. "The civilians must be mobilized. If they are warned to evacuate the war zone, that should cause exactly the congestion you want."

"Certainly, but we must not warn them until the bombing begins. We know it may be a sacrifice for some people, but it's an important sacrifice—to help win the war. The civilians will create mass confusion for the Nazis, but it will actually benefit them. They will be out of harm's way in a day or two."

Mitch could see the Mayor looked doubtful. "I have a good deal of influence, as you apparently know, in Normandy, but not much in the Pas de Calais."

"We understand, your honor, but most of the German reinforcements are in Chartres and Caen. They will funnel through your area when they realize where the attack is taking place. Of course, we would welcome any outright sabotage that you can arrange through your influence—such as cutting phone lines and railroad tracks. But our primary objective is to create as much general confusion as possible on the roads leading to Calais. You understand me?"

The muttonchops were quivering now. Mitch thought, I'll bet he thinks he'll receive the Croix de Guerre for this.

"Of course. I understand. Absolutely," the Mayor answered.

With some difficulty, Mitch and Raoul broke off the conversation with the effusive mayor and bid him adieu. His honor had some important rumor-spreading to do.

Much as Mitch would have preferred to move on to St.-Pierre, curfew time had arrived, and they needed a place to spend the night. The school's janitor closet would have to do.

ST.-PIERRE-DU-BOIS, FRANCE

On a sunny but windy morning of June 4th, Mitch bicycled through the familiar countryside on the way to St.-Pierre, while Raoul headed back to the caves.

Mitch stopped to pick a bouquet of wild flowers and was once again struck by the pastoral beauty of the fields, orchards, and vineyards of Normandy. He thought it a terrible shame that this beautiful country would be torn apart by war again. Finding columbine, honeysuckle, and morning glory, he put together a many-colored bouquet, which now protruded like a fountain from the top of his backpack.

Lost in thoughts of seeing Renee, Mitch whistled a happy tune as he passed German soldiers and workmen on the road. Surely a fellow whistling, with flowers sticking out of his pack, couldn't be much of a threat to the Third Reich.

As he circled St.-Pierre, he looked around carefully before veering off across the fields and disappearing into the bushes along the creek, which led to the Brousard farm.

Mitch peered out through the bushes and spotted Renee in the distance, working in the cabbage field, hoeing weeds, but he didn't dare call to her. They were too close to the German headquarters where a steady stream of soldiers tramped in and out. He waited impatiently, watching her graceful movements. The wide-brimmed hat and the sack-like dress may have been some kind of disguise to discourage unwanted attention, but all Mitch could see was the grace of her movements and the occasional glint of sunlight on the golden hair.

After what seemed an eternity to Mitch, she walked slowly to the house. He waited until there were no Germans in sight. Only then did he approach the back door and knock, using Henri's signal, three short knocks repeated three times.

Wide-eyed, Renee stood rooted to the spot, staring at Mitch in disbelief. "Thank God," she finally managed. He could see her choking back the tears.

Mitch sailed his hat across the room and grinned. "Brought you some posies."

Sweeping her into his arms—at the same time trying to avoid crushing the flowers—he felt the silky hair brush against his cheek like a kiss. She clung to him like a drowning person, hanging on for dear life, finally pushing away long enough to take the flowers. "They're beautiful," she murmured.

At first speechless, they both started talking at once. "Let's find a priest," Mitch said, "and get married. War or no war. To heck with the war. You're all I care about. I'll love you and take care of you forever. Please say you will, Renee."

"Yes, of course. Yes, yes," she said and kissed him hard. "I know Father Francois will marry us without worrying about bans and all that sort of thing. If we can get to the church without attracting attention, we can do it tomorrow. I'm sure he will do it."

Mitch had almost forgotten. There were things that needed to be said. "Renee, I meant to say ..." His lips went numb as he searched for words. "First off, how terribly sorry I am about your father and your brother. You've been through hell since I left you."

"There have been times," her voice shook, "when I thought I couldn't go on. It would have been easier just to die. Thinking about you is all that kept me going. The memories of you. I'd have died without that."

Mitch held her close. "We've got to go on as best we can in spite of this damn war and life's cruelties. You've had more than your share. Now you're entitled to some happiness. This terrible war can't go on forever. But right now, I want to take you away from here. We'll come back later when it's safe."

"I don't know." Renee hesitated. "There's my mother—and Roger. I've been fixing his food, you know. And the farm is about to be lost to the bankers. They want their loans paid back in spite of the war, and the Germans are paying hardly anything for the food they take."

Mitch felt a tear running down her cheek. "I hate to say it, Renee, but you should be marrying some rich Frenchman." He hesitated. "Someone who can take care of you—and the farm. You realize you could have any man you want, don't you? You're so beautiful and desirable. And to be perfectly honest, I'm poor as a church mouse."

Renee gave him one of those determined looks, which reminded him he was proposing to a lady with a mind of her own. "Don't talk nonsense. You're the only man in this world for me, and I'm not going to let you get away. We both know the two of us together can overcome anything." With which she gave him a bewitching smile followed by a passionate kiss. Disoriented for an instant, Mitch laughed, realizing the power she had over him.

Much as he hated to destroy the magic of the moment, he knew that Roger had to be brought into the discussion and the invasion plans discussed. If the invasion was to be on schedule, the twenty-four hour warning would come tonight.

Called down from the attic, where, for too long, he'd been holed up like a mole, Roger looked pale and red-eyed.

"You look terrible," Mitch said with a grin. "How's it going up there in your crow's nest?"

"Lousy, but at least I can tell you the transmissions are goin' through without an 'itch."

Knowing everything was about to explode around them, Mitch spoke haltingly as he explained what he could about the invasion plan. Even to Smith and Renee, he talked of a dual invasion—here and Calais—knowing tens of thousands of lives were at stake.

"When you hear the Autumn Song on BBC," Mitch chose his words carefully, "you'll know the invasion will begin in twenty-four hours. More than likely the signal will be heard tonight."

Roger stared at Mitch. "So soon?"

Mitch rubbed his forehead. It hurt. "The real question is whether to evacuate the two of you. This whole area is going to be bombed and fought over. I'd be much happier if you—and your mother too, Renee—were at least fifty kilometers south of here, or else in the caves."

"I can't leave," Roger said. "They're bringin' me messages to send every day, important stuff. The *Maquis* are dependin' on me for their supplies; and they've been bringin' in all kinds of valuable intelligence, the kind of stuff SHAEF really needs, like where the Panzer divisions are 'oled up and the build-up at Calais. Even if the invasion is successful, they're goin' to need me for a while, probably more than before."

"I guess you're right, but I want to get Renee and her mother out of here. In the meantime, we should dig a bomb shelter for you, whatever we can do in one day."

"I suppose we could expand the root cellar, dig it deeper," Roger suggested.

"It would be better to dig it outside by the creek if you want my opinion. The house is liable to become a fire trap."

At 6:00 p.m. they turned on the radio, and, sure enough, the strains of the Autumn Song came through loud and clear. Following a few minutes of news, it was repeated.

"No question about it. This is it," Mitch said. "We'd better start digging that shelter, and you'd better talk to your mother, Ren ..."

He was cut off by the rumble of trucks on the gravel outside, then blinding lights and discordant shouting. Searchlights flashed against the house and flooded in through the windows. Two trucks full of soldiers rumbled up to the front door, and a bullhorn sounded, "Come out! Hands up! You are surrounded. Come out immediately, or we'll shoot our way in."

Mitch reacted quickly. "Roger, you hide in the attic. I'll go out. Renee, you stay put. They know you're here, but they don't know about Roger." Before they could protest, he pushed open the door and stood in the doorway with his hands in the air.

Seconds after Roger rushed up the stairs, Otto burst into the house, followed by half a dozen blackshirts. Two of his men grabbed Mitch. "*Ja. Ja.* What we have here?" Otto gloated. "You the slippery British spy I try to catch for a year now." He spoke in broken French with a smug smile. "We finally catch you. You not get away this time."

"*Monsieur*, you are mistaken." Mitch gave his best French impersonation. "Here are my papers. I am just a carpenter."

"We see about that. We follow you here from underground meeting with that traitor, *le Maire de Chabeaux*. We wring confession from him, and we will have confession from you too. Have no doubt about that."

Turning to Renee, he added. "You harbor spy. You know penalty for—"

"No, No," she broke in. "*Monsieur* is only here for carpentry. You have the wrong man."

Otto stared hard at Renee, gradually softening. "Him I want," he said, jabbing his finger in Mitch's midriff. Then he turned to his men. "Take him to my headquarters," he ordered in German. "We'll get the truth soon enough."

Losing her self-control, Renee screamed. "You killed my father. You beast! You monster! Now you want to kill my ..." She stopped and bit her lip.

"So, this man is more to you than just a carpenter. We find out soon enough. We have our ways." Turning his back on Renee's protests, he stormed out the door with Mitch in tow.

At headquarters, Otto ordered his captive tied to a chair and posted two guards behind him for good measure. "You not get away this time," he repeated. "You the same one that escaped before, *Ya?*"

"Certainly not, sir." Mitch had been coached to make a show of respect. "You must see my papers. They will show you who I am— just a carpenter. Do I look like the spy you describe? Certainly not."

Otto squinted at his captive, showing doubt. "We check papers. Let's see what we have here." He studied the identity papers with a scowl. "It says you a carpenter from St. Flour. We check tomorrow. In the meantime, you my prisoner. Guards have orders to shoot if you make slightest move."

Mitch was bound tightly to the chair with two German soldiers posted behind him. When Otto left the room, he consciously tried to will himself to sleep, knowing he would need his wits about him in the morning. But, his mind in turmoil, the world of sleep escaped him.

On the morning of June 5, Mitch watched Otto, pacing the floor, apparently waiting for the information from St. Flour. Mitch noticed the twitching eye and the hands clasping and unclasping. *The man is obviously a nervous wreck. Is there some way I can work on that?*

Half a day went by when Otto's radio operator strode into the office and saluted. "A message from St. Flour, *Herr Kapitan*." Although in German, Mitch understood the gist of it when the Corporal read it aloud. "The St. Flour records are difficult to access. We will continue to pursue your request and make every effort to find the information you require." Mitch watched Otto's face turn red. He knew the town of St. Flour had been under the control of the Vichy French government for two years, and its records were probably a mess. Henri had chosen St. Flour for a reason.

Otto left the room, leaving the guards with orders to shoot to kill if the prisoner made the slightest attempt to escape or even move. Two hours passed while the bonds gnawed painfully into Mitch's wrists. He tried, in his broken German, to ask the guards to loosen them, but they only stared back in silence. They had been ordered not to speak to the prisoner.

Finally Otto returned, shakily holding a sheaf of official-looking papers in one hand. He ordered the bonds removed. "Stand at attention," he barked. "I have St. Flour records. No carpenter with your name. Your address not exist."

Mitch tried to protest, "There must be some mistake. I can explain. I—"

"No mistake. You are spy," Otto interrupted, pointing his finger at his victim and then at the papers. "I will have confession, unless you wish be torn apart in small pieces, fed to dogs."

At this point, Mitch believed the Gestapo did, indeed, have proof of his fake identity and reasoned that his only chance of survival was to string them along with the Pas de Calais story. He would withhold just enough to make it worth their while to keep him alive, but he'd have to make it convincing.

Otto ordered his captive tied to an overhead beam so his toes could barely touch the ground, a standard Gestapo interrogation practice. "We'll leave you there for a while to think it over," he growled. "When I come back, you may feel more like signing a confession?"

Knowing it would sound phony if he gave in too easily, Mitch endured two hours of isolation in a dark room with the agony of ropes cutting into his bleeding wrists. Almost as bad as the pain were the gnawing hunger pains and thirst. He hadn't eaten for nearly two days.

Nearly unconscious by the time Otto returned at 11:00 p.m., Mitch had to be prodded into full consciousness. "Now, I have here confession for you sign," Otto said, thrusting a paper at Mitch. "Frankly, you no have choice. It does not matter whether you guilty or not. You will sign—unless you want die very slowly, very painfully."

Mitch groaned. "Cut me down. I can't sign anything tied up like this."

"That better," Otto said with a smile that reminded Mitch of a hyena. Otto nodded to his corporal. "Cut him down and tie him to the chair again."

Otto ordered his own dinner brought to the interrogation room, which he proceeded to eat slowly, all the while watching his captive and grinning between bites.

Slumped over in the chair, Mitch needed a quarter of an hour before he was in any condition to read the "confession," much less sign it. Huskily, his first utterance was, "Water. Something to eat."

"After you sign," the Captain said, taking another mouthful and then leaning back in his chair with his arms folded.

"I can't sign this," Mitch spoke slowly in French after reading the document. "It's a pack of lies."

Otto turned to his corporal. "Tie him back up."

"Wait," Mitch groaned, "I'm not a hero. If I sign this, you'll shoot me anyway, won't you?"

Otto responded with a steely stare. "I promise you it is better to die by firing squad than by slow torture."

"I don't want to die," Mitch said with conviction. "If you shoot me, you will not learn some very important information I have—the invasion plans. If you let me live, I can give you information that can make the difference between Germany winning or losing the war."

"So you are British spy. You admit?"

"I will tell you that, but I won't put it on paper, because you will shoot me as soon as I do, won't you? On the other hand, if I tell you what I know about the invasion, you'll be the biggest hero in the Third Reich."

Otto leaned forward in his chair and stared at his captive, his eye twitching furiously. "How I know you tell truth or invent story to save skin?"

"The things I tell you can be checked with the Abwehr. They will fit exactly in the puzzle. Your Abwehr has most of the pieces, but not quite all. I was on General Eisenhower's planning task force, and I can fill in the missing pieces. I know every detail of the invasion plan."

The Captain continued to stare at Mitch. "Tell me something to convince me."

"All right, I ..." Mitch hesitated. "I can tell you this much right now. The first landings will be in Normandy, but that will only be a feint. The real invasion will be in the Pas de Calais, and the First U.S. army under General Patton is ready to attack with the largest amphibious force ever assembled in the history of the world."

Mitch could see doubt in Otto's face. *Surely he knows this could be the greatest intelligence break of the war. At the very least, he has to notify the Abwehr of the possibilities before executing me. Besides,*

I'm an obvious candidate for double agent. But that's the business of the Abwehr, not the SS.

At 1:OO a.m., the verbal fencing had become heated, when suddenly the wail of sirens shattered the night calm, then the thud of bombs and screeching alarms. Screeched outside the SS headquarters.

D-DAY

Tied to his chair, Mitch watched bedlam erupt around him, the screaming of orders, troops grabbing their rifles and pouring out of the building, rifle fire, grenades exploding, shouting in German. He could see Otto's face, frozen with fear and indecision.

Otto rushed to the entrance, only to be met by a volley of rifle fire that crashed against the partially opened door. Dropping to the floor, he yelled, "Take cover." Then he screamed at his radioman, "Find out what the hell is going on."

Half a minute later the radioman shouted back over the din, "Report, *Herr Kapitan.* Allied paratroops dropping all over Normandy."

"Get through to Rommel's headquarters."

"The lines are dead, *Herr Kapitan.*"

A grenade smashed through a window in the storage wing of the building. Mitch could hear secondary explosions, followed by sounds of collapsing walls and screams in German.

Otto collared three of his men and rushed out the back door, while Mitch crawled part way under the Captain's desk—as best as he could with the chair still tied to his back.

Three American soldiers crashed into the room, and a burst of gunfire blindly sprayed the room, grazing the desk inches above Mitch's head. He screamed, "I'm an American. Don't shoot."

"Keep him covered," the Sergeant yelled to one of his men.

"The Krauts went out the back door," Mitch shouted.

The GI kept a gun trained on him. "What the hell are you doing here?"

"It's a long story, but boy am I glad to see you guys. I was just about to be shot as a spy," Mitch said with a twisted grin. "I guess the truth is I was a spy."

"Sounds like horseshit to me. What d'ya mean a spy?"

"Working for British Intelligence, believe it or not."

The GI's mouth hung open. "Okay, I guess you sound like an American, but you'd better tell me something to convince me, like who's in the world series, 'n what's your rank and serial number."

Mitch had no trouble convincing the Sergeant, who shouted at him, "Wait there," then sprinted through the back door with the two other GIs. Mitch heard a burst of gunfire. Half a minute later, the Sergeant came running back into the room, took a large knife from his belt and cut Mitch's bonds.

Mitch talked the Sergeant into going with him across the yard to the farmhouse and checking out Renee and Roger. "They are some of the most important Allied agents in France," Mitch pleaded. "You've got to help us."

But Germans, who had scattered and taken cover, were still sniping at the paratroopers. A burst of fire whined inches from the Sergeant, and the two men pitched flat to the ground. Seconds later, they got up to a low crouch and scuttled across the yard to the Brousard house, which so far appeared to be unscathed.

As Mitch expected, the front door was bolted. There was no answer when he pounded on it and shouted, "Renee. Roger. It's me, Mitch." Every joint in his body ached as he hurried around to the back of the house and pounded some more, using the special knock. Still no answer. In a near panic, Mitch and his adopted GI sprinted to the creek and worked their way up stream under cover of the shrubbery.

He was about to give up, when a familiar voice came out of nowhere. "That you, Mitch?"

"Yeah, Roger, is that you? Is Renee with you? Are you okay?"

"We're okay." The voice was Renee's. "It's you we're worried about. Are *you* all right? I'm jammed into this hole so tight, I can't see you."

Mitch felt his pains melt away. "You sure fixed a good hiding place. I practically fell into it. Yeah, I'm okay, but damned sore and hungry. You don't have anything to eat, do you?"

The GI pulled a chocolate K-ration out of his vest pocket. "Thanks," Mitch said with conviction. "I haven't eaten for two days."

The sounds of battle had faded into the distance, but the Sergeant figited. "Who the hell are these people?"

Mitch explained as they squeezed out of the foxhole.

Miraculously, the four of them were unscathed, but Mitch knew their troubles had only begun. The invasion plan called for the paratroops to join up with the landing force by fighting their way together. He was worried. The Germans were bound to contest the area. They would certainly regroup, bring up reinforcements, and make a fight of it. God only knew how long it would take the Allies to secure this sector.

"What's your rank?" Mitch asked the GI.

"Staff sergeant," was the hesitant reply.

"Well, Sergeant, I'm a lieutenant commander in the U.S. Navy. D'you suppose I could order you to stay with us for a few days? This lady, and Roger Smith here, have been the most valuable intelligence sources the Allies have had for the last two years. It would be a disaster if they were picked up by the Krauts."

"I don'no sir. My C.O.'d probably have me court-marshaled for desertion. I gotta find my unit and tell 'em what's going on."

"Okay, I suppose you're right. We're going to be holed up here or in that house." Mitch pointed to the Brousard farmhouse. "If there's any way you can talk your C.O. into giving us some support, we'd sure ... Oh, what the hell. Forget it. You've got a war to fight."

"Look, I gotta go," the Sergeant said with a half salute. "I'll try to get back to you, but don't count on it." He disappeared into the night, running.

With the American paratroopers in pursuit, the Germans had evacuated the town. Now there was an eerie silence.

"There are weapons lyin' all over the place," Roger observed. "We oughta pick up a couple of rifles and a few grenades. We may need 'em."

"Good idea," Mitch agreed. "Renee, you and your mother stay

out of sight. Roger and I'll see what we can find."

Renee wouldn't let him go without a hug. "Be careful, Mitch. You've had enough run-ins with the Krauts."

Hunched over, they ran across the compound to what was left of the German headquarters. Fearful there might be some Germans left behind, they circled the building and cautiously peered in the windows. Nothing but destruction. With the sidewall blown open, the furniture, papers, telephones, light bulbs, and loose wires intermingled crazily in a broken mess. Groping in the darkness, Mitch tripped over the body of a dead German.

Roger stripped the German of two grenades and a rifle. Mitch grabbed a pistol and an ammunition belt. They stumbled over two more bodies and stripped them likewise. It was all they could carry.

CANNON FODDER

Otto Streikler had always known, without question, the SS were the elite of the German fighting forces. He knew they came from the toughest, meanest Aryan raw material. They would fight the hardest and win the toughest battles. Now they were being put to the test. However, after five years of secret-police work, operating concentration camps, and acting as official executioners, they had lost some of their ability to function as ordinary soldiers.

Taken completely by surprise on D-Day, Otto's SS company retreated in panic. At this point, the German High Command, which Otto knew had always been contemptuous of the SS, directed them to take orders from the Wehrmacht.

Having lost a third of his men and most of his arms and supplies in the surprise attack, Captain Streikler was now ordered to counterattack. Angered and embittered, he found his pleas for arms, trucks, and supplies falling on deaf ears. He was going to be cannon fodder.

Cannon fodder perhaps, but Otto would never know that his life had been in much greater peril from the single bullet of an assassin than from the battle with the Allies.

On June 4th, Heidendorff had returned to Bernau to clean up a few loose ends of a personal nature after months of distractions over the Atlantic Wall. His aide-de-camp, Gestapo Major Rikker, brought him up to date. "Herr Marshal, there are a number of matters here that need your attention."

"Yes, yes, of course. Have you found a safe storage for my Rothschild collection? Utmost importance. The utmost."

"Certainly, Herr Marshal." He handed a bound packet to the fat man. "Here is the complete inventory of your collection and all the safe storage areas listed in detail. There are two hundred and fifty pages."

While the Marshal thumbed through the packet, immersed in his favorite passion, the Major cleared his throat. "Sir, one small matter you should be aware of. You may recall you gave me an assignment to eliminate a Captain Streikler when he came to Bernau last year."

"Yes, yes." Heidendorff was trying to concentrate on the packet.

The Major cleared his throat twice more and shifted his feet. "Sir, I have to tell you that something went wrong and Streikler escaped."

"What did you say?" Heidendorff looked up from the papers and frowned. "Streikler escaped, you say? How could that have happened?"

After a thunderous dressing down, the Marshal issued new orders. "Do not fail this time, Rikker, or you will be court-martialed and demoted to the rank of private. This is of the utmost importance. The utmost. Do you understand me, Major?"

On June 6th, which turned out to be D-Day, the Major set out before dawn for St.-Pierre-du-Bois.

Heidendorff received the report the same day. Rikker's command car was spotted by an RAF Spitfire in the early morning light and blown to pieces. In the confusion of retreats and defeats during the next few months, Heidendorff lost track of Otto. The Captain had been granted a second reprieve.

LONDON

In the underground headquarters of MI-6, Sir Charles tracked the D-Day action in every detail. Through the Ultra-Enigma intercepts,

SHAEF and MI-6 were reading every move of the German High Command, OKW[9].

It was immediately obvious on the morning of June 6th that the Germans had been taken by surprise. The OKW, Field Marshal Rommel, and his division commanders appeared to be thoroughly confused and frustrated. They had received no warning, no sightings of any kind, before the landings began. The gliders and paratroops, landing all over Normandy, had revealed no evident pattern, and now the bombing of Calais was attracting most of their attention. In London, Enigma intercepts painted a picture of German Intelligence reports, pouring into Rommel's headquarters, telling him that the attack in Normandy was a feint. The real invasion would be at the Pas de Calais. General Atwater smiled. Their hard work and years of planning had paid off.

Rommel had been away from the front to celebrate his wife's birthday on June 6th, believing the weather too stormy for an Allied attack. Upon receiving the news, he had rushed back to his headquarters in La Roche-Guyon to find nothing but confusion and inoperative telephones.

One Enigma intercept read Rommel's frantic request to Hitler and to the OKW. Rommel wanted to bring up his Panzer divisions immediately, but von Rundstedt would not allow it, at least not without the concurrence of Hitler. On the morning of June 6th, the Fuehrer slept until 10:00 a.m., as was his custom. When he was finally informed, he went along with von Rundstedt, overruling Rommel, refusing to release the Panzers. Hitler had also been taken in by the Pas de Calais deception.

Sir Charles received a stream of reports from the Resistance, many of them transmitted through Roger Smith. On June 7th, they reported that the 2nd Panzer division had been sighted moving southward to the Dordogne, apparently to put down some minor *Maquis* sabotage. It would be a matter of weeks before these fearsome tanks would be turned around and deployed on the Normandy battlefields.

Held in reserve at Chartres, six critical days went by before the other Panzer units finally started toward the front. Even then, their progress toward Caen slowed to a crawl as they dodged around mines and stopped to repair blown tracks. The cow-pie mines were working. According to radio reports coming in from Roger, German tank crews were seen stopping to examine every strange object on the road, adding days to their redeployment.

Atwater now had over a thousand pins on his map of France, each representing an SOE agent attempting to work with the Resistance. The reports poured in to MI-6 headquarters. Denis's *Maquisards* had been at work. They had succeeded in scrambling the telephone wires at Roche-Guyon. German generals had been observed screaming at empty telephones. Every main rail line between Marseilles and Paris had been cut in at least ten places. Similarly the rail lines between Paris, Le Havre, Caen, and Cherbourg were cut and re-cut as soon as they were repaired. A dozen radar stations and four key bridges over the Orne River had been destroyed, and half a dozen trains, attempting to move troops to the front, had been derailed.

Then began the retribution, which Charles had feared. The Nazis, using the SS, burned whole villages, in one case with the villagers locked in their homes to be burned alive. But he knew the French were energized now. Nothing would stop them.

One month after D-Day, SHAEF and Allied Intelligence sat down to evaluate the results.

The U.S. 1st and 29th infantry divisions, which had landed on Omaha beach, had been mauled cruelly by the German shore batteries. They would take issue with the observation that some areas had been lightly defended. However, the other four beaches, in fact, had been lightly defended, at least compared to what would have been the case had the Panzers been there; had the Germans not kept a major part of their forces in the Pas de Calais; had Hitler not made dozens of unwise decisions; had von Rundstedt not also been duped; had the Germans not left 27 divisions in Norway and Denmark fearing a landing there; had Hitler not been deceived into believing the Balkans would be attacked, therefore stationing 24 divisions in Greece and Yugoslavia; and had the French Resistance not effectively sabotaged German rail lines, roads, radar installations, bridges, and telephone lines.

"The list is impressive," Atwater pointed out. "It's testimony to the planning, preparation, and execution of the plan." He looked around at the faces and saw them nodding. "But it's also testimony to the terrible sacrifices made by those killed and wounded in the landings—and to the bravery of the Resistance, and our SOE agents."

These leaders acknowledged there were certain facets of the landings that had gone wrong, and men died that need not have died. But in the end, the fighting on the first day of the invasion, D-Day, resulted in less than 2,500 Allied men killed, one quarter of the number predicted by SHAEF.[10]

For a month, Rommel's troops fought fiercely and held a tight line around the Allied beachhead, inflicting some terrible punishment; but gradually they were ground down to battle-weary half-strength units by the shear weight and numbers of the Allied forces. By August 20th, the Germans had suffered 450,000 casualties and the Allies 209,000.

After taking a frightful beating trying to capture Caen, the British and the Canadians were held to a standstill. Then, with a lightning thrust, the Americans, under General Patton, broke out on the west flank and surrounded the Germans defending Caen.

SHAEF couldn't believe their luck when they intercepted Hitler's orders to his army to stand and fight in the pocket around Caen and Argentan. It had the effect of trapping them under a rain of artillery fire and bombing from the air, a total disaster for the Germans.

NO MAN'S LAND

From their foxhole by the creek, Mitch, Renee, Roger, and Annette watched the seesaw battle. They dug in deeper and kept out of sight.

Despite the Allies' initial paratroop landings, St.-Pierre-du-Bois became a no-man's-land. The troops of both sides were using the houses for cover and for machine gun nests. Half the houses had been destroyed, and the other half were full of shell fragments. Civilians, caught in the crossfire, retreated to their basements and prayed.

Mitch and Roger pulled branches over the top of their foxhole and took turns keeping watch, peeking out through gaps in the twigs. They could hear the whine of bullets overhead and feel the ground shake from grenades and artillery. They watched men being killed, fighting their way through the hedgerows, tanks burning, trucks abandoned, and weapons strewn around the fields.

After dark on D-Day + 1, a brief quiet settled over the battlefield. Mitch whispered to Roger, "For the life of me, I can't figure out what's going on or who's winning. What do you think, Rog."

"You got me. But I'm goin' to take advantage of this let-up an' see if I can find us somethin' to eat." Roger gingerly climbed out of their hole and crept back to the farmhouse. A few minutes later, he returned with a handful of carrots and a jar of water. "'ope you like the gourmet menu," he said with a grin.

Located half a kilometer from the edge of the village, the Brousard farm was not subjected to the same house-to-house fighting as the houses in the village and luckily remained standing, although riddled with bullet holes. The barn and the SS headquarters building were completely destroyed.

On D-Day + 3, an eerie silence again fell over the town with troops of neither side in sight. Mitch and Roger crawled over to the farm house, following the hollow of the creek, and searched for food. Fortunately, the root cellar remained intact, and they were able to gather up an armload of vegetables. It would mean munching on carrots and cabbage for the foreseeable future, but the raw veggies would taste like champagne and caviar to the hungry foursome.

Roger scurried up the stairs to find his transmitter damaged by a single bullet. "Any chance you can fix it?" Mitch asked.

"Yeah, sure. No problem."

Arms loaded with vegetables, they heard the gunfire start up again and then a frightening rumble. Peering out the paneless window, they made out a German tank rolling down the road, coming directly toward them.

They rushed out the back door, scrambled back to their foxhole, clutching the vegetables, pulled the branches over their heads, and prayed. Their prayers were answered. A tank could have wiped them out with one round.

During the next seven days, they occupied their time digging their hole deeper, whispering to each other, and venturing out on brief forays to the farmhouse whenever the coast cleared.

On June 17th, D-Day + 11, St.-Pierre-du-Bois fell silent, finally secured by the Americans. Shell-shocked, the local populace cautiously poked their heads out of basements and makeshift shelters. The worst of their ordeal was over.

Renee, Mitch, Roger, and Annette climbed out of their hole, stiff, sore, and hungry and looked around in a daze. Roger and Annette stumbled back to the house, while Renee and Mitch hurried into the town to join in the celebration.

Pouring into the streets, crowds began shouting, "*viva La France*," cheering, and waving tri-color flags, which had been hidden away for four years. Someone found an American flag and hung it from the *Hotel de Ville*. Two American soldiers in a Jeep were mobbed and hoisted onto the shoulders of the crowd.

Then the retribution began. Renee gripped Mitch's arm as she watched two young women, who had fraternized with Germans, being hoisted onto a platform in the town square, their heads shaved, their breasts bared and painted with swastikas, while the crowd shouted epithets. A mob of young patriots pulled the Weasel, whimpering, from a basement where he had hidden and dragged him down the main street feet first. Fortunate not to be shot on the spot, he was spat upon, kicked, and finally dragged off to jail.

Renee thought she had been anonymous all these years and watched from the back of the crowd. Then she heard the Mayor calling her name, shouting above the din, "Where is Mademoiselle Renee Brousard?"

She was pushed forward, and a dozen men hoisted her onto the same platform where the collaborators had been humiliated, along with Madame Lazzard and half a dozen *Maquisards*. The Mayor hung a garland of flowers around her neck, and the crowd screamed, "Cheers for Renee. Cheers for Renee. Cheers for Renee."

Like the vast majority of Frenchmen, the Mayor of St.-Pierre-du-Bois had kept a low profile during the war and followed orders from the Nazis. He was hardly a hero, but he was not considered a collaborator, and everyone knew he hated the Germans as much as the rest of them. On this occasion, he climbed on the platform, waved his arms and called for quiet. "My fellow countrymen, we are free at last." The cheers drowned him out. "We owe a great debt of gratitude to those brave ones who took up the cause and risked their lives." More cheers.

The Mayor went on to tell how Madame Lazzard had not only hidden and sheltered unfortunate girls, but had provided a safe house for the Resistance and escapees. Then he recounted how Renee had supplied the *Maquis* with food and provided the secret radio communication with London and had been a courier for the Escape Line. He kissed both of them on both cheeks, Renee four times—which seemed a bit overdone to Mitch. "I promise to see that you receive medals for heroism," he proclaimed, holding their arms in the air, one on each side of him.

"How on earth did he know what I was doing," Renee asked Madame Lazzard when the cheering quieted down enough to hear themselves talk.

"My dear, everybody in town knew. When you came to my house to take Michelle away, do you think I didn't know?"

"*Mon Dieu*, it's a miracle the Germans didn't find out."

"I've often wondered about that in my case too," Madame agreed. "I could be shot for saying this, but I think there were some decent Germans who suspected and didn't say anything. Not the SS, of course. They were all bastards, but some of the others. When it came to women, they didn't want to see a woman killed, and they certainly weren't going to tell the SS anything."

"I wish the real heroes—my brother and Denis and all the others—could be here for this," Renee said in a subdued voice, looking into the distance. "Henri is dead, and the others are still fighting. Joined up with the Free French troops, you know."

After the jubilation died down, and the hard realities of their situation sank in, the populace went to work cleaning up the rubble and ministering to the injured.

Mitch and Renee hurried back to the farmhouse to find Roger and Annette inspecting the mess. Roger immediately set to work with bits of wire and solder to repair his transmitter, while Mitch and

Renee straightened things up and boarded the shattered windows.

A trip across the yard to the demolished SS building produced a supply of building materials. Mitch surveyed the clutter. "I think the house can be fixed good as new—maybe better—given time to do the job. I just hope they let me stay long enough to be some help."

He told Roger not to hurry with the transmitter, knowing a message to London probably would result in an order to return immediately. In the meantime, the remains of the SS building yielded useful materials—lumber, tools, food, flashlights, ropes, petrol, and even welding equipment.

Although the village looked as if a tornado had torn it to shreds, the summer sun warmed the land, and the crops Renee had planted earlier in the spring were sprouting. Wild flowers grew in the scars left by tanks and bombs. God had not forsaken them altogether.

That night, after a hot dinner, the first in weeks, Mitch led Renee out onto the back porch. He held her hand and listened to the crickets chirping and let the warm summer evening flow over them. "Renee, lets talk about our wedding. It's what we both want, isn't it?"

"Yes. You know it is. It's the most important thing in the world to me."

"Me too, but should we go ahead with it right now? I won't be able to stay in St.-Pierre for more than a day or two. London will order me out. There's still a war to be fought, both in Europe and in the Pacific."

"Damn the war. I hate it. Isn't there any way ...?"

"Once we're married," Mitch explained, "I can arrange to bring you to England, or wherever I'm stationed, just so it's not a war zone. It all depends on where they send me. Of course, they won't let me bring you, unless we're officially married."

"I want to marry you more than anything I have ever wanted in my life, Mitch, but I've got a problem, and I don't know what to do about it."

"Whatever it is, I know we can work it out," Mitch insisted.

"I can't bring myself to leave the farm, Mitch. It means too much to me. Now that both my father and Henri are dead, I'm the only heir to a tradition going back more than five hundred years. And there's my mother. She would be heartbroken if I left permanently."

Holding her, Mitch said, "I know the farm is terribly important to you—and to me too—but trust me, we'll find a way."

There was a long silence while he tried to think of what to say. "I love you, Renee, and we're going to get married. Nothing is going to stand in the way." He stopped and chose his words carefully. "But I've got a few things to work out too. For one, I've got to report back to London. Then, after the war, I have two more years at Princeton to finish my architecture degree. I owe it to a very dear man, Bradstreet James, who's given me a full scholarship. On top of everything else, I've got to help my family. My father's had a stroke, and my mother's in desperate financial straits."

Mitch's heart ached as he watched Renee staring at the ground, choking back tears. Was there any way around the dilemma? "We should see Father Francois in the morning and ask his advice," Mitch said softly.

"Yes, Father Francois will know what ..." Renee responded in a near whisper.

Renee stood with her arm around him and looked into the distance. "I almost forgot," she added after a long pause. "Do you remember? I told you about the mysterious steel boxes that vile Gestapo captain buried. He was very secretive about it. And I think he killed the two men who were helping him."

"Yes, I remember. You told me about it when we were bicycling to Vire."

"Do you think we ought to dig them up and have a look?"

Mitch thought for a moment. "It's on your property. I can't see why not. It didn't look to you like there were explosives or booby-traps, or anything like that, did it?"

"No, I don't think so, but it was foggy. I could hardly see what they were doing. Frankly, I'm not sure of anything. The whole thing could have been my imagination."

Mitch scratched the back of his neck. "You've got my curiosity up. We'd better have a look anyway."

"If we do dig it up, whatever it is, I think we should do it at night, don't you? We might want to keep it our secret?"

"We'd better do it tonight," Mitch said. "I don't know how much longer I'm going to be able to stick around."

After Annette had retired, and Roger was tinkering with his transmitter, Renee and Mitch took two shovels and went to work. With a little moonlight, they were able to see just enough to work, but by the time they had dug down four feet, the bottom of the hole was totally dark.

"Are you sure we're in the right place?" Mitch asked wiping away the sweat.

"I think so," Renee whispered, "unless my imagination is playing tricks on me."

Then Mitch's shovel struck something hard. "Point your flashlight down here," he whispered.

At arm's length, Renee pointed the flashlight down into the hole, and Mitch scooped more dirt away from a hard, metallic surface. "I think we've hit it," he muttered and dug deeper, down and around the object. He gradually made out the outline of a steel box. Then there were two more. In all there were six.

Mitch tried to pry one loose. "Good God, it's heavy," he grunted, "and so is this," he added, trying a second one. He leaned on the shovel. "We'll have to rig up a sling and see if the two of us can get them out one at a time."

He climbed out of the hole. "Bring the flashlight, Renee. I think I know where there's some rope left by the Germans." Five minutes later, they had succeeded in rigging a sling, and Mitch had it worked under the first box. "You take one side, and I'll take the other." He handed one end to Renee. "See if we can do it."

Accompanied be a few grunts and some hard pulling, they finally hauled all six boxes up to surface. Mitch was sweating and out of breath. "Holy cats!" he gasped. "They look like pirate's treasure chests."

Renee held the light and ran her hand over the sides of the boxes. "Looks like they're welded shut. How're we going to get them open?"

"I saw an acetylene torch in the rubble of the SS building. If it's working, I can cut the welds. But first, I think we should get them over to your house where they're out of sight."

They dragged the boxes, one at a time, around behind the house.

Then Mitch went back to look for the acetylene torch. "It might not be a bad idea to refill that hole," he said. "Somehow, I think we shouldn't attract a whole lot of attention to this."

"First, let's find out what's in the boxes. The hole can wait." Renee was breathless.

"I'll see if I can get this torch to work." Mitch tried the spark-starter and twisted the valve handles of the unfamiliar equipment. Wearing welding goggles, obligingly provided by the Germans, he finally managed to get the torch ignited and went to work cutting open the first box. He looked across at Renee, who appeared to be holding her breath. "It's loose, but I can't get it off. Help me pull. Okay, here it comes." As the lid came off with a jerk, they stared speechless at the contents. "Quick, get the flashlight," Mitch said.

He reached into the box and lifted out a shiny bar. "Good God. These are gold," he gasped, gingerly lifting out one bar at a time. Feverishly, they went through the whole box, counting twenty bars. Mitch guessed each bar weighed more than twenty pounds.

Sitting on the second box, slightly dazed, he stared at Renee. "If this is what it seems to be, there must be a million francs' worth of gold in this one box."

"What are we going to do?" Renee whispered. "Do you think we can keep it?"

"I don't know what to say," Mitch responded slowly.

"Will we get in trouble?"

"Certainly nobody is going to say, 'Give it back to the Nazis.' Anyway, let's open the other boxes."

Renee held the flashlight while Mitch cut open the remaining five boxes. They tugged off the lids and pulled out a dozen cloth bags. Closed with twisted wire, they were easily opened. Mitch reached into the first bag and pulled out a handful of sparkling stones. Shards of light, reflected from the flashlight, shone on their faces. "They're diamonds!" Renee gasped. "Look at the size of some of them."

Hurriedly, Mitch went through the bags. They found more diamonds, then gold Krugerands and the currency of six nations: Germany, France, Denmark, Norway, Czechoslovakia, and even some English pounds.

"I don't know what we should do," Mitch repeated for the third time, feeling sheepish.

Renee put her hand to her forehead and whispered something he couldn't make out.

Mitch broke the silence. "I guess we'd better hide it for now and think about it. We'd be incredibly rich if we kept as little as a hundredth of it, but I'd feel a lot better if we knew where it came from."

Renee continued to stare at the treasure and murmured, "Yes, of course, hide it for now, but..."

"We know your SS Captain buried it, but we don't know where he got it."

"I suppose we could hide it under the boards of the root cellar," Renee said. "I don't think we're going to need the hiding place for food any longer. Or we could hide it in the caves."

"The caves wound be a good idea, but the boxes are ungodly heavy."

Renee sat on one of the boxes and ran her fingers over the sides. "They sure are."

"I don't know how we'd get them down those narrow shafts without some help. Besides, I'm sure to be ordered back to London right away, so I don't see how we'd have the time to move them anyway."

"You're probably right."

A jumble of thoughts tumbled through his mind. "Do you realize what this could mean for us," Mitch put both hands on top of hers. "I could send money to my parents, which they desperately need. You could pay off the mortgage on the farm and even hire some help. We could get married and live wherever we want—at least after the war ends—without worrying about the farm or my family. We could even come back here and live our lives and raise a family." He stopped abruptly, realizing what he had just said. Had he committed himself to living on a farm in Normandy?

"Oh Mitch!" Renee exclaimed, throwing her arms around him. "Those are the most beautiful words I've ever heard."

"Let's get married today before anything else happens. Before I'm sent back to London. You know, my orders could come any minute."

In late June, dawn came early, and the first rays awoke them to the urgency of doing something with the boxes. Mitch asked, "Do you have any wooden crates or cardboard boxes around the house? These steel ones are too heavy."

"No, but I think I saw some in the SS building."

"You take a look, while I start unloading these."

Renee made three trips to the rubble of the SS building and collected a dozen wooden boxes. Sweating from excitement as much as from handling the heavy bars, they transferred the contents to the lighter containers then carried them to the root cellar.

Mitch dumped the empty steel boxes back into the hole, back-filled the dirt, and smoothed it over.

Exhausted, they sat down in the parlor and talked like a couple of excited school children. "Remember," Mitch said, laughing, "this is our wedding day—if we can talk Father Francois into it. But we're going to be a couple of basket cases."

"I don't care if you have to carry me to the church." Renee was talking a mile a minute now. "We're going to get married. What could be better than being married on the longest day of the year, Mitch? I'm so happy. It's just as well we stayed up all night. I couldn't have slept anyway."

Mitch grinned at her while she carried on. "We can't go like this," she said breathlessly. "I'll start the water heating, so we can bathe. I'll scrub you off, if you'll do me," she said blushing, "and we'll have to find some decent clothes."

An hour later, Roger gave them a startled look when he came down for breakfast. "You two look like a couple of cats that just swallowed a whole cage full of canaries. And all dressed up. It isn't even Sunday."

"We're getting married—if we can persuade Father Francois," Mitch said, "before something else comes along and puts us off again."

Annette appeared just as excited as her daughter when they told her. She had some special things and her own wedding dress saved for the occasion.

Father Francois was wreathed in smiles. "I've been looking

forward to this day, ever since the Christmas service when I blessed the two of you. You do remember, don't you?"

"Of course," Renee responded. "How could we forget? That was a very special service and a brave sermon."

"Normally, I would insist on publishing the bans for three days and giving you three days of instructions, but I understand the urgency. Monsieur Carter—or should I address you as Commander—you may be called back to duty elsewhere at any minute. Is that not correct?"

"Yes, Father," Mitch replied. "We are ardently hoping you will marry us today. The worst of the war may be over in France, but the Nazis aren't beaten yet, and there's still the war in the Pacific."

Seeing to the paperwork, Father Francois told them to come back at 2:OO p.m.. He would have a little wedding service. "But you will, of course, have to get your civil wedding license first at the *Hotel de Ville,*" he added.

Somewhat bigger than her mother, Renee wouldn't fit into the cherished wedding dress. "Never mind," Annette offered. "I can fix it. You'll see." Sewing furiously, she managed to refit it flawlessly to her daughter. "You are so beautiful in that dress, I could cry," she exclaimed when it was finished.

In the meantime, Mitch went off to the city hall to get the license. But there he hit a snag. The petty official insisted that the law required a three-day waiting period. "Yes, I understand the urgency," he said, "but the law is the law, and I can lose my job if I break it." Mitch glared at the official but finally accepted the inescapable. The wedding would have to be put off for three days.

Grumbling to himself, he went back to see Father Francois, who promised to reschedule the wedding for three days hence. But the hard part was breaking the news to Renee. She'd been floating on a cloud. Now she would have to come back down to earth.

"Some day, I'm going to strangle that stupid bureaucrat," she muttered when Mitch told her. "But never mind the formalities, Mitch. They can't put our wedding off for ever." She kissed him and led him upstairs. "Come here, you handsome dog," she whispered as she worked on the buttons.

Twenty-four hours later found them still in bed, when they

heard Roger bumbling around downstairs, making an unnecessary ruckus.

"Cut it out, Roger," Mitch called out with good humor. "You're messing up our honeymoon."

Coming to the closed door of the bedroom, Roger apologized, "I 'ate to tell you this, ol' buddy. Didn't want to say anythin' on your supposed weddin' day, but you've got orders. You don't want to get court-martialed do you?"

"Damn," Mitch kissed Renee for the hundredth time. "Damn, damn, damn. The Gods have conspired to keep us from getting married." He climbed out of bed, threw on some clothes, and stormed down the stairs.

"What kind of orders?" he yelled at Roger. "I thought I told you not to get that damn transmitter fixed for a while."

"Sorry 'ol man. Actually I 'aven't fixed it, but the orders came in on the BBC. And in case you're wonderin' what 'appens next, there's an SOE agent on 'is way 'ere to escort you out. Supposed to arrive any time now. Figg'red you'd rather be dressed than found in the sack."

"Did the orders say anything about where I'm going or when?"

"Just that you're to go to Cherbourg for evacuation immediately," Roger replied. "They want me out too."

With time running out, Mitch and Renee had one last serious conversation. "I'll write to you as soon as I know where they're sending me," Mitch said, "and I'll write my parents and tell them I am marrying the most wonderful and most beautiful woman in the world. Then I'll get permission to come back as soon as possible, and we'll get properly married."

"Don't worry too much," Renee said. "What matters most is that you're safe. This horrible war can't last much longer. Just don't go and get yourself killed."

"About the money and the gold and all," Mitch hesitated, "I don't see any reason why you shouldn't use a small amount of the French francs. I wouldn't use very much, because it would attract attention. Someone might think you've been a collaborator, but enough to hire some help to fix the house and work on the farm. You can't go on doing it all alone. Then get yourself a telephone so I can talk to you."

Renee looked worried. "Do you think we can get in trouble using the money."

"I don't see how. We won't use very much for now, and we could pay it back someday if we had to. But I can't imagine paying it back to the Nazis."

"I suppose you're right, but I am—or rather I should say we are—going to lose the farm to the bankers if I don't make a couple of back payments on the mortgage."

"The only possible hitch I can see," Mitch continued slowly, "is if the Nazis should try to recover it secretly. They probably think it's undiscovered. And with that amount of money involved..."

"I've got an idea," Renee suggested. "I'll pile a bunch of old building materials over the hole. There'll be plenty of that sort of thing from the clean-up. If anyone comes poking around in the middle of the night and tries to start digging, he'll make a lot of noise."

Mitch nodded. "Sounds like a good idea. One other thing—keep your doors locked day and night, and I want you to have this pistol. It's okay. I've got another one. Keep it with you all the time—and by your bed at night. I don't care what anybody thinks. I want you safe 'til I get back."

CHAPTER FIVE

1945

PATTON OPENS A NEW DRIVE
INTO NAZI'S FLANK;
WESTERN TIP OF SALIENT
AGAIN SMASHED BACK;
HITLER BARS A SURRENDER, WARNS
DEFEATISTS
New York Times, Jan. 1, 1945

LONDON, ENGLAND

Captain Ames peered across the room at Mitch and pointed to a paper on his desk. "This report just came in from General Bradley's headquarters. It's an odd coincidence. Seems one of our most-wanted Nazis had a connection with St.-Pierre."

"May I see it please?" Mitch squinted at the teletype. "I have a pretty good hunch who that might be."

Ever since the Germans had been driven out of France at the first of the year, MI-6 had shifted some of its resources from working with the Resistance to identifying and locating Nazi war criminals. The whereabouts of (and the case against) Hitler, Himmler, Goering, and his principal henchmen had become a prime concern. They were also developing dossiers on scores of others such as "Ivan The Terrible," the "Beast of Belsen," and certain perpetrators of barbarous medical experiments.

Along with dozens of other dossiers, Mitch had seen the beginnings of one on a Gestapo captain responsible for dozens of murders and the plundering of Holland in 1940, but he had not noticed the name Streikler.

As he read the report from General Bradley, he became increasingly certain it was the same man. Bradley had been particularly incensed by the Malmedy atrocities, and had ordered an immediate and thorough investigation. The half dozen survivors had described the black-shirted Captain, and intelligence cross-references had confirmed Streikler's involvement at Malmedy. A captured Nazi had even named him.

According to the file, Streikler had also been connected to atrocities in Austria. This latest report moved his case into the "most wanted" category.

HEIDENDORFF'S TREASURE

Death and destruction no longer had any meaning to Otto. He had seen his comrades blown to pieces, and he had killed without feeling. The smell of death, together with the bitter cold, had numbed his senses. Furthermore, he had recently become aware of his own failing mind.

Nevertheless, his mind still functioned well enough to realize that the Third Reich was collapsing around him. And he still feared the Marshal. The fat man would surely try to escape and retrieve his treasure when the Allies closed in, and his first order of business would be to eliminate the only other person who knew about it.

Huddled in his tent behind the battle lines in Western Germany, he reasoned that he had best stay out of sight. His life wouldn't be worth a pfennig if Heidendorff tracked him down. One of the few soldiers who had any kind of shelter, he stared at the drops of water, dripping through a tear in the canvas of his tent and brooded about his situation.

What were his options? Stay with his company and be killed. Get lucky and survive long enough to be assassinated by the fat man? Desert and disappear? Of course, it was his only chance.

The thought of the treasure, buried at St.-Pierre, haunted him. *If those steel boxes contain anything like what I think they contain, and if I can get my hands on them, I can live like a king. I can buy my safety anywhere in the world. On the other hand, if I return to Germany, I will probably be executed for war crimes by the Allies— unless Heidendorff kills me first. But if I can unearth the treasure, I can buy my escape. There would be enough money to buy about anything—a new identity, a new life in South America. I will be a tycoon, have servants, everything.*

At the moment, he needed to move quickly while the confusion of battle made the border between France and Germany meaningless. He knew it would be suicidal to attempt to work his way through the battlefields of the northern sector. If not killed by the enemy, he would more than likely be shot as a deserter.

Nevertheless, his only option was to desert and do it now. The remaining question—how to get through the lines and back into France and to St.-Pierre? All things considered, the mountainous, heavily forested southwest corner of Germany offered the best escape route.

Otto checked his watch. 12:3O a.m. He donned his rain slicker, loaded his field pack, pocketed a compass, strapped on his Luger, and stepped out into the rain. The sentry saluted him, as he left the camp and walked rapidly in a southerly direction.

Wehrmacht control had broken down. In the gloom, Otto could make out refugees moving away from the front. The Germans were retreating to the east, but the French ex-forced-laborers and even some escaped Allied prisoners were trudging south and west. Apparently they had come to the same conclusion as he.

Unrecognizable in the dark rain, Otto stood by the side of a muddy road and waited. He did not have to wait long before he spotted what he was looking for, a lone straggler who appeared to be about his size. The emaciated Frenchman was no match for the Gestapo Captain. With a single punch, Otto knocked him out, and stripped him of his coat, outer clothes, and papers, which identified him as a French prisoner of war, an escapee from Hammelburg.

Otto stowed the man's clothes in his field pack, but decided to continue wearing his Gestapo uniform a while longer. It would be useful in frightening German civilians into providing him with his needs. But in the black uniform, he knew his life would be in danger around French nationals. He would switch to the stolen prisoner's clothes at the French border.

Shouldering his pack, he looked back at the prone figure on the ground, curled in a fetal position, clad only in his underwear, the cold rain running over him. Otto hesitated, then turned back and muttered under his breath, "Sorry, Frenchie. I had to do it." He took off his heavy Gestapo coat and wrapped it around the man. Pulling on the Frenchman's threadbare wool coat, he started down the muddy road at a near run.

Otto worked his way south, demanding food and shelter at isolated farmhouses, and then thanking his farmer-hosts in the morning by robbing them at gunpoint.

In the southwest corner of Germany, the Black Forest and the tiny town of Lorrach share the headwaters of the Rhine River with Switzerland and France. There, Otto put on the stolen clothes over his uniform for warmth as well as disguise.

His first challenge was to cross the partly frozen over Rhine. Now guarded by Allied troops, the bridges were out of the question. He didn't know how to swim, and the water was prohibitively cold, so he set out prowling the east bank in search of a small boat.

Frustrated after half a day's search, he was about to give up, when he spotted a small boy, fishing from a rowboat. From the shore, Otto hailed the boy, who smiled, waved, and responded with a cheerful, *"Guten Tag."* Beckoning to the boy, Otto asked if he would take him across. "Sure, jump in," the boy responded, reeling in his line. He backed the small boat against the icy bank, and pointed to the back seat. "Be careful. It's tippy," he added.

The Rhine is narrow near the headwaters, and they were across in five minutes. Otto wondered whether he should kill the boy but finally decided it was not necessary. He grunted, "danke."

Once across, he climbed up the steep west bank and immediately found himself in a heavily wooded pine forest with several inches of snow on the ground. Otto began trudging in the southwesterly direction toward the setting sun until the light gave out. He looked in vain for shelter, but finding none, huddled under a tree. Unable to sleep on the snowy, cold ground, he clutched every item in his pack against his body and covered himself with fragments of dead ferns and broken branches.

After two hours, he began to shake like a wet dog and realized he would freeze to death if he didn't start moving again. The moon rose above the trees, and stars began to illuminate the forest. He consulted his compass and resumed his plodding westward toward France. The steep cliffs and deep ravines conspired to make the trek a nightmare, but at least the exertion kept him warm. He recalled having been told that the precipitous terrain was the reason why invading armies had never taken this route, precisely the reason it was now available to him. He also knew that only about twenty kilometers separated the Rhine River from the nearest town in France, Mulhouse. But those kilometers would be some of the roughest in Europe outside the Swiss Alps.

On the second day, Otto continued to fight his way westward up and down steep cliffs, through deep snow and dark woods. He had now consumed his last morsel of food and was nearly frozen when he stumbled upon a woodcutter's cabin. He pounded on the door with a numb fist and, receiving no response, tried the latch. Frustrated, he looked around for some way to break in, but the windows were barred, and the door was securely locked. Chilled to the bone, he went in search of the owner, following some recent tracks in the snow and the sounds of wood chopping. He found the owner nearby, ax in hand, delimbing a tree. In his poor French, Otto called to him, *"Pouvez-vous m'aider. Je me suis perdu et tres froid."*

A big, raw-boned man with a heavy red beard, the woodcutter stared suspiciously at Otto. The response, in French, came slowly in curt monosyllables. *"qui etes-vous?"*

Otto fished out the papers he had stolen from the French prisoner-of-war and tried to sound like a Frenchman. *"Voici mes papiers."*

The woodcutter grunted without looking at the papers and pointed to the trail toward the cabin, indicating that Otto stay in front of him. As they walked back to the cabin, Otto could see him gripping the ax in front of him with both hands.

"Put your hands in the air," the woodsman ordered as he

unlocked the door.

Obviously the home of a single male, the one-room cabin was warm and comfortable. Shelves of books lined one wall. A rifle hung over the fireplace and copper pots hung from hooks above a wood-burning stove.

Otto moved close to the stove and warmed himself, while the silence between them hung like a steel curtain. The woodcutter, still wearing his heavy wool cap, made tea in a large pot and watched without blinking as Otto accepted a cup of brew that tasted slightly of pine needles. Otto wrinkled up his nose and, sinking gingerly into a chair by the stove, drank it slowly.

With steely eyes, they stared at each other. This was not a man to trifle with, Otto decided. Rising carefully from the chair, he slowly backed out through the cabin door without so much as a thank-you.

He peered at his compass, calculated his westward direction again, and wondered if he would make it to civilization. For one thing, he would have to keep his mouth shut around Frenchmen. He longed for a map, but nearly out of the high country now, he knew he was somewhere near Mulhouse. He pulled his coat tightly around him, put his face down into the collar, and continued to trudge through the snow. Three hours after leaving the woodcutter's cabin, the terrain began to flatten out, and he came across a narrow dirt road. Without regard to its direction, he decided to follow it. Anything was better than slogging through the deep snow. Only a short distance down the road, he spotted a dilapidated barn. Exhausted, he pushed open the creaky barn door, covered himself with some musty hay, and fell asleep instantly.

At dawn the next day, Otto, nearly starved, staggered out onto the dirt road and pressed on with his journey westward. Half a kilometer down the road, he came upon an intersection and a weathered road sign pointing to Mulhouse.

Faint with hunger, he rubbed his face to stay awake and then felt the gun in his pocket. There must be a farmhouse somewhere. His best disguise, he decided, would be that of a decrepid old man, not expected to speak more than a word or two.

He approached the first farmhouse on the outskirts of Mulhouse and knocked on the door. A middle-aged woman, wearing an apron, opened it promptly and reached out to help him. Hunched over, he stepped into the warm kitchen as the odor of baking bread assaulted him. The woman, prematurely gray and quite petite, surely would not give him any trouble. Besides, there was no man in sight. Otto straightened up, pulled his gun from his pocket and snapped, "I'll kill you, if you make a sound. I need food. That loaf of bread," he said, pointing to a long French loaf on the kitchen table, "and your money."

When she stood motionless and silent, he raised his hand to strike her, but held off when she jumped back and thrust the bread into his hand.

"And your money," Otto repeated, jabbing the gun into her face.

She reached for a purse in the top kitchen drawer. Otto extracted the contents of the purse, tied the woman by her apron strings to a door handle, and ran out the door. There had been no one else in the house, no telephone wires, and the house was isolated, so Otto was confident the woman would not be able to raise an alarm quickly.

Fifteen minutes later, he found the Mulhouse train station and examined the money—seventy francs, enough to buy a train ticket to Paris and then to Rouen. He was in luck. A train was leaving for Paris in ten minutes.

Twenty-four hours later, Otto stepped off the train in Rouen. There was no train from Rouen to St.-Pierre-du-Bois, which was only a few kilometers away, but he knew the area like the back of his hand. He waited until dusk and stole a bicycle, which was obligingly leaning against the wall of the railroad station, the young owner having taken half a minute to use the unisex toilet.

Bicycling to St.-Pierre-du-Bois, Otto went unnoticed among the thousands of refugees trudging along the roads, returning to their homes.

ST.-PIERRE-DU-BOIS

Renee rose early as usual and hustled outside to the chicken coop to gather two eggs for breakfast. She stopped short. Something was wrong. The pile of building materials had been moved.

She hurried back to the house and found her mother in the kitchen. "Who moved the pile of materials by the barn?" she asked.

Her mother looked up from the stove. "I have no idea. I assume it was Pierre."

Renee forgot about breakfast. She ran back outside and carefully inspected the ground where the treasure had been, but could not detect any signs of digging. Puzzled, she went off to talk to Pierre who was already at work in the fields.

"*Bonjour, Pierre. Comment ca va.*"

"*Bien. Bonjour, Mademoiselle. Ca va bien.*"

"Pierre, did you move the pile of lumber by the barn?"

"No, certainly not, Mademoiselle."

"Do you have any idea who did?"

"No, no idea at all."

"That's really strange. Well then, would you please help me put it back?"

"Right now?"

"Yes, we must do it immediately."

* * *

Otto looked around carefully. It was dark now. No one in sight. It was his second night back at the Brousard farm.

The previous night, he had discovered the pile of lumber over the place where he had buried the steel boxes, the place where he planned to dig. Late at night, he had come out of his hiding place by the creek and had begun to move the pile slowly, careful not to make any noise. But dawn and the arrival of Pierre had put an end to his efforts before he could finish and start digging. He had crawled back into his cold, damp hiding place by the creek.

Now he was ready to try again. He found a shovel in the barn and planned to start digging. But to his dismay, he discovered that the pile of lumber was back in its place over the treasure boxes.

"*Ach, Scheisse,*" he muttered under his breath. "The damned workman must have put it back while I was in the village."

He had gone into the village, disguised as an old man, to buy food at the alimentation store. Then, in the afternoon, he had tried unsuccessfully to get some sleep, lying on the cold ground.

Now it was finally dark enough. Grumbling to himself, he laid the shovel aside and went to work moving the pile for the second time. Damn, it was hard not to make any noise. He would have to go at it carefully and slowly.

He had hardly started when a car drove up to house, and the headlights swept across the barn. Otto jumped behind the corner of the vine-covered outbuilding and crawled back into his hiding place. He saw a bearded man with a gun strapped to his belt get out and enter the house. With growing frustration, he watched the lights in the house and the car parked in front until early morning. He didn't dare work on the pile now.

Cursing his luck, he pounded the ground and tried to control the shaking in his hands.

*　　*　　*

After four years of hiding and fighting, Denis LeCoc had come home at last. In 1944, most of the able-bodied *Maquis* had joined the Allied forces to help drive the Germans out of France. Now they were entitled to a rest and some kind of celebration. The home folks had been too exhausted to provide much of a homecoming. Nevertheless, Renee broke out her best bottle of wine and insisted he stay for dinner. They talked into the late hours of the night, telling of the events of the last four years.

"What happened to Michelle LaRoth?" Renee asked.

"She's just fine," Denis answered. "Turned into one of our best fighters, hard as nails. Married one of my lieutenants. He's a good man, and I'm sure they'll do very well. But tell me, what happened to Madame Lazzard? Did the Nazis ever catch on to her?"

"She was special friend of the Mayor, and he hid her somewhere outside of St.-Pierre. She is a survivor."

And so the conversation went on into the night, but gradually a shadow settled over Renee's countenance, and the conversation stalled.

"What is it, Renee? You look frightened. You know I will always help if you have a problem."

"I know that, Denis," she hesitated, "but I don't know whether I really have a problem or even how to tell you about it."

"Is everything all right with you and Mitch?"

"It's nothing like that, but I do have a problem—maybe not exactly a problem—just call it a situation, but I have to swear you to secrecy."

"Of course, Renee. Whatever you say."

Unnerved by the mysterious moving of the pile, she felt she had to confide in someone, and Denis was the only person she could turn to at the moment. She hoped Mitch would understand.

Haltingly, she told him the story of the Nazi treasure and the curious moving of the lumber pile, but not the part about the attempted rape. She didn't give him any idea of the size of the treasure. He would see for himself.

"I think you should have a look," she said, "but remember to keep it secret."

"Of course. Of course, but what can possibly be so secret as all that?"

Leading the way to the root cellar, she removed the boards that had done such a good job of hiding food from the Germans.

"Here, Denis, help me lift out a couple these boxes. They're heavy. You take that end. All right. That's it. Now, let's take them up in the light where we can get a better look."

When they had dug into the first box and spread only a small part of it on the floor, Denis let out an exclamation. "Holy Jesus, there's a king's ransom here—just in this one box!"

Half way through the second box, Renee watched him turn rigid. "You know what this is?" he gasped. "My God, it's the gold and diamonds stolen from the Jews in Holland and from melted-down gold fillings. See this box. You can tell by the color of the metal. This came from the gas chambers at Auchwitz and Dachau. There's currency here too, but you can be sure that was stolen from the Jews just like everything else."

Renee recoiled in horror. "Are you sure? *Mon Dieu*, if that's true, I won't touch it."

"Yes. I'm sure. I've seen this before—when we liberated

Ravensbrueck. We had Jews in the Maquis who had escaped from Dachau—witnesses to it—also a few lucky ones who escaped from Holland. It fits exactly. The Nazi SS stole every last diamond, every last bar of gold, everything of value from the Jews in Holland in 1940, then murdered them in the concentration camps, and ... Well, you know the rest."

"That's horrible. I don't want any part of it in that case, and I'm sure Mitch won't either."

"Maybe not," Denis agreed, "but don't do anything hasty. You and Mitch'll want to think about it—talk it over."

"We'll give it back. There must be some organization ..." Renee closed her eyes and buried her face in her hands. "But, as you say, I have to talk to Mitch before we do anything."

"Does anyone know about this besides you and Mitch?"

"No, not that I know of, except the German that buried it. But I'm terrified, having all that gold and money right here in my house."

Denis frowned. "Yes, of course. You've got to move it somewhere else."

"Then I ask you, why would the pile of lumber have been moved, unless someone's looking for it? There's enough money here to finance a small country, and the only people who know about it are the German and Mitch and me—and now you."

"You'd better get a phone call or a telegram through to Mitch tomorrow," Denis said, "and keep your door locked."

After helping Renee put the boxes back in their hiding place, Denis put his hand on her arm, "Do you have a gun?"

"Yes. I keep it by my bed."

"I think you should carry it. Keep it with you all the time."

Renee shrank from the idea of carrying a gun, but nodded anyway.

"You should try to contact Mitch in the morning. In the meantime, I'll see if I can find some organization in the business of resettling the Jews."

When he finally departed, well after midnight, he tried to kiss her on the mouth, but she turned her cheek. "I'll check back with you in a couple of days," he said, waving adieu.

Renee could not sleep that night. Was she in danger from some mysterious intruder? Could she and Mitch ever be married without the money? Could she ask Mitch to give up his Princeton education and his architecture? Would the marriage be put off forever?

*   *   *

Otto stayed in hiding and watched the lights of the house. The man with the gun was staying late, and it was after 1:OO a.m. when he finally emerged and drove away. Otto realized he would not have time to move the pile again and start digging before dawn. He would have to wait still another day. But he assumed that nobody knew about the treasure except he and Heidendorff. All he would have to do was dig it up and move it into the bushes by the creek, one box at a time. Then he would take out enough money to buy an automobile. And after that ...? He would worry about the next step later.

*   *   *

The next morning, relieved to see the pile of lumber still in place, Renee bicycled into the village. The only public telephones were at the Post Office.

"*Bonjour, Monsieur Charlon .*" She smiled at the Postmaster, whom she had known all her life. "I need to place a phone call to England. It's rather urgent."

"Bonjour, Mademoiselle. I'm afraid you must have military clearance. You know it's required for overseas calls."

"I didn't know. Perhaps a telegram then?"

"Certainly, Mademoiselle. Here is a form."

Unable to explain everything in the telegram, she asked Mitch to telephone her at the St.-Pierre postoffice at 9:OO a.m. the next morning. She felt certain he could obtain the necessary authorization to make the call from his end.

*   *   *

That night, Otto went to work, moving the pile of lumber for the second time. Then he started digging with a vengeance.

At 3:OO a.m. his shovel struck the first box with a hollow thud. Digging furiously around it, he pulled it loose and hoisted it to the surface. Even before he opened it, he knew something was wrong. It was too light. Exhausted, he ripped off the lid, which was no longer welded shut. Nothing. In frenzy, he dug further and repeated the process. Still nothing.

Nearing dawn, Otto knew he would not have time to fill the hole and replace the lumber. Someone had found the boxes. But who? Someone had placed a pile of lumber over the hole. But who? And the same someone had replaced the pile only yesterday! The obvious answer jumped at him—the French woman.

He uttered obscenities and felt his features distort in rage. His fist pounded on an empty box. The hollow sound mocked him. Grabbing the shovel in one hand and his Walther in the other, he stormed over to the Brousard house and pounded on the latch of the front door. Finding it securely bolted, he threw his weight against it. When it wouldn't budge, he pointed a shaky pistol at the door and shot the lock to pieces with two blasts.

He climbed the stairs two at a time and burst into the French woman's bedroom. In the faint glimmer of moonlight coming from the window, Otto could make out her outline, sitting on the edge of the bed, juggling a gun with both hands.

"Drop it," he barked, at the same time firing two shots into the floor at her feet.

She dropped the gun on the floor and stared at him mutely.

"So we meet again, Fraulein," he kicked her gun to one side. "You cause me great trouble, Fraulein. You think I not know about your part in Resistance? Of course, I know."

He shoved the gun back in its holster and gripped her arms. "Why you think I let you get away with it? Let's just say I like you. I wanted you." He put his face up close to her's. "But no more. You found boxes, haven't you?"

"You're mad," Renee croaked. "I don't know what you are talking about."

"You know what I talk about. You dig up boxes and put dirt back in hole. You had workman pile lumber on top. Don't try to deny it.

I've been watching for three days. You two are the only people here."

"You're crazy," Renee said, shaking. "You'd better get out of France in a hurry or the Gendarmes will arrest you. They will kill you."

In the dim light, Otto could see her cringe. He read the fear in her voice. "Don't play games," he said quietly. "You must tell me where it is. But first, I think we finish what we not finish last time. You remember? Of course, you do." He grabbed the front of her dress, and ripped it apart. The buttons went flying. He continued to hold her arms in a bruising grip and stared at the bare breasts. She began to scream and pound his face and tried to kick him in the groin.

Damn this woman, Otto thought, pushing her onto the bed. *She fights like a swarm of hornets and screams like a Banshee. But I want her. I want her.*

"No. No," she gasped. "I'll tell you where ..."

Suddenly there was a running noise, and an older woman stumbled into the room. Barefoot, with her long hair streaming behind, she screamed incoherently, "Renee, Renee. What is..."

"Go back to your room, mama," Renee shouted. "He'll kill you like he did papa."

"No." Otto commanded, pointing his gun first at one and then the other. "Both of you. Down on floor. Face down."

When the women did not move, he fired two more bullets into the floor inches from the older woman's foot. "Now!" he shouted. "Or I'll put the next one into you. Down on the floor. Face down. Hands behind back."

Pulling a sheet off the bed and ripping it into strips, he tied their hands behind their backs, then snapped, "Don't move or I kill you both."

"That's better," he hesitated and stared at Renee's half-nude body. "Now, are you going to show me where the boxes are?"

"You beast, I'll ..." Renee sputtered.

"You'll what?"

"I'll ..." She closed her eyes and started to speak. Then stopped and started again. "I'll show you where it is," she said in a steady voice.

Hunched over, eyes wide, the mother seemed to be in a state of shock. Otto tied her feet together and warned her not to move. Removing the ties from Renee and stuffing them in his pocket, he pushed his gun against her back and ordered her to lead the way.

She pulled the shreds of her nightdress across her front and showed him to the root cellar, then silently pointed to the loose boards. Otto pulled off the boards, lifted the first box up into the light, and feverishly pried off the lid.

"Mein Gott," he gasped, forgetting about Renee. When he dove into the second box, she began to back away, then broke into a run. She got only as far as the kitchen door. Otto heard the footsteps behind him and, in a matter of seconds, caught up with her, spun her around, and knocked her to the floor with a backhand blow across the jaw. He retied the bonds.

She lay motionless, and Otto found her limp body difficult to move. Impatient to get back to the boxes, he tied her feet as well as her hands and decided to leave her, a motionless heap on the floor.

The first rays of dawn streamed through the half-open door to the root cellar. Otto was sweating like a hog in heat, partly from the physical strain of wrestling with the boxes and partly from the mental strain of trying to figure out what to do next. What should he do with the women? *Should I kill them, take them hostage, or tie them up and leave them? Obviously, the only sensible thing is to kill them. But damn. I want the French woman.*

Gun in hand, he went back to find Renee struggling frantically with the bonds on her ankles and wrists. Pointing the gun slightly to one side of her head, he pulled the trigger. He would frighten her into submission. CLICK. The gun clip was empty. He had used all the bullets shooting open the door and putting holes in the floor.

He stared at Renee. She stared back, abject terror showing in her blue-green eyes. Once again the image of Ilsa. *I can't hurt her. I want her."* He stood mesmerized and stared into her eyes. *"Mein Gott,"* he muttered to himself.

"You come with me," he said gruffly.

Shaking like a wounded bird in a snowstorm, she closed her eyes. "I'm cold," she said in a hoarse whisper.

He brought her a coat from the hall closet, then doubled up the ties on her wrists, put a gag over her mouth, and tied her to a chair. "I leave you now for a time. If you move even one inch, I kill you when I get back."

Otto extracted 20,000 francs from the first box and stuffed them in his pocket, then went outside, made a half-way effort to hide the evidence of his digging, and replaced the lumber pile. He hurried to the bushes by the creek where he had hidden the stolen bicycle, then rode into the village.

As Otto suspected, automobiles were almost impossible to come by in the summer of 1944, and the only car dealer in St.-Pierre was able to name his price. In spite of the shortage, the dealer had for sale a few pre-war, well-used models that could be had for twice their original price.

The dealer, no doubt accustomed to considerable haggling and tire-kicking, smiled broadly and exuded felicitations when Otto paid him the asking price for his most expensive car without even driving it. Otto, hunched over, spoke only in grunts and nods.

"You forgot your bicycle," the dealer yelled after him as Otto drove off.

*   *   *

Renee knew that Pierre would come to work in the fields promptly at 8:00 o'clock in the morning, but normally he would only come to the house at noon for a lunch break. Still, she prayed he would notice something wrong and look in.

She heard a car pull up and prayed. Perhaps it was Denis or a neighbor. Her hopes quickly shattered when Otto burst in, looking totally pleased with himself.

Renee watched with mounting fear as the German went to work loading the boxes into the car. He checked her bonds, then ran up the stairs, apparently to check on her mother and recover her gun, which still lay on the floor. She knew it was loaded with six bullets.

When he came back down the stairs and pointed her own gun at her, Renee was certain he would shoot her. Instead, he removed the bonds from her ankles and ordered her to walk to the car. With a gun at her back, he prodded her into the right front seat. The back seat was stuffed to the ceiling with the excess boxes that would not fit in the trunk.

He squinted at her, one eye twitching badly, "Even the smallest move, and I shoot you. I should have done it back there, you know. I may change my mind. You be nice to Otto. Don't make trouble. You stay alive."

Terrified, Renee closed her eyes and prayed. He no doubt meant what he said. She could understand why he would want her dead. She would be much less trouble.

*   *   *

Familiar with the geography of northern France, Otto headed west toward the seaport of Brest. He had been told Brest was the largest fishing port in Northern France. Surely there would be a fisherman who would take him to Portugal for the right price. If necessary, he could buy the whole boat. From Portugal, he would buy his passage to Argentina—and a new life.

As he drove, his mind formed pictures of a magnificent estate with horses and cattle and servants—and this beautiful Frenchwoman. But the last thought troubled him. *Can I tame her? Can I keep her in line? Will she revolt and prove to be my undoing? If I offer her so many good things she can't possibly refuse, will she come around?*

LONDON

Mitch frowned as he read the telegram for the second time. **LUMBER PILE MOVED DURING NIGHT UNEXPLAINABLE.   PLEASE CALL ME AT ST.-PIERRE POST OFFICE STOP PHONE 21-13-33-48 9:OO AM   TOMORROW. URGENT STOP LOVE RENEE.**

At 9:OO a.m. sharp, Mitch called the number. The phone rang for several minutes. There was no answer. He hung up and tried again and every ten minutes thereafter. Still getting no answer, he was becoming alarmed, when on the ninth try, the St.-Pierre Postmaster picked up the phone.

"*Allo, Monsieur Charlon ici.* I'm not supposed to answer the telephone, but—"

Mitch broke in, "I'm sorry, *Monsieur*, but this is an emergency. I need to talk to Mademoiselle Renee Brousard."

"I have not seen her today," the Postmaster responded. "You say it is an emergency? How serious?"

"I think she could be in great trouble. Is there any chance you could have someone—perhaps a Gendarme—look in on her, and call me back? I'll pay you for the call and for any inconvenience."

"I don't know. I'm alone here, and I can't leave the post office. You say it's an emergency? Well, I'll try to find someone. Normally, I'm not supposed to do anything like that." He hesitated. "But, after all, she was a special heroine of the Resistance. I'll call you back when I find out something—this afternoon in any event."

Giving his telephone number, which had military clearance, Mitch thanked the man profusely.

Mitch had been pacing the floor for two hours, when his phone rang. "This is Sergeant Mausant of the St.-Pierre-du-Bois Police." The voice sounded serious. "I have just returned from the Brousard residence, and there is, indeed, a problem. May I ask, what is your connection with this?"

"Please tell me what has happened? Is Renee—Mademoiselle Brousard—all right?"

"Sorry. You must tell me your connection with this."

"Mademoiselle and I are engaged to be married." Mitch felt somewhat inadequate in the explanation.

There was a long pause. "Are you, by any chance Trout, the American who trained the Resistance?"

"Yes, but please, I must know what is going on."

"In that case, we will do everything in our power to help. You may not remember. I was with Denis and Henri when you trained us. It is a great pleasure to speak with—"

Mitch cut him off. "Please tell me what happened."

"We are not exactly sure. We found Madame Annette Brousard

bound and gagged, tied to a chair, but we did not find Mademoiselle Renee yet. Madame was quite incoherent, and we were not able to make any sense of what she was saying. We have taken her to the hospital where she is under sedation. I'm sure she will be all right."

"Yes, but what about Renee. Where is she?"

"I'm afraid we don't know," the sergeant replied, "but we are searching. I have two men on it."

"Did Madame say anything at all? Did you find any clues?"

"She said something about a man with a gun. And the front door lock had been shot to pieces. Also there were bullet holes in the floor."

"Anything else?" Mitch asked. "I might be able to give you some idea of who you're looking for."

"We talked to a workman on the farm. His name is Pierre. He said he saw a car drive up at about 9:30 this morning and drive away a few minutes later. He wasn't too sure, but thought it was a Peugeot. A dark color, maybe green."

"Please. Please do everything you can," Mitch urged. "If it's humanly possible, I'll come and help you search. In the meantime, would you get hold of Denis LeCoc. You know him. He'll help and may know where to look. One other thing. I'm almost certain the man you are looking for is a German, a Nazi Gestapo captain, who is possibly in disguise. He is a big, heavy-set man, blond, about twenty-five years old, and extremely dangerous. He is the same man who was chief of the SS in St.-Pierre for two years and is well known to Denis and many others in your town."

"How do you know this?"

"I can't tell you everything, but I can tell you this much: I am with British Intelligence, and we have a dossier on this man. His name is Otto Streikler, and he's on the list of Nazis, most wanted for war crimes."

After obtaining assurances from the Sergeant that he would do everything in his power, Mitch rushed into Captain Ames' office without knocking.

The Captain looked up from his desk with obvious irritation. "This'd better be important. I'm in the middle of–"

"Sorry sir," Mitch cut in. "But this is a real crisis. I've got to get into France—by air—today. I'll parachute in if there's no other way."

"Slow down, Commander." Ames held up his hand. "Tell me what's going on."

"It's Streikler, the Nazi we talked about just the other day. He has kidnapped Renee Brousard and made off with a fortune in stolen gold and diamonds and currency—enough to buy him just about anything. This has only happened in the last few hours, and my guess is he's trying to escape the country."

"How do you know all this?" Ames asked.

"It's a long story, sir," Mitch responded, talking fast, "and I don't have time. Streikler is the same Gestapo captain that captured me last year—would have killed me too if I hadn't been rescued by paratroops on D-Day. I don't have time to explain it all now. The man has a four or five hour head start, and we can't waste a minute. I've started the French police looking for him, but they're going to need me too."

"Are you the right man to go after him?" Ames asked. "Maybe you're too emotionally involved."

"I have to go." Mitch replied. "I'd go crazy sitting here, knowing that insane beast has Renee. Besides, I know the country and I can get Denis LeCoc and his *Maquis* to help. Nobody else can do that like I can. I've got to get on the stick—now. I need you to authorize an airdrop for me though. Can you do that for me?"

"Okay," Ames agreed hesitantly. "I hope you know what you're doing. I'll send Roger in behind you, as backup, as soon as I can find him."

"Might be better if you held him ready to go when I telephone. Can you keep your phone manned around the clock for the next few days? One other thing, I'll need some French francs. Two thousand ought to do it. Can you give me a requisition slip on that? I think I have everything else ready to go."

"All right, I'll write it out, then I'll drive you out to Bromley field as soon as you get your gear together." Ames reached for his telephone. "While you're doing that, I'll call ahead and have a Lizzy ready."

"Give me thirty minutes," said Mitch.

Like the other men in MI-6, his chute and pack were always at the ready, but it would take a few minutes to requisition the two thousand francs.

NORMANDY, FRANCE

Two and a half hours later, Mitch was leaning out the jump hatch of the Lysander, yelling at the pilot to circle first a little one way and then the other. Parachuting in on the small field behind Denis' house was not going to be easy, but it would save a great deal of time. With no wind and good visibility, he knew he could do it.

Checking his gear one last time, he signaled thumbs up to the pilot and jumped.

BRITTANY, FRANCE

Otto had a problem. He wanted this woman—the mother had called her Renee—almost as much as he wanted the money, but, the more he thought about it, the more he realized she spelled trouble.

Driving as fast as he dared without attracting attention or being stopped by the police, he lectured to Renee. In guttural French, he spoke of the future idyllic life he envisaged in South America. "We will have everything," he gloated, "a huge estate, servants and horses and cattle and anything else you can think of, everything you can possibly want. All you have to do is be nice to Otto." He pulled over for a short stop and removed the gag, then stepped hard on the gas pedal and sped on. From time to time, he peered across at Renee's ashen face, trying to read her reaction.

So far, she had stared straight ahead, expressionless. Otto frowned. She had better show some signs of cooperation, or I'm going to have to kill her.

She turned slowly and her eyes seemed to look through him. He wondered if she was forcing herself to look at him—play-acting—to save herself?

"That's better," he said. "We can get along. You will see."

Near the town of Avranches, Otto stopped. "I get something to eat. You like wine?"

When there was no answer, Otto muttered, "Yes, of course, all Frenchies like wine. You wait in car and not move or make a sound, or I ..." He did not need to finish the sentence. Pressing the gun against her ribs to emphasize his point, he re-tied her ankles and hurried into the small cafe.

Returning minutes later with bread, cheese, and two bottles of wine, he grunted his satisfaction as he found Renee still immobilized as he had left her.

With a jerk and a noisy grinding of gears, he restarted the car and headed westward, then turned away from the coast and veered off in a southerly direction onto a web of back-country dirt roads, which soon led to the rocky hills and farmlands of central Brittany. After three nights without sleep, Otto was exhausted and fought to stay awake. He knew he would fall asleep at the wheel unless he found some stopping place soon, a place off the beaten track.

As the Renault bumped along on the dirt roads, pocked from the winter rains, Otto yawned, rubbed his eyes, and looked from side to side for a place to hide out for the night. The light had begun to fade when he spotted an isolated farm, which looked promising. There were signs of life in the house, but the barn appeared to be deserted. It would do, he thought, just so long as there was no dog to raise an alarm. But he knew that hardly any dogs had survived the war in France. They had all been eaten. He drove to the backside of the barn and looked around. There were no dogs. And the car would be hidden from the house.

"I have to relieve myself," Renee said in a near whisper, her first words since being forced into the car.

"Ah, so Fraulein can talk." Otto removed her ties. "Do not try anything you will regret," he added, pointing the gun at her.

She retreated behind a haystack, while he stood, shifting from one foot to the other, impatient.

"That's enough time," he called.

When she emerged the wrist ties looked a bit loose. He frowned, muttered something in German, and retied them, but this time in front of her.

Otto pushed open the barn door and peered into the dark interior. When his eyes had adjusted, he focused on the bales of hay and grunted something in German. The barn would make a tolerable place to sleep. With the gun at her back, he prodded his captive into the barn and nudged her onto a hay bale.

"Sit," he ordered and returned to the car where he picked up the two bottles of wine, the bread, and cheese. He placed these on a hay bale in front of Renee and loosened her wrist ties slightly so she could reach the food. Using his pocketknife, he pried the cork out of one of the wine bottles, took a large swig, and offered it to Renee. She shook her head. With an irritated frown, he drank some more, then cut into the bread and cheese.

Renee could not bring herself to drink from the same bottle, but accepted the bread and cheese, partly out of fear of antagonizing him and partly because she needed her strength. She was becoming faint with hunger. In the meantime, she watched the German making short work of the wine. She noticed his fist clenching and shaking and the wine splashing out of the top of the bottle, dribbling down his unshaven chin.

Otto made slurping noises, burped, then started on the second bottle. As he consumed the last of the wine, he reached out to her and seemed to be trying to form some words, "Sshlet's smake luf" Instead, he collapsed in a stupor and, in a few seconds, was snoring like an angry lion. The wine and lack of sleep—she knew it had been at least two days—had caught up with him.

Renee carefully disengaged his arm, then sat rigidly still, listening to the snoring for a full minute before daring to move. Along with the car keys, the gun was in his right pocket. Did she dare try to remove them, or would it be better just to make a run for it?

With her hands still tied, she couldn't get at the gun without practically sitting on him. She had no use for the car keys. She didn't know how to drive. Of course, it would be a good idea to deprive him of both the gun and the keys, but she decided it wasn't worth the risk.

Slowly rising and tiptoeing toward the barn door, she heard a particularly loud snore and saw his arm flop over on his other side. She froze. But the regular sounds resumed. The barn door made a frightening squeak as she eased her way through the opening. She started running, stumbling along the dirt road, at the same time working her wrist ties. She had not dared to rouse the nearby farmhouse for fear Otto would force his way in and recapture her. He would probably shoot her this time.

A faint glimmer of starlight illuminated the bumpy road in front of her, the same road she and Otto had taken earlier. Fortunately, the early spring weather had turned warm, but all Renee could feel was terror as she ran for miles through the deserted countryside with no idea of direction, until exhaustion overcame her. Her last reserves of energy gone and no farmhouse in sight, she collapsed on a haystack. Burrowing inside, she fell asleep to the accompaniment of frightful nightmares.

*   *   *

Otto thrashed like a boxer. He grunted and shouted garbled orders in his sleep. His fist twitched and pounded the hay bale next to his head. Then everything changed. The dream turned to a small play-field when he was a boy. The fist opened and a smile formed on his sleeping face. *The little girl with the blue-green eyes and yellow ringlets ran after the ball. She squealed and rewarded him with a smile when he pushed the other boy aside. Now there was the beautiful Frenchwoman with blue-green eyes and golden hair. The little girl looked up at the bigger woman with adoration. She held out her hand, and the woman took it. They walked slowly, slowly, slowly, up to Otto and knelt at his feet. "Please be nice to us. Please be nice to..."*

Otto woke up muttering. He sat bolt upright staring into the tines of pitchfork a few inches from his face.

"What are you doing here?" the farmer demanded, jabbing the pitchfork closer.

Otto made an effort to be polite. "*Pardonez-moi, Monsieur,* I got lost last night and needed a place to sleep."

When there was no response from the farmer, and the look was far from friendly, Otto continued, "Sorry if I trouble you. I be on my way, but can you give me directions to Avranches?"

Still skeptical and obviously suspicious of the foreign accent, the farmer pointed down the road with his pitchfork. Brushing off the hay, Otto handed the farmer a ten-franc note, thanked him for his trouble, and ran to the car.

Otto's face contorted. *Where the devil is the girl? Damn. I wanted to tell her ... I want her to like me. I got careless and drank too much. Damn, damn, damn. She's nothing but trouble.*

Otto tramped on the accelerator and spun the wheels.

ST.-PIERRE-DU-BOIS

"How'd you get here so fast?" Denis asked. "I just heard about this not more than an hour ago. Sergeant Mausant said you were in England."

"I parachuted in," Mitch replied. "Landed dead center in your back yard."

"I'll be damned!" Denis pumped Mitch's hand like a well handle. "Anyway, I'm sure glad you're here."

"Any word on Renee?" Mitch asked.

"No. The police've put out a dragnet all over Normandy. Nothing yet. But we've got to get busy. I've got three of my lieutenants supposed to meet me here. Then we're going over to the *Poste de Police.*"

Fifteen minutes later, the five men rendezvoused with Sergeant Mausant and two of his men at the police station. It was now 4:00 p.m.

A tall, gangly man with a neat mustache and a dour countenance, Mausant wasted no time getting down to business. "All we have to go on is the car," he pointed out. "Pierre identified it as a green Peugeot. That checks with our car dealer who sold a green Peugeot to a strange man with a German accent. And we know the license plate number, 403AB14."

Mitch interrupted, "I can add to that. Like I told you on the phone, I'm certain it's the same man. His name is Otto Streikler, one of our most-wanted Nazi war criminals. He's about 190 centimeters tall,

110 kilos, blond, 25 years old, and extremely dangerous."

"We've got to move fast," Sergeant Mausant said. "Judging from Pierre's statement, our kidnapper drove off at about 9:30 this morning. That gives him a six and a half hour head start."

"Have you radioed alerts to other police in the area?" Mitch asked.

"I'm afraid not. Our equipment is out-of-date—due to the war, of course." The sergeant shrugged. "I've had to rely on telephoning each of our stations separately, and I've done that. But now we have the description and the license number. I'll call them again."

"You'll probably want to stay here to be a central clearing point for telephone messages," Mitch said, "but I suggest the rest of us break up into four parties—two of us in each party—and start driving in the most likely directions, and start searching. We can call in every hour to see if there's any information. That way, at least one of us should be in the right area to make an arrest if the car is spotted."

Mausant nodded his approval.

"Can you supply us with four police cars?" Mitch asked. "We'll need to bust the speed limit and then some."

"I'll make my personal car available, and we have three others. You'll need deputy ID cards and police ration cards for petrol. And I'd better show you how to work the sirens."

While Sergeant Mausant went into his office to make the phone calls, Mitch and Denis studied a map. They decided on the four routes to take: one toward Rouen to the northeast, which would lead to Belgium and Holland; one toward Paris; one south toward Le Mans; and one west into Brittany.

The four police cars were gassed up and brought around. Three would be driven by policemen with one of Denis' men assigned to each. Mitch teamed up with Denis and elected to take the westerly route to Brittany. He had a hunch the Nazi might try to escape by boat.

It was getting late. There was no time to waste. Mitch and Denis sped along the road toward Avranches at 90km/hr., the best they could do on the narrow roads, which were still pocked with unrepaired bomb craters. Fortunately, the traffic was light. Few

Frenchmen had acquired cars by the spring of 1945, and petrol was in short supply.

With two hours of daylight left, they would only have time to search Avranches and St.-Malo before dark. Then they would phone in to Sergeant Mausant.

At 6:OO p.m., discouraged and frustrated, Mitch telephoned Mausant from Avranches. The Sergeant had nothing new to report.

Mitch and Denis put their heads together and studied the map of Brittany. They decided to search the seaport towns along the coast in spite of the darkness, asking at petrol stations and cafes, "Has anyone seen a green Peugeot driven by a large heavy-set man with a foreign accent accompanied by a young blonde Frenchwoman?"

After searching the coastal towns without success until past midnight, they finally agreed to take a break and sleep in the car for a couple of hours.

At daybreak, Mitch telephoned the St.-Pierre police station and then checked with the police stations at St.-Malo, Avranches, Brest and Quimper. Still nothing.

BRITTANY, FRANCE

Renee awoke from a frightening nightmare and glimpsed the first rays of morning light through the strands of hay. Was the loathsome Nazi still stalking her? Should she stay hidden? Did she dare to go for help? Stiff and sore, her wrists still tied, she stayed in the warmth of the haystack and wrestled with the bonds. With the help of her teeth, she finally worked them free.

Renee worked up her courage, wriggled out of the hay, and started walking again, but with no sense of direction. She had walked for less than ten minutes when she heard a sound in the distance, but coming closer. She jumped into the shelter of a hedgerow, then peered out cautiously, searching for the source of the noisy squeaks and rattles. Relieved to see a farm cart loaded with hay bumping along the road, she examined it closely from her hiding place. An ancient nag, its gray head hanging down, was pulling the cart at a snail's pace, but to Renee, it looked like a chariot from heaven.

She stepped out into middle of the road, waived her arms, and screamed, *"M'aider. Au secours!"* The cart creaked to a halt, and the farmer stared at her, but said nothing.

"Monsieur, s'il vous plait, I need help. Can you give me a ride?" Renee pleaded.

The farmer's nod was barely perceptible.

"I have had a great trouble. I must get to the nearest town."

The driver simply pointed to the seat beside him, and Renee climbed in. "I must find some place where there is a telephone," she explained. The farmer only grunted in response. Even after she explained her predicament, he showed no emotion. "Take you to Fourgeres," he muttered, but made it clear he was not interested in conversation.

On any other day, Renee would have been enchanted by the beauty of the spring morning and would have chuckled to herself over the taciturn farmer. With his slouched hat and long pointed nose protruding from a bushy beard, he was a comical figure. But not this day. Renee, still shaking with fear, hunkered down on the wooden seat.

They had not gone half a mile when a green Peugeot screamed over the top of the hill ahead. It was coming toward them at breakneck speed, kicking up a cloud of dust.

The farmer called, "Whoa," and pulled to the side of the road. Renee dove down on the floorboards as the car roared past. She turned and poked her head up to watch it disappear behind. That was her mistake. Otto must have seen the movement in the rear-view mirror. The car skidded to a halt, spun around, and half a minute later it was blocking the wagon.

The farmer sat like a toad on a rock, while Otto, gun in hand, hauled Renee off the wagon seat and slammed her into the car. He locked the door from the outside, then shoved gun hard against her side. "One move—one move of any kind—and I'll put six bullets into you."

The farmer remained motionless, as if asleep, until the green car was out of sight. Then he gathered up the reins and snapped his buggy whip on the rump of the old nag. It responded with a smart trot.

Ten minutes later he pulled up to the Fougeres *Poste de Police* where he knew the gendarme, Armand Gierrot, an acquaintance since childhood. An aging, portly man, Armand, slouched behind a battered desk, looking bored. There hadn't been any excitement in Fougeres since the Germans had been driven out the year before.

The taciturn farmer never wasted words. "A French girl was just kidnapped by a big, ugly man. Sounded like a Kraut to me."

Armand sat forward in his chair. "What did he look like? How old?"

When the farmer described him, Armand reached for the telephone. "Sounds like the man I've been getting calls about. One of the most-wanted Nazi war criminals."

Armand clicked the receiver half a dozen times. "Allo, allo, operator. Ring me through to Sergeant Mausant in St.-Pierre-du-Bois, *tout de suite*. Yes, yes. It's an emergency. Top priority. Break in if you have to."

The farmer could only make out Armand's half of the conversation. "I have a report of a kidnapping. A large man with a German accent. Kidnapped a French woman. Yes, she was blonde. In her twenties. Yes, the car was a green Peugeot. Yes, yes. That's the one. Headed west toward the coast."

Armand turned to the farmer. "Sounds like the man we're after all right. Anything else you can tell us."

"Nope."

BREST, FRANCE

Otto glowered at the huddled body, gagged and bound on the front seat. With his head pounding from too much wine and his stomach growling, he decided to stop at a small cafe for a roll of bread and coffee. He offered Renee a piece of the roll, but she shook her head. Slamming his door, he jerked the car into gear and sped westward toward Brest.

The French girl stirred his anger. He pounded the wheel with his fist. She would not even look at him, and he could see her shaking. Now he too began to shake, and the car swerved. "You mustn't hate me, Ilsa. I want to help you. Yes, I know your name. I know everything about you, about you, about you." The voice trailed off.

He looked at her too long and nearly went off the road. Damn. His mind snapped back, I'd better be careful. Don't make a mess now. I'm almost there. Almost free.

After a minute of silence, he started in again. He was stuttering now, "I do this for you, Ilsa. Want you be happy. I want you have everything. We'll have horses and cattle and ... You like horses, Ilsa? Yes, you like horses. I know you do. Don't shake so much. I won't hurt you. I want you to like me. I want ..." The words trailed off again, but the muttering continued all the way to Brest.

Otto saw her turn her head slightly and stare at him with a blank expression. His grip on the wheel shook, and he stared straight ahead like a sleepwalker. Drops of sweat ran down his face and dripped from his chin.

When the fisherman's wharf came into view with countless nets strung about, the fog began to clear from his mind. *I must think clearly now. I must be careful. No one must see her.*

Parking the car behind a large fishing boat, which was up on blocks, he started making inquiries. The first fisherman looked at him as if he was crazy. "I don't care how much money you offer. I'm not going to Portugal. They'd impound my boat and throw me in jail."

Getting the same reaction from two others and becoming increasingly worried about the scene he was creating, Otto decided on another tack. "Would you take me as far as St.-Nazaire for 2,000 francs?" he asked.

That was another matter. "*Certainement Monsieur,*" responded the owner of the next boat he approached, "but I will not be ready to cast off for at least four hours."

Otto scowled, then pulled five 1,000-franc notes out of his pocket and held them within inches of the fisherman's face. "Would this be enough to persuade you to leave now—right away?"

The fisherman smiled broadly and repeated, *"Certainement Monsieur."*

Otto noted the name of the boat painted on the transom, LE POISSON BLEU. The fisherman radiated enthusiasm. *"Je m'appele Georgio, Monsieur."* He held out his hand, which Otto ignored. "I'm glad to cast off any time."

Pocketing the money—as much as most fishermen cleared in an entire year of good fishing. Georgio loosened the mooring lines.

"One moment, Monsieur, I have a passenger." Otto strode back to the car and drove it onto the pier right up beside *Le Poisson Bleu.*

"You can't leave your car there," Georgio said. "It's not allowed."

"Never you mind," Otto growled as he unloaded six heavy boxes onto the dock. "Stow these," he ordered.

While Georgio stowed the boxes below the deck, Otto pulled the gagged and bound Renee onto the dock and dragged her to the boat. Georgio emerged from below and jumped in surprise. "What's going on? Who is—?"

"She's been a bad girl. I take her to St.-Nazaire."

"I can't—"

Otto did not have time to argue. He pointed a gun at the fisherman. "You'll take her," he barked. "And stay quiet, or I'll blow a hole in you. Now move." He nudged Georgio with the gun and pushed the hobbled Renee below deck.

The fisherman hesitated, but a second nudge with the Luger convinced him to cast off. In a windless, glassy sea, Georgio steered his craft slowly out of the Brest estuary. Otto immediately subjected the fisherman to a battery of questions about his boat. How far would it go on a tank of fuel? What kind of fuel? How to start, stop, and reverse the engine?

Of course, Otto had no intention of going to St.-Nazaire. He would dispose of the fisherman when they were far enough from shore and take the boat to Portugal on his own. But he was now berating himself for not insisting on bringing extra cans of petrol. He would have to find some place along the coast to re-fuel.

QUIMPER AND BREST, BRITTANY, FRANCE

At 9:00 a.m. Mitch telephoned Sergeant Mausant from Quimper. The Sergeant sounded excited. "We have a tip from a gendarme in Fougeres. He says Streikler has been spotted heading for the coast, probably Quimper or Brest."

"What about...?" Mitch wanted to ask about Renee, but Mausant was too excited about catching the German.

"Haven't got time to talk. You've got to move—*vite*."

"What about your other men?"

"They're all too far away. You and LeCoc will have to go after him. You say you're calling from Quimper? I'd be willing to bet he's gone to Brest. But first check the docks at Quimper and then go on up to Brest. It's only twenty minutes from where you are."

Mitch and Denis gave Quimper one more quick inspection. They found no signs of Streikler, so they turned north along the coast, pushing the police car as fast as it would go and reached Brest in less than half an hour. With rapid-fire questions, it took only minutes to figure out what had happened. The green Peugeot, license 403AB14 was parked on the Fisherman's wharf. A few inquiries quickly established the particulars. *Le Poisson Bleu* had shoved off only twenty minutes before.

Described as a brick-red boat, *Le Poisson Bleu* had a single gaff-rig mast, occasionally used to support a sail. The owner, Georgio, was generally regarded as a fine fellow, but not too bright.

Mitch and Denis split up and asked several fishermen, "Do you know of any boat here that is fast enough to catch up with Georgio?"

The answer was "No." Apparently the only such boat was not in port at the time, and "No, the other fishing boats are all about the same speed as Georgio's."

"You should try the Allied military pier at the end of town," one of the fishermen offered, pointing to the north. "It's only a supply base, but they may have something."

Brest had been almost completely destroyed by the Germans when the Allies had overrun it in July of 1944. Eight months later, the fishing wharf and the small Allied pier were among the few facilities that had been restored. Mitch thought they would at least have a telephone. Maybe some kind of a ship could be pried loose.

Mitch, who was in uniform, had no trouble getting into the base, but Denis had to wait outside. No time for formalities. Explaining the urgency to the Petty Officer at the desk, he asked to see the C.O.

The officer of the day, who happened to be the same rank as Mitch, stomped out of his office. "What's all this about an escaped Nazi?" he asked with obvious irritation.

When Mitch explained, the O.D. grumbled, "We've got nothing but emergencies around here. We're trying to get supplies to the front. For Christ sake, man, we can't divert a ship for some crazy manhunt. I don't care what kind of a son-of-a-bitch you're chasing."

"I haven't time to argue with you," Mitch said. "Let me use your phone. I've got to get through to MI-6."

"Ames, here. What's up, Carter?"

"I'll make it as brief as I can," Mitch said. "The Nazi has taken off with a fishing boat from Brest—about forty-five minutes ago. I think he's headed for Portugal. Odds are ten to one he'll kill the fisherman and commandeer the boat."

"Can you come up with a boat to go after him?" Ames asked.

"So far, no luck. I'm at the military supply dock at Brest, and they can't or won't give me any help. Have you got any ideas?"

"Let me check with the Navy. I'll see what they've got in the area. Give me your phone number, and I'll get back to you as soon as I can. There's one thing in our favor, though. Those fishing boats are slow. It'll take Streikler at least two or three days to get to Portugal. We ought to be able to intercept the SOB easily enough—if I can come up with anything from the Navy."

While he waited impatiently for Ames to call back, Mitch called Mausant and filled him in. He also arranged a pass to get Denis into the base. He would need him.

With both the British and American Naval Group Commands, Captain Ames' requests carried considerable weight. Mitch had been well aware of it for the last year. Whether there was any truth to it or not, Ames' close association with McDonald was generally interpreted as providing him with some kind of direct authority from Eisenhower.

In this instance, it took Ames less than half an hour to clear an American PT boat from its patrol off the Channel Islands and send it at flank speed toward Brest.

Ames called Mitch back, "I've pried loose a PT-boat. Should get to Brest in slightly less than three hours. It'll do thirty-five knots. Seems to me you ought to be able to catch Streikler if you have a description of the boat."

"Yes, I have a good description, but it may be dark before we catch up with him."

"You'll have radio contact from the PT, and I want you to keep me informed. If you don't catch him by tomorrow, I'll send more help."

At 3:OO p.m., Mitch, Denis, and the PT boat with a crew of six men were speeding out of the Brest estuary at thirty-five knots. With a calm sea and good visibility, the PT skipper calculated they might be able to catch the fishing boat before dark.

Having the advantage of radar, Mitch figured all they would be able to spot a lone fishing boat easily enough. At about 5:OO p.m. they began picking up multiple blips. There were nearly one hundred of them, and when they closed in on the whole fleet, they found it nearly impossible to distinguish any boat by its color because of the poor light. Besides, half had gaff rigs, and at least a quarter were various shades of red. No single boat stood out alone. As the usual mist settled over the fishing grounds, and the light gradually faded, most of the boats headed back north to the ports of Quimper and Brest. But about a third of them stayed out for another day's fishing.

"Streikler isn't going to be heading back north," Mitch shouted to the skipper over the noise of the engines. "*Le Poisson's* got to be one of the boats that's still out here. Have your radarman keep an eye out for any blip that breaks away from the group and begins moving south."

The PT slowed down and coasted through the fleet of fishing boats, shining its searchlight on the faces. They called out, asking for Georgio and *Le Poisson Blue* but with no results. Increasingly puzzled, Mitch and his PT crew scrutinized every boat. He could not understand how the red boat with the gaff rig could simply disappear. Mitch radioed to Captain Ames at 6:00 p.m.

"Keep looking," Ames said. "He has to be there somewhere. In the meantime, I'll check with the navy and see if there is any other U.S. ship in the area that can help."

Laboriously they went back over every boat and hailed each one with a bullhorn, "Have you seen Georgio's boat?"

At 6:30, they finally got a response. One of the fishermen shouted across the water, "We pulled him out of the water half an hour ago." When the PT pulled closer, the fisherman added, "He was unconscious and half frozen."

"Has he said anything yet?" Mitch called back. "Can I talk to him?"

"He's still unconscious. Hasn't said a word, but I think he's coming around."

"What about his boat? Has anyone seen his boat, *Le Poisson Blue*?" Mitch persisted.

"No, I can't explain why it isn't here. I'd recognize it easily. But come along side. Maybe you can give him better first aid than we can."

With a grappling hook and bumpers over the side, they tied up, and Mitch jumped over to the fishing boat. "Is he conscious at all?" he asked.

"He's been groaning. Starting to come around, I think," the fisherman offered.

Mitch went below and leaned over Georgio. He could see the dried blood matted on his still-damp hair. Mitch rubbed the limp hand. "Can you hear me, Georgio?"

Georgio groaned.

Holding up the damp head and giving him a few sips of coffee, Mitch finally succeeded in getting some response. "Can you hear me now. Can you tell me what happened?"

"He hit me—the German," Georgio gasped.

"Then what?"

"Pushed me over the side. Hit me real hard. Tried to kill me."

"Do you have any idea where he went with your boat?"

"No." Georgio sat up and gingerly touched the back of his head. "I suppose he might have gone to St.-Nazaire. That's where he asked me to take him."

Of course, Mitch thought. That's why we can't find his boat. He must have gone ashore.

"Georgio, it looks like you're going to be all right. I've got to run now. We've got to catch that bastard, but we'll come back later to be sure you're okay."

Mitch leapt back onto the PT boat and shouted to the skipper, "Head for St.-Nazaire, full speed."

St.-Nazaire was directly east of their position, about five kilometers straight in shore. At thirty-five knots, they should reach the harbor in ten minutes with at least another half-hour of twilight left.

ST.-NAZAIRE, FRANCE

Disposing of Georgio was easy. When his back was turned, Otto bashed him on the head with a wrench and tipped him over the side. But then he'd had to handle the boat by himself, which worried him. Did he have it right?

When Georgio's body floated out of sight behind the boat in a calm sea, Otto stopped the engine and looked around. *Le Poisson Bleu* drifted slowly in a southerly direction, and he could make out the faint images of a dozen other fishing boats on the horizon. He had smiled to himself. *I'm free at last. No one will ever find me now.*

Muffled noises emanated from below deck where Renee was kicking her feet against the bulkhead and making choking sounds. Otto went below, sat on the end of the bunk and studied his captive. Suddenly disoriented, his thoughts turned to jelly—a feeling like vertigo. He felt like a boy again. *She is so beautiful. I can't stand it. Every time I look at her, I get an erection.* When he collected his thoughts enough to speak, the sounds came out in a small boy's voice. "I sorry I had to gag you, Ilsa. Really sorry. I had to do it. I take it off now where nobody can hear."

Renee closed her eyes, avoiding his gaze, kicked her feet harder, and wrestled with her ties.

"All right. I wait until you calm down, Ilsa. I wait. I want you to like me, Ilsa. I do all this for you, you know. We will have everything— you and me—everything. Argentina a wonderful place. You will love Argentina. You will love me. You will. Just give me a little time."

Renee stopped struggling long enough for him to remove the gag. "You beast. You killed him!" She strained to sit up and look out through the hatch where Georgio had been.

"I do it for you, Ilsa. He was in the way. You understand, don't you? We must get to Portugal. I do it for us. For you. For us. I want you so much, Ilsa. You will see when I make love to you. You will see how much I love you. You will see how much you love me." He reached down and pulled at a button on the front of her dress.

Renee screamed.

"I can't show you when you act that way, Ilsa. I have to put the gag back. You will see. You will see. If you don't love me after ... I let you go. I promise."

With the gag back in place, he held her head still with one hand and slowly undid the buttons with the other. Then with lingering reverent movements, he slid the bra down, exposing her nipples and finally her breasts. He stopped and stared for a full minute, then began to caress them gently.

*　　*　　*

Otto turned the boat toward St.-Nazaire. He would purchase enough fuel to get to Portugal. A good-sized port, St.-Nazaire had been a major submarine base during the German occupation. It was bound to have petrol.

Arriving late in the day, Otto made a clumsy landing, banging the boat hard against the pier. He tied up the boat and went below to be sure Renee was securely bound and gagged. He found her slumped in the corner of the cabin, curled up in a fetal position, eyes closed, her ashen face turned to the wall. He frowned, grunted some

German words under his breath, and clambered up the hatchway, then went in search of petrol. There was none to be had on the pier at that hour, so he hurried into the town and searched for a petrol station.

A mechanic was in the process of closing up shop when Otto hailed him, "*Monsieur*, do you have any diesel I can buy?"

Obviously in a hurry to close up, the mechanic was terse. "No. I don't sell petrol. You'll have to find a station."

"I have an emergency, and all the stations are closed," Otto said holding up a 5OO-franc note. "I can pay you whatever you ask."

The mechanic frowned and stared at Otto. "For five hundred, you can have all the diesel I've got, but what are you going to put it in?"

"I'll have to buy some fuel cans," Otto said.

"That'll be extra," the mechanic replied with a take-it-or-leave-it shrug. "I've got a couple of twenty-liter cans, but they'll cost you an extra hundred."

"I'll take them." Otto pulled out another 5OO-franc note. He did not have anything smaller, and the mechanic didn't bother to make change.

"Wait here," the mechanic said and disappeared into the back room while Otto paced the floor. Five minutes later he reemerged lugging two large cans. "They're heavy," he warned.

Without a word, Otto shoved the two five hundred franc notes at the man, grabbed the cans, and hurried down the street.

Straining under the load, he arrived back at the docks just in time to see a gray motor-torpedo boat, flying an American flag, nosing its way into the harbor. Suddenly it picked up speed and bore down on the red fishing boat. Otto frowned and squinted at the fast-approaching boat. *Could they be looking for me? Is it possible they could have tracked me this fast?*

Seconds later, his question was answered. A searchlight swept the bay and quickly settled on his fishing boat. Then the boat came straight toward him at full speed. Otto, trembling and exhausted, dropped the fuel cans and ran back towards the town. Where to hide? In a frenzy, he rattled shop entries but found only locked doors and extinguished lights. Panting like a dog on a hot day, Otto ran on.

He rushed headlong into the old part of the town, then spotted an ancient church with massive wooden doors. He pushed open the small entry door-within-a-door and found himself in a cavernous nave with a dirt floor. But the church was not entirely abandoned. It had a few pews and an altar.[11]

He quickly explored the interior of this dark building and discovered an anteroom. Hanging neatly in a closet were choirboy robes and a minister's vestments.

"That's the boat!" Mitch yelled over the noise of the engines. "Close on him. Full speed."

"Aye, Aye, sir," the boatswain responded. "I see someone running." He pointed at the street behind the dock.

Mitch shouted orders. "That's him. Tie up alongside. Denis, you come with me, and we'll need two more of the crew to help track him down. The man's dangerous. Be sure you're armed. Have your guns loaded."

Without waiting to tie up, Mitch leapt onto the fishing boat. He spotted the boxes and shouted at the skipper, "Put a guard on these boxes, but don't touch them. They're classified materials for MI-6."

Then he heard a faint pounding noise below deck. He shoved his head through the small door of the cabin and saw Renee banging her feet against the wall and making frantic muffled sounds.

"Renee, it's you, *ma cherie*. Thank God." He pulled off the gag, grabbed a blanket off of Georgio's bunk, and wrapped it around her, then yelled for one of the sailors to help cut the bonds on her wrists and feet. "Are you all right? Tell me, you're all right, my love. Dear God. I've been sick with worry."

She put her arms around him and started to sob incoherently. He gently lifted her to her feet. "It was..." she choked. "I c-can't talk about it. I'll tell you later when I can, but I'm all right. Right now you've got to catch him, don't you?"

"I don't want to leave you."

"I'll be all right, but you've got to catch him. But be careful. He's dangerous. He's got a gun—keeps it inside his coat—and a big knife on his belt."

"I'll be careful. I've got Denis and a lot of help."

Mitch yelled at the skipper to take good care of her and rushed to catch up with Denis and the two sailors who had already begun searching the town.

They started asking questions, "Has anyone seen a large, blonde-haired man running." Several locals pointed in the direction of the old part of the town. They split into twos. Denis and Mitch, each with one sailor, ran through the cobblestone streets. But the light was fading, and the trail went cold.

They knocked on doors, looked down all the alleys, and even searched churches, including a venerable old church with a dirt floor. Half a dozen locals had seen a large man running near the church. Denis peered into the closet where he made out a rack full of choirboy smocks, but it was too dark to see anything else.

"Damn," Mitch muttered, "He's got to be around here somewhere."

One lone street light penetrated the darkness, and this deserted part of town offered no other sources of light. Mitch cursed himself for not bringing flashlights. "We'll have to wait until morning to continue the search," he said to Denis reluctantly. "In the meantime, we'll just have to keep watch all night."

The next morning, which happened to be a Sunday, Mitch sat on a stone bench across from the church and rubbed his eyes. He yawned and watched the minister, a small man, arriving early and noticed the sign on the massive door, COMMUNION SERVICE, 6:OO a.m. He watched the small group of worshipers trickle in and forced himself to stay awake as he watched the doors close, then listened sleepily to the faint sounds of organ music.

The service was short. At 6:3O, a score of devout Protestants filed out, saying a few words of thanks to the preacher. When the last of his flock had left, the Reverend turned back inside.

Denis appeared around the corner, looking exhausted.

"Anything yet?" Mitch asked.

"Nope. You see anything?"

"No. Afraid not. Why don't you see if you can rustle up a cup of coffee? I'll stick around here a little longer."

Just as Denis started to walk away, a large figure emerged from the church, wearing preacher's vestments and a black hat. At first, Mitch paid no attention, but then he noticed the arms and legs. They stuck out a foot beyond the cuffs.

Pulling out his gun, he shouted, "That's him—Streikler—Halt, you're under arrest."

The bizarre figure broke into a run. Mitch fired a shot over the head of the fleeing figure, then hesitated for a fraction of a second. *It would be pretty horrible if I shot a priest,* he thought. *But that's no priest.* He broke into a run and fired a second shot.

Hearing the shots, Denis whirled around and joined the chase.

Otto Streikler may have been strong, but he was not fast. Mitch got to him first with a flying tackle. Otto's hulking body went down hard, knocking out his wind. Denis pinned the arms while Otto gasped for breath. In a fury, Mitch grabbed the Nazi by the throat with his left hand and raised the butt of his gun to bash the hated face. "I'll kill you, you bast..."

With a sudden violent lurch, Otto threw both men off. In one motion he swung his fist in an arc and knocked the gun out of Mitch's grip. While Mitch staggered off balance, Otto threw a punch at Denis who fell and lay still on the stone pavement. Blood trickled from a gash on his forehead. Mitch dove for his gun as a massive fist slashed by his face. His ear stung. Then he saw the knife flash in Otto's hand.

Mitch juggled the gun and frantically felt for the safety catch as he jumped backward. In the same fraction of a second, he nudged the trigger and a bullet ricocheted off a cobblestone inches from Otto's feet.

Otto stopped short, and they faced each other. Otto held the knife and Mitch the gun.

"You raped her, you filthy bastard. I should kill you for that," Mitch yelled, jabbing the gun toward Otto's chest.

"I ... I was going to let her go," Otto sounded almost plaintive.

"Liar."

"I was going to let her go."

"You're a Goddamn-son-of-a-bitch liar."

With a growl Otto leapt straight at Mitch, thrusting the knife. Mitch jumped sideways and fired point-blank at the chest. The massive body catapulted on top of him, and they crashed to the pavement together. The knife stabbed the cobblestone next to Mitch's shoulder.

Alerted by the sound of the gunshots, the two American sailors came running. They rolled the limp body off of Mitch and helped the dazed Commander to his feet. Denis sat up and felt the gash on his head.

"You okay, Denis?" Mitch asked.

"Yeah, I'll be all right," Denis responded slowly, inspecting the blood on his hand.

"Is Streikler dead?" Mitch's voice shook.

"No. Don't think so." Denis put an ear to the mouth and felt for a pulse. "He's still breathing, and there's a heartbeat."

"Where'd the bullet enter?"

"Let's see—here." Denis pointed to the slowly spreading pool of blood just below the shoulder.

A small crowd had gathered, and Mitch had to explain they had just captured a dangerous Nazi. Denis whispered in Mitch's ear, "Let's get the hell out of here before we get involved with the police."

To the approving murmurs of the onlookers, the four of them carried the body to the PT boat where the boat's pharmacist mate took over. "The bullet's gone clean through," he pronounced. "He's damned lucky. Just missed the lungs, but there are a couple of bones shattered." He dressed the wound. Then it took four of them to roll the unconscious body onto a bunk.

"I want two armed men guarding him," Mitch ordered. "Don't trust that snake for one minute."

Mitch finally had a chance to talk to Renee. He held her gently. "Are you all right, darling? Are you all right?"

"It was..." her voice faded, "I can't talk about it."

"I can find a hospital—here in St.-Nazaire."

"No. No. Just hold me. I'll be all right. Just give me a little time. I want you to hold me, Mitch," she whispered. "But I don't think this is the place. All these men."

"To heck with them," Mitch said. He held her and kissed her anyway. The crew cheered, and Renee couldn't help but smile weakly.

They radioed to Ames and headed back out to sea. After returning the fishing boat to Georgio and making sure he was all right, they set their course for Brest. Georgio waved from the deck of the *Poisson Blue*, clutching his 5,000 francs as the PT boat sped northward.

Mitch took possession of the mysterious boxes. "It's a matter for British Intelligence to sort out," he informed the PT skipper. As the ranking naval officer on board, Mitch directed the skipper to deliver him, Denis, Renee, and their captive back to Brest. He would take it from there with the help of the French Police.

THE WAR IN EUROPE IS ENDED
SURRENDER IN UNCONDITIONAL
GERMANS CAPITULATE ON ALL FRONTS
New York Times, May 8, 1945

ST.-PIERRE-DU-BOIS

Dusk had settled over the Brousard farm when the police car pulled up in front of the house. Locked and deserted, the house looked threatening to Renee as memories of Otto flooded back.

Denis had been dropped off at his house, a short walk from the Brousard farm. Renee would visit her mother first thing in the morning at Denis' house where she was being cared for by Denis' parents.

Now, at her own home, she hesitated, shook her head, and rummaged for the latchkey, which was hidden under a brick. After unloading the boxes, Mitch thanked the two Gendarmes. Streikler, his hands and feet tied, lay slumped unconscious in the back seat of the police car. "Take him to the hospital and keep a double guard on him," Mitch said. "I'll come around in the morning and discuss the next move with Sergeant Mausant."

When the car drove away, Renee threw her arms around Mitch.

"At last! Let's pray we never see that beast again."

He hoisted her in the air. "The bloody war is over," he exclaimed, "and we're together finally." With so many things to talk about, they both started talking at once, and kept talking breathlessly.

"The important thing is you're okay," Mitch said in a serious tone. "Actually, you look like a dream. It's incredible after all you've been through."

Renee put a finger over his lips and smiled. "Before we talk any more, I have something to show you. Come on. It's a beautiful warm night. I want to show it to you."

Leading the way, walking at first, then breaking into a run, Renee scampered across a field of wild flowers twinkling in the moonlight. Mitch caught up in seconds, but didn't say anything. Caught in the magic spell, he conjured up wood sprites in his mind, but the fragrance of the wild honeysuckle was real. They stumbled onto a narrow path, barely passable, that led through some thick woods, then ducked under an arch of wild roses and finally came out on a stream.

"I had to show you this, Mitch. There's a wonderful swimming hole right up here—just a little farther. We have to push our way through this brush."

Breathless, they broke out onto a sandy place by a still, deep pool. Moonlight glittered on the tiny ripples.

"It's beautiful," Mitch murmured.

"It's my secret swimming hole. I used to come here when I was little, sometimes with Denis. But this is the first time since I went off to England. Do you realize it's been six years? So much has happened. So much confusion. The war. The Nazis."

"Forget all that." Mitch took her in his arms. "You're safe now."

"Let's go for a swim," Renee said, stripping off her clothes quick as a rabbit. She jumped in the water before he could answer. Mitch laughed. It took him two seconds to follow suit.

"How're we going to dry off?" Renee laughed when they hauled themselves out onto large rock and sat dripping in the warm May night.

Mitch reached out and ran a finger lightly over her breast.

"Do you have any idea how beautiful you are with those tiny pearl drops gleaming all over you?" he said, gently brushing away a few pearls. "More beautiful than any painting. More beautiful than any flower."

"Thanks, my love. You look pretty good too," she laughed and kissed him. "But those pearl drops are making me cold. I'm afraid they're really goose bumps."

"I'll just have to sacrifice my shirt," Mitch chuckled as he went to work drying her off. Then he picked her up and carried her to a patch of wild flowers shimmering in the moonlight. He set her down gently in the bed of flowers. And kissed her gently. And they made love gently, for fear of offending the wild flowers.

The moon dropped below the trees, and the flowers lost their twinkle. Mitch held her tightly. "Now, let's talk about the most important subject. When can we get married?"

Renee's features clouded over as she pulled on a shirt, and Mitch thought he saw her brush away a tear. When there was no answer, he gently cupped her face in his hands and repeated the question.

"This is all I have thought about ever since we said goodbye last time," she choked on the words, "but I showed Denis the treasure, and he..." She stopped and started again. "Marrying you is all I want in this world, but..."

"You are everything to me too," Mitch replied, perplexed, "but why the buts? What is it?"

"I may have made a terrible mistake," Renee answered slowly. "I told Denis about the treasure, and showed it to him when that Nazi came prowling around. I didn't know what to do, and you weren't here." She was shaking now.

"You were right to show him, but he should have stayed with you."

"Maybe you're right, but Denis looked at the gold, and said it is mostly melted-down gold fillings from the gas chambers of Auchwitz and Dachau and Ravensbrueck. He says the diamonds and the other gold bars and the money were stolen from the Jews, murdered in the concentration camps."

"Good Lord, that's horrible. Is he sure about it? How could he know?"

"He says he's absolutely certain. His men liberated Ravensbrueck, and he had Jews in his *Maquis* who had escaped from Dachau. They know exactly where it all came from—all stolen and taken from dead bodies by the SS."

"We can't keep it then," Mitch said firmly. "We have to give it back. The French government must have some way to repatriate the survivors—to return whatever can be returned—although God knows there's no adequate way."

"That's exactly what I said to Denis." The words kept tumbling out. "I ... I don't see how we can get married without the money. I can't deprive you of your architecture. Your college education. And I can't leave the farm. You have an obligation to the wonderful man who gave you the scholarship. And your father's had a stroke,and .... and your family. You have to go back."

Mitch tried to break in, but the words kept coming, and the tears ran faster. "I should probably marry Denis. I don't love him, but I—"

"Whoa. Slow down," Mitch interrupted. "Put all those ideas out of your head. We're going to find a way. We are made for each other, and if I live to be one hundred, I'll never find another I love the way I love you. Denis is a fine fellow, but don't marry him. Trust me, Renee, we'll find a way to work it out."

Silently, they walked back to the house hand in hand. The magic of the night had evaporated.

"Renee, I have to get to a telephone," Mitch mumbled, barely audible.

"Now? At this hour?"

"I'm sorry. The war may be over in Europe, but I'm still in the navy, and there's still the war in the Pacific. I'm liable to be court-martialed for being AWOL."

"It's late. You can't get to anyone now, can you?"

"I'm afraid my C.O. is watching the phone. Said he would man it around the clock. I hate to admit it, but it was my idea. He's going to insist on a report about Streikler."

"You'll come back right after...?"

"I'll try, but I'm not sure."

Their eyes met. He touched her lips lightly with a finger as if to stop the words.

"Don't go," Renee pleaded, "We've said goodbye too many times."

Unable to answer, he closed his eyes and held her. And she clung to him.

"I have to go, my love. I have to." He choked on the words.

Gently prying her arms loose, he kissed her softly, picked up his hat, and opened the door. With the faint moonlight behind him, he became just a dark outline to her. He raised his arm half way in a goodbye gesture and whispered words, "I love you."

*   *   *

"Captain Ames, here. Is that you Commander?"

"Yes, sir. I'm in St.-Pierre. At the police station."

"What the devil are you doing there? You're supposed to be on a PT-boat, headed back here."

"I had to turn Streikler over to the French police. Also the boxes of Nazi loot."

"You should have talked to me first. That's a top-level decision."

There was a long pause while Mitch tried to think of some response. "Would you like to talk to Sergeant Mausant about it?"

"No, but I want you to get your ass back here *tout de suite* before I report you AWOL. Something important has come up. On second thought, let me talk to Mausant."

The Sergeant picked up the phone. *"Bon soir, Capitaine."*

"Good evening, Sergeant. Captain Ames here. I need your help. It's important."

"But, of course, *Capitaine.*"

"Can you provide transportation for Commander Carter to Cherbourg?"

"Certainly, *Capitaine.* Tomorrow?"

"No. Right now. Tonight. It can't wait."

There was a long pause. "You say it's important? *D'accord,* tonight then."

LONDON

"These orders came through yesterday." Ames handed the papers to Mitch. "They are the reason I had to get you back immediately."

Mitch scanned them with dismay. "Good God, I'm supposed to leave tomorrow—for Washington."

"McDonald set this up," Ames said, placing his hand on Mitch's shoulder. "I'm sorry. I'm going to miss you. Want you to know, I think you are the best."

Mitch looked the other man in the eye. "Thank you, sir. It's been an incredible three years, hasn't it?"

"Sure has. We've accomplished a lot—you and I. We've been a good team."

Mitch nodded.

"I'll drive you out to Bromley. Seems they're giving you the VIP treatment. Going to fly you via Greenland. Guess they want you in Washington to tell them how to run the rest of the war."

Mitch interrupted, "I have to talk to Renee. She'll think I've run out on her."

Ames nodded and pushed the telephone across the desk. "Sure. I understand."

Mitch tried to reach Renee by calling Sergeant Mausant, but he didn't have the number. The overworked operator informed him they did not run an information service unless it was classified military business. He tried to call the St.-Pierre Post Office, but nobody was able to give him a number for that either.

He realized with a shock, he didn't even have her address, other than the name of the town. Would a letter get through? Would it be censored? Would it take forever to be delivered? Nevertheless, he wrote a long letter, telling of his love and promise to marry, but still being part of the Intelligence service, he could not tell her of his new orders. He addressed it to Mlle. Renee Brousard, St.-Pierre-du-Bois, France.

Early the next morning, Mitch opened the office to clean out his desk and sort through his gear. He grimaced. He wouldn't be needing his parachute or the L-pill in Washington.

Ames found him hunched over a pile of papers. "Good morning Mitch. I see you're hard at it. I'll take you to Bromley at eleven hundred hours—in one hour."

"Mornin', Captain. I'm going to need your help with these. Some of it can be thrown out, but you'll want to keep most of it."

"Yes, I think so. By the way, did you see this in the morning London Times?" Ames held out a neatly folded section of the morning Times.

CHARLES DE GAULLE AWARDS
50,000 FRANCS TO FRENCH
HEROINE OF THE RESISTANCE

Calling her a "modern-day Joan of Arc," General Charles de Gaulle presented a 50,000-franc award to a young heroine of the French Resistance, Mademoiselle Renee Brousard, who discovered an immense Nazi buried treasure. While the exact amount of the treasure was not disclosed, it is believed to be valued at more than 100 million pounds. She has turned the entire treasure over to the Jewish Resettlement Fund.

ST.-PIERRE-DU-BOIS

"You might as well face it." Denis held her by the shoulders and looked into her eyes. "He's gone, and he won't come back. Even if he wanted to, there's no way he can come back."

"I don't know. I just don't know." Renee leaned against him for support.

"You can't waste your life waiting for him, Renee. I can give you a good life. Marry me, and you'll be happy, and I'll be the happiest man in the world. We can put our farms together. We'll have one of the best farms in Normandy."

She had known Denis like a brother since they were small

children, but now she felt she was seeing him for the first time. She took in the thick red hair, carefully slicked back, and the dark blue jacket, the same one he wore to church. She admired the square jaw, but realized she had never seen him smile.

Denis cleared his throat. "Well?"

"Oh, Denis. I don't know what to say. Of course, I'm honored. I'm flattered. You're a wonderful friend. But I just don't know. You'll have to give me some time."

*   *   *

Renee stared out the window and fingered the small handkerchief balled up in her lap. She had been feeling poorly for a week now. Something was wrong.

The nurse-receptionist smiled. "Doctor Rouleau can see you now."

Renee rose slowly and followed the nurse into the office. "Good morning, Doctor," she mumbled, avoiding the doctor's inquisitive look.

"It's always a pleasure to see you, Renee. What can I do for you?"

She had been rehearsing what to say, but now the words wouldn't come. Rouleau gazed at her troubled features and tried again. "You know I'll do anything in my power to help you, Renee. And, of course, anything you tell me is confidential."

Renee took a deep breath. "I don't know much about these things, doctor."

Rouleau walked around the desk and put a hand on her shoulder. "Pleased don't be embarrassed. I think I understand. I know where your heart is."

Renee remained silent, and the damp handkerchief flicked across her eyes.

The doctor squeezed her hand. "I think we all came to love him as much as you did."

The brief examination confirmed what they both already knew. Renee was two-month's pregnant.

Annette moved about the kitchen fixing dinner for the two of them. She had been painfully quiet since both her husband and her son had been killed. Renee could feel the sadness like a shroud hanging over the house. How could she tell her mother without adding to the gloom?

"Mamma, I don't know how to tell you."

"Yes, Renee. You can tell me whatever's on your mind. I'm sure it will be all right."

Renee put her arms around her mother and blurted out, "I'm pregnant. I'm so ashamed. Two-month's pregnant. I've been to Doctor Rouleau. It's true. I don't know what to ..."

"Hush, daughter. I already knew. You looked so radiant, I could tell. It's the American, isn't it?"

"Yes, I loved him so much. But now I don't know."

"And he's disappeared? You haven't heard from him? You don't even know where he is?"

"Yes. It's been two months, and I haven't heard anything. I've tried to send letters, but I don't have any address other than the U.S. Navy."

"He seemed such a fine man. I can't believe he would abandon you. But these things happen in war all the time. You must face reality."

Renee continued to hold onto her mother but said nothing.

"Denis has proposed, hasn't he?" Annette asked. "He'll make a fine husband if he'll still have you. Of course, it would be much better if you married him right away before everyone in St.-Pierre knows. But you'll have to tell him about the baby and ask his forgiveness."

Renee could not sleep. Even the tears wouldn't come anymore. She stared at the gun Mitch had given her. *It would be so much easier just to end it.* She picked it up, looked in the chamber, pushed the safety off, then put it down again.

ST.-PIERRE-DU-BOIS

Mitch felt his nerves prickle as he walked the familiar road to the Brousard farm. He slowed down as he approached the house and went over in his mind the things he would say.

But she was not in the house. Conscious of his heart beating too fast, he felt a moment of panic. Please, God, let her be there. Then he saw the figure in the distance, a floppy hat, a baggy smock, working a hoe at the far end of the field. He dropped his duffel bag and started running.

The figure straightened up and put a hand across the forehead to shield the sun. She took a hesitant step. Then broke into a run.

The arms reached out. "It's you. It's really you." The tears began streaming down her face as she threw herself into his arms. "I had almost lost hope."

He forgot his prepared speech. Choked up, he was only able to whisper, "I love you so much. I tried to telephone, but I couldn't get through. I wrote dozens of letters, and they all came back."

"I was beginning to think you would never ..." She stopped and put her hand over her mouth. "How did you get here?"

"They sent me to Washington. I had to turn the whole U.S. Navy inside out to get here."

"How long can you stay?"

"I only have two days, but we can see Father Francois and get married tomorrow." Mitch grinned. "Our three-day waiting period ought to be over by now."

"Oh, yes, yes, Mitch. How I've dreamed about it, but there is something I have to tell you first."

Mitch put a finger to her lips. "We'll talk about the 'buts' later. We've said goodbye too many times. Right now we're going to see Father Francois."

-

EPILOGE

1987

CHRISTMAS

ST.-PIERRE-DU-BOIS

The table was set for eight, and the aroma of cooked goose permeated the house, while Christmas tree ornaments sent reflected shafts of light from the fire dancing across the room.

Surrounded by miniature holly wreaths, eight little red candles centered the table and gave off just the right glow to make everyone look younger. "Renee, you look twenty again," Mitch said, "beautiful as always." He watched in appreciation as she bustled back into the kitchen.

"The compliments are unnecessary, Mitch. Don't get impatient. The goose is coming. Just a couple more minutes."

Mitch chuckled and turned to his eldest son who was warming his hands by the fire. "Anton, how is your work going at the Foreign Office? Your mother and I are very proud of you, you know."

"Very well, father. I think I'm up for a promotion to Second Consul next month."

"That's wonderful. You are a great credit to us."

Anton, imposing and fair with pale blue eyes, always popular, nevertheless rarely smiled. He inquired about his father's architectural work, and Mitch assured him it was going splendidly. Just then, his younger brother, Claude, tall and thin like Mitch and with the same mischievous brown eyes, entered the room, proudly carrying the Christmas goose.

Mitch held a chair for Renee. Anton and Claude sat on either side of their mother. Anton's two children sat on either side of their grandfather. The remaining grandchild, Claude the third, and Claude's wife, Clarissa, sat opposite each other in the middle. Anton's wife had been unable to come, tied up with government business in Paris.

Mitch said grace, ending with, "and thank you God for our wonderful children and grandchildren."

The grandchildren dug in like hungry bears and started talking, all at once. Mitch smiled and held up his hand. "Whoa, one at a time."

Young Mitch looked at his grandfather, "Tell us the story, Grandpapa, about how you caught the bad German, and about the treasure."

"Yes, Grandfather, please," echoed his little sister.

"I would rather not tell it at Christmas time," Mitch replied. "You see, I hated the violence, and I even felt sorry for what I had to do. If I hadn't shot him, he would have killed me, so I'm afraid I had to do it. The German was a terrible, evil man, but he was brought into a world of hatred and ordered by Hitler to do terrible things. How could he be anything else? Christmas is a time of love and forgiveness, so this is not the time to talk about things I can't forgive.

"Please, Grandpapa, tell us the story anyway. Everyone at school talks about it, but you never tell us."

"Another time, children, when you're older. Right now let's have your grandmother tell about the wedding." Mitch smiled and looked at Renee. "Please, honey. It was such a beautiful wedding."

Renee smiled. "Yes, the wedding. It *was* a beautiful wedding. Your grandfather was so handsome in his white navy uniform. The whole town came. Father Francois gave a very special service and told about all the things we had done in the war. Lily, the wonderful lady who had saved your grandfather, came from Le Mans. And Sir Charles, a very important man who had been in charge of British spies, came from England. And the Mayor of Chabeaux. Oh, Mitch, why don't you tell that part?"

Mitch chuckled. "It was really rather funny. The Mayor looked so sad. His mutton-chop whiskers were quivering, and he could hardly speak. He took me aside and said, `I have a terrible confession. I must get it off my conscience.' He asked if I remembered the day I was captured—the day before the D-Day invasion. Of course, I remembered. Then he said, `I was captured the same day, and they were going to torture me to find out everything I knew about the Resistance. I confess I told them the secret things about where the invasion would be. It was the only way I could save my life.'"

Mitch stopped and laughed at his own story. "Well, the poor man didn't know that he had actually done us a great service. It was all to fool the Germans, and it worked. I had to explain it to him about five times before he would believe me."

"Mitch!" Renee jumped out of her chair and pointed at the window. Seven heads jerked around.

A wrinkled, unshaven face was pressed against the glass, the grizzled head covered with snow. Circular wire rimmed glasses magnified large round eyes and thick eyebrows.

*   *   *

Otto Streikler wiped away a small patch of snow and pushed his face hard against the frozen windowpane. Shivering, he stared at the blazing fire and the steam rising from the roast goose. The tall man was carving the bird while the children gesticulated, obviously carrying on an animated conversation.

Otto's face twisted in pain. *He's stolen my Christmas, my life. While I spent forty years in prison, he's had my woman and my children. This should have been mine.* With shaky hands, he felt for the gun in his pocket and shuffled toward the entry door. *It's all coming back to me now. The damned American, the one he had come for. And the woman—Ilsa—or was it...?* He recalled the day he had shot the lock off the same door—but now the door opened on its own. *They must have seen me.* Otto stood frozen in place. *I won't have to shoot the lock.*

The woman reached out to help him, but Otto was too cold to move his feet. The man took his arm and propelled him toward the fire with small steps.

"On Christmas of all days," the woman exclaimed as she reached out and took his other arm. The American said, "Come out of the cold before you freeze."

Otto became vaguely aware of the woman's voice saying, "Mitch, the man is hardly breathing. I'll call the doctor. Anton, get him some hot tea. Mitch, you stay with him while I call." She hurried to the telephone.

Two minutes later she returned. The man, whom she'd called Mitch, pulled off his boots, which had been locked to his feet with ice. The young man, called Anton, tipped the hot tea to his lips. Otto slowly lifted his head and stared into the fire, then at Mitch. He could see the American studying his face, apparently trying to remember. *He'll never recognize me with the beard and my prison haircut.*

But the woman leapt back. "Oh my God! It's him. They've let him out of prison."

The American shook his head. "Streikler? It can't be. Doesn't look like..."

"It's him. I know. Dear God, I'd know. I'd know."

"I don't know," the American stared hard at Otto. "Even if it is him, we can't put him back out in the snow. He's half dead now. Not on Christmas. What'd the doctor say?"

"He was busy. Emergencies. Said he would come as soon as possible. Maybe half an hour."

Mitch rubbed the frozen feet. "Anton, bring a blanket. Claude, see if you can find a little brandy."

Otto slowly turned his head toward Renee, his eyes straining to focus. He moved his lips, trying to form the word. "Ilsa." He put his hand out toward her. "Ilsa."

The woman shrank back. Mitch gripped his arm.

As the American started to ask, "Who is Ils...?" Otto summoned a sudden spurt of energy and rose with a jerk. His shaky hand fished in his pocket and finally succeeded in pulling out the gun. Using both hands, he wrenched it around and pointed it at Mitch.

In the same instant Anton leapt between the two men. "No!" he shouted and slammed the gun with his fist. A bullet crashed into the floor as the weapon flew out of Otto's shaking hands. The gun skidded across the floor and landed at Renee's feet. Kneeling, she grabbed it with both hands, turned it on Otto, and fired. She dropped the gun on the floor, clasping both hands over her face.

Otto slumped to the floor, blood oozing from his side. He stared at Anton and gasped, "My son. You are my s..." and reached out to touch Anton. Instead, mouth open, he collapsed on the floor with a crash.

Anton knelt down and felt for a pulse, looked up at Mitch, and shook his head, then buried his head in his hands. "My God, is it true? Tell me the truth."

Mitch put both arms around Anton and held him close. "Yes, son. I'm afraid it's true. Your mother and I knew from the beginning, but it didn't make any difference. We love you as much as anyone in this world. You are our son. We are very proud of you, and God bless you. You've saved my life just now."

Renee, sobbing and shaking, put her arms around both Mitch and Anton. "Dear God, what have I done?"

"Renee, my love, you have put a end to a terrible cancer—finally. The world is a better place without him."

FOOTNOTES

[1]. William L. Shirer, The Rise and Fall of The Third Reich (New York: Simon and Schuster, 1960), 943-945.

[2]. Credits equal to about 2/3 of the Netherlands national income. William L. Shirer, The Rise and Fall of the Third Reich (New York: Simon and Schuster, 1960), 943.

[3]. Reference: Anthony Cave Brown, Bodyguard of Lies (New York: Harper and Row, 1975), 570.

[4]. Fast German armed patrol boats.

[5]. The Gestapo was an arm of the SS. Heinrich Himmler was chief of both.

[6]. Based on the true story of a Dutch painter, Rene Duchez, but fictionalized somewhat here to fit the plot. One reference (among many): Russell Miller, The Resistance (Chicogo: Time-Life Books, 1979), 48.

[7]. Actual title a British Ambassador at the time. The name in the middle is fictional.

[8]. Acronym for Supreme Headquarters Allied Expeditionary Force.

[9] Acronym for Oberkommando der Wehrmacht, the German High Command.

[10]. Douglas Botting and the Editors of TIME-LIFE Books, The Second Front (Chicogo, 1978) 161.

[11]. Not uncommon in some ancient French towns, these churches had been built in the twelfth century, more as fortifications to protect the townspeople from marauding crusaders than as places of worship. Now, many of them were used by itinerant ministers to preach a service once a week, or sometimes only once a month.

Printed in the United States
102941LV00002B/87/A